Billionaire Daddy Series
Books 1 to 5

S.E. Riley

The Redherring Publishing House

ISBN: 9798365652293

Table of Contents

CEO Billionaire Daddy (Book 1)

Blurb

Lillian Miller has loved Atticus Moore since they were younger, but she is certain he thinks nothing of her. Atticus has thought of her as nothing more than his best friend's little sister – but she's not so little anymore.

Atticus has fought hard to build his business. He is grateful for what he has, but he can't help but think his rougher emotions have led him to live an isolated life. He wants something more.

Lillian is trying to build a life for herself, so she jumps on the chance when a job opportunity presents itself. The only thing that complicates matters is that her boss is the only man she has ever truly loved. And worse yet, her brother's best friend.

Her shyness prevents her from boldly claiming her feelings until Atticus makes the first move.

Would they betray the closest person to them for love?

Prologue

Lillian stepped into the Poet's Brew coffeehouse and inhaled the heady aroma of brewing coffee and buttered scones. It had been too long since she'd come in here. When had she last been in here? Probably a year ago, when she was with her older brother Tyler for the Christmas holidays. He'd made her feel like his kid sister all over again despite all the growing up she'd done, and while she loved him dearly, she was glad he wasn't here to make her feel that way today. He was only seven years older, but he made a big deal of it, and she wanted time to celebrate this milestone as an adult. Tyler forgot she wasn't the little kid he'd raised alone after their parents died in a car accident. Being here alone for once made her feel more like the adult she was, and it seemed like the perfect way to celebrate her return home.

She stepped up to the counter and placed her order, heading over to the pickup counter with her gaze fixed on her phone screen. Job hunting had proven difficult, and she hoped the employer she'd interviewed with last week would call back with a job offer. As she scrolled through emails, she ran into a solid, warm shape.

Gasping, she looked up to see who she'd run into, an apology on her lips. The apology died when she saw familiar gray eyes and dark, neatly combed hair that always seemed to curl at the ends. She shivered, remembering how those gray eyes had fixed on her the summer she'd had a gap year to save for college. He hadn't been able to stop looking at her when they'd gone to the pool or taken runs together.

Tyler had griped about it teasingly, and she'd daydreamed that those looks meant more than they probably had. She doubted the man who'd been like a second older brother when she was a kid had developed a similar crush on her as she'd had on him during high school. Still did, if her inability to think of something to say was anything to go on.

She finally managed to stop gaping like an idiot and squeaked, "Atticus?"

He frowned down at her. "Lillian? When did you get home?"

"Two days ago. I've been busy job hunting," she admitted. "I should've thought to call and let you know I'd come back."

"That would've been nice." His gaze raked over her. "But it's not as if you're still a little kid texting your brother or your brother's best friend to tell them you made it to the theater safely when you were a senior."

She flushed and stared down at the ground. "I hated it when you two made me do that."

He laughed. "I know, but we wanted to know you were safe."

True, she understood why he and Tyler were overly protective of her, but she hadn't wanted Atticus to see her as a little kid he needed to watch out for. She still didn't, but running into him probably didn't help solidify her image as an independent woman he no longer needed to baby.

"Do you have a minute?" Atticus's low voice snapped her out of her thoughts.

She looked up at him with a smile and tucked an unruly auburn curl out of her face. "Yeah. Do you?"

"I can make one. Perks of being the CEO of a successful company."

"And yet you're still in here getting your usual." She eyed his cup. "Hold on. I need to get my order."

He walked her to the counter. "It really is good to see you, Lil. I see you haven't changed your habits one bit. Still glued to walking while staring at a screen or a book."

The tips of her ears heated. She looked away and went to collect her order when they called her name. Behind her, she thought she heard Atticus mutter something about making a rule against walking and reading at the same time if she were his, but she shook off the idea.

He wouldn't say something like that.

Atticus saw her as the little sister he'd never had. Being ten years older, he probably wouldn't see her as a twenty-three-year-old woman with an interest in finding the right man to settle down with. He could have anyone, anyway. He wouldn't want the girl he'd grown up with and saw as a kid's sister.

"So, what are you doing these days? You mentioned job hunting. Didn't you finish your degree in interior design?" Atticus took her elbow and steered her toward a table.

She let him pull her chair out and push her in once she was seated. "I did, but I'm not having any luck with jobs."

"Any examples you can show me?"

"Promise not to laugh." She set her phone on the table.

He eyed her. "Why would I laugh, Lillian? I'm sure you've worked hard on your work, just as you always have. Let me see."

She opened the folder with photos from some of the redecorating and design work she'd done in school and handed him the phone. Sipping at her coffee while he looked, she tried not to squirm in the seat. A flush warmed her ears and then her cheeks as he looked through everything in silence. Finally, he pushed the phone back across the table and took a sip of his own coffee, his gaze fixed on her.

"It's not very good, I know," she whispered. "That might be why I'm not—"

"They're very good, Lil. Top notch work, actually. Your inability to find a job has nothing to do with your talent." He continued to watch her for a moment, those gray eyes searching. Lillian squirmed some more in her seat. Then he pulled a business card from his pocket and handed it to her. "Use the email on the card. Send me your resume and portfolio."

She frowned. "Why?"

"Because my head of design needs an assistant, and I think you'd be perfect."

Lillian steeled for a moment. "This seems like a huge coincidence...I don't know."

"Sometimes coincidences happen. I wasn't expecting to run into you or hear that you're still looking for work, but this right here..." he tapped on his business card that was in front of her, "...seems like a good solution to both of our problems."

She didn't want handouts. Besides, a position as assistant to a director? She was fresh out of school and couldn't possibly be qualified. Furthermore, there was the little problem of a clash between her career and the desire for him that obviously hadn't faded. Seeing him again forced her to admit he'd only grown more attractive to her over time. This would be a disaster.

"Atticus, come on...I—"

He raised a brow. "I wasn't asking, Lillian. You need a job. My design director needs an assistant. She'll like you. Apply. I'm not handing you anything. You'll have to interview her and impress her yourself. I don't make a habit of handing things out to anyone, especially not without proof it's merited."

That much was true. Atticus never handed anything to anyone, just as no one had ever handed anything to him. It's what he'd always liked about her brother—the two of them knew what it was to claw their way to the top and to fight tooth and nail to survive.

Atticus had been better at it, but the two had held their own together through the years. If he was telling her to apply, not just politely suggesting it, then he wanted her there because he thought she could do the job.

The heat in her cheeks traveled down her neck. She must look like a cherry tomato by now. That only worsened the situation. He thought too highly of her. She wasn't the right one for this.

"Is there a reason you don't think you'd be a fit for the job?" he murmured.

She squirmed in the seat. Why did he always have to be so perceptive when it came to her? "Well..."

"Besides an abominable lack of self-confidence, Lillian."

She couldn't tell him she was worried she'd never be able to focus if she had to work with him, and she *did* need the job desperately. If he would not hand her anything and she'd either stand or fall on her own merit, she could be professional for the sake of her career, and mounting bills and debt.

"No," she admitted quietly. "I guess there's not."

He stood with a broad smile. "Good. I can't guarantee you the job. That's not how my company runs. If you're the best candidate, though, I can promise you'll get it. I expect the resume and digital copies of your portfolio in my inbox by the end of the evening, little miss. Got it?"

She ducked her head, hating the sound of that childhood nickname on his lips; *little miss*. That confirmed it. He still thought of her as a kid sister, not as a woman he might see himself dating.

She needed to get over this silly infatuation with him. He'd never see her the way she wanted him to, and she was setting herself up for heartbreak if she didn't stop hoping for it.

"Got it."

"Good." He walked away.

She sat there a moment longer, wishing she could get Atticus off her mind and out of her imagination.

He wasn't meant for her.

Tyler would have a fit if anything ever happened, and Atticus would never risk Tyler's wrath, even if he saw her as more than a little girl now.

Any chance with him was doomed already. Sighing, she finished her coffee and left the shop. She'd turn in her resume tonight. Even if she could never have him, she could still have the job he'd offered if she tried.

Chapter 1

Two years later

Lillian stood on the pier waiting for him when Atticus disembarked from his private charter ship. He descended the gangplank, watching as she stared at him for a long moment before shaking her head and stepping forward with a smile to greet him.

He spoke first, beating her to a greeting. "Lil. How do you like my island?"

"It's..." She laughed. "I guess I should've known it would be spectacular. Every other location you've built has been, and you did, build a private getaway on the other side of the island. But I have to admit I was a bit shocked when I saw it."

"Wait until you see the main island. Those resorts and hotels were built before you started with us, and they won't be as modern as this one, but I think you'll like them."

"I didn't realize we were planning a trip over there."

"I was." He smiled down at her. "I thought it would be nice to go together, just us."

She looked away, flushing. "Oh...I...is there time?"

"We'll make time. I want to show them off a bit, especially since you'll be taking over Marie's position as design director next year."

Her shoulders relaxed. "Oh, I see." Lillian looked around before changing the subject. "Was it a good trip, boss?"

"Atticus," he corrected mildly. "This counts as off work, Lillian."

She lifted one shoulder in a half shrug and ducked her head, the setting sun glinting off her red-gold hair as she returned to her earlier discomfort.

He frowned at her dismissal. After two years of working together, she still seemed uneasy with him outside of the formalities of the office. They worked together wonderfully, and in a few more years, when his head designer retired, she would take over that role. He loved how easy it was to work with her, but he hated how tense she became when he tried to make things more personal.

"A verbal response, not a shrug, Lil."

He still remembered the first day he'd seen her again after two years of studying abroad. She'd no longer been the little girl he remembered from childhood. She'd been much more outgoing with him back then. Sweet, innocent, and talkative. Now she was reserved, and anxious outside of work. He disliked the change and often wondered what had caused it, but he couldn't seem to tease it out of her, so he'd backed off.

She stared at the ground and shifted, but didn't answer.

"Very well. Are we pushing buttons today?" He almost wished the answer was yes, because at least then she'd be acting more like the girl he'd known since they were younger.

"No button pushing today, I promise." She smiled shyly, her green eyes flicking up to his and then away. "I'm on the clock, remember? You made me promise not to clock out before I drove over to pick you up."

He suppressed a groan. He'd only told her to convince her to come in place of his chauffeur. The drive back to the hotel was long, and he'd wanted to get her alone before they really dove into the project. His reasons for being here went beyond overseeing the final touches on designs and the first month of operation. This time, he would use this trip to perform a miracle.

He was done waiting for Lillian to realize that he was interested and trying to subtly hint it to her, too. He'd be cautious in his approach and ease her into the idea, but he was almost certain that the young woman currently unlocking her little sedan was also interested and just didn't want to admit it. She needed coaxing, but she was interested. He'd caught her sneaking glances when she thought he wasn't looking.

Lillian Miller liked him but had convinced herself she couldn't have him, just like she always convinced herself she couldn't afford to eat that last piece of cake on her birthday. He needed to deal with that misconception soon. "I made you promise because I wanted to compensate you for the drive out. I did not tell you that because I wanted to spend the drive home in business mode."

She opened her car door but paused, that lovely flush back in her cheeks. "You didn't?"

"No, I did not." He held out a hand for the keys.

She backed away a bit to look up at him. "You're paying me to drive."

"Not anymore. You're off the clock now, little miss." He crooked a finger. "Keys, please."

She bit her lip and glanced at the car, as if uncertain what to do. He waited quietly, trying not to think about how much he wanted to pull her lip from between her teeth and kiss her senseless.

Finally, Lillian dropped the keys into his outstretched hand, a tiny shiver working through her slight frame. "Yes, sir."

"Do we need to have another chat about not behaving like an employee when it's just us? We're friends too, Lil, not just employer and employee."

The blush deepened, nearly hiding her freckles. "Why did you want me to drive over if you didn't plan on resting?"

"Because I wanted time to talk to you on the trip. You know I dislike chauffeurs." He rounded the car and opened the passenger's door for her. "Hop in, please."

She brushed past him with another tiny shiver and climbed into the car. He reached across to buckle her in, catching the tiny hitch in her breathing when he did so with a tiny smile.

He shouldn't tease her about it, but he couldn't resist. "Something the matter?"

"No, s—"

He raised a brow.

"No," she murmured. "Can we go back to the hotel now?"

"Better idea. We'll go back to my mansion on the other side of the island. I was going to invite the staff to stay there in the extra rooms until the hotel is finished, anyway." He pulled away from the docks and headed inland.

Lillian toyed with her skirt's hem. She often did that when she was alone with him, and he wasn't sure if she was nervous or simply needed something to occupy her hands. Reaching over, he laid a hand over hers, guessing that it was nerves, not the need to occupy herself.

"You seem nervous. What's wrong?"

"I'm just..." She sighed and shivered. "I'm fine. Just nervous about the project. Like always...The last few weeks before a grand opening are always stressful."

"I see. Perhaps we can ease the stress. Did you pack a swimsuit?"

A furrow appeared between her brows. "I...why?"

"I thought we could relax in the pool at my place."

"Oh." She stared out the window. "If you like."

"It's not always about what I like, Lil. Do you want to?"

She pursed her lips. "You're sure it would be okay?"

"More than okay."

"Then yes, I would." A tiny smile softened the corners of her mouth.

He gave her some space, briefly letting the silence stretch between them. Then he confronted the strange tension that had been building between them over the last two years. He'd promised himself he was done waiting and meant it.

"You're nervous around me when we're not in a work setting."

"What?" Her head jerked up. "No, I—"

He frowned at her. "Lillian Miller, the next words out of your mouth had best not be a lie or an excuse."

"I...Well, what if I am?"

"I don't like that very much, and I hate to think I might be the reason. Am I?"

"Not exactly." Her voice barely rose above a whisper. "You've been a great boss..."

"Only a great boss?"

"And a good friend."

"No one would know that, looking at how you act around me outside of work. What is it that puts you on pins and needles with me as soon as I'm not playing the role of your boss?"

"I just..." She pulled her knees to her chest. "I don't know, Atticus. I feel like you see me as that little kid that tagged along with you and Tyler, and I don't know how to act with you in private now that I'm...well, I'm not a kid. You still call me little miss, like you did when we were kids, so obviously—" She cut herself off with a sigh.

He glanced over to find her attention fixed on the road ahead instead of him. "I do not see you as a child, Lil. You became a lovely young woman in the time you were away, something I am very much aware of. I call you that because it's always been an endearment between us, an endearment that has more to do with your height than your age. I didn't know it upset you."

She blushed and turned her face away from him. "It...well, if you put it that way, I guess it doesn't."

He pulled into the driveway of his mansion and stopped the car, turning to face her. "I want this awkwardness to end, Lil. I don't like it and intend to remove every reason for it. Is thinking I see you as a child the only issue?"

She wouldn't look at him.

"You don't have to tell me now. That's your choice, but think very carefully before you try to lie to me again," he warned. "You know I don't tolerate lies to avoid difficult truths."

"I can't...I can't talk about this." Her voice shook, and she reached for the door handle.

"I'll come around to open it for you. We'll table this for now, but Lil?"

She finally turned her gaze back to his.

"It's not being tabled forever, understand?"

She nodded, looking anywhere but him.

He ignored the lack of verbal response just this once. He climbed out and went around to open her door.

Then he retrieved her suitcase and guided her inside. He'd dig into her anxious response to him more deeply later. He'd clearly failed to make his interest apparent, but he'd rectify that situation quickly so that there could be no doubt in her mind that he saw her as a woman—a woman he respected and wanted. For now, he just wanted to get her to bed, so she'd be well-rested for what lay ahead.

Chapter 2

A week after their arrival on the island, Atticus knocked on the doorframe of the main office of his new resort and hotel. Lillian sat at a desk bent over design plans. This was the first project for one of his chains of resorts and hotels that she'd taken the lead on for her direct supervisor, Marie, and he'd never seen her so tightly wound. Her shoulders were hunched, and she was going through the swatches of paint colors and carpeting options. She'd been reviewing them last night too.

At his knock, she jumped, her gaze flying to his. "Boss!" She put a hand to her heart. "I hadn't seen you there."

He stepped inside and closed the door. "You went over those same swatches last night. Is something wrong?"

"No, no. Just making certain these are our best options before I present them to you. We need to send them off to the team for final purchases. The paint crew's coming in three days, and they need to mix the paint batches before they come over here."

"I approved the colors last week and sent them off to the team already." He strode over to the desk and bent over to look, brushing her arm with his casually. "You're worrying too much."

She twisted to stare up at him. "You did what? But sir, those were preliminary options. I just wanted you to let me know what you thought. I hadn't decided for certain that they were our best—"

He laid a finger on her lips with a slight smile. "Shhh. First of all, we're in private, Lillian. We don't need titles. Second, they were the best. This isn't the first chain hotel or resort I've opened, nor is it the first luxury resort. I know what I'm doing. Besides, you showed me all the options months ago and sent me the one you thought might be the best choice. I agreed and sent it off. Then I told you I thought it was a solid choice."

"But solid doesn't mean the best," she whispered against his finger.

"It does when I say it." He picked up the swatches and dumped them into the garbage can beside the desk. "I have already decided, little miss. Stop worrying. The crews will be here with all the essential supplies over the next week or two. Let's focus on supervising and planning for the grand opening."

She stared at the garbage can for a long moment, a protest clear in the tight press of her full lips.

He reached out and took her chin, turning her face and her gaze back to him. "Eyes on me, not the trash can. Everything in there is no longer of importance. It's been handled. Now, what do you have for the grand opening?"

Her stare seemed a little unfocused, as if she was shocked by his boldness today. Well, little surprise. He'd abandoned his usual subtlety to be very clear with her as part of his new goal to have her as his by the end of this trip. She was probably still a bit confused since he hadn't yet declared that intent. He wasn't yet certain of the right moment to do it and was hoping to ease her into it with clearer hints to give her time to refuse if he'd read her wrong. So far, she hadn't protested his overtures, though she'd protested plenty about the design and showed more of that shy side he'd only ever seen when she was with him.

Atticus would tell her soon. There was little doubt in his mind now that he'd read the situation correctly.

"Lillian," he pressed.

"What?"

"The grand opening."

She flushed and tried to pull away. He didn't let her.

"Atticus," she whispered. "What are you doing?"

He grinned. "Asking you to share your thoughts on arranging the grand opening. We only have two months to put it together while the decorating crew are finalizing on things."

Her blush deepened, and she dropped her gaze to his Rolex. "That doesn't...you don't need to...I mean, this isn't very professional."

He put her out of her misery and released her, watching her shoulders slump in relief. He didn't leave her to revert to her usual professional self, and he pulled his chair around the desk to sit closer to her than was technically necessary. If she didn't like it, she could say so and put an end to his flirtations. Otherwise, he didn't plan to give her time to retreat into her shell of propriety to escape his intentions or her feelings about them. "Show me what you've worked out."

She fiddled with the portfolio's pages, her hair falling in a sheet to hide her face from him. The unruly curls never stayed put, even when she put it up. Today, her hair was loose in its usual wild self. He reached out to tuck it back behind her ear with a smile. He'd always liked that hair of hers. It was easily one of her best features.

Her fair skin flushed again, momentarily washing out the freckles. "It's fine in my face. I don't mind, really."

"I know that. The plans?"

She slid the portfolio over. "I thought we could open the casino attached to the hotel to the clients. Serve champagne and hoers d'oeuvres before dinner and end the evening with a nice catered dinner."

"That sounds like a good plan." He leaned closer until he could smell the rose perfume she liked to wear. "What else? Any specific plans for the meal or before dinner refreshments?"

"Since the clients will be wealthy, we should plan to dazzle." She settled a little, though she still cast him uneasy glances when it became clear he wasn't interested in leaving the usual space between them as they worked. "Armand de Brignac for the champagne before dinner and a glass of sparkling wine for those who would prefer it. I thought we could serve caviar *crème fraîche* tartlets and figs with bacon and chile for the *hoers d'oeuvres*. It gives two options in case anyone's averse to caviar."

"All excellent choices."

She glanced over at him. "May I ask why you wanted me to plan this instead of your marketing team or personal assistant? I know Marie often helps pitch in, but...I'm not Marie, and I don't do this stuff much."

"You've watched Marie do it, and since I plan to give you her position in a year when she retires, you should learn. You're doing a wonderful job. We'll let the team handle sorting out who will cater and all the finer details. I just want you to help design the party, the decor, the flow of the meal, that sort of thing."

She bit her lower lip. "I don't know if I can—"

"You don't have to. All that matters is that I'm confident you can and have you on the job." He leaned closer, frowning. "I don't want to overload you, but I know you can handle it, Lil. You're good at this, and you've already put together exactly what I'd hoped you would."

Her gaze dropped to the desk, and her head dipped, sending her hair into her face again. "Really?"

He brushed it behind her ear once more with a fond smile. This woman really was something else. She had an air of innocence and humility about her that was attractive, but it left a twinge of frustration deep inside every time she talked down about herself. Once she was his, he would make sure that stopped. "Really. Do you think I'd lie to you?"

She lifted one shoulder. "As my boss or as my..."

He raised a brow.

The adorable flush was back. "N-no."

"Good. Then accept the compliment because you've earned it."

"Yes, sir." She shuffled through the papers.

He watched her in silence for a long moment. The way her mouth tightened in uncertainty left him wanting to kiss away the stress that left her so concerned she'd mess this up. If he didn't know she needed a bit of time to become accustomed to how he'd changed his behavior, he'd do it too. "Good girl. Let's take a look at the rest of these plans, then, shall we?"

She peeked up at him through her lashes. "Atticus?"

He smiled encouragingly, pleased that she'd called him by his name instead of using more formal addresses for him. "Yes?"

"You're...something's different today, isn't it?"

"Yes."

"It was yesterday too."

"Yes."

"What's changed?" Her teeth worried at her lower lip.

He reached out and gently pulled her lip free from her teeth with the pad of his thumb before she could cause any damage. "Don't you know?"

A hint of a blush tinged her cheeks as she nodded no.

"I see." He leaned back, giving her a little space. "You know. You just want to hear me say it."

She ducked her head, shifting in her seat. "No, never mind. It was a silly question."

"No, it wasn't." He tipped her chin back up. "Why don't you want to vocalize what's changed, Lillian?"

She swallowed hard. "I...we're at work, Atticus."

"So if we were in my home or my apartment back in New York, you'd ask what you really want to know?" He narrowed his eyes. "No lies, Lillian, remember? That's the first rule of engagement with me."

She chewed on the inside of her cheek and then sighed. "I don't need to know," she finally muttered. "Let's just focus on work."

He laughed. "I think you're just afraid of the answer and what that answer might mean."

He didn't say anything more, just grinned. He'd let it go, for now. He turned his attention back to the high-level planning for the grand opening. Time enough to whittle away at her objections and defenses over the next couple of weeks they'd be here. He didn't have to rush, though he could admit a large part of him wanted her as his as soon as possible.

Chapter 3

Lillian sat at her desk in the manager's office, laptop open, but she wasn't thinking about anything on the screen. Instead, she was contemplating Atticus's behavior in the last week. She couldn't lie to herself or Atticus, even if she could refuse to give Atticus answers to his probing questions of late. She couldn't avoid the answers in her own mind, though. His behavior had been decidedly aimed at getting her attention.

Since their conversation in the car on the trip up here from the docks and their first meeting in this office, he'd taken every opportunity he could to touch her, though he remained professional in front of the rest of the staff. In private was another matter. She blushed, thinking of his teasing and featherlight touches in contrast to his firm tone of command and demand for her attention. There was no question of whether he had her focus. He definitely did.

There were a thousand reasons she shouldn't—no, couldn't—give in. Even though it had been a fantasy of hers to have him notice her this way, she couldn't actually reach out and grasp at it now that it was in front of her. He was like a brother.

Tyler, her real flesh-and-blood brother, would probably kill her and Atticus too if he ever caught wind of anything between them. She didn't want to disappoint or anger Tyler. Not after he'd paid half her way through college and done everything in his power to take care of her after their parents' deaths, it had been hard for him, and he'd made many sacrifices.

It was the main reason he wasn't rich like Atticus.

Taking care of her had knocked him back a few years in his law career, and even now, looking out for her had prevented him from climbing the corporate ladder at his law firm as quickly as he might have wanted to. Worse still, Atticus was her boss. It wouldn't be professional.

She knew all the reasons she shouldn't, but the truth was that all the reasons paled when he touched her or spoke to her in that low, commanding timbre. She didn't want to move away or say no, which was the problem. She shifted in her seat with a sigh. He had to remain the subject of her fantasies and dreams, not the subject of real life romantic attachment.

A knock at the door startled her out of her reverie. She looked up to find the object of her musings standing in the door in a crisply ironed dress shirt, an expensive suit, and his usual Rolex. His gray eyes remained firmly on her, and his lips curled into a slight smile of greeting. What would it be like to kiss that full mouth of his? Would he be a gentle kisser or demanding and passionate as he was in his work? The thoughts were as intrusive as the blush that rose unbidden to her cheeks as she stared at the man she'd been fantasizing about for more than a decade. These thoughts had no place in her job. She needed to get a grip, but for the life of her, she couldn't stop staring. She opened her mouth to say something and then closed it.

He raised a brow and walked into the small office. "Something to say, Lillian? You look a little flushed."

She stared down at her lap, the heat in her cheeks intensifying. "I...good morning, boss."

"Good morning, Atticus," he corrected. "But good morning to you, too, little miss. I came to see if you were ready for the tour of the presidential suite and a check up on the painting crew's progress."

Was it that time already? She glanced at the clock on her

computer and shoved away from the desk with a gasp. "We're behind schedule! We were supposed to meet about it an hour ago. I am so sorry. I should've been at your office on time. I forgot." She rambled, as she rushed past him.

He caught her arm and tugged her back into him. "Lillian, slow down. I had a meeting that ran long. You're not in trouble, and there's no need to rush. The suite and the painters will still be there in a few minutes. No need to endanger yourself running through a construction site."

She settled, the blush returning. "I...I'm sorry."

He tucked a wayward curl behind her ear with a soft smile. "No need to apologize. I told you. You aren't in trouble. Now, let's walk to the elevator with a little less need for speed. Maybe I need to start calling you my little speed demon instead."

The blush turned to a fire in her ears and cheeks. "I'm not a speed demon!"

"You're right. Much too well-behaved for that. I guess we'll just have to stick with your established nickname, hmm? Little miss..."

She shivered and looked away. "Can we go?"

"Of course." He released her and offered an arm. "Shall we, milady?"

"What is wrong with you?" She laughed, but linked her arm through his. "We look silly, and people are going to stare."

He tugged on a strand of her wild hair where it had escaped her ponytail. "Do I look like I care?"

She pulled back, jerking her arm out of his. "You should."

He frowned. "I never have before, and I'm not about to start now. Come on. We should go check on the painting crew's progress and see how the suite looks now that it's fully decorated."

Sucking a deep breath to steady herself, she tugged her skirt down and hurried after him with a tight smile. She had to stop giving in to the temptation to go with the flow he established. If she didn't, she could endanger her professional image, not to mention her standing with her brother. She'd worked far too hard at work to have her team talking behind her back about gaining promotions by sleeping with the boss, and she didn't want Tyler angry at her either.

He took her by the elbow and guided her out of the room, giving her no chance or room to protest that someone might see. His stern look when she tried to adjust herself shut down any attempt at it very quickly. She remained silent the rest of the way to the presidential suite.

Once they reached the suite, she drifted through the room, looking at the decor. It was stately and simplistic, though she knew the paintings on the walls alone cost thousands of dollars. The rug under her feet was lush and an inviting shade of blue. The bed was piled with pillows and partially obscured by the canopy on one side. She drifted over, brushing her fingers over the cherry wood frame supporting the canopy.

Atticus stood in the doorway, hands in his pockets. "It looks lovely. Should we check the bathroom?"

She headed that way, stepping into a massive bathroom that boasted a whirlpool bath, a shower, and a steam room. The sinks were marbled granite with gleaming platinum fixtures, and a gilt gold mirror hung over them. The muted cream paint job brought everything together well. Turning back to the mirror, she found Atticus standing behind her, a slight smile on his lips.

"Everything to your liking?" she whispered.

He gave her an appraising look. "Maybe. I might need a closer look."

She turned to face him, heart thudding. He wasn't talking about the room anymore. Of that, she was certain. His gaze flicked to her lips and then back to her eyes. A shiver worked its way down her spine. If he just leaned in a little and pressed his lips to hers, it would turn into the same fantasies she'd dreamed about for years.

He stepped closer, reaching out to run his thumb over her cheek in slow circles. "A much closer look, I think," he whispered.

The shiver intensified into a wave of longing. Her gaze fell on his full mouth, and she wondered for the second time that day what it would be like to have his mouth on hers. He bent his head until their foreheads touched, and when his hands drifted to her hair, tangling there, she closed her eyes with a sigh. She shouldn't let him do this. She should stop him.

She didn't.

His mouth brushed hers in a maddeningly brief moment. She whimpered when the contact disappeared. Then she was rewarded with a real kiss, his lips caressing hers as he tugged on her hair to pull her head back so he could really kiss her. His mouth demanded her submission, and when he urged her to let him deepen the kiss, she opened to him with a sigh. He groaned, his hold on her tightening. His free hand gripped her hip and dragged her into him. She flushed when the close contact left her without doubts about his interest in her and their kiss.

When he finally pulled back, she sucked in a shuddering breath, goosebumps trailing down her arms. She stared up into his dark gray gaze and then back to his mouth and the attractive shadow of stubble gracing his jaw, fingers going to her lips. The shock gradually gave way to panic. What had she just done? She'd let Atticus Moore kiss her. She'd liked it every bit as much as she'd imagined she would.

She backed away, the small of her back pressing into the marble sink's counter. "That..."

"...was amazing," he murmured, his gaze returning to her mouth.

She flinched even though she desperately wished she could voice her own agreement. Instead, she forced herself to shake her head and disagree with him. "That can't happen again, Atticus."

"Why not? Didn't you like it?" He reached out to toy with a strand of her hair with his long, slender fingers.

"We can't. You're my boss, and Tyler—"

"...can screw off," Atticus said bluntly. "I love your brother like my own, but I'm not going to forgo pursuing what I want to please Tyler."

She shrank away from him. "My professional image..."

"I will not do anything to damage that, little miss." His tone and gaze softened. "I promise you your job won't be in jeopardy."

"But it already is," she whispered back. "T-this changes things."

"For the better, I think."

She brushed past him, nerves frayed. How could fate be so cruel as to give her what she'd wanted for years at precisely the moment when she could least afford to let herself have it? She wanted so badly to go back into his arms and let him soothe her fears with another of those sizzling kisses, but she couldn't. He was her boss, and there were too many obstacles. "I don't think so."

"You do. You're just afraid to admit it."

"This can't happen again, Atticus." She turned and fled the room, leaving him to himself. She wasn't sure if she was relieved or disappointed when he let her go without comment.

Chapter 4

Atticus found her in the pool in the early afternoon after work was over for the day. It had been a few days since their first kiss. That kiss was all he could think about for days, but he'd forced himself to give Lillian a little breathing room. Tonight, that room ended if she'd let him have his way. He was going to show her that as scary as it was, he could help her soar if she'd just let go and let him have control. She didn't need to worry about her professional image or Tyler, and he would take her somewhere where neither would intrude if he had any say.

Lillian lay floating in the water, her unruly hair wrapped in a thick braid around her head. She'd never liked lounging on the pool floats like many other women he'd known, claiming she preferred the feeling of the water cradling her. He smiled and tucked his hands into his pockets, watching for a long moment while she was unaware of his presence.

Finally, he decided to break the spell. "Lillian?"

She startled, splashing out of her relaxed pose and coming up to tread water, eyes wide. When she spotted him, she relaxed with a groan. "Really, Atticus...was that necessary?"

He shrugged. "How else would I get your attention?"

She swam in lazy strokes to the steps and climbed out, water streaming over her lithe frame. He watched her, shifting his weight from foot to foot a bit. The woman had no idea what she did to him or how infuriating it was to wait for her to towel off when he wanted nothing more than to seduce her here and now, showing her how flimsy all of her excuses were.

He restrained himself with a tiny growl. No. He was not a savage, and he could wait. He would wait until tonight after dinner. He'd timed this carefully to make certain they wouldn't be done in time to return after dinner. There would be no seduction until he'd taken her to dinner and eased her defenses with a reminder of how well they'd gotten along in the past before he'd become her boss. If he pushed now, she'd only rebuff him again and refuse to attend dinner.

"What did you need?" She unwound the braid from her hair and started toweling it dry as she approached.

He eyed the slippery floor and her quick steps, his protective instinct rising. "Slow down before you slip, little miss."

She slowed immediately, cheeks flushing. "I'm not a child."

"I think we've well established that." He crossed the distance between them and took the towel from her, helping her dry the water out of her hair.

"Thank you." Her tone was hushed and shy.

He smiled. She'd always liked it when he helped her with her hair after pool parties when they were kids, too. Now it had a much different tone than it had then, but he still enjoyed caring for her as much as she seemed to enjoy letting him do it. So few people took care of the little girl standing in front of him, she least of all.

Tyler had tried, but he'd been spread too thin acting as both breadwinner and single parent. Atticus was older than Tyler by three years, more settled by then, and able to be around to help his friend out after Tyler and Lillian had lost both parents in a car crash. Tyler had relied on Atticus to help when he couldn't. Back then, looking for the family his own had never been, he'd been only too happy to give someone else what he hadn't had, and he hadn't minded helping Tyler out. Tyler had been the brother he'd never had, after all. Now, even though Tyler hadn't asked him to take care of the young woman in front of him, and would probably kill him if he saw the shift in Atticus's motives for doing it, he still found himself wanting to make sure she was cared for and happy. Once in a while, it would do her good to let someone—preferably him—look after her.

"What did you come for?" she murmured, relaxing into his touch with a sigh.

"I'm taking my yacht out to the big island. Come with me."

"What for?"

"Dinner. Maybe to go see some of the other resorts and casinos I built there. You've been working very hard, Lillian. Let me do something nice to reward you."

She pulled away, turning to face him. "Just us?"

"Just us."

"Why isn't anyone else coming? They've worked hard too."

He took her by the hips and pulled her close, wrapping the towel around her shoulders as a shiver wracked her. She was dampening his suit, but for once, he didn't feel any urge to fuss about the damage or the mess. He could afford to replace it if the cleaner couldn't remove any water stains, and he liked how she trembled when the finely woven wool cloth of his suit jacket scraped along the bare skin of her belly and ribcage. After making her wait a moment for an answer, he finally said, "I want to spend some time with just you, that's why. Do you have plans?"

She rested her palms against his chest and resolutely stared down at her hands. "No."

"Then come with me."

Still, she hesitated.

"What are you afraid of, Lillian?"

Her chin lifted, her beautiful green eyes finally meeting his. A sheen of uncertainty veiled them.

He cupped her cheek in his palm with a frown. "Lillian? What is it? What's wrong?"

"It's not fair," she whispered. "It's not fair. Life dangling this in front of me when I can't have it."

He dipped his head to brush his nose against hers. "Lillian Miller, life isn't dangling anything in front of you. I'm right here, within easy reach. I'm not going anywhere, and you most certainly can have me, if you'll just let go and let me take charge."

She closed her eyes with a sigh. "I c-can't."

"Can't let go or can't let me take charge?"

"Neither." Her voice was raw. "I can't have you."

He kissed the tip of her nose. "Not true, little miss. Let me prove it to you. Go to dinner with me."

She lifted her gaze to his. "I want to..."

"Then you will." He scooped her up and headed outside the pool house into the muggy summer air.

She clung to him with a sigh. "It's not that easy."

"Oh, but it is." He grinned. "Let go, remember? I'll prove to you it's much easier than you think."

***

Lillian sat at the dinner table in his yacht's private dining room, watching in shock as a waiter settled a dish of perfectly cooked salmon in a lemon butter sauce in front of her. When Atticus had said he wanted to take her to dinner, she hadn't expected this. He'd parked the yacht on his private docking pier and brought the restaurant from one of his resorts to her. She stared at him from across the table, unable to quite form the words for the situation.

He smiled back as another waiter placed a steak in front of him. A dish of seasoned vegetables and a salad were placed between them at the center of the table. The two waiters poured them both full glasses of the same Ace of Spades brand she'd recommended using for the grand opening's champagne selection. This one was their Rosé.

She watched the waiters pour in numb silence. A bottle of this stuff costed at least three hundred dollars. It wasn't something you just popped open for a private two-person dinner like this. Not in her world, anyway.

When the waiters retreated, she took a tentative sip of the wine, savoring the sweet fruity flavor and the hints of smoky grilled notes behind it.

"Good?" Atticus asked, sipping his own as he watched her with his keen gray eyes.

She nodded, stomach rumbling. The salmon smelled wonderful too. The two of them ate in silence for a while until she finally worked up the courage to ask him what she'd been wanting to ask since the pool house. "Atticus?"

"Yes?"

"What did you mean when you said you'd show me how easy it is if I let go?"

He smiled at her with the affectionate look she'd only seen directed at her. It softened the angular planes of his face and the sharp look in his eyes. "I meant I'd show you it's easy to be with me. Physically, emotionally...in every way that counts. I know you have fears, Lil. I know you're unsure how we would balance things to avoid wrecking your career, and I know you're scared for other reasons that you won't share. This is real...we are real."

She picked at the rest of her salad. "How can I be sure? I'm risking so much if I say yes to this, Atticus. My relationship with my brother, my job, you..."

"First of all, you're not risking your job," he replied. "That will not be affected by anything between us no matter what happens. If you decide after tonight, you still don't want to move forward and can honestly say it's not just because you're afraid. Then I'll leave this be and will remain nothing but professional in private or otherwise. But if you can't..." His look turned from affectionate to ravenous. "Then I will have all of you, Lillian, whether or not you are afraid. In exchange, I promise you will have all of me and everything I can offer. But that can only happen if you're willing to take a risk tonight."

"What kind of risk?"

"Let me prove to you we have the chemistry to make this work, not just the comfortable camaraderie we had as children or the easy friendship we have when working together."

She blushed, shifting in her seat. Could she really do that? If she did, she'd be crossing a line she'd never crossed with her ex. In truth, she wasn't just afraid of this because she feared Tyler's reaction or endangering her career. She knew Atticus well enough to know he'd do nothing to hurt her professional image. Even if she didn't want to remain with the company, he'd find her something else and make sure she would be okay there.

This was something more.

It was about past wounds and her fears that if she trusted Atticus, it would do more than garner Tyler's ire or start rumors in the office. She feared it would break her in much worse ways than having the one man she'd trusted in college sleep with her college roommate and close friend because she wasn't ready to put out.

"What's going on in that head of yours, little miss?" Atticus asked softly.

"Atticus, if...I don't want it to hurt."

His brow furrowed in concern. "Don't want what to hurt, love?"

"When it falls apart...I...I just don't—"

He was up in an instant and crossing to her side. Kneeling, he took her hands in his. "Lillian, listen to me. I have no intention of going anywhere. If you want me, I'm going to take you. You know I never give up until I have what I want, and that's you this time."

"But what if it's not me tomorrow?" she whispered, heart aching.

"I don't work like that." He squeezed her hands. "You know I don't. If there's anything you should be afraid of, it should be that I will consume you until you don't know which way is up and which down. I never do things in half measures. Let me prove it to you in just a small way tonight."

She lowered her head to hide behind her hair, a tremble in her voice. "Atticus, I...I might mess up."

"Mess up?" He reached up to cup her cheek in his palm. "Little miss, there is no way you could do that tonight unless you demand I take you back to the island and refuse to try to trust me. Even if you do that, I will not be angry."

Her eyes remained permanently fixed on their intertwined hands. "You d-don't understand," she said. This was harder than she could have imagined. Her past fears were at the fore now, and there was no way she could suppress them. She had to deal with this. It was now or never.

He sighed and pulled her from her chair into his lap, cradling her to his chest. "I'm trying. Help me to, Lillian."

"I t-trusted someone else not to be angry with me f-for not knowing what to do, and h-he ditched me for my friend," she admitted.

"What?" His tone hardened.

"I wasn't ready, so he said h-he'd find someone who was." She curled into him, a deep sense of relief warring with shame at the confession.

"Oh, Lil," he whispered, his grip tightening. "That man was an idiot and a jerk. I promise you I'll never be angry at you for inexperience or for saying no if you're not ready. I will understand if you don't want to be with me like that tonight. I promise. If you do, I will consider it an honor."

She clung to him, the shame easing. "You really mean I can't do anything wrong?"

"I really do." He stood and picked her up, heading for the bedroom on the yacht. "If you want this, all you have to do to please me is let go and let me take charge. I'll take care of you, Lillian, just like always."

A tiny shiver skittered through her, and she wrapped her arms around his neck with a sigh, relaxing. She wanted this badly. She could have this, just as Atticus had said. He didn't mind her inexperience, and she didn't know anyone she trusted more than him to be her first. "You'll be gentle? I...it's my first time."

He sucked in a sharp breath, setting her down on the bed and staring down at her with an inscrutable expression. "Really?"

"Really..." She looked away, afraid to see his reaction.

The bed dipped, and he sat beside her, turning her face up to his and kissing her thoroughly. When she was breathless and melting against him, he released her mouth and said, "I'll be gentle, baby girl. You just have to trust me, and I'll make it as good as I can."

She nodded, sagging into him. "I trust you."

Chapter 5

Lillian woke in the warm cocoon of the sheets and comforter on Atticus's bed. She stretched, smiling at the slight soreness the movement provoked. They really had gone through with it last night. She'd given Atticus her virginity, and in the warm light of the morning sunshine streaming in through the window, she felt like she was floating on cloud nine.

Atticus had already risen, but his side of the bed was warm, so he'd only been up for a few minutes at most. She heard murmurs of conversation from the office connected to the yacht's master bedroom. Sitting up, she located the dress she'd worn last night and pulled it on, wishing she'd brought a change of clothes to go home with. Creeping to the door, she raised a hand to knock when she heard Tyler's voice in the small office. Peering in, she saw Atticus was focused on his laptop. Tyler must have called.

"...not going to just stand aside while you screw around with my sister. You're nearly ten years older than she is! What are you thinking? Or are you thinking at all? You'll ruin her! She's practically your sister."

Atticus cleared his throat, silencing even Tyler's tirade with a thunderous look. "Tyler Miller, your sister is a grown woman, not a little girl. She is not my sister, however close we all were growing up, and what I feel for her is certainly not brotherly affection. I am not screwing around with her, as you so rudely put it, and she didn't seem concerned with the age gap, so I don't think you need to concern yourself either. You are my best friend, but that woman out there is my heart and soul." Atticus's voice sharpened. "I will not lose her in order to make you feel more comfortable. I only called because I thought it right to inform you before you find out some other way."

"I can't believe you!" Tyler's voice rose in disbelief and anger.

"Believe it. You know how much I care about your sister, Ty. I always have. I'd never do anything to intentionally hurt her—"

"You keep up with this, and that's exactly what you'll do! What do you think will happen when you tire of her and leave?"

"Tyler Miller!" Atticus's tone sharpened. "Suggest that again, and we'll come to blows when I next see you. Your sister isn't a fling, and you know full well I take relationships seriously."

"I don't give my approval. Doesn't that matter to you at all, Atti?" Tyler's tone was almost pleading now. "She's my baby sister."

"The only thing you have right about that, Tyler, is that she is your sister. But she hasn't been a child in a very long time. Your problem is that you can't see it. I do."

"You know what, Atticus?" Tyler's voice tightened. "If you won't quit playing games with my sister, I don't want to hear from you again, and you can bet Lillian will be hearing from me."

Atticus growled, low and menacing. "I'm not playing any games with Lil. You'll be waiting a very long time to hear from me again if this is how you're going to behave!" The laptop screen slammed down with startling force.

Lillian backed away from the door, chest tightening. What had she done? She'd done precisely what she'd been trying to avoid—coming between two best friends and angering her brother. She never should have given in to Atticus, vulnerable and needy or not. She'd wanted him so badly last night and let him have her without protest. She should have known better.

She fled to the bathroom, turning on the shower to hide her heavy breaths. Now, even though it killed her even to consider it, she had to walk away from Atticus. She couldn't get between them, and she couldn't risk her career for it either. Atticus would understand, wouldn't he?

His words to Tyler came back then. That woman out there is my heart and soul. How had she not noticed Atticus Moore was in love with her? She'd known him nearly all her life, and she knew he wouldn't lie to Tyler, even if he wouldn't say the words aloud. She stood under the hot water, body shaking. It figured that the one man who really loved her for who she was happened to be the one man she couldn't let herself have or want.

She swiped at her eyes filled with tears threatening to fall, and got out of the shower. No sense in prolonging this. She needed to steel herself for this, and find a way to lie to Atticus about how she felt about last night. It hurt so badly to consider lying to a man she knew trusted her to be honest, and was banking on her honesty to pull them through the initial hurdles toward a future. Now she had to crush it to keep their relationship from ruining one he'd always held in high regard. She wouldn't get between Tyler and Atticus. There were other men to love.

She knew it wasn't true even as she thought it. There might be other men to love, but there were no other men she would ever love. She'd tried with her ex, and her fixation on Atticus had been the subconscious block that kept her from sleeping with her ex, ultimately leading to his devastating betrayal. Trying again wouldn't see better success now, not after she'd let Atticus have her body as well as her soul.

Pinching some color into her cheeks, she took a few steadying breaths. It didn't matter that this would rip her heart out and break his for a time. She had to do this for his sake. If she really loved him, she couldn't be why he lost the few genuine and close relationships he had in his life.

***

When Lillian came out of his bathroom, he knew something was wrong with one look on her face. He was still seething over the call with Tyler. The man could be so bull-headed sometimes, and this was an occasion where he'd decided to be just that. He hated that the call had to end on such bad footing, but he wasn't budging on this. Lillian was his. Tyler would have to deal.

Seeing Lillian's distant expression, which didn't quite hide the regret and pain in her eyes, wiped away all concern over Tyler. He froze, unsure what could have happened between last night and this morning. "Lil?"

She looked away. "I want to go back."

"We don't have to hurry back. I told the team we'd be out until late this afternoon."

Her jaw tightened, as she continued avoiding his gaze. "I want to go back, Atticus. Now."

"Are you okay?"

"No. Last night..." Her voice wavered. "Last night was a mistake. I...I felt vulnerable, and it sounded so...I shouldn't have given in."

A low growl built deep inside of him. She was doing it again. Refusing herself things she wanted and had no reason to push aside because she thought she shouldn't. "This had better not be like turning down the last piece of cake on your birthday, little miss."

"Don't call me that," she hissed. "You're nothing more than my boss, and it needs to stay that way."

"No, it most certainly does not, and you weren't saying that last night in my bed." He shoved his hands into his pockets to hide the way they were shaking. Why was she doing this? "You promised me not to run from this if last night went well. You're many things, sweetheart, but a good actress isn't one of them."

"I don't want more between us," she insisted.

"You do. You just don't want to risk everything else to have it."

He stalked closer, grabbing her chin and forcing her to look at him. "What did I tell you, Lillian? First rule of engagement. What is it?"

"No lies," she whispered, meeting his gaze.

"Are you lying to me?"

"No."

"I don't believe you. Tell me the truth."

She sucked in a sharp breath, color rising into her cheeks from how close they were. Flashes of last night came back to her, unrelenting.

No! she thought as she shoved him away. "How dare you accuse me of lying on purpose? This isn't a game, Atticus."

"No, it most certainly is not." He gritted his teeth. "I know you enjoyed last night. Tell me the truth. Why are you pushing me away?"

Her hands trembled at her sides. "Stop, Atticus. Please..."

The word, soft and broken, stabbed him to the quick. What was wrong? Had he done something to cause her pain and her anger? "Come on, little miss," he whispered in a plea of his own. "Talk to me."

She shook her head and turned her back, wrapping her arms around her torso. "Take me home, Atticus."

He sighed. "Lil..."

"No. I mean it. Take me home right now. This...whatever this is...is a mistake. I don't want to talk about it. I don't even want to think about it. I want to go back—"

"We can't," Atticus said, voice strangled.

"Maybe we can't," she agreed before delivering the final blow. "But I can. I want to go back to the hotel and work, sir."

Shoulders slumping, he slipped past her. "Very well."

Chapter 6

Atticus made it through a week of burying himself in work and avoiding Lillian before he had to ask her questions that texts or phone calls couldn't answer. He was about to knock when her phone rang inside the office, insistent and demanding her attention. The ringing stopped. She must have picked up.

"Tyler, what's up?"

"Lillian." Tyler's voice was clipped and irritated on speaker. "I think you know why I'm calling."

"I'm not sure..."

"Don't play coy," he snapped. "What is the matter with you? He's ten years your senior, and he's your boss. Besides, he is like an older brother. How could you possibly—"

"Tyler, first of all, it's none of your business who I do and do not get involved with."

Atticus's hopes rose. Maybe last week had all been a misunderstanding. Maybe she'd panicked and said the first things that came to mind in order to get some space. If that was the case, she'd have to learn that asking would get further with him than anything else.

Her next words dashed his hope. "But if you must know, we're not an item. I made a mistake last week, and we slept together. That is not the same as being together, and you can rest easy knowing I've come to my senses," she snapped. "So, please...don't call to rub my face in my own rash behavior."

Tyler heaved a sigh over the phone. "You know this will complicate things for you. If you end up needing a job, my firm—"

"Atticus is mature enough not to let what happened impact my job. He'll get over it."

"He didn't seem inclined to get over it when he called last week. He seemed to believe you were the one."

Lillian remained quiet for a long moment.

"Lillian? You made sure he knew you weren't interested in more beforehand, didn't you?"

"Of course I did."

Atticus held back a growl. She'd done no such thing. In fact, she'd agreed to trust him, had promised to give them a chance if he could prove to her it was worth the risk. He'd thought he'd done so, but now he wasn't so certain. Maybe he'd made a huge mistake.

He left and headed back to his office, not wanting to hear more. She'd lied to her brother. Had she also lied when she'd told him on the yacht that she didn't want more between them? She seemed to be insistent on keeping her distance.

They hadn't talked at all on the ride home, and in the past week, she'd barely spoken to him if she could avoid it. When they saw one another in meetings, she was coldly professional, and when they ran across one another in the hotel, she quickly headed the other way to avoid him.

It cut deep. He couldn't think of a time they had been this uncomfortable around one another. And every time he saw her, he spotted the signs of exhaustion and misery in her.

He longed to reach out to brush her wayward curls out of her way in meetings or pull her aside to demand she take a day off to sleep long enough to remove the dark smudges of weariness beneath her eyes.

He resisted the urge even though it killed him to do it. She'd made herself clear, and any other attempts at conversation since the morning on his yacht had ended in disaster.

Anger and pain warred with one another inside, and he slammed his office door, stalking to his computer to turn on his out-of-office email notification. The team didn't need him for the rest of the afternoon. He was going back to his mansion. He'd work out in his home gym and then take a dip in the pool to cool off some of his anger. Maybe some physical pain could take the edge off this emotional pain.

Never in his life had he experienced such pain. He'd gone through countless injuries in his younger years thanks to his reckless nature, but not one of them had ever hurt this badly. He wanted to scream and beat something to a pulp. Maybe Tyler.

He was almost certain she'd overheard his conversation with her brother. Even if she hadn't made up her mind before that to put distance between them, no doubt that conversation solidified it. And now that she'd lied to her brother, it would only be a matter of time before she chose to end things formally before they even started.

If he wanted any chance to salvage whatever small spark was left between them, he needed to blow off some steam and then confront her about avoiding him.

At the very least, he needed to be certain she was really being honest about how she felt about him if Tyler and her concerns about work were removed. If she hadn't lied to Tyler about her concerns over her job, then he knew at least that concern was not at the heart of the issue.

But hearing her lie to her brother so smoothly left him uncertain of even that much. If she could lie to him so easily, who knew what she'd told the truth or chosen to lie about?

For his own sanity, though, he needed to deal with this. He didn't run from his problems, and while Lillian had a habit of it, he was done putting up with that particular habit. She'd have to tell him face to face that she wanted to end the relationship.

He felt a pang deep in his chest at the thought of things ending.

He'd respect Lillian's wishes if she truly thought they were a mistake, but he hated the idea with every fiber of his being.

Somehow, he'd already come to think of her as his, and what had happened that night on his boat only crystallized that for him. If she didn't think the same way, then for the first time in his life, he might actually find an obstacle he couldn't surmount. He might actually find himself heartbroken, not just disappointed, too, and the thought terrified him.

Chapter 7

A knock at her bedroom door pulled her out of the book she'd snagged from Atticus's library. Sighing, she threw her legs over the bed and stood, shuffling to the door to open it.

Atticus's butler, Graves, stood on the other side, hand poised to knock again. He lowered his arm with a smile when he saw her. "Miss Miller, Mr. Moore has requested your presence in his office."

She frowned. "What for?"

"He wishes to go over something about the hotel with you over dinner, unless you've eaten already."

Her stomach grumbled, reminding her that she hadn't eaten anything since lunch. She'd been too engrossed in her work and then too tired right after work to bother. "Just to go over the designs, right?"

"I believe so, Miss Miller. Shall I tell him you'll be up after you change?"

She glanced down at her yoga pants and t-shirt. Maybe she should change. Atticus was probably accustomed to wearing more formal attire to dinner, given his status, but she wasn't. He could deal with it. She wasn't trying to impress him. Besides, she sort of wanted to see his response. Would he be shocked? Off kilter? Or amused? "No. I'll go as I am. I can find my own way, Graves. Thank you."

He bowed and left, disappearing down the hall to return to his tasks. She sighed and returned to her room, putting a bookmark in the book she'd been reading. Then she pulled her hair into a high ponytail and trudged out of the bedroom to go see what Atticus needed this late. It was well after work hours, but it shouldn't surprise her. He spent most of his time working anyway, and he'd been worse than usual since their argument on the yacht.

She padded barefoot down the thick wine-red carpet that blanketed the oak floorboards of the mansion. Trailing her fingers along the banister, she looked down at the chandelier of the entryway and shook her head. He really did have a lot of money. She couldn't imagine owning a house with one chandelier, let alone one that had four like Atticus's mansion here did.

When she reached the heavy oak door of Atticus's office, she paused, collecting herself for a moment. She could still turn around and leave, and part of her wanted to. Still, he'd called her here to discuss their project. It would be childish and unprofessional not to appear when her boss called her. She might've ignored dress protocols because it was after hours, and they had known each other for so long, but she shouldn't refuse to show. Raising a hand, she knocked.

"Come in," Atticus called.

She opened the door and stepped inside.

He had two plates of chicken marsala and two glasses of chardonnay already resting on the desk, with the rest of the wine in a bucket of ice. A candle sat lit in the center, giving the whole scene a warm glow when paired with the dull orange light of the lamps around the room.

She didn't see any papers or his laptop, and she frowned. "Wasn't this supposed to be a business dinner?"

He stared back at her. "I had something I wanted to speak to you about, but you've been difficult to catch of late."

Flushing, she trailed over to the desk and sat across from him. "This looks romantic, not professional."

"Trust me. It's nothing of the kind," he muttered, voice

sharpening. "I wanted you here to ask you a very blunt question, and I want the truth, Lillian."

Her heart hammered in her chest. "What are you talking about?"

"Us. You've been distant since the yacht, and I don't think it's because our night together wasn't good for you." He frowned at her. "I think you lied to me because you were spooked and overthought the situation, and I want the truth now. If you really want us to be over, I want you to look me in the eye and tell me that."

"I told you that on the yacht," she snapped, feeling ambushed.

"You were nearly in tears as you did so, which leads me to believe you didn't really want to say the words. If you can tell me that you want to end what's between us right now without looking near tears, I will let it go." He sipped at his wine, regarding her over the rim of his wineglass.

"I can," she whispered, heart aching. "As I said, we can't do this." She waved at the candle and the meal on his desk. "Any of this. I have a professional image to maintain, and—"

"Bull," he snapped, setting aside the wine. "You're using that as an excuse. You know full well I'd never let anything that happened between us hurt your career or your authority with those you're managing."

"People talk." Her voice rose in frustration. Why couldn't he understand this? Even if she knew he wouldn't intentionally jeopardize anything, he shouldn't dismiss her fears. "This is a hard limit for me, Atticus. I won't have my employees or coworkers claiming I got my position or upcoming promotion because I slept with my boss!"

"No one would say that. Everyone knows how hard you work. They respect you, and more importantly, they like you. Not one of them would dare imply that."

"They might not dare do so openly, but there'll be muffled gossip around the water cooler. They'll be thinking about it if they don't say it. It's just a bad idea!"

"Others have made it work. This isn't the problem at all, Lillian. Something else is at the root of this obstinance." He leaned back in his chair and crossed his arms, candlelight throwing his high cheekbones into sharp relief. "What's the real reason you don't want to be with me?"

She stood, throwing her hands up in exasperation. "You know what, Atticus? This is enough of a reason! You don't need an explanation at all, actually. I'm giving one out of respect for our friendship, but I didn't have to. You need to hear me spell it out? I don't want you. I don't want a relationship. I want to remain nothing more than an employee. Is that clear enough?"

A muscle in his jaw ticked as he stared back at her, but after a long moment, he looked away with a curt nod. "Fine. Get out."

"Really?" She shook her head with a huff. "Look, we still have to work together. We need to figure out how to do that despite—"

Atticus stood, towering behind his desk. "Lillian, leave. I'm not asking. You don't want to be anything more, and I will respect that, but I don't want to talk about it further, and I definitely do not want to eat a meal while pretending nothing is wrong. Take your food and the wine with you, and just go."

She contemplated the tired slump of his shoulders and the pain in his expression. He was hiding it better than she'd hid hers the morning after he'd taken her virginity, but it was there. Her choice was breaking his heart, something she hadn't really expected of Atticus. He was usually so composed and cool. It ached to watch him hurt, but this was for the best. She nodded, collected both the plate and the wine glass, and left him alone.

Chapter 8

The month remaining before opening slipped away at an agonizingly slow pace. Lillian couldn't shake the ache that had settled into her chest since she'd told Atticus they wouldn't see each other anymore. Tyler had called a few more times, but she'd barely spoken to him at all. Now the grand opening night was upon them.

She glided through the ballroom where they'd set up refreshments and over to the adjoining room of poker and roulette tables by a gleaming bar. Everything seemed to be in order, and the guests would arrive in a few minutes. Atticus would kick the evening off with the ribbon cutting to symbolize the hotel's opening, and then they'd have refreshments and a bit of friendly gaming near the bar.

Her phone rang in the pocket of her slacks, and she pulled it out. Tyler. Sighing, she flicked it to send it to voicemail. A minute later, the phone rang again. She rolled her eyes and picked up. "Tyler, I'm busy."

"You're always busy," he remarked. "I wanted to check in on you. You've been clipped and quiet every time you've picked up, and over the last month, you've ignored half of those calls entirely."

"Because I'm—"

"Busy?" Tyler finished.

"Yes. Much like now. I don't want to talk, Tyler. You've done enough."

"What?" He sounded confused.

She pinched the bridge of her nose and sighed. "I didn't...never mind. I'm just a bit tired and stressed. The grand opening will start seating for the opening ceremony in three minutes, and I need to be on stage in twenty. What do you really want, Tyler?"

"Initially, I just wanted to know things were really okay with you. Now I want to know what you mean by 'you've done enough'. What's going on?"

"You know what, Tyler? If you don't know, I don't want to share."

"I don't understand, Lil. What did I do?"

"Tyler," she snapped. "I don't have time to deal with this or with you. Really, I'm in no mood. I have to go on stage in twenty minutes with Atticus, and the guests are starting to arrive. I don't want to...It's going to be a long enough night without adding this to the list of things I have to find a way to slog through. Got it?"

"This is about Atticus, isn't it?" he asked quietly. "That's what you mean when you say I've done enough. You overheard us talking. I'm the reason you broke things off with him, aren't I?"

She swallowed hard and collapsed onto a bar stool as guests started trickling into the next room. Her feet already hurt thanks to these stupid heels, and Tyler was dredging up even more emotional pain. Even though she knew he deserved more grace because of all he'd done to raise her and care for her through the years after their parents' deaths, she couldn't muster the energy to be forgiving. "What does it matter, Ty? You got what you wanted."

"I—"

"Tyler, I really do have to go," she murmured.

"Sis, maybe—"

"Bye, Tyler. We'll talk some other time, but not if you decide to bring this up again. I'm not talking about it with you." She hung up, tucking her phone into her pocket. It buzzed again. Tyler was probably calling back, but she didn't have the energy for this.

It hurt badly enough to be forced to stand on the stage, smiling beside Atticus, when the mere sight of him sent pain slicing through her chest. She knew they didn't look happy when they were around each other anymore. They never really looked content or happy like they had before. Despite Atticus's promises, their quickly ended romance was already impacting both of their images. She just hoped she could put on a good show tonight so it wouldn't be obvious to the high-paying clients here.

***

Atticus stood still while Graves adjusted his tie and then disappeared to go help with the refreshments. He was grateful to his old friend and butler for being here to support him. He would've liked to have Tyler here instead, but his best friend was otherwise occupied, and after the way Tyler had come between him and Lillian, Atticus found himself disinclined to see the man.

His phone buzzed in his pocket, and he pulled it out to check the caller ID. Tyler. He rolled his eyes and picked up. If this wasn't an apology, he'd hang up as soon as he could get a word in. Now was not the time to deal with an argument. Lillian would be in any minute. As soon as he picked up, the other man lit into him.

"Why didn't you pick up earlier?"

An argument, then. He sighed. "I was busy. I'm sure you are aware we had the grand opening tonight."

"Yes, but...I need to ask you about Lillian. She's been avoiding my calls or answering them, but keeping everything brief and terse. It's not like her," Tyler said. "I'm worried."

Atticus ground his teeth for a moment before he replied. "You should be, Tyler."

"Excuse me? You sound like you think this is my fault!"

"You think it isn't, you idiot? If she hasn't told you so, it's only because she can't bear to upset you." His temper rose with his voice. "You knew very well that Lil would give up anything to make you happy, Tyler Miller! She loves you. More than that, she looks up to you and feels indebted to you because you raised her so she wouldn't end up in foster care after your parents died."

"Come on, Atti, it's not—"

"I'm not done, Tyler. The only thing she cares about more than her job is you, and you barged into our business, making her feel like she had to give up a chance to be happy with me to make you happy. I don't want to hear it from you." He blew out a heavy breath, softening his tone a fraction. "Tyler, she's miserable. She has dark circles under her eyes like she's not sleeping. I'm pretty sure she's lost weight. She looks worse than death warmed over. Don't you dare tell me this isn't your fault. She overheard you chewing me out for sleeping with her and intending to make her mine. I'm certain of it now, and she lied to you that day on the phone, by the way. She didn't tell me it was a fling."

Tyler remained silent, as though he didn't know what to say.

"Did you actively talk her into breaking things off, Ty?"

"No...I mean, not in as many words. It took me a week to cool off enough to talk to her, and when I did, I just asked her to confirm or deny it. I didn't talk her into it."

"But you planned to?"

The other side of the line went quiet. Finally, Tyler heaved a sigh. "Yes."

"She's miserable, Tyler. I hope you understand what you've done."

"Look, Atticus," Tyler snapped. "I get that you think I've done the wrong thing. She's probably not nearly as miserable as you think, and she'll get over it if she is. She's better off leaving early on before she gets hurt."

Atticus's fingers went stiff, and he barely got the words out when he replied. "That's not fair to me, and you know it. I'm not the sort of man who would take a relationship with her lightly."

"I know my sister," he stated. "And I know you. It'll end with her getting hurt. This is for the best."

"You know what?" Atticus snapped. "You don't know what's best for her, Tyler. Not anymore. You know full well I never would've done anything to hurt her, and you know once I make up my mind, it's made up. She is the only one who would've walked away, and she did because of you, not because it was best for her."

"She decided herself."

"You know what, Miller? Don't call me again, or I'll block your number. You can call Lillian to apologize. We won't be speaking again if you don't intend to apologize to her. You don't have to worry about my relationship with her screwing up our friendship. You've done that yourself. We're through unless you fix your giant screw-up, understood?"

"Come on. Be—"

Atticus hung up with a growl. He clenched his fingers around his phone, tempted to hurl it at a wall. That wouldn't do much. It was Tyler's face he wanted to smash. His phone didn't need to withstand his wrath. After what he'd just heard from Tyler, he was certain he'd screwed up too by letting Lillian go. This was done. He was through waiting for this.

After that call, he needed time to steel himself before seeing Lillian and knowing he would forever feel that sharp blast of pain, longing, and regret that blew through his walls every time he saw her. There wasn't any time left, though. The low buzz of the crowd's chatter filled the space, and he glanced at the clock on the wall above the stage entrance. It was time.

Where was Lillian?

His frustration rose.

He could understand her need to push him away because of Tyler, but she should've just said that. He probably would've taken his anger out on Tyler and forced him to stop being such a moron about the issue, but he would've understood. Instead, she'd lied, which made him almost as furious with her as he was with Tyler.

The door to the casino opened, and she appeared, dressed in a pair of fitted slacks and a ruffled white blouse that dipped just low enough to expose a tantalizing glimpse of her cleavage. He stared for too long, wishing he could remind her of how good things were between them, so she'd stop pushing him away. But he'd promised to respect her decision, so he dragged his gaze back up. "It's time. You're late."

"Sorry," she whispered.

He dared a glance at her face and found nothing, but his own misery reflected on him. Nothing about her tense shoulders, the tight set of her jaw, or the weak attempt at a smile she offered spoke of a woman happy with her life. He'd never seen her look so lackluster as she did tonight. His anger softened a bit when he realized her lies had hurt her even more than they'd hurt him. She'd dished out her own punishment for the dishonesty. They still needed to talk, but he needed to tread gently with her to avoid making this worse.

"Let's go." He offered Lillian an arm. "Smile for me?" he whispered. "Just for tonight? I...you look miserable, little miss."

She looked away, but not before he saw the sheen of tears in her eyes. "Don't call me that, Atticus. I can't...I don't like it."

"Just one smile, Lil. Just while we're on stage," he begged.

"If you can manage one, then so will I."

He nodded, wishing that wasn't such a difficult thing to accomplish. Taking a deep breath, he shoved the pain back into its safe deep inside his heart and plastered a smile on his face. He'd put on a smile for her for tonight, but they would deal with this little issue and her lies when this was over. With a deep breath, he led Lillian into the dazzling lights.

Chapter 9

Lillian hid in the library, trying to avoid everyone, especially Atticus. The rest of the crew would be going back to the States tomorrow. She was supposed to stay on to help Atticus begin some other design work for a set of rental condos he wanted to construct near the hotel to provide more permanent vacation housing on that side of his island. It would be a month of torture being so close to him with no one else to take his attention off her.

A throat clearing caused her to jump to her feet, dropping the book she'd been pretending to read with a thump on the blue carpet. She stared up into familiar gray eyes, heart thudding in her chest. Words failed to come to mind as she tried to think of something to say. He looked ready to explode with anger, and she wasn't sure if it was directed at her or something else. She dropped her gaze, fiddling with her blouse's buttons.

"We need to talk. You'd best answer the questions I'm about to ask honestly this time, because I'm really not in the mood for lies."

She gasped, lifting her gaze to his with heat rising in her cheeks. "What?"

"You heard me. I believe I've made it clear how I feel about lies." His expression softened a little. "The truth, if you please."

"I..." She shifted from foot to foot, nervous about where this was going. "I don't know why you think I've been lying."

"I asked you if you really wanted to end our relationship in my office last month," he said quietly.

Oh. That was what this was about. She stared down at the floor without a word.

"I already know you lied to me. You didn't want to end anything. You did it because you knew Tyler didn't want us together, and you were afraid to wreck his relationship with me or to lose him yourself."

There was nothing left to say. He was right, and shame filled her. She should've been honest about why she wanted to end things, but instead, she'd run. In truth, she hadn't wanted to end it at all. That one night with Atticus had replayed in her dreams countless times since, leaving her sleepless many nights. She was miserable without him now that she'd tasted the fantasy she'd held since she was a teenager.

"I'm sorry." Her voice hitched, and then the stress and pain from the last month came to a head, as she collapsed into the leather armchair. "I'm sorry."

He sighed, motionless for a long moment.

She squeezed her eyes shut and buried her face in her hands. He probably hated her now. She'd known how he felt about lies and had lied anyway, not once, but twice. Firm, gentle hands picked her up and dragged her into a warm embrace. Then she was nestled on Atticus's lap as he sat down in the chair with her. "Thank you for being honest with me. Now this time, I want the truth, Lil. Do you or do you not want to take a chance on us?"

She buried her face in his chest. "If you still want m-me after this."

He stroked her hair gently. "Of course I do. I never stopped wanting you, but from now on, you will tell me the truth when something's wrong instead of running. We will find our balance, baby girl, even if it takes time. You just have to work with me. Promise me?"

"I promise."

"Good. Now, we're making a weekend trip to go see Tyler. You're going to tell him yourself that we're together, and he can screw off if he doesn't like it."

"What?" She sat up. "But he'll—"

He scowled, a touch of his earlier anger back in his angular features. "If he knows what's good for him, he'll apologize. I've already informed him that if you don't get an apology, I'm through speaking to him."

She stiffened. "But Atticus, he's your best friend?"

"No one comes before the woman I love, little miss." He smiled at her affectionately. "Not even your brother."

***

They arrived at Tyler's small condo back in New York City in the early evening hours after an eight-hour flight on Atticus's private jet. Atticus propelled her up the steps and reached out to ring the bell when her hands were shaking too much to do so. She hated conflict with Tyler, and this news was certain to cause just that.

Tyler opened the door with a frown, eyes widening when he saw the two of them on his doorstep. She looked back at Atticus, who was standing there with his hands in his pockets and a stern look on his face. Then she looked back at Tyler and played with the strap of her purse. "T-Tyler..."

"Lil." He scowled at Atticus. "What are you both doing here?"

"Visiting to share some wonderful news," Atticus said, resting a hand on the small of her back. "Lil?"

Tyler groaned. "Oh, God, please no...Lil, don't tell me you're...didn't you...well, you know?"

She flushed. "Tyler Miller! I am not sharing those kinds of things with you."

"Well, someone's got to ask," he snapped. "Mom and Dad would have, but they're gone, so now I have to. If you mess up and get knocked up, I'm the one you'll be coming to."

Her temper washed away any trepidation she'd felt. "After

how you handled the news of my involvement with Atticus? You've got to be delusional! I'd go to Atticus before I'd go to you, whether he and I were involved. But I'm not here because he knocked me up. I'm here to tell you I've done some thinking and want to pursue a relationship with Atticus. Nothing you can say can talk me out of it. I let you do that once, and I was so miserable I didn't think I could keep going through it for another day."

Tyler scowled and crossed his arms. "Did you put her up to this, Atticus?"

Lillian didn't give Atticus a chance to answer. "No, he did not. Get your head out of the sand, Tyler. Stop allowing your protectiveness of me and your prejudice against Atticus because of his age and your discomfort with your best friend dating your sister to turn you into a jerk. It's not becoming. I'm standing here telling you I have decided to be with Atticus. I decided, not him. You either live with it or don't. It won't change what I do."

Lillian huffed out, drawing closer to Atticus. Seconds later, her eyes softened. "This man was there for me in every way he could be when we were dealing with Mom and Dad's deaths. He helped you when you couldn't cope with everything, and even though he now sees me as a woman instead of a child—something you ought to try—he still stands up for me and does his best to care for me. I love you, but I won't walk away from a man who loves me like that just to make you happy."

Tyler stood there in stunned silence for a few moments, staring at her as if she'd grown two heads. Finally, he cleared his throat and nodded. "Okay. Okay, I get it. I...I don't like it, but you're right. This isn't my decision. I'm sorry I tried to get involved, Lillian. Atticus...You hurt her, and I will rip you to pieces, best friend or not. Got it?"

Atticus laughed. "Got it. You going to leave us on the doorstep all day?"

Tyler sighed and glanced at Atticus's Maserati. "No. Bring the car into the garage. Can't believe you brought such an expensive car into this neighborhood. Hurry up and get it out of sight before someone gets ideas."

Atticus took her hand in his and drew her into him, kissing her temple. "Go inside and talk with your brother, little miss. I'll be in after I park the car."

She nodded with a soft smile.

When he was out of earshot, Tyler eyed her. "You really love him, don't you?"

"I do."

He nodded. "I'm sorry, Lil. Really...I should've known better. Should've trusted your judgment."

"Yes, you should've." She linked her arm through his and tugged him inside. "But I won't hold it over your head forever. Now come on. We have catching up to do."

Epilogue

A year later

Lillian rolled out of her side of the king-sized bed in Atticus's New York City penthouse apartment with a moan, clapping a hand over her mouth.

Atticus stirred and sat up. "Are you all right, love? You're not coming down with something, right before the wedding, are you? This is the third day in a row you've woken up feeling queasy."

She shook her head, fighting down the rising wave of nausea. It wouldn't settle, and it intensified instead. She shot to her feet and ran for the bathroom, making it just in time to heave into the toilet. Nothing much besides bile came up, and she was thankful she hadn't tried to eat anything yet.

Atticus's fingers scraped her hair back and off her neck. He tied it off with a ponytail with a sigh. When the heaving subsided, he handed her a glass of water. She took it with a tired, grateful smile and took small sips to settle her stomach, staring at the glittering diamond on her ring to ground herself. It would soon be replaced with a much more expensive gold band of small diamonds surrounded by rubies, but she liked the small single diamond encased with delicate gold prongs and filigree.

"Maybe we should see the doctor. Do you think we'll have to postpone the wedding next week?"

She shook her head with a grimace. "No. It's in the afternoon. I'll be fine by then."

He raised a brow. “You can time the puking?”

A weak laugh escaped her. “No, I can’t time the puking, Atticus. It’s better in the afternoons.”

“It is?” He eyed her dubiously. “That doesn’t make sense. Either you’re sick, or you’re not.”

“I’m not.”

He gestured to the toilet with a shake of his head. “Then what does this classify as?”

“Morning sickness?”

He opened his mouth to say something and then stopped, eyes widening. “Wait...you mean...”

She smiled. “Pretty sure, yes. I took the test last night, but you came home too late for me to tell you.”

“We’re going to have a baby?” he whispered.

“Yeah.” Her smile faltered. “You’re...You’re okay with that, right?”

“Okay with it?” He cupped her face in his hands and kissed her. “I’m more than okay with it.”

She relaxed against him with a contented sigh. “Oh, good. We hadn’t talked about it, so I was worried...I mean, you seemed less than thrilled, so...”

“I’m just surprised. I didn’t expect it quite so soon. We weren’t trying, and you were on birth control, so I thought you wouldn’t...”

“So did I, but I missed a dose by accident. Sometimes this stuff happens.” She pressed her palms to her belly. “You’re glad it did, though, right?”

“Yes, little miss.” He kissed the tip of her nose. “Are you?”

“Well, I could do without the morning sickness.” She laughed. “But yeah...yeah, I am. It took a few hours for it to really sink in after I had the test results staring back at me, but I’m more excited than I’d expected.”

He grinned. “We’re going to be parents.”

“I’m just glad the wedding is in a week,” she muttered.

"Otherwise, I'm pretty sure Tyler would kill you for this."

He chuckled. "He could try."

"I'd rather he didn't. I'm not interested in losing you for a long, long time yet." She leaned up to kiss his cheek. "I rather like the idea of becoming Mrs. Atticus Moore in a week. If Tyler tries to screw it up, he'll be the one in fear for his life."

"Such a hellion when you set your mind to it," he murmured, drawing her into an embrace. "Don't worry, though. Tyler's already agreed to be my best man. I'm pretty sure he's not going to kill me."

She stared at the big steam room with longing and sighed. "Good. Atticus?"

"Hmmm?"

"We can't use the sauna anymore until the baby's born. I read that online last night." She groaned, pressing a hand to her lower back. "And I ache everywhere."

"Come on then, silly girl." He tugged on one of her unruly curls with a laugh. "I'll knead the knots out for you if you come back to bed."

With a satisfied smile, she let him draw her into the bedroom and back to bed. When he did as promised and began working the knots and kinks out of her back, she relaxed into the mattress with a contented moan. How she'd ever been lucky enough to have the man she'd wanted since her high school days, she didn't know, but she would forever be grateful that he'd chosen her. She couldn't imagine a life without him, and they would exchange the vows that would bind them for the rest of their lives in a week. She looked forward to that and to whatever riding off into the sunset would bring their way next.

Lawyer Billionaire Daddy (Book 2)

Blurb
Elijah Clarkson knows which buttons to push to elicit a debate from Sophia Anderson. But Sophia has yet to realize why Elijah is keen to see her heated.

Elijah loves to get a rise out of Sophia. He loves her, point blank. He sees her potential and has waited until she made her dreams come true by becoming a lawyer before revealing how he feels. He has waited long enough and isn't afraid of a challenge.

Sophia has always looked up to Elijah. His career as a lawyer has always inspired her. As soon as she graduates and begins her career, she notices a shift in how Elijah treats her. It's all she's ever wanted, but the stakes are too high. Especially when they are opposing counsels on a high-profile case with media attention.

Elijah suggests a one-night stand to ease the tension.
The fix fails. They both want more.

Can they give in to the forbidden for more? Can they risk their careers and hearts by giving in?

Prologue

Sophia Anderson stepped into the stuffy meeting room with a spring in her step. This would be her first real case since passing the bar. Finally, she had achieved her childhood dream, and she was part of an incredible team, alongside junior partner, Maria Martinez, her idol. She had previously worked with Maria as a paralegal and admired the woman greatly. To be invited to work with her as an associate on this case was a dream come true.

Sophia took her place at the table with a smile, leaning over to greet Maria. The older woman smiled back and nodded to her. The door on the opposite side of the room opened, and she settled into her seat, trying not to squirm like an excited schoolgirl. She knew this wouldn't be nearly as exciting in a week or two, but she'd loved her work as a paralegal and expected to love this too.

Her gaze lifted to the people entering from the other side of the meeting room. This would be the other team, the people they would have to beat if they wanted to get their client acquitted. When Sophia saw a familiar tall frame with piercing brown eyes and neatly combed dirty blond hair, she tensed and tried to stifle a gasp. Her breath hitched, strangling in her throat.

His gaze fell on her, and she spotted the tightening of his jaw. It was probably imperceptible to anyone else, but she knew it well. He was surprised too. He was better at hiding it than she was, though, and he moved to the head of the table across from

Maria without missing a step.

Maria leaned over with a tight smile. "Try not to be intimidated, Soph. His bark is worse than his bite."

Sophia forced a laugh. His bark was certainly *not* worse than his bite. Elijah Clarkson was not a man to be trifled with and was a good lawyer. Well, spectacular, actually, given his quick rise to senior partner at his firm. Why hadn't she realized a high profile case like this might draw him in? She was so screwed. Seeing him now brought the old feelings she'd held for him into sharp focus once again, and she shifted in her seat, avoiding his gaze. "I'm sure it is."

"I'd know," Maria murmured. "I dated the hard-nosed pain in the—"

Elijah's gaze was firmly on Sophia, weighing her down in the chair until she wanted to sink into it and hide. Whatever Maria was telling her in quiet murmurs was lost in the gravity of that look, and she couldn't help looking back. This was so bad.

Back in the day, since she was 8 and him 16, she and Elijah could argue until kingdom come, and the few times he'd been by to visit since his graduation from high school had proven their debates hadn't changed much. She didn't fear that she wouldn't be able to counter his arguments before the jury and judge.

Now, at 24, she feared her professionalism would be wrecked, losing her place in this case because of their past. She had to keep a lid on her attraction to him, that had been growing since she turned 16, and avoid letting on about their personal connection. Thankfully, Maria had no idea they'd known each other as children.

The meeting started, and Sophia tried to focus on taking notes as usual, but with Elijah's gaze boring a hole in the top of her bent head, she found it increasingly difficult to focus. The minutes ticked by in slow torture, and she was acutely aware of the clock's ticking behind the low murmur of the voices in the room as requests for information were handed over, and other official business was dealt with.

Finally, Elijah stood. She straightened in her seat, unsure why she felt the need to snap to attention when he did so. His movement signaled the meeting's end.

"Any further requests may be sent directly to me or my paralegal," he informed the room in his warm, low voice.

She suppressed a shiver and doodled on her notepad to distract herself.

"Sophia, may I speak to you in the hall?"

She looked up to find him standing next to her chair and stiffened, glancing at Maria for help.

"Why do you need to talk to my associate, Elijah?" Maria's voice held suspicion but remained professional in tone.

"She assisted as my paralegal a few times while going through law school. I haven't had a chance to congratulate her on passing the bar exam," he replied smoothly, waving his own gawking team out of the room. "I'll catch up," he told them.

"You can't congratulate her in here?"

"I had a small gift for her, and I see no reason why I need to explain myself to you, Maria. If Sophia has no objections, you shouldn't either. It's hardly unacceptable practice to give a newly minted lawyer hearty congratulations, regardless of which team she's playing for." His gaze returned to her. "Sophia? May I give you the gift privately? I didn't think you'd wish me to embarrass you in front of the entire team. Unless you've changed your opinion of making a display of gifts and congratulations for your work?"

She flushed and pushed away from the table. A bark worse than his bite, indeed! She had tremendous respect for Maria, but the woman clearly hadn't come to know Elijah like she did. If Sophia didn't cooperate, he'd give the gift—if there was one—here and leave her to squirm as he heaped on the praise in front of her team. "No, I haven't. We can speak in the hall."

"Soph," Maria warned.

"I won't take the gift in front of everyone in the court building, Maria. Don't worry. I know better than to make it look like I'm compromised or colluding with the other team."

Her boss nodded and sat back in her seat, seeming satisfied. "I'll see you back in the office."

She followed Elijah out into the hall with trepidation. When they had found a relatively private alcove by the windows on the left side of the building, she stopped and crossed her arms. "Well? Are you trying to make me look bad in front of Maria? I've worked too hard for this to let you screw it up for me, Elijah."

He smiled gently. "I have no intention of screwing it up for you, Soph. I really did want to congratulate you." He pulled a small box from his pocket and handed it to her. "I'd intended to stop by your floor in the building after the meeting to give it to you. I didn't know you'd be here today, but no sense in waiting. Open it later. I need to speak to you about the trial now while we have a moment."

She tucked it into her purse and waited with a raised brow. "Out with it, then, Elijah Clarkson."

He grinned. "My station and rank mean nothing to you, do they?"

"Not in private," she said. "Well?"

"Can you really handle working against me on this case?"

Though his question hit hard at her private doubts and fears, she rolled her eyes. "Have I ever had a problem arguing with you?"

"No, but that's not my concern, and you know it."

She looked away. No, it wasn't his concern, and it wasn't hers, either. Both of them knew the real question was whether she'd be able to remain professional and distant without falling into the usual patterns of their debates where they'd amicably make up and return to their usual close friendship. Seeing him as someone other than a friend had been difficult enough when she worked with him. Now she had to work against him, and she couldn't allow any indication they were friends to slip if she didn't want to risk accusations of misconduct and collusion.

"I can handle it, Elijah. Worry about yourself. I'm not the only one with habits of familiarity. What you just did in there...don't do it again if you intend to keep us both on the trial."

He tucked his hands into his pockets with a nod. "Very well. Soph?"

She lifted her gaze back to his.

"I meant what I said. Congratulations on passing the bar. I always knew you would."

She laughed, some of the tension between them easing to give way to their familiar warmth. "I have a habit of getting what I want."

"As do I." He grinned. "I suspect it's what makes us so good at butting heads."

"I suspect so. I suppose I'll see you at the next meeting or during depositions." She pushed past him, trying not to notice the warm cinnamon and spice of his cologne, and hurried down the hall toward the exit. Whatever happened in that courtroom, she had to maintain her distance. If she couldn't, they were both going to be in trouble.

Chapter 1

Two years later

Elijah stepped into the courtroom with a weary sigh. This trial had dragged on for two years, and he was more than ready for litigation to end. This was why clients usually tried to resolve disputes about breach-of-contract before they ever landed in court. Unfortunately, these two hadn't been able to resolve the differences, and his client's opponent had refused arbitration. So, here they were. Two long years of courtrooms and meetings to try to resolve the problems. Two long years of working against Sophia when he'd come to want nothing more than to have her on his side again.

Speaking of Sophia...

He eyed the brunette as she strode in and settled next to his ex, Maria. Sophia had been burning the midnight oil again. She had dark circles, ill-concealed by her makeup, under her eyes, and her shoulders slumped a little more than usual. He wanted to march across the courtroom and tell her to go to bed early today, but he shook off the urge. She wasn't his, and she couldn't be during this trial.

He'd be lying if he said he didn't wish it were different. He'd watched Sophia Anderson's lightning rise to the top with pride and interest since she entered law school. He had known how bright she was since she was eight, just as he knew she would be, and she was good at her job. Too bad. If she and Maria hadn't been so good, his team wouldn't have been forced to appeal the first two rulings. However, his client deserved a resolution in his favor, and Elijah refused to lose that for the man. The client and his family had been through enough. He needed to focus on that, not the overwhelming desire to drag Sophia into his bed to see if she was more than a temporary obsession borne from wanting what was forbidden.

Unfortunately, he couldn't get her off his mind, and he was desperate to deal with this increasingly uncomfortable attraction to the petite brunette with piercing gray-blue eyes. Every time she looked at him, he hardly managed to keep his focus on whatever he was meant to be doing. It had been torture trying to maintain his usual persona in the courtroom with her there, and he suspected Maria knew it, though she had the good grace not to mention it. Sophia seemed the only one out of the three of them who *didn't* know the power she held, which only made her that much more appealing.

This most recent appeal should be over in a month or two, and it would be the last any of them made.

I could have her then, he reminded himself. He was legendary for his patience and persistence. So why did two or three months seem like an eternity? In all his 34 years, Elijah had never been this way with women, but with her, he was. That was the most worrying thing about this.

He settled into his seat beside his associate and tugged at the collar of his dress shirt.

"Everything all right, boss?"

"Fine. Just a little warm in here today."

The associate cast him a dubious glance and then returned to his work with a shrug. Elijah rubbed his temples and tried not to look at Sophia. He had to make it through two more months. Just two more. He was merely infatuated with Sophia, not in love, and he could wait that long to quench his thirst—if she proved amenable. He hoped that for once, she'd understand he didn't want to debate the merits of his wish to act on this urge and would give in. He'd watched her over the last two years, and he was confident he wasn't the only one interested, however oblivious she was to his own interest. Yes, two more months. Two more, and he could have her.

***

Waiting another two months proved impossible. Elijah found he lacked the necessary self-control for the first time in his life. He shouldn't be doing what he was doing, but he'd called Sophia up to request her for documents she'd been asked for earlier in the week. She was supposed to send them up by courier in a week, but he'd made up some excuse to get her to bring them up herself. He waited impatiently for her to take the elevator or the stairs from her firm's offices two floors down to make her way to his office.

The two of them could face serious consequences for what he was about to do if she agreed to it. Even if they weren't disbarred, the whole trial might have to be retried, which would cost everyone dearly. That was why no one was going to find out.

There was a knock at his office door.

"Come in."

The door opened, and Sophia stepped in with a frown on her face, clutching a folder with the files his team had requested from theirs. She shut the door behind her and shuffled in, dropping the folder onto his desk. "Elijah."

"Sophia," he murmured, eyeing her wrist where the bracelet he'd gifted her for passing the bar always rested. "Thank you for bringing them."

"Your excuse was one of the dumbest I've ever heard." She crossed her arms. "What did you really want, Elijah?"

He cleared his throat and smiled tightly. "You always did see straight through any of my nonsense. You want it straight?"

"Have I ever wanted anything else?" She sat in the chair across from him and crossed her legs. "*Summoning* me up here like this is going to raise questions."

"No, it's not. You can just say I demanded urgent delivery of the files, and you didn't have a courier, so you brought them yourself. You're not the junior partner in this case. People would probably believe it."

"Fine." She recrossed her arms. "Spill, then. Why did you really call me up here?"

She wanted it blunt and unequivocal, as usual. For once, he wanted to dance around it. What he was about to say was crossing a line he couldn't uncross. "Soph...what I'm about to say might sound somewhat indelicate, but you'll give me a chance, won't you?"

She raised a brow. "Elijah Clarkson, are *you* tongue-tied? This is a first!"

"I want you," he blurted out, hating that there was no better way to say this now that he'd started. "And I'm sick of waiting for the trial to end to say it."

Her eyes widened, and she stiffened, barely breathing. "W-what?"

He groaned and rounded the desk, grabbing the arms of her chair and leaning close. "I can't put this much more bluntly, Soph. I want to sleep with you. You're like a drug I can't get off my mind. I want it too badly to keep waiting. Two years of waiting is enough."

She gasped, cheeks coloring. "Elijah! You...you can't possibly be serious."

"I am." He eyed her with a frown. "I didn't misread you, did I? You want me to, don't you?"

She didn't speak. He waited, heart hammering in his chest. She did, didn't she? She had to. He'd known her since childhood. He couldn't have mistaken the signs.

"Sophia?" he prompted softly. "Please tell me this wasn't a horrible mistake...I...I made one back when I got involved with Maria, and I'd never forgive myself if—"

"Elijah, we can't."

"Because you don't want to?"

She flushed and looked away, but she didn't say yes. "It isn't right. We could end up disbarred if anyone finds out."

"No one will. I promise. Besides, Soph...I'm asking you for a few nights."

Her blush deepened. "Seriously? You're not only asking me to risk my license and career, but you're asking me to risk it for a few nights with you?"

"What would it take to convince you?"

She looked away, hurt flashing on her face. "Elijah, I...I don't know if I can do this."

"Then let me help you decide..." He could tell she wanted him, but she needed a push to give in.

He leaned the last few inches to caress her mouth with his. She whimpered, but she didn't push him away, and her hands went to the lapels of his suit coat. That was all the proof he needed, but he wanted to hear her acknowledge what she wanted aloud. She tried to pull him closer.

Elijah smiled against her mouth and then pulled away just enough that she couldn't easily recapture his lips with hers. "Do you want me or not?"

"I..." The red in her cheeks crept to her ears as she tipped her face up to his. "I sh-shouldn't."

"I don't care about shouldn't, Sophia. Obviously, I don't, or I wouldn't have kissed you or asked you any of this. I think that kiss proves you want me, but I want to hear you say it. Do you want me or not?"

"I do," she whispered softly.

"Then say yes. Come see me at my place. It's a gated community. My staff can pick you up; no one will ever know."

She shifted in her seat, staring down at her lap. "You don't know what you're asking of me."

"Are you afraid you won't enjoy it? I promise our secret will be safe, Soph. You can count on it."

She looked near tears. "I'm afraid you won't give anything more. You're asking me to settle for being your toy."

He flinched. "That's not how I meant it. If you didn't want me, I'd apologize and beg you to forget I ever brought it up. I'd spend an eternity trying to make it up to you. But you do want me, and I want you."

She laughed sadly. "I've always wanted to hear you tell me that. Only you could find a way to make it the last thing I'd hoped to hear."

"Soph..."

"Fine," she whispered. "Is that the only way I can have any part of what I want?"

"I..." He sighed. For now, it was, and he wouldn't lie to her about that. "Yes."

"I guess I'll take what I can get. But Elijah? I'm not going to settle for warming your bed forever. If that's all you'll ever give me, don't expect me to stay."

He didn't. He just needed to burn her out of his system. Once he did that, they'd go their separate ways. But the pain in her expression tugged at something deep inside and made him wish he could promise more, wish that he hadn't been so badly burned with Maria. His girl-next-door deserved more. If he were a better man, he'd give it to her, but he wasn't going to lie to her about who he was now. He'd never lied to her, whatever other pain he'd inflicted at times. "I don't expect you to. Frankly, I think this is a matter of wanting the forbidden for both of us. We'll deal with it and move forward before one of us does something foolish."

She stood with a sharp nod. "Very well. Maybe you're right."

Maybe? He was. He'd never been wrong about these things. Except with Maria...he'd been wrong with her. Could he be wrong here? He opened his mouth to ask her something, but she turned and walked out, leaving him to contemplate her parting statement.

Maybe you're right. With Sophia, that always meant, *but you're probably not*. He sighed and shifted in his chair. This time, he would prove her wrong. He was right about this. He had to be because to have anything more meant risking too much. Their careers, their licenses, their hearts. That wasn't a risk he was prepared to take.

Chapter 2

Sophia stepped out of the car and strode to the steps of Elijah's enormous mansion on the outskirts of Chicago. She'd never seen a private estate this big. He'd purchased the land surrounding it and had turned it into a fair imitation of an old Victorian estate in England with the sort of privacy he'd promised he could offer. At least he hadn't lied about anything, even if he had ripped a little piece of her heart out in the office earlier that day.

She'd hoped to hear Elijah Clarkson tell her he had wanted her since her late teenage years, and now, when he finally said the words, they'd come in all the wrong ways.

Part of her still screamed. This was lunacy. Agreeing to this cheapened her to nothing more than a thoroughly desired lay he'd cast aside in the end. She knew agreeing would only bring devastation in the end, that they'd never regain their friendship after crossing this line.

Still, she'd said yes because a bigger part of her hoped that she'd read her old friend correctly, that he was lying to himself by claiming he only wanted to burn her out of his system. Perhaps in time, he might change his stance and offer her his heart, not just his body. That was the real reason she was here, ringing the bell and listening to the tinny sound echoing inside the enormous mansion. The door opened, cutting off any reverie. Elijah stood on the other side, a warm smile on his face.

"You came."

"I said I would."

His smile fell, and he stepped aside, drawing her inside with him. "Sophia, listen...I know how I asked wasn't very delicate—"

"It could've been worse." She smirked, trying to cover the raw pain the reminder brought with sarcasm.

He sighed and scrubbed a hand over his face. "I'd first ask you out on a date or two if we could do that, but we can't. I couldn't wait anymore, Sophia. I hate seeing you on the other side of the courtroom and knowing I can't show you just how easily you snap my self-control."

She laughed and shook her head. "Elijah, you've demonstrated perfectly how easily I apparently snap that already. Where is the bedroom?"

He grimaced. "We don't have to go straight to—"

"You didn't want anything other than sex, Elijah Clarkson. Renegotiate the terms of engagement if you don't like them."

"I suppose I deserve that," he murmured. "Fine." He pulled her into him and pressed his lips to hers in a teasing kiss. "Is this better?"

She shivered. Even though she hated how they'd ended up here, she couldn't deny that she wanted him or that she loved even that brief touch of his mouth on hers. "Maybe a bit, but you can do better."

"Hmmm." He smiled slightly and trailed his lips from her mouth to her jaw and down her neck. "How is that?"

Her skin tingled everywhere he touched, and she moaned gently. Even his teasing touch was enough to fog her mind, though she retained a deep-seated sense of hurt and pain at the knowledge that there might never be more than sex between them. "I still think it could be better," she whispered.

"Better?" He shook his head. "Hard to please much, woman? Very well. What do I need to do to redeem myself?"

She smiled sadly at the familiar bantering between them. Why couldn't he see that she loved him, that she wasn't Maria and didn't want anyone else? Didn't want anything more than she wanted Elijah Clarkson to take charge and love her. She wanted this, but she knew it wouldn't be enough on its own.

She needed more, needed to know he saw her in his future as more than a fun lay or merely a friend.

Now wasn't the time to focus on that, though. In time, he might open up and come to see her as more than a desire he could burn out of his system.

For now, she wanted him to soothe both the ache of need he'd created and the pain of longing he'd ignored.

"There are too many clothes in the way for my liking." She played with the buttons of her blouse. "You want to redeem yourself, Elijah? Perhaps we can move this to the bedroom?"

He scooped her up with a smile. "Demanding little thing, aren't you?"

"Demanding and little, maybe. A thing? Most certainly not," she replied gravely. "You need to stop thinking I'm a thing you can use and toss away."

"I meant the remark kindly," he muttered, heading for the bedroom. "Don't take it the wrong way. Are you still pouting over how I asked you over here? If you want to argue over methods, I'll oblige. I'd much rather strip you and kiss you senseless before I take you, but I'm not insensitive. We can talk first."

She turned her face away. Once he started kissing her in earnest, she'd lose herself in the need she also felt for him. She wouldn't want to talk anymore. She didn't want to talk now, either, though. She'd agreed to take what she could get, even if it should be degrading to even consider agreeing to such a proposal. "No. We agreed. Sex only. Nothing permanent. I don't want to talk."

"We always used to talk to each other before this. I'd like to think we're still friends."

"You can't cross the Rubicon and pretend everything's the same on the other side, Elijah. Either we're friends, or you're sleeping with me for a fun fling."

"You mean more to me than that, Soph," he whispered, hurt flashing in his gaze. "I'd never..."

"You don't like to imagine that's what you're doing, and maybe I do mean more to you than that, but you certainly aren't proving it with your actions."

He set her on the bed in his master bedroom and stepped back as if she'd bitten him. "Don't be unfair. You agreed."

"Yes, I did." She reached back and unbuttoned her skirt, shimmying out of it before starting on the buttons of her blouse. "Well? Are you going to help?"

He chewed on his lower lip, watching her with a mixture of lust and uncertainty. "I think maybe we should talk."

"There's nothing else to talk about. You want me. I want you. There's nothing more to it. Your words, Elijah. Not mine."

"Fine." He stalked over and stood between her thighs, pressing them further apart. "But don't say I didn't try to be a gentleman."

"I'm under no delusion that you are a gentleman. A gentleman wouldn't have asked me what you did."

He reached out and grasped her chin in his long fingers. "One last chance, then, love. Do you want me, or don't you?"

She smacked his hand away with a bitter smile. "Don't you dare call me that. As for wanting you, I may hate myself for the rest of my life for it, but yes. I want you, Elijah Clarkson. Now for God's sake, stop slapping me in the face with it. Make me forget that desire has made me stoop so low or so help me God. I will walk out right now."

He smiled sadly and cupped her cheek. "If that's what you want."

As he stripped her out of her blouse to expose the lacy black bra she'd worn for him, she closed her eyes and wished desperately that were true.

If her wish were his command, she'd have more than this stolen moment with him.

His lips trailed a line of fire from her jaw down, and she surrendered to the sensations, letting his touch wash away the pain his refusal to give more than this left deep inside.

Later she would let herself hurt over it, knowing full well she'd go back if it meant having just one more taste of Elijah. She wanted him too much to say no. If she was his drug, he was her kryptonite.

Chapter 3

When she next faced Elijah, it was in the courtroom. She watched him enter, but he didn't acknowledge her, and she sank back in her chair, ripping her gaze away from him. Of course, he wouldn't give her the time of day in public. She was his dirty little secret, and he'd never be seen treating her as a lover in public, even if he wanted her as such. He'd made it clear. He didn't have room in his heart to love her like she wanted to be loved, and any hope for it was foolishness.

"Are you all right, Soph?" Maria eyed her with concern.

"I'm fine," she whispered, watching people filter in as the jury took their seats.

"You don't seem it. If you need to step out, I can handle the case today."

She straightened, pulling her jacket taut and buttoning it. "No. I'm fine. I just...I blew off some steam with some guy last night, and it didn't go like I'd hoped."

Maria's brows rose. "Straightlaced Sophia Anderson and fling do not go in the same sentence. What happened?"

"I'm not a fling sort of girl." Her cheeks burned in shame because that wasn't entirely true; for Elijah, she was. What did that say about her? "And that's precisely why it didn't go as I'd hoped."

Maria made a sympathetic sound of understanding. "He didn't tell you he didn't want more?"

"No, he did." She slumped in her seat. "I agreed anyway, and now I'm kicking myself."

"Girl, you have it bad for this guy if you agreed to sleep with him knowing he wouldn't give you the commitment you wanted. Either that, or you were drunk. Were you?"

She gaped at the older woman, who had become a friend as well as a role model in the last few years. "No! Jeez, Maria. What do you think I'm doing at night? I don't go out drinking when I have to prepare for court the next day."

Maria shrugged. "Just asking...so it's the first. Who is this guy?"

She forced herself not to look at Elijah, even though she could sense he was staring at her. "No one, you know...anyway, I didn't have a chance to tell you yesterday, but Mr. Clarkson has those files he'd asked about. I had to take them up. The man-made some stupid excuse to have me running documents like a courier." She rolled her eyes. "He thinks too highly of himself."

Maria snorted. "Sometimes, but Elijah probably just did it to see you."

"What?" Her heart hammered in her chest. Could Maria suspect? "No, I don't think so...I think you're imagining things. Mr. Clarkson wouldn't be interested in me. I'm sure I'm not his type."

"Right. Sophia Anderson, you can't possibly be that naïve! The man's had his eye on you for the last two years. I'm surprised he hasn't made a move yet. He has more self-control than he did with me. In fact, it's impressive, considering that he's been pining after you for as long as I've known him. It was always Sophia that and Sophia this when we were together. It grated after a while."

She knew...

Sophia swallowed hard, wondering why Maria hadn't said anything all this time.

If she had known Elijah and I had had a past, why did she ask me to be on this case? Sophia mulled.

"We were...he and I were childhood friends, Mar, and I was his paralegal while I was studying for the bar. He probably just talked because he was proud of me and still feels some of that older brother sort of affection he had for me when we were kids. He's probably not interested." She sneaked a peek at him and found him watching her discreetly too. "It would be highly unprofessional for him to make a move, even if you're right. He knows better."

Maria pursed her lips. "Maybe, but he's not known for always playing by the rules."

"You can't seriously be accusing him of breaking rules and cheating!" She was momentarily distracted from trying to throw Maria off this train of reasoning. "He wouldn't."

"No, but he's not afraid to exploit loopholes or engage in risky behavior. He hasn't had any complaints from clients or other lawyers. He's good at doing things quietly when he needs to." Maria frowned at her ex. "But I know him well enough to know he's interested in you, Soph. Maybe it's that he's not sure you're interested, but if he asks while we're on trial, I'll rip his head off. This is your first major trial, and if he messes it up for you, I'll personally make sure he's the one disbarred."

Sophia shrank down in her seat. "That's...that's probably not necessary, Maria."

"It is absolutely necessary. Costing you your license on accusations of collusion is unacceptable. He might or might not lose his license normally for it, though he'd be in trouble. If he tries, I want you to tell me." Maria stood as the judge entered the room.

Sophia followed suit. It was a little late for that. He'd already asked, and she'd already agreed. There was no way she'd ever tell Maria that. She wouldn't risk getting Elijah in trouble, especially when he'd promised her he'd keep *her* from getting caught. However she felt about their arrangement, and however angry she was with him for his methods and refusal to offer her more, she'd never go that far. He was a good lawyer and didn't deserve to lose his license for being a blind fool when it came to her.

***

Elijah caught up with Sophia and Maria in the parking lot. He wanted to pull her aside and speak to her privately, but the expression on Maria was thunder. He didn't know what he'd done to tick her off now, but he wasn't going to give her a good reason for being angry by conversing with Sophia privately and giving the appearance they were friendly with each other.

Not when they were so close to the end of this miserable trial.

Besides, he was only indulging himself with Sophia to rid himself of this pesky desire so they could go back to the way things were meant to be as friends.

The thought rang hollow even to him as he stared at the woman he'd had writhing underneath him the previous evening. He already wanted her in that position again, staring up at him with those vulnerable, wide eyes.

This time, though, he wanted her without the tears that had come last night as they lay in bed together. She'd been quiet, and he suspected she thought he'd gone to sleep, but he hadn't. He'd listened to her sniffling for a while until she was asleep, and he lay awake long after, questioning everything he'd done.

He should've understood this would hurt her that day in his office when she'd told him she'd take what she could get. It had been such an obvious remark, such an obvious hint that she had liked him for some time.

He'd brushed it aside because he hadn't *wanted* to think that as much as she wanted sex with him—it would destroy her to give up her body in addition to her heart without any chance at having his in return.

"What do you want, Clarkson?" Maria asked in a clipped tone. "If you're here to congratulate Sophia again like you did two years ago and again at the end of the last appeal, you can get lost. You're going to start rumors if you keep this up. Lawyers from opposite teams don't congratulate one another on wins that cost them and their clients. You're no different except with Sofia."

A warning note echoed in her last remark, and he bowed his head in acknowledgment. "I needed to speak to Sofia, Maria. I promise I'll be brief and discreet."

Sofia gasped. "Mr. Clarkson, I—"

He shot her a warning look.

"What do you need to discuss with her?"

"Does it matter?" Elijah stepped past Maria toward Sophia.

His ex stepped into his way with a scowl. "Elijah, so help me...you're not pulling this secretive bull you always did when we were an item. What do you want from Miss Anderson?"

He fixed her with a glare of his own. "Nothing that pertains to the trial."

"Not good enough." She crossed her arms. "Well?"

"Fine," he growled, knowing she wouldn't move without a good reason.

Maria wouldn't tell anyone about their prior friendship, given how long ago it had been, and there was no reason not to use that information to spin a small lie to get her off his back.

"*Miss* Anderson and I are old friends, if you have to know, and she was my paralegal while she studied for the bar, which you well know. We've been professional about the situation to avoid a conflict of interests, but it's been two long years of working in that courtroom with a friend and keeping my distance. Can't you give me five minutes? I have something private I need to talk to her about, and it has nothing to do with the trial. I wouldn't ask if it weren't important, Maria."

Her eyes narrowed. "Five minutes, then, Clarkson."

He didn't need to be told twice. Grabbing Sophia's arm, he tugged her away from her boss and toward the corner of the building where they could talk without appearing too cozy. At least if he had her there, and they spoke quietly, it would seem like he'd caught up with her to ask for something related to the case. It was believable enough.

Sophia followed along without a word, glancing at the empty parking lot. The hearing today stretched past the normal dinner hour, and few people were still around. He could practically hear her worrying about this publicity and what people would think. He stopped on the steps off to the side in Maria's line of sight. "Stop worrying about what people will think. Look at me."

She did, but she couldn't seem to hold his gaze for very long.

"You were crying last night."

"You must've been dreaming." She laughed and looked away. "What we did...it was fun. Why on earth would I be crying after that?"

He scowled. "Sophia Anderson, I have never once lied to you. I expect the same courtesy."

Her cheeks heated, and her hands balled into fists at her sides. "Stop this, Elijah...we're in public, and I don't want a scene."

"Then just admit you were crying and tell me why."

She glanced at Maria and then met his gaze, eyes glassy with unshed tears. "If you don't know, Elijah, then you're a fool. Think for five seconds, and maybe you'll figure it out. When you do, maybe you'll know why you should apologize."

"Come to dinner over the weekend," he murmured. "We can talk about it then."

"Why should I?"

"I'm trying, Soph." He didn't want to say he already knew why she was upset and wanted the privacy to make her admit it, to try to make this right. He also didn't want to admit that one night with her hadn't been even close to enough. So much for burning her out of his system.

"You didn't want anything more than what we had last night," she murmured. "Dinner isn't part of that."

"It could be. We could renegotiate terms."

A spark of hope lit in her expression before she tamped it down and looked away, hiding her feelings from him as best she could. "You don't negotiate. You decide and expect everyone else to agree, just like you had yesterday when we first spoke about this. How is that now different?"

Because he'd realized how much of a fool he really had been to think she could keep emotions out of this. He wanted her so badly but didn't want to ruin her. If she told him she couldn't handle it without getting entangled with him so badly that she'd break when he'd finally managed to burn this desire for her out, he would back off and deal with it on his own. He cared too much about the woman in front of him to push her to do something she didn't want or couldn't bear.

"It's different because you're...I care about you. You're a good friend, and we need to talk. I messed up yesterday, maybe more than once, and I'm not taking no for an answer on this, Soph. Come to dinner."

She sighed and looked at Maria, who was tapping her wristwatch with a frown. Then her gaze returned to him, and she nodded. "Fine. Dinner over the weekend. Goodbye, Mr. Clarkson."

He shoved his hands in his pockets to keep himself from reaching out to her and watched her walk down the stairs to rejoin Maria. She murmured something to the other woman that seemed to satisfy Maria's curiosity and then strode to her car.

He stood and watched until she was out of the parking lot before walking to his own car with a low curse.

What was he doing?

He'd said nothing more than sex. Now here he was, asking her to come over for dinner and trying to renegotiate something that would offer her what she needed. He didn't *have* what she needed, though, and it wasn't a good sign that he hated the idea of walking away.

Groaning, he climbed into his Ferrari. He could be an unfeeling jerk at times in this business. That's who he had to be on the outside. It wasn't who he was inside, or at least, he hadn't thought so.

Now, when Sophia really needed him to walk away from her because he wouldn't give her his heart––which was what she desperately wanted and needed––he couldn't find that legendary self-control of his long enough to let her go.

This was insanity and couldn't end well, but here they were.

Sighing, he took off, heading for home. There was too much he needed to sort through, and it didn't feel like there was enough time for it.

Chapter 4

Sophia stepped into the entry hall of the mansion, staring up at the chandelier she'd failed to notice last time she'd been here. Elijah had a habit of distracting her, even from things she should face, and didn't wish to—like the reasons she'd cried herself to sleep next to him a few days ago after he'd taken her the first time. He'd made the physical intimacy memorable and almost sweet at times, but by the end, that had only been salt in an open wound. It reminded her that she would never have his love and heart. Only his lust.

She turned her focus to the paintings on the walls. He had a Rembrandt on display in the entryway.

Just how much money did Elijah have?

She trailed along, looking at each painting in turn. The names on these were only slightly less recognizable than Rembrandt. A piece, these cost more than she made in a whole year. Being one of only two senior partners at a firm paid a killing, it seemed.

"You like them?" Elijah's low timbre filled the entryway, bouncing on the marble floor and wood-paneled walls.

"You display wealth like a peacock struts about displaying feathers," she muttered. "How much was the Rembrandt?"

He shrugged. "I don't remember. Dinner awaits. Shall we?"

She stared back at him. He waited, hands in his pockets, as if he wanted her to come to him. Tensing, she considered walking back out. Having this dinner was a slap in the face after his proposal that they have no-strings-attached sex. As if sleeping with Elijah could *ever* be no-strings-attached to her.

"Come, Soph," he murmured. "We agreed."

She stiffened. "I know what we agreed. But maybe we should just have the conversation now and skip dinner."

He gave her a long-suffering look. "Really, Sophia. I'm not a patient man, but I'm trying."

For you, the tone seemed to imply. Could he really be trying to temper his usual intensity for her, to talk to her like he'd once done when they were young?

"Why?" she whispered.

"Because I care."

About her? Or just about making certain she was willing to continue warming his bed? She straightened further and walked to him, heels clicking on the polished stone. "Fine. I can endure dinner."

He put a hand on her shoulder. "Endure? I'd hoped you might enjoy it."

"Have you given any thought at all to what I said on Thursday?" she asked coldly.

"A great deal. That's why I asked you for dinner. I want time to discuss things without the temptation to ignore our chat in favor of my bed." He tipped her chin up. "Wanting to burn you out of my system doesn't mean I don't care. I just..." He exhaled softly.

"You just what?"

"I don't want to feel like this."

"Like what?"

He released her with a groan, scraping his fingers through his hair. "God only knows...for once, I'm not sure what to do, Sophia."

She cracked a smile and tried to lighten the mood. "I can tell you what you *shouldn't* do."

He eyed her with a shake of his head. "I don't doubt it. Look, Soph...I don't want to *want* a woman I've known since she was a little girl. I can't get you off my mind, and I'd hoped sex would help."

"Did it?" She crossed her arms. "Are you content now?"

"No. It made it worse."

"What a shock," she remarked flatly. "But I thought you wanted to eat."

"I do, but you're angry now, not just hurt. Tell me what I've done. Tell me how to fix this."

"You can't."

He flinched.

"You can't because you don't want to risk what it would take to fix it. Now I'm hungry. Let's finish this discussion over dinner," she added.

He looked away and headed down the hall. They walked in silence until they reached a door at the end of the hall. He opened it to reveal a warmly lit dining room with candles on the table, flames dancing merrily, and soup bowls full of piping hot soup set across from each other. "Dinner, then?"

She let him guide her inside and seat her, her gaze fixed on the candles. Why had he lit these? What was the point? It added a romantic flair that she doubted he'd intended.

"Don't you like them?" Elijah took his own seat across from her and fiddled with his napkin. "I lit them for you."

"Romance hardly fits into our situation."

"Sophia..."

"Look, you wanted to know what was wrong. How to fix this?"

"Desperately."

"Do you love me? Is that what has you scared about your interest in me?"

He blanched and stared down at his soup. "I don't know. Once, I thought I loved Maria, but I was wrong, and she didn't love me like I'd thought. The relationship was a nightmare, even if I let her go amicably."

"What makes you think she and I are even vaguely similar?"

"I'm the same person. What if I'm wrong again?" He lifted his gaze to hers. "I don't think I could let you go like I let her go, Sophia. I already don't want to let you go now, even if I know I should. Even knowing you can't keep feelings out of it and that it may break you, I still want to hold on."

She looked away, pondering both the words and her response. If he couldn't let her go like he'd let Maria go, that meant he felt more strongly about her than he did Maria or others he'd been with. "Are you normally this possessive?"

He barked out a laugh. "Not usually, no. Maria will have told you about the string of women after her."

"You've set your sights on me, but I'm different than the rest."

"Yes, God help you..." His voice sounded strangled.

When she glanced up, she found a mixture of shame and frustration in his gaze. "You'll do anything to have me, even if you know having your bed and not your heart will break me? Really, Elijah?"

He didn't answer, and he dropped his gaze away from hers.

"You're crueler than I remember." She pushed away the untouched soup, appetite gone. "Why, Elijah?"

"I don't know." His voice tightened. "I don't understand why I...Soph, I don't want to hurt you, but I need to know why I feel this way."

"Maybe you're lying to us both tonight," she suggested softly.

He stared at her like she was a lifeline, even as he claimed he needed nothing but her body. Even this dinner said there was more to his feelings than mere lust. He wanted something, but he was afraid to name it, and his fear would be the end of them both at this rate.

"I'm not like her, Elijah," she whispered. "But if you keep pushing me away and holding me at arms' length, you will break me, and I will either walk away or become a shell of my former self trying to be the elusive ideal you crave."

"I don't want some elusive ideal," he murmured back. "I want you. I just don't know if I want you like *that*. How can I know? It could be mere infatuation, the longing for the forbidden."

She rose and set aside her napkin. "Well, let me know when you've decided. I'm too tired to warm your bed tonight. I'll see myself out."

"Soph..." He stood and reached out for her before letting his hand drop back to his side.

"Figure out what you want before it ruins us both. No more of this if you only want me in your bed. I can't bear it," she whispered hoarsely.

"I'm sorry."

"I know. Just not sorry enough to let me go if you don't want me here permanently." She smiled sadly. "I hope you know what you're doing."

"I don't," he admitted. "I don't, Soph, and it terrifies me."

"You know where to find me if you want me. Call. Text. Email. Just do me a favor. Don't ask me over again until you figure out how to untangle it all." Turning her back on him, she walked out, her heart breaking with each step.

Deep down, she knew she'd return to his bed if he wanted her, and that terrified her more than anything. How much of her would be left when Elijah was through with her? What if she was making a terrible bet in believing that, given time, he would realize he wanted her permanently? What if she'd misread his conflicted, pained replies tonight, and he wasn't struggling to recognize love? It would break her, but she couldn't let go of the hope. Not yet. Not even if it would wreck her in the end.

Chapter 5

Elijah spent nearly four weeks thinking about what Sophia had said. He'd struggled to keep his distance and fought with himself over calling her, but he'd forced himself to respect her wishes. Once he knew what he wanted, he'd call.

Four weeks of pure torture later, and he knew for a fact that he'd done both of them a massive disservice by failing to consider his own emotions more closely. He was terrible with personal relationships for all his success in business. He'd never regretted that more than he did now, but hoped that Sophia wouldn't hold it against him.

The trouble now was that he didn't know how to tell her things had changed. He didn't want to come out directly and just say he was in love, but how should he go about it otherwise? Maybe it was best he simply admitted it in as blunt a fashion as he'd suggested he take her to bed. He entered the courtroom and caught her gaze across the divide between the two teams. They were presenting closing arguments in another two weeks, and things were dragging on too long. He was ready to be done with this, and the look on her face said she was too.

Guilt warred with the relief that he could now proceed, knowing what he wanted. He'd put her through an emotional wringer, and she hadn't deserved that. It had been callous, cruel, and foolish to suggest they engage in no-strings sex to begin with. He owed her an apology, and he'd probably be apologizing for his stupidity for the rest of his life if she'd even have him. What if he gave her everything, as he'd done with Maria, and she fled? He'd already made such a mess of this. Maybe one more mistake would be the last straw. He stared down at his notepad with a frown.

"You all right, boss?" One of his firm's senior associates leaned over and handed him a coffee as he sat down. "You seem…tired."

"I'm fine," he murmured. "Thanks for bringing the coffee."

The door to the judge's chambers opened, and he rose along with everyone else, waiting until the judge sat to flop back into his seat. He'd been fighting for a dismissal of the previous ruling on the grounds of mistrial and failure to consider all of the evidence for a while. New information had come to light in the meantime, and now they were going over all of that too. The back and forth was becoming obnoxious.

"Wish the judge would just call it in favor of our client." Another senior associate settled into her seat with a groan. "It's obvious the defendant breached contract at this point, if it wasn't two years ago."

"It's just how these things go. Everything goes through a fine-toothed comb before a decision is made if we want to win this without another appeal." He rubbed his temples with a sigh. "But I know what you mean…hopefully, in a few weeks, it'll be the end of it."

"I hope so," she muttered, sipping her coffee.

That was the end of conversation as the judge called on them to present the last of the evidence. They'd adjourn court until the final arguments were made on the court date in two weeks. This was their last chance to lay out anything they had. Hours dragged by before they adjourned for lunch.

He cornered Sophia as they were leaving the courtroom and bent to murmur, "Dinner at my place tomorrow night at seven."

She looked up at him with a searching glance and then nodded. The crowd surged around them, and Maria pulled her away with a perfunctory glance at him. He let her go. They'd sort this out.

Now that he knew she was it for him, he'd do whatever was necessary to have her.

***

Sophia stepped into the mansion for the first time since their argument over the last dinner. Why had he invited her this time? He'd kept his distance for four agonizing weeks, leaving her to wonder what he was thinking and where they stood. Now he'd swept back in and ordered her over in that commanding, expectant tone of his. He'd commanded, and she'd obeyed.

Elijah stood waiting in the dining room when his butler showed her in. He held the back of her chair, candlelight dancing along the planes of his face and casting shadows over his skin. When she entered, he lifted his head to stare.

Something about the stare was different than usual. She couldn't put her finger on it exactly, but she knew it was different. There wasn't anything on the table yet, either. Just Elijah and the candles gleamed in the center of the table. She shifted, suddenly self-conscious, and pulled at the hem of her short black dress. "You asked me to come, so here I am," she murmured, the words sounding deafening in the room's stillness.

His gaze roamed over her before settling on her face. "Thank you. I thought we could take a walk before we eat."

"Where? You never want to be seen with me in public unless you think it can be excused as some professional interaction."

He frowned. "Doing otherwise would risk your career and mine."

"I'm aware." She pulled her sweater closer. "Where did you want to walk?"

"I thought we could walk in my aviary."

"Not outside then."

"No," he murmured, eyeing her as though he anticipated this was a trap. "Why?"

"You don't even want to be seen with me in the privacy of your own gardens." She frowned. "I know we can't risk the trial, but it's private on your property, and there are places well out of the city we could go. I'm not so hurting for money that I can't afford to go to some out-of-the-way town in the cornfields to spend a free weekend relaxing with you. You've never once suggested it."

His lips pressed together, and he looked away. "It didn't occur to me."

"Why is that?" She crossed her arms, shivering. "Are you ashamed of me?"

He frowned. "This isn't how I wanted dinner to go, Soph. I brought you here to tell you something important."

"You've decided then?" If he had, should she read into his behavior right now?

He stepped over to meet her and cupped her cheek in his hand. "I have, but I...I'm not ready to say it yet. I wanted to show you the house, though."

She smiled softly. He wanted to let her in. The house was merely a gateway into his life. It was his way of saying he was willing to take a risk, even if he wasn't yet ready to name the emotions he felt toward her. "I need to know what you want this to be soon."

He stroked her cheek and bent his head to capture her mouth with his. His lips caressed hers gently at first and then more urgently, as if he were trying to convey everything he couldn't say in that single kiss. When he finally released her, she was breathless and staring up at him in surprise. He'd never kissed her like that before. The behavior was confusing. Elijah wasn't one to hide from what he wanted once he knew, so if he knew how he felt about her, why didn't he want to say? Was it that he felt guilty for what he'd done to her?

"I know. What I want isn't what we had. I am so sorry for how I handled this at the start, Sophia. I never should've treated you like that." Guilt flashed in his eyes, and he dropped his gaze from hers, stepping back. "I want to make it up to you, make it right somehow."

She wrapped her arms around her torso, any happiness at the step forward dimming. "Is all of this because you feel guilty for what happened? I don't want a relationship based on lies or on guilt."

His head jerked up. "No! It is absolutely not because I feel guilty. How could you even think that's what this is about?"

"Can you blame me after how you convinced me to come to your bed, Elijah?" She stared at him, hurt, warring with confusion, and then anger. "You start by telling me you're ready to give us a chance, the one thing you know I want, and in the next breath, you're apologizing for what you've done and pleading for forgiveness. It seems like all of it is geared toward not losing me."

"It's not about keeping you!" He raked his hands through his hair. "I mean, not keeping you in my bed...I want to keep you *with* me. I want the chance to learn to love again. Maybe you're the one I can do that with." His voice softened. "Maybe this time I can give everything and not lose the one I loved."

"Then prove it's about more, Elijah," she whispered back. "You want to have a fresh start? I'm willing to give it, if you can show me you aren't trying to hide me away. Let's go do normal couple stuff. Far away from here to minimize risks, but if you aren't trying to hide or make things better to ease your guilt, it shouldn't be a hard request to honor."

He bit his lip and stared at her. Finally, he nodded. "We'll go somewhere for the weekend. Pack a bag and tell Maria you're taking a short trip to see family further instate. I'm taking you to dinner at one of my favorite childhood places."

Chapter 6

Sophia hurried to the private runway, wondering where they were going. She'd met Elijah after he'd moved into her neighborhood here in Illinois near the Chicago suburbs, but she knew only that he'd moved from neighboring Indiana to come here when his father had taken a surgeon's position in Chicago. His father had since moved back to retire out here, but Elijah had remained in Chicago for his law practice.

He didn't speak much about his childhood, perhaps because his mother had walked out on them when he was young, and his father had struggled to care for a young teen while working in a demanding hospital environment. Even after he'd moved in next door in his teens, her mother often took him into their home when his father couldn't make it home until the early morning hours. He'd practically grown up treating her mother as his.

The downside to that was that she had no idea what to expect. Elijah had asked her to pack warm clothes for the fall weather, so she assumed they'd be outside some of the weekend. Butterflies rioted in her stomach. This was straight out of her childhood and teen dreams featuring Elijah and a romantic getaway, but she was afraid to let herself hope he might be coming to see her that way. Or that he was doing this because he genuinely meant it when he said he wasn't trying to hide her and wasn't ashamed of their relationship––or whatever was going on between them.

She walked to the hangar door and found him lounging inside

by the steps into the plane. He pushed away from the side of the jet and strolled to meet her, his long legs eating up the distance and his hair uncharacteristically tousled. A smile curled his lips, softening the harsh planes of his face.

"Here. Let me take the bag." He didn't wait for her to protest, taking it from her and lifting it easily.

"Thank you," she murmured. "You're certain the staff here won't say anything or leak this to the press?"

"I'm certain, Soph." He stopped and cupped her cheek, leaning down to kiss her gently. "Stop worrying."

She released a soft sigh and leaned into him for a moment. This was really happening. Elijah was letting her see something from the childhood he never spoke about, the years before her. That was big, especially for Elijah, who was used to keeping even the smallest things private from most. He was letting her in, just as she'd wanted. It left a warmth deep in her chest that spread to everything else.

He kissed the top of her head. "Come then. We're ready to take off."

At his wave toward the cockpit, the plane roared to life. She hurried to follow after Elijah, clambering up the steps onto the plane. He stowed her luggage and led her to the back, where there was a small door into a private compartment. "It's going to be about an hour long flight. I told the pilot to take the...scenic route." He offered her a roguish grin. "I thought we could take advantage of the private quarters."

She stared at the giant round bed in the center of the room and flushed. "Won't the owner of the plane mind?"

He laughed. "He doesn't."

"You know him that well?" She turned to find him grinning.

"Sweetheart, *I* own the jet."

Her breath hitched, and she spun in a slow circle, taking in the gleaming chrome, and oak surfaces and the small windows with shades pulled over them. "You own *this*?"

He walked over to the bed and sat down, patting the space at his side. "Is it really that hard to believe?"

"I...I don't know." She joined him and laid back on the bed, staring up at the white plastic ceiling. "I just never imagined you were rich enough to own a jet."

"I don't flaunt my wealth." He dropped back to lay beside her. "Now...about availing ourselves of the facilities..."

The plane shuddered and began pulling out of the hangar. He sat up and pulled her over to the seats near the window, buckling her in. Then he buckled himself in beside her with a smile. "What do you think?"

She glanced at the door with a frown. "Are the doors soundproof?"

"No, but the flight attendant knows not to disturb me unless I call him with the intercom. He'll stay up at the front of the jet. He's not going to hear anything." He placed a hand on her thigh. "If you don't want to, we won't. We can curl up and watch a movie instead."

She bit her lip with a smile. "I think this time you should work for it, Mr. Clarkson. Can't let you think I'm easy."

He grimaced. "Sophia Anderson, I would never...no one who knows you would make such an error."

And yet he had with his ill-conceived, harebrained scheme to get her into his bed without letting her in. At some point, however, she had to let that go. It had been stupid, but he was here now, trying to make it right. It was clear he'd rethought his position, at least a little bit. "I expect dinner first when we land."

He nodded. "Movie it is, then."

They settled as the plane leveled in the air. Once it was steady, Elijah unbuckled them both and scooped her up, carrying her over to the bed. They spent the remainder of the flight nestled in pillows and blankets, her head on Elijah's chest and his fingers stroking her hair.

By the time they arrived at the airstrip near Elijah's childhood home, she was ready to eat. He guided her out of the plane, retrieving their luggage on the way out and laughing at her eagerness to disembark. She didn't care if he found it amusing. She was ready to see this part of his life, the one part he'd never allowed her into. "How far is it to the restaurant?"

He unlocked a Maserati and packed their luggage into the trunk with a shake of his head. "Not far."

"Why is it your favorite?"

He bundled her into the passenger's seat with a smile, but he didn't answer her until they were out of the airfield and on the road through cornfields and stretches of open country. "My mother used to bring me to the place I'm taking you when we went to pick my father up from the airport." His smile faded. "It's the last place she took me before she disappeared."

"Oh..." Her enthusiasm softened to sadness mingled with curiosity. She pushed aside her interest to think about how he might feel toward the place. "Elijah, we don't have to—"

He reached over and pressed a finger to her lips. "Hush. I chose the place, remember?"

"But it's...it's so personal."

"That's why it's perfect." He pulled off the road into a parking lot in front of a quaintly decorated diner with neon signs and climbed out.

She frowned when he rounded the car and opened her door. "What are you doing?"

"Taking you to dinner. You wanted me to, didn't you?"

"Here?"

"Is something wrong with here?" He tensed. "I told you it was a childhood favorite, so I figured you'd realize it wasn't anything fancy...if it's not—"

She leaned in and wrapped her arms around his neck to kiss him. "No. It's fine, Elijah. It wasn't what I expected. I've never seen you outside of ritzy restaurants, bars, and law offices in Chicago. It's a shock to be reminded that you were a normal kid once."

"Good. You had me worried for a minute." He kissed her back, relaxing into her touch.

She relished the warmth of his lips on hers, his mouth exploring hers eagerly. Then she pressed gently at his shoulders, breathing shallowly and rapidly when he obeyed her silent command and pulled away. "We should go in, or we'll never eat."

"As you wish, my lady." He offered her an arm, grinning like a child.

She laughed at the silly gesture. How long had it been since she and Elijah had been playful with one another like this? She'd forgotten he could be anything besides serious or seductive. Taking his arm, she let him guide her inside.

The interior was warm and inviting, though the people were mostly wearing beat-up jeans or overalls. Farmers, probably. It wasn't a place well-off lawyers went to eat, but that made it that much more special.

It was self-seated, so Elijah guided her to a booth in the back where they'd be hidden from view of the rest of the restaurant's patrons. He helped her into the curved bench and slid beside her, his hand going to her thigh in promise of what would come after they ate.

Soon, a middle-aged waitress drifted over to take their drink orders. She stopped when she saw Elijah. "Elijah? Is that you?"

He frowned in concentration and then smiled politely in recognition. "Mol?"

"One and the same. It's been ages! I've been following your case on the TV. Everyone talks about little Elijah Clarkson making it big. No one thought you'd go into law instead of medicine, but we sure are proud."

He cleared his throat and shifted, adjusting his tie. "Really?"

"Really! If you have a moment while you're up visiting your father, stop in again and say hi. I'd love to catch up." She flicked a glance over at Sophia with a polite smile. "You look familiar.

Have I seen you somewhere?"

Sophia shifted to slouch in the seat and stared at the table. In jeans and a t-shirt, she probably didn't look much like Sophia Anderson, associate lawyer for defense council, but it still left her unsettled that this woman had recognized Elijah so quickly and had watched the case on TV. What if she recognized her and took it to the press? They'd be in so much trouble. "I just have that sort of face, I guess," she mumbled.

Elijah took her hand with a tight smile at the waitress. "Mol, we're in a bit of a rush tonight. My father is on a cruise, and he asked that we get to the rental in time to make sure the cleaner had the check he left for her. I'd love to stay and chat, but I can't. After we get back to his place, I have meetings. I can leave the city, but no matter how far I run, the clients don't stop demanding attention."

She laughed and flipped her ponytail off her shoulder. "Guess you're in high demand. I'll get the drinks. You ready to order?"

"Two double cheeseburgers, everything on them, and fries to go with. Thanks, Mol."

The waitress wrote it all down and left with a backward glance at Sophia.

Sophia groaned. "You took me somewhere everyone recognizes you?"

"Not everyone. I didn't think anyone in the diner would, Soph. We'll be fine once we get to my father's bungalow for the weekend. He said to make ourselves at home, but there won't be the usual maid service to disturb us."

"Good," she murmured. "I don't want the vacation ruined by a media firestorm."

He took her hand in his and brushed his lips across her knuckles. "That's not going to happen."

"I certainly hope not," she said, pulling her hand back with a sigh.

Deep down, though, Mol's obvious interest in the two of them left her worried. What if the woman told someone they'd been here? She didn't like the way Mol had stared at Elijah either. Too much keen attention, and her dismissive attitude toward Sophia nagged at her. She could've *tried* to be as friendly to Sophia as she was to her...

She hesitated and glanced over at Elijah to find him watching her closely. Her what? Boyfriend? Friend with benefits? Enemy in court and lover at night?

"You're overthinking, Soph. Just enjoy dinner."

She nodded and focused on trying to absorb everything about the little diner instead. This was her first and closest look at Elijah's childhood. He was right. She needed to enjoy the experience and have the amount of trust it took for him to show her all of this.

***

The weekend flew by in a blur. They were back on the jet to Chicago in no time, and she watched the Indiana landscape fall away from the plane window with a sigh. Once they were able to leave the seats, she curled up on the bed beside Elijah. He didn't ask her if she wanted to make use of the bed this time. Instead, he just spooned her and laid gentle kisses down the side of her neck and her exposed shoulders where the sweater had slid off to reveal her skin. He didn't try to take it any further, and she relished the warm, comforting moment with him. Soon, they would have to return to the façade they'd been maintaining for the last month and a half or so.

When the quiet announcement that they could turn on WIFI came over the speaker, she reached for her phone. She should check on her notifications to see what was going on. Maria might have tried to contact her since she knew Sophia was returning today. Others could've messaged about personal or work things too.

Elijah groaned behind her and tangled his fingers in her hair, pulling gently to grab her attention. "That can wait, love."

"It's been waiting all weekend, Elijah." She shifted to face him, pressing her hips against him and throwing a leg over his hip. "I just want to check it quickly."

He ground his hips against hers in a distracting rhythm. "I can make it worthwhile to wait a little longer."

She rolled her eyes and logged onto the internet with the plane's WIFI signal. "Stop it. It'll only be a minute."

His hands drifted to her hips and then to her butt, kneading and pinching gently. "Come on, Soph. Don't spend the little time we have left like this on checking emails."

She was about to answer when the notifications started pouring in, along with one notifying her of a new report on the trial. She'd set up alerts about those for the major news outlets. Nothing should've been happening while she was gone, though, so she wasn't sure what it could be. She clicked on the notification to read more.

INNOCENT OR GUILTY? POSSIBLE COLLUSION BETWEEN LAWYERS ON HANSON CASE TAKES EVERYONE BY SURPRISE.

Her entire body went cold, and she froze when the photo in the main article loaded. It was a bit grainy, but it was clearly a photo of her with Elijah in the little family diner they'd visited. The phone slipped from her hands and fell face down on the bed. "Oh, God, please, no..."

Elijah stopped teasing and sat up. "What's wrong?"

Her lower lip trembled, tears filling her eyes. "You promised this wouldn't happen!"

"What?" Confusion flashed across his face, and he picked up her phone. Then understanding mixed with fury shifted his expression. "How did they get their hands on this?"

"I don't know, Elijah. Ask Mol, maybe," she spat. Elijah

dropped the phone back onto the bed with a scowl. "Let me off on the runway. I'll walk back. I'm not going to be seen with you. It'll wreck my career and everything we've worked on these last two years."

He stiffened, his face going hard and blank. "I will not. It's not safe."

"I'll be fine."

"You have luggage."

"Keep it," she snapped. "You've done enough damage. I think I can bear the loss of my luggage to save my career."

"It's one story. No one has any proof."

"They have photos of us cozied up to each other looking like a couple." She stared out the window as the fury rose higher. "I'd say that's enough for everyone to believe them, even if the teams we're on don't."

"I'll fix it, Soph." His expression turned to pained pleading. "Please, get off at the hangar."

"No."

"The pilot can't stop on the airstrip. It's not allowed."

"Then let me off and wait to leave so we won't be seen together."

"No one will talk."

"People already have." She jammed her phone into her purse and stalked to the door. "I'll spend the rest of the trip in the main cabin. I don't want you anywhere near me, Elijah. Not until this is over. Maybe not ever if this goes really badly. I..." The tears pressed in then threatened to make an appearance.

He stood, starting toward her.

She shook her head. "Don't. Don't you dare. This is all your fault. You couldn't wait. You just *had* to proposition me, even after you knew I didn't know how to say no to the man I've wanted since I was in my late teens. You knew what could happen, and you did it anyway."

He scowled. "You insisted I take you out in public, Sophia! I didn't suggest that. If you hadn't—"

"I was a fool. A fool to believe we could work. A fool to say yes in the first place. A fool to ask for the fairytale I obviously can't have. But at least I wasn't the jerk who could justify asking the unthinkable and risking a friend's career."

"Soph..."

She raised a hand and turned, jerking the door open. "I don't want to hear it, Elijah. This is over until the end of the trial, and maybe forever."

He didn't try to stop her this time, and she slammed the door behind her before collapsing into one of the long, leather seats of the main cabin, the tears finally making their presence known. She curled into herself and cried, wishing someone would hold her and tell her it would be okay, but the only man who could do that was Elijah, and she couldn't bear to have him near her after what had happened.

That headline was the last straw; in this state, she simply couldn't handle looking at him, let alone having his hands on her. Her heart felt like it was breaking in two, and she didn't know if it would ever get better. If this cost her her license, she was going to be devastated. She should've known not to cave to Elijah's request. Now she was paying for her stupidity.

Chapter 7

Sophia hurried toward the front door of her building to go over final preparations for the trial with Maria. What had started out as one headline a week ago had morphed into a firestorm of media attention. She'd spent most nights seeing the trainwreck unfold in front of her. The worst part of all of this was the pain of being alone and missing Elijah's steady presence. Up until they'd parted ways when he went to college, he'd been her steady place. He'd listened to countless silly problems and given his support and friendship to draw her through them to a point where she too could see they had been silly, however big they'd seemed then. Now she didn't even have that, and she'd pushed him away for the sake of professional appearances.

A lot of good that had done. There were whispers in her office now too, and she suspected the rumors were flying on the two floors above that housed Clarkson and Holden Law. She didn't know how much longer she could handle this. She might as well take her relationship with Elijah public at this point; no one was arguing she hadn't been involved with him after seeing those photos. The only thing they were arguing about was whether any collusion had happened along with the incredibly unprofessional emotional entanglement. When the verdict came out on that, she might well lose her reputation, worse yet, her license.

A crowd of reporters in plain clothes lingered on the side of her office building, waiting for her or Elijah. They mobbed around her at first, shoving mics in her face and asking questions. She pushed her way through them before the tears and breakdown she felt coming on could make an appearance on national news. Before she lost it, though, the reporters pulled back and changed focus.

She turned to find Elijah standing there, hands in his pockets, looking sad—though to the reporters, he likely looked thunderous. She could see a hint of anger at their treatment of her boiling in the look he leveled on them. It said more about how he felt about her than any words ever could have. When his eyes met hers, though, she ducked her head and scurried inside. There were many people around to risk a grateful smile or even a nod. It would only give more weight to the rumor mill the press was running.

Her chest squeezed with a combination of emotional pain and panic. She'd been so foolish to think she could come out of this the same or even in one piece. It quickly became obvious to her that she needed Elijah, even if she couldn't have him. If she hadn't, she never would've agreed to his demeaning first request, let alone forgiven him for it. She made it to the bathroom and into a stall before she broke down in tears.

The whole affair was one humiliation after another, and she'd done it to herself. If she hadn't insisted Elijah prove he didn't want to hide her away, this never would have happened. She'd caused this problem. She'd been so stupid to think this could have a happy ending. Actually, she'd been foolish for going along with it all even though she knew it couldn't. She let herself hope it could end well when Elijah had invited her to dinner the second time, but she should have known better than that.

She tried her best to remain quiet as she cried to avoid adding further humiliation by letting everyone in the office know it was getting to her, but she must not have been very successful because, after a minute or two, she heard a knock on the stall door.

"Sophia?"

Maria. Wonderful. Could the tiled floor just open up and swallow me whole?

She straightened, wiping at the tears and clearing her throat a bit, hoping she didn't sound like she'd been crying for the last five minutes. "Sorry. I'll be out in a minute. I know I'm running late."

"I'm not upset about you running late. I'm concerned about your change in demeanor and the fact that one of the other girls came to tell me they heard you crying in the bathroom. Can you come out here, please?"

Great. Maria would probably lay into her for ever getting involved with Elijah once she knew the truth. She'd be furious at Sophia for endangering her license and risking the entire trial just to get into bed with a man who hadn't even been willing to admit his feelings to her and had chosen to deflect by making her his toy instead of a lover. She couldn't put it off, though, so she stood and straightened her clothes before opening the door to the stall.

"Come on. We'll talk in my office." Maria handed her a tissue. "Your mascara ran, by the way. Why don't you clean up a bit before we walk over?"

She nodded, her voice failing her, and went to the sink to blow her nose and wipe away the streaked mascara on her cheeks. Waterproof would've been her best option today. She'd thought about it and decided it wasn't needed. Another bad decision to add to the string of them she was making lately. When she'd cleaned away most of the traces of her tears, she turned to Maria. "I know I messed up," she whispered.

"We'll discuss it in my office." Maria took her arm gently and led her out of the bathroom through the halls.

The other employees were kind enough not to stare, though some stole little glances at the two of them as they passed. She flushed and stared at the ground. Could this get much worse? By the time this was over, she might be too embarrassed to even set foot in this building, assuming she had a license to practice when this was done.

Maria pushed open her office door and guided Sophia inside, closing the door behind them and locking it. "Why don't you sit down? You look like you're ready to collapse." She took a seat in one of the spare chairs and gestured to the one beside hers. "I'm worried about you, Sophia. I've seen the headlines, but I assumed they weren't true. That maybe you'd taken that photo with Elijah before the trial, and someone was trying to sabotage our last appeals. But you seem too upset for that to be the case. What's going on?"

Sophia dropped into the offered chair and buried her head in her hands, the tears threatening to make another appearance. "I've screwed up so badly, Maria." A sob hitched in her throat. "I'll be disbarred for sure."

"The collusion charges are true then?" Maria sounded horrified.

"No! No, they're not. But..." She looked up at Maria and sighed, "...I did get involved with Elijah..."

Understanding replaced the confusion and despair on Maria's face. "I knew it. I knew it was you he had his eye on. Honestly, I think the man was in love with you back when we were dating, which might be why he never seemed really happy."

"You don't understand!" Sophia wailed. "I know you think he was in love with me then, but he wanted it to be only sex, and now the papers are dragging our names through the mud because I slept with him."

"Please tell me you had the good sense to demand more than a one-night stand from the man." Maria looked aghast at that rather than the issue of the media. "He's not good at admitting his feelings, and if you let him, he'll just try to burn you out of his system. When it doesn't work, he'll panic and make stupid decisions."

"Sounds like it's something you know firsthand," she muttered. "Well, that's how it started, at least...It...I agreed to it, and it was more like any night he wanted than it was a one-night stand...I think it's more now, but he never had the chance to tell me. I was so stupid. I insisted he take me out in public to prove he wasn't ashamed of being with me or trying to hide me away like a dirty little secret."

Maria smothered a laugh. "Really, Soph? Why didn't you just ask him about it instead of insisting he prove it?"

"I guess I just wanted hard evidence." The tears slipped past her lashes. "Then, when I saw the headlines, I was angry and hurt. He'd promised this wouldn't happen, and here we are anyway. I can't be seen with him or be near him. It'll destroy my career and the trial."

Maria stopped laughing and reached out to take her hands. "Soph, we walk a tough line as lawyers, and often, we don't find a good work-life balance. You have a man who understands exactly how hard that balance is, understands exactly how hard you have to fight for your place in this sort of world, and he respects that."

Sophia stared at their hands in her lap.

"That's worth a lot. Elijah drives me crazy in the give-me-five-minutes-with-him-and-a-brick kind of way. But I see how he is with you, and it's not even close to how he was with me. He's protected you in this as much as he can by keeping the reporters at bay."

That much was true.

"The man's brilliant in a courtroom, but put him into interpersonal situations, and he's a bull in a china shop, but he'd do anything to make this right. I know both of you, remember? I've never seen him so miserable, not even after I ended things with him."

Sophia looked up at her boss and mentor with a frown. "You mean that?"

"I do. Knowing Elijah, he's either scheming or wracking his brain for the solution to win you back. Leave this in his hands, Sophia. He'll find a way to make it work if he wants you. When he does, give him the chance to make it right. I can see your love for him in the pained, longing way you look at him whenever you cross paths now. No job is worth losing that kind of love."

She stared at Maria with wide eyes. Had the woman who hated Elijah Clarkson's guts *really* told her to give him a chance, to risk her career if necessary, to take a shot at what Elijah was offering her? What was it that Elijah was offering, though? Until she knew that, she couldn't promise she *could* give him a chance. He might not be worth risking her job for rather than the other way around.

"Promise me you'll give him a chance and, by extension, yourself a shot at happiness." Maria squeezed her hands and let go. "You may not get another opportunity if you walk away from this one now."

Sophia swallowed back tears. "I'm scared."

"I know, but for all his flaws, when Elijah loves someone, he's the safest place to land, Soph. He will not drop you, but you have to trust him. He doesn't do well with people who fight him for control, but when someone hands it over, he would sacrifice even his life to make sure that trust is honored. I'm guessing that, unlike me, deep down, all you want is to trust him and let go."

Her cheeks warmed. "I'm a competent professional. I don't need to let anyone take care of things."

"Need and want aren't always the same. It's not a shame to be a pugnacious lawyer in the courtroom then go home to submit to a man who cherishes you. Don't let fear or pride get in the way."

She sucked in a deep breath. "Can I really submit to him and still keep a professional image?"

"I don't know. You might have to work for a firm that's not connected to him or what happened here, but I will gladly help you find that position if it's necessary. Knowing Elijah, he'll find a way to make sure it isn't. Just trust him, Soph."

"Okay." She peeked up at Maria from beneath tear-soaked lashes. "You're really not angry at me?"

"No, I'm not. Whatever they want to say about collusion, Sophia, there's no way you could successfully collude with him without my help since everything passes through me. Anyone who knows this trial knows I'd rather be raked over hot coals than collude or cooperate unnecessarily with Elijah." She smiled. "At least my reputation for hating him is useful for something."

"Thank you, Maria," she whispered.

"What are friends for?"

"I expected you to yell at me for my indiscretions."

"I'm not the yelling sort." Maria stood. "Well, shall we go over the final details and put this issue out of our minds for now?"

Sophia nodded, relieved to change topics. She filed Maria's advice away for later, though. The older woman had made some excellent points, and though she was still scared of committing if Elijah did find a way to fix this, she didn't want to let go of him, either. Maybe Maria was right. Maybe she could take a leap of faith and find a safe place to land in Elijah's arms.

Chapter 8

Elijah chased off the news anchors mobbing around him the moment Sophia had fled. With her safely inside, he didn't need to hold their focus any longer, and he hadn't decided how to handle this yet. Until he did, he wouldn't say anything to these people. Once he'd decided how to proceed, he could determine if a press conference would be of any use.

For now, he had a meeting with his partner. The two of them had to discuss the narrative the media was spinning and figure out how to handle it. He strode into the building and took the elevator to his floor. Stepping off, he walked through the quiet office space and past meeting rooms filled with lawyers working together on other cases his firm had taken on. He stopped at the end of the hall where his office and his partner's stood side by side and knocked on his partner's door.

Liam Holden opened the door with a grim look. "You always have been good at stirring up hornets, Eli."

"Good to see you too, Liam."

"Don't even start." Liam stood aside and ushered him in. "What were you thinking, man?"

"That I've been slowly going mad over the last two years watching her in that courtroom. Things got out of hand. I need to find a way to fix this."

"Fix it?" Liam whistled and shook his head. "Has it occurred to you the best way to 'fix it' might be to distance yourself from her?"

"Not an acceptable solution."

The word distance niggled at him, however. He needed a way out of this, distance from the problem. But he didn't need or want distance from his woman. That wasn't an acceptable route to take.

"I know that look." Liam groaned. "What are you thinking about now?"

Elijah pursed his lips. "Liam, I need a solution that doesn't involve letting go of Sophia."

"She avoids you like the plague now, I've noticed. Haven't seen her come up to deliver anything in weeks. Not since you returned from your trip to Indiana. Let me guess...that's where the picture was taken."

"Yes." Elijah hated laying out personal details like this, but Liam was his partner. Liam would have to take over if this went belly up on him.

Liam would have to *take over*. It hit him like a thunderclap. "Wait...I think I might have an idea. Liam, I know this is a bit unusual, but what if you took over the case?"

"What?" Liam pushed back from his desk and shook his head. "But you're handling it. You know more about the situation and the files."

"I'll help you behind the scenes. You'll have all my notes, all my case files, everything. But if I remove myself from the case and do a press conference to explain I want to pursue Sophia without the accusations of collusion or concerns about the conflict of interest, we could solve this whole mess."

Liam settled in his chair with a frown. "I don't know, Eli. It's a big risk. If you admit that you were involved with her previously, you're risking *confirming* in the minds of the public that there was something untoward happening."

"There's zero evidence of it."

"Not yet, but you know there could be a mistrial claim filed over these accusations if Maria decides to pursue it."

"She won't."

"She hates you," his partner pointed out.

"But not enough to stoop to that level. She won't believe the press. Even if she believed I could cross that line, she *knows* Soph wouldn't."

"Soph, is it?" Liam shook his head. "You have it bad, Elijah."

"I've 'had it bad' for a long time," he admitted. "But that's not the issue right now."

"Does she know?"

"Liam, I value you a great deal as a partner, but you know I don't do personal chats."

"What I know is that it's Clarkson and Holden Law Services we have on our sign, not just Holden Law. What you do affects the business just as much as mine does. My name's not the only one connected to the prestige this company enjoys, and this whole personal matter has become very public, risking our careers and our firm." Liam crossed his arms with a raised brow. "So I'll ask again. Does she know, Elijah? Does she know you're in love with her, and is it worth trying to fix this?"

Elijah shifted in his seat, hating that he felt like a bug under a microscope. His personal life was his own, and he didn't want to lay it bare before anyone, not even a man he'd come to consider a friend. Liam was right, though. It had become personal. "No, she doesn't know. I didn't have a chance to tell her."

"One would think you'd *open* with that, Elijah," Liam drawled.

"Well, I didn't," he snapped. "Can we just leave it and focus on a solution?"

"Not yet." Liam's eyes narrowed. "Why are you so defensive about this? Why *didn't* you open with that?"

Elijah looked away, ears burning. "Fine. I don't want to talk about it because I bungled it all up at the beginning and then managed to bungle it even worse by taking her someplace people knew me when I'd promised her it was safe. I thought it was, but I was wrong, and now she's hurting because of me. *Again.*"

"Again?" Liam looked aghast. "What in the world did you do in such a short time that could cause pain worse than what she's going through with this media debacle?"

"I proposed we have no-strings-attached sex so I could burn her out of my system even though I knew she was infatuated with me and would say yes to anything that gave her some small scrap of my attention," he admitted with a sigh. "Yes, I know. I was an idiot."

"I had another word in mind," Liam remarked coldly. "What would possess you to do such a thing?"

"Not thinking clearly. I...look, it's no secret Maria's leaving messed me up badly. I didn't want to risk anything. I was going to tell Sophia I'd come to my senses and was in love with her when she misunderstood my reasons for apologizing and demanded I prove I wasn't hiding her away in shame."

"So you took her to dinner back in Indiana and spent the weekend there with her?" Liam groaned and rubbed his temples. "And your solution to this is that I take over the trial so you can try to patch things over?"

"A rather oversimplified way of putting it, but yes...I need to fix this; I can't do it if I stay on the case. By the time the case is over, assuming it even ends on time in a week, I'll have lost her. I can't do that, Liam. I'm asking as both your friend and your partner...help me out on this."

"Fine. But you'd better make things right with that poor woman. You've hurt her enough, Elijah. Don't make it worse." Liam pointed a finger at him. "Hold a presser tomorrow and fix this. Then go sort things out with your woman."

Elijah rose with a nod, relief coursing through him. "Thank you, Liam. I'll owe you one."

"Yes, you will. Now go figure out what you're going to say. That interview will probably make national news." Liam waved him out.

Elijah left, wondering if he was going too far and if Sophia would let him fall without catching him. For once in his life, he depended on someone else to catch *him*, and he was terrified she wouldn't. Despite the fear and uncertainty, though, he had to do this. He had to try to make things right by her. Honor and love demanded it. His need for her demanded it. It didn't matter if she was there to catch him in the end or not. He'd never forgive himself if he didn't try.

***

Elijah sat under the bright studio lights with the news anchor from the station he'd contacted. They'd been the first to break the story about him and Sophia, so it seemed only fitting that they'd put this misunderstanding to bed with his interview and announcement.

The camera light blinked to green, a steady pulse marking the passage of time much like every rapid beat of his heart. He looked to the news anchor with a raised brow as if to say, *Well, get on with it.*

The anchor, a middle-aged man who was balding and red-faced as though he were perpetually angry, straightened in his chair and leaned forward with an engaging smile at the camera. "Folks, we have Elijah Clarkson live in the study with us. You heard that right. Live in the studio. The man who has been avoiding the press like the plague has finally come out of hiding and offered us an exclusive interview."

Elijah smiled begrudgingly at the camera when the man behind it gave him a wave, the cue to look at the camera and look pleasant. They'd been over the details before he'd taken his seat up here behind the long frosted surface of the table.

His host turned to him. "Well, Elijah, we're delighted to have you here today."

He just bet they were. What news agency wouldn't be given the recent manufactured scandal? "I'm honored to be here."

"So tell us...when you contacted the studio, you said you

wanted a chance to air the truth about you and Miss Sophia Anderson. So what is the truth, Elijah?"

"The truth is that we were not involved during the trial. I hate to disappoint viewers, but we weren't colluding or even romantically involved."

"But the photos—"

Elijah held up a finger. "Ah, yes. The photos...an old friend's claim to fame gone wrong, sadly. I took Sophia home to Indiana for a weekend to ask her if she would consider a relationship with me. You see, I've known her since we were both younger, and I've wanted her for a long time. This trial, as everyone knows, has dragged on for an interminable amount of time, and I've grown tired of waiting."

"So what did she say?" The news anchor leaned forward in his seat as though hanging on Elijah's every word.

A cheap trick for the audience. What he was saying might fly in the face of the media's wild speculations, but it wasn't all that riveting. "I never had an answer from her on my question," he admitted quietly. "Your story jumped the gun, broke a story that misunderstood our involvement, and scared her off."

The news anchor made a sympathetic sound. "That's a tough break, my friend. Are you going to try again?"

"Yes, but not before I ensure the collusion issue is out of the way. We've both worked too hard on our respective teams to have the case declared a mistrial on speculation." He smiled tepidly to show there were no hard feelings about it, though that was a lie. He'd like to strangle whoever had messed everything up between him and Sophia with that ill-conceived article. "I'm going to hand my case over to my senior partner, Liam Holden, so that I can pursue Sophia without endangering the integrity of the trial."

"You must really love her to do something like that. This is a big case and a big client for you."

He stared down at his hands. The first time she heard him say those words shouldn't be on TV in some scripted interview. The anchor was going off script, and he didn't have to answer. "That's between me and Sophia. I came here to clear both of our names by speaking up about what was really going on. That's all."

The anchor took the hint and smiled broadly at the camera. "Well, that's all for today, everyone. We'll see you back at the top of the hour for the weather report."

The camera light blinked red, announcing the end of the broadcast, and Elijah rose, hurrying down the steps. The anchor tried to stop him, but he had somewhere to be and someone to apologize to. He just hoped what he'd done up there on stage would be enough to convince her he meant business and wasn't playing around anymore.

Chapter 9

There was a knock at her door around nine the evening before the final hearing. Sophia frowned and rose. Who would call at this hour? She glided to the front door and opened it to find Elijah standing on her doorstep in a t-shirt and jeans, looking more casual than she'd seen him in a long time. Dressed like this, it was as if he'd shed his usual persona of Elijah Clarkson, business lawyer extraordinaire, for her Elijah, the one she'd known as a child and loved as much as a naïve little girl could. "Elijah?"

"Soph. Can I come in?"

She hesitated, glancing back at the messy apartment and noticing the lingering scent of Chinese takeout. The place wasn't suitable for visitors.

"I won't be long if you don't want me here, but I need to talk to you." He stepped closer, his chest brushing hers. "Let me inside."

This time it was a command with a hint of underlying uncertainty. She didn't like seeing him unsure. He was always so confident, so in control. To see him vulnerable at all left her unsettled. She stepped aside and let him in, closing the door behind him. She remained facing the door, hand on the doorknob as she wrestled with the emotions that seeing him always brought up. A new one flooded over the old ones, though. Hope. She'd seen his interview and knew he was serious about fixing this. But she was terrified that if she trusted him now, he would break her to pieces.

"Soph," he whispered behind her. "Look at me, please."

Tears filled her eyes, and she shook her head and then lowered it to hide behind a curtain of her wavy hair. His hands settled on her shoulders, turning her gently. Then she was enveloped in his embrace. He smelled of his usual cologne––fresh pine, and earthy cedar tickled her nose.

He scooped her up and carried her to the sofa. When he sat down and cuddled her close, laying down so that she could lay on his chest, she knew he had no intention of hiding from his own feelings or hers anymore. He stroked her hair gently, whispering soothing nothings until the tears subsided. After the tears had gone, she lay in silence for a long while and listened to his steady heartbeat, letting the rhythm lull her back to a steady calm.

"I came to apologize for how I started this whole mess," he murmured. "I never should have done that. I never should have lied about my feelings or what I wanted."

"No, you shouldn't have," she agreed.

He tugged at her hair just enough to make it sting. "Brat. I'm groveling here, and I never do that. Let me do it in peace, would you?"

She lifted herself to stare down at him, straddling his hips to sit more comfortably. "You shouldn't have. I'm not going to disagree and argue you did nothing wrong."

He soothed her with a nod of agreement. "All right. I'm sorry for everything I did, Sophia. I'm sorry for how I hurt you and for being the dumbest man alive about this stuff. I'm sorry, but I'm hoping you'll let me make it right."

"Didn't you do that when you gave the trial to Mr. Holden?"

"That wasn't enough. I want you, Sophia. I love you."

She tensed. He couldn't have said what she thought he had. Earlier, while watching his interview, the anchor had implied as much and tried subtly encouraging Elijah to say it on air, but he'd refused, claiming it was private. Had he really just told her the anchor was right? "What?"

"I love you," he murmured. "I love you even if you won't forgive me and give me a second chance, but I'm pleading with you to do both, Soph."

Calm replaced the tension. She was afraid, but Maria's warning came back to her before she opened her mouth to tell him she wasn't sure. If she didn't trust Elijah, she would never have what she wanted. He was a safe place to land, but she had to trust him enough to jump first. "I want to try, but I'm scared...Promise me you'll catch me if I fall? That I can...That I can..."

"Trust me?" he whispered.

She nodded.

He leaned up and kissed her softly. "Always and forever, from now on."

"Okay. I'll give you a second chance, but if you mess this one up..."

He kissed her more thoroughly. "I won't, but I never want you against me in the courtroom again, Soph. It wouldn't work out well. Come work for me instead, so we never have a case between us again."

She straightened and shook her head. "No. I need to make my own way, Elijah. We'll just have to work things out because I won't have people thinking I grew my career by doing my boss. I'm sorry..."

He sighed. "I figured that would be the answer. Very well...we'll find a way to make it work. Together, Soph. I promise it'll work out."

She smiled down at him. "I'm going to hold you to that."

***

Sophia dropped her keys into the bowl at Elijah's front door and kicked off her shoes. She shook her head at the Van Gogh painting he'd recently mounted with a sigh. The man really did spend ridiculous amounts of money on art.

Elijah ambled out of his den and down the hall toward her, a welcoming smile on his lips. "How did it go, Soph?"

"You don't know?" Thinking about it brought a rush of frustration. "I thought you'd watch it live."

"I wanted to hear it from you." He wrapped her up in his arms and kissed her forehead. "But based on the look on your face, I'm guessing it didn't go well."

"No, it did not. I lost. We lost"

"I'm sorry."

"Really? Your former client won."

"Well, I'm not sorry he won," Elijah amended. "He was the wronged party. But I'm sorry you lost your first big case."

She sighed and rested her cheek against his chest. "I hate losing."

"I know. But Soph? You've just had your first and most important lesson since you passed the bar."

"I have? It feels more like a punishment than anything..."

"Certainly not." He tangled his fingers in her hair and tugged her head up so he could see her face. "Don't ever think that about losing a case. It happens. But in this case, you lost fair and square because your client was guilty. Sometimes, Sophia, it is all right to lose the case so that justice can be served. You have a duty to give your client the best defense you can, but when there is no defense for their actions, and the evidence shows it, don't ever feel guilty for losing."

She bit her lower lip. "That's not what we're taught in law school."

He kissed her mouth gently. "I know. Consider it rule number one from Elijah Clarkson's school of law."

She laughed and shook her head. "All right then. Dinner?"

"Absolutely. I'm famished. If you want to rant, you can tell me more about the case while we eat."

"No, I think I'm all right. I don't want to think about the case tonight."

"Good. I have other things we can discuss and other things we can do."

She rolled her eyes and headed for the dining room. "I'm sure you do, Elijah. I'm sure you do."

Epilogue

A year later

Sophia couldn't wait to share her news with Elijah. She was a bundle of nerves and excitement, and she hoped he'd share in that excitement once she told him. Insecurity mingled with her joy, dimming her enthusiasm.

What if he wasn't happy?

What if he didn't want this as much as she did?

It would bring a great deal of change into their lives, and he might be unhappy about that.

Elijah strode in, carrying the gourmet takeout and caramel apples she'd asked for. He took one look at her face and placed the takeout on the counter to rush to her side.

Cupping her face in his hands, he looked her over, trying to decide what had caused the distress.

"Are you all right, love?"

"I think so."

"Good. You look a bit pale, though. Why don't you sit down on one of the stools while I plate the food? I have something to ask you, and I don't want you fainting on me."

She fidgeted with her sweater and stared at her lap.

Elijah pinned her with a more stern look, crossing his arms. "All right. Out with it, Sophia. Why do you look nervous? Did you do something I should know about?"

"I..." Her ears warmed, "...well, it's more what *we* did than anything," she admitted.

"What we did?" He went from stern to confused. "I don't understand."

"Well, okay. Sort of part what we did and part what you did."

"I am not in the mood for riddles, love."

Well, there was no time like the present. "I'm pregnant."

The words were out in a rush and hung in the air, waiting for an acknowledgment from Elijah. He stood, staring at her in mute shock for a long moment. Then he blinked and shook his head.

"What?"

"I'm pregnant," she repeated.

She had to resist the urge to shy away in fear of his judgment. He didn't speak for a long moment, just staring down at her.

She stared up into his gaze as he processed her confession. Then a slow smile spread across his lips. "Really?"

"Really."

He bent and kissed her. "You really know how to one-up a man."

"One-up?" She frowned.

He dropped to one knee in front of her, pulling a small black box from his pocket.

Oh. She covered her mouth with one hand as he took the other and opened the box.

"The baby announcement has kind of stolen my thunder, but I guess I can forgive the kid," he teased. "Marry me, Sophia Anderson."

As usual, he wasn't requesting. He was demanding. But underneath the command, she heard the note of vulnerability, just as she had on the night when he'd come over to ask for a second chance, which she'd given despite her fears.

Now she was glad she had.

Tears filled her eyes, and she nodded. He slid the ring onto her finger with a broad smile and pulled her hand away from her mouth, leaning up to kiss her.

"You've made me a very happy man, Soph."

"And you've made me a very happy woman," she whispered. "Thank you for being a safe place to land, Elijah."

He kissed her more thoroughly and murmured against her lips, "Forever and always, love. Forever and always."

Ex-Military Billionaire Daddy (Book 3)

Blurb

Liam Beckett would give everything he has to be the recipient of Madison Haye's affection – but she never saw him that way. Madison's focus is on her son, Trystam. When her ex is back in the picture, Madison is torn between doing what's best for her son and following her heart.

Madison loves her son more than anyone else, and she would give and do anything for his happiness and safety. So, when her absentee ex comes back into her life, Madison is at an impasse. However, she can't help but feel pulled toward Liam, her best friend's brother, who never left her side and is always so tender with her.

Liam has always been in Maddie's corner, feeling protective over her and her son. He would do anything to ease her struggles, but the woman is stubborn, insisting on doing things her way. If only she could let him take care of her like she takes care of everyone else.

When things take an unexpected turn, Liam must act fast to show Maddie the kind of life she deserves with him by her side.

Can Liam still prove to Maddie that she can count on him when her ex becomes a danger to her and her son?

Prologue

Maddie Hayes surveyed the lavish spread of food on the table. When Liam had asked her to come over for dinner with her three-year old son Trystam, he'd asked what she wanted to eat. She'd told him she missed the luxury of a good steak and potatoes, but she hadn't expected this. The cook had prepared fresh, made-from-scratch mashed potatoes, perfectly seared steak garnished with parsley and lemon, steamed vegetables, and crème brûlée for dessert.

"Is everything all right, Mad?" Liam's sister Jessica settled a moderate portion of steak and potatoes on her plate before passing the dish to Liam. "You're staring at your plate of food like you can't quite believe what you're seeing."

Maddie looked up from the plate, heat flushing her cheeks. "Oh...everything is fine. More than fine." She met Liam's attentive gaze and cleared her throat, shifting in her seat. "It's more than I imagined when Liam asked me what I wanted for dinner."

Jessica laughed. "You know my brother doesn't do things halfway, Maddie. Of course he'd make sure dinner was spectacular."

Liam smiled indulgently. "I had to do something special to convince you to come back. Good food seems to be the only way I can coax a visit from you these days, and with my busy schedule at the security firm, I can't exactly drop in whenever unannounced. I'm glad you could make it."

She smiled back and dropped her gaze to the plate of food in front of her. Liam had done so much for her. She couldn't quite believe he still wanted her around after all he'd seen her through. Trystam's father leaving for a job opportunity in another state while she was a few months pregnant had devastated her, made worse by him saying a child would only slow him down. But Liam—who had just returned from a long, difficult tour in Iraq—had stepped in to help as soon as he heard what had happened.

He'd been starting up the security firm in those days, barely a year into operating it, yet he'd often spare time from his schedule to look after her.

He'd show up to check that she'd had lunch and taken her vitamins, staying over to keep an eye on her in the early days when she was sick often. And he'd taken her to the hospital when labor hit.

He'd been there even though she'd wished the man who'd put her in this position was instead, and he hadn't once complained about her late-night rants or the emotions that followed as she struggled to move past her ex.

Liam had been furious with her, offering to drag her ex back and set him straight, but she'd refused to give him her ex's details, including his name.

Even after all that, he still made time for her and wanted to see her and Trystam. She glanced at the baby monitor on the sideboard across the room and cut into her steak.

"Don't worry about him, Maddie," Liam murmured. "You're here to take a break. He's sleeping in my room, and he's fine. He's getting big now, and he can handle getting up and calling for us if he needs you."

She nodded and released a slow breath before digging into her food with enthusiasm. She hadn't had a good meal like this in a long time, and she certainly hadn't been eating anything close to it in the last few months. She and Trystam had been surviving off macaroni and cheese, peanut butter, and toast. Sometimes she managed a little chicken, but things were tight right now, and she rarely had the money to afford it.

"So, how are things at the vet?" Jessica asked before taking a bite of her vegetables.

Maddie swallowed the bite she'd taken, her appetite ebbing. "Oh…they're…fine, I guess."

Liam's eyes narrowed, his usual response when she lied to him. He hated it when she kept secrets and told half-truths or outright lies. I

f she'd been his to care for, she expected he'd have taken her to task for it more openly and sternly, but the expression on his face perfectly conveyed his irritation and disappointment, anyway.

"Maddie," he murmured in a warning tone. "Just fine?"

She shifted in her seat and swallowed hard. "All right…they closed a few months ago."

"Oh…" Jessica frowned. "Well, have you been able to pick up more hours at the diner?"

"I've tried. They don't have the hours for me."

Liam scowled. "So what have you been doing to pay bills and put food on the table, missy?"

"What is this? The Spanish Inquisition?"

"You'd know if it were an inquisition," Liam drawled. "Right now, I'm just asking."

Jessica stifled a smile. Maddie shot her a glare. So much for sisterly solidarity from her best friend.

"I'm waiting." Liam set down his silverware. "Maddie?"

"All right, all right." She heaved a sigh. "I haven't found anything to make up for losing the secretarial position at the vet."

"But what are you eating, and how do you pay bills on the pay from the diner?"

Maddie flushed and stared down at her plate.

"Maddie Hayes," Liam rumbled. "You should have said something. You know I'd have helped."

Her cheeks warmed further. "You shouldn't have to bail me out all the time."

"I'm not." Liam sat back and crossed his arms. "I have a position open for a secretary, and I haven't been able to fill it yet. If you'd told me months ago, I would've offered you the job right at the beginning."

She bit her lower lip. "Liam, I can't...I won't take a job just because—"

"Don't you dare finish that sentence, missy." Liam glanced over at Jessica. "Jessica, I'll understand if you don't want to sit through this conversation. I can go discuss this with Maddie in the library."

"No," Maddie snapped. "I'm not a wayward child to be taken into hand, Liam. I don't want handouts, either."

"It isn't a handout," Jessica murmured with a bemused smile. "Not when Liam's offering the job. He'll demand his money's worth out of you just like he does any other employee."

Maddie's annoyance ebbed a bit. Jessica was right about that much. Liam didn't accept half measures any more than he offered them.

"I want you in my office at eight tomorrow morning," Liam told her. "I need a secretary, and you need a job, Maddie. The only answer I want to hear from you is 'yes, sir'. Understood?"

The blush returned with a vengeance. "All right."

He pinned her with an impatient stare, one brow lifting in expectation.

"Yes, sir," she mumbled.

Liam nodded, and the other two returned to their meals. She followed suit shortly after, wishing she didn't feel so embarrassed by her situation. She'd hoped to have a solution *before* Liam discovered she'd kept her financial difficulties from him so that it could remain her secret. He'd done so much for her already.

Sighing, she consoled herself with the reminder that this would be a job. He wasn't handing her the paycheck; she'd have to earn it, and every cent of that check every two weeks would be hers, fair and square.

He was helping out, but he wasn't taking her independence from her or asking her to rely on him for everything.

For that, she was grateful.

Chapter 1

Two years later

Liam Beckett climbed out of his Maserati and headed into the building that housed his private security firm. He opened the door and nodded to the receptionist at the front door, who smiled back with a quiet greeting. He made his way up to the top floor where his offices were located and found Maddie waiting at her desk with his coffee and hers in a cardboard drink holder on her desk's neat surface.

"Maddie," he murmured.

"Liam." She looked up from her work and grinned, snatching his coffee from the drink holder and handing it over. "I've finalized your meetings. Unless anyone stops by unannounced and without an appointment, you have a light load for meetings today."

He took the coffee from her, his fingers lingering on hers a little longer than strictly necessary. She caught the lingering touch and looked away, withdrawing her hand quickly.

A frown furrowed his brow before he could stop his reaction.

A cute, delicate blush brought color to his cheeks and soothed the sting her haste to pull back had caused. He smiled at her again and moved past her toward the office door behind her desk. "How is Trystam doing?"

He leaned against the doorframe and sipped his coffee, watching her face for any signs of distress or trouble.

She gave him a broad smile. "He's doing well. All over the sniffles from his cold, and he's chattering incessantly about your promise to take him to the science museum."

Liam laughed. "That boy loves science more than any kid I've ever known. Like mother, like son, in this case."

She shifted and stared down at her keyboard. "What's wrong with liking science? I know it might be nerdy, but he'll make good money if he chooses to pursue the interest into a career."

Liam pushed away from the door and walked back to the desk, setting the coffee down on the desk and crouching in front of her. "Hey, I wasn't making light of it. There's nothing wrong with it at all, Mad."

She bit her lower lip and stared down at him. "You mean that?"

"I do. You know me well enough to know I wouldn't tease or make fun of you or Trystam for it, missy. Why the defensiveness?"

She sighed and relaxed. "I'm sorry. I just...old habits die hard."

"Yes, I can see that. This is what? The hundredth time I've had to tell you there's nothing to be embarrassed about?"

"In my defense, I've been teased and given a hard time about being the...nerd since I was a schoolgirl. People at work think I'm odd for being so interested in it still at 27, and...and..."

"And he used to mock you for it, didn't he?" Liam clenched his jaw and looked away, furious to learn of yet another way the man who had abandoned her after knocking her up had left scars. "You know, I'm still happy to track this jerk down and make a point."

A tiny laugh escaped her. "It's a little late for that, Liam. Leave it alone. And thank you for reminding me that at least one person doesn't think I'm crazy, nerdy, or weird."

"Well...I think you're nerdy," he murmured, reaching up to brush her hair from her face. "I just happen to think it's cute rather than weird."

The blush returned, and she didn't respond to the remark.

He stood and retrieved his coffee. "Someday, you'll stop bristling when I make comments about this. It might take more time, but I'll find a way."

She snorted. "Liam, it's been what? Five years...it's a habit."

"A habit you can unlearn. Don't you trust me?"

The look on her face was torn. So she still feared what might happen if she trusted him, but at the same time, her experience told her he could be trusted.

Maddie was too independent and stubborn to just let him take care of things, to trust him to take charge and not run out like her ex had. The man had left deep scars, and even though Liam had stuck around and made it clear he intended to keep doing so, she still looked at him like she was afraid he'd leave at any moment when he finally understood the kind of person she was.

He knew full well who Maddie Hayes was, though, and he had zero intention of walking away.

It would just take time to show her that he wasn't helping out of some sense of duty to his sister or even to her and Trystam but because he genuinely cared and wanted to be there.

He was in this for the long game.

He wanted her, and he loved her son like his own. There was no way he'd give that up, even if she never chose to see him as he'd come to see her.

"Let me know when the first appointment arrives, and make sure you take your lunch today, Maddie. I don't want to see you eating over your work when I take my own lunch break, understood?"

"Yes, sir."

He smiled at her once more and then spun on his heel and headed for the office before he let her know just how much he liked it when she was sweet and obedient instead of stubborn and mulish. She wasn't ready yet.

He needed to ease her into the idea of going beyond friendship, not toss her off the deep end. He'd find a way to do this slow and right so he wouldn't send her running for the hills.

***

Liam's phone rang, cutting through the quiet in his office. The outer office was empty. Maddie had taken the afternoon off to attend a parent-teacher day at Trystam's school, and the receptionist at the front desk had been handling his meetings and calls. He answered it absentmindedly. "Yes?"

"Your next appointment is here to see you, Mr. Beckett. Mr. Alyx Marlin?"

"Send him up, then." Liam pulled up his email and glanced over the email Marlin had sent. The man was a high-powered district attorney dealing with a gang-related issue and wanted extra security to protect him from a slew of threats and a few assassination attempts.

There was a knock at the door.

"Come in."

His floor's receptionist entered along with a thin, nervous looking man with eyes that couldn't remain fixed on one place for long.

"Mr. Marlin, sir," his receptionist said.

"Thank you, Bessie."

The receptionist left the room. He ushered Marlin to a seat, immediately disliking the man. His personal unease and dislike for a client didn't matter, though. Marlin could pay well, and although the man wasn't the DA for their little part of the state and held no sway here, it didn't hurt to have friends in high places. "Tell me about the situation, Mr. Marlin."

The man rubbed his hands together with a grimace. "I've been dealing with the organized crime case going on in Minneapolis. I told you in my email I've received death threats and had attempts made on my life. My own security detail hasn't really stopped the issue, so I want extra outside help."

"Do you believe your own security detail is compromised?"

"I suspect so, but I can't prove it, and proving it is everything." The man smiled wanly. "I've barely been able to sleep for fear they'll try again, whoever they are. I want them handled and my life safe and stable again."

"You've come to the right place for security. We'll need to discuss further details, though. You need to keep a closer eye on the security team you already have, and I'll be reviewing any footage from your security system that might help. How many members of the team do you already have?"

"Three. I have an armed escort whenever I need to go somewhere, but those are the three who handle security for me and my home twenty-four-seven."

"I see. All vetted carefully?"

"Of course." The man straightened his jacket. "What do you take me for? A fool?"

Perhaps if you imagine safety and stability were possible in a DA's position, Liam mused.

"I'd like to see the background checks, and I need a list of everyone who has a key or access to your home and personal office. The first two attacks happened in your home, correct? Bombs, if I recall?"

Marlin paled as the attacks were brought up in more detail, but he nodded. "You've done your research."

"What do you take me for?" Liam smiled, though the smile was more teeth than it was a friendly gesture. "A fool? You came to me for a reason, Mr. Marlin. It was because I am the best, not just here but in several states, and my firm is renowned for its excellence across the country."

"I didn't mean any insult by it."

"It's not as though the details were difficult to find," Liam murmured. "I will assign two of my men to escort you. I think it would be best if you stayed in a safe house until we can sort out this issue."

"I won't be kept from going about errands and daily life by these thugs, Mr. Beckett."

"I don't expect that, for now, but I want you in a place I control until we know the threat is past. I cannot afford to try to protect you from your own men in a place where they have a home court advantage, if one of them is indeed involved. These thugs have proven resourceful enough to find their way into your home despite your security. Clearly, that location is not safe."

Marlin grimaced and nodded, but he pressed his lips together in a tight white line, looking ready to explode in frustration.

"I won't fight with you over your safety, Mr. Marlin. If you don't like how I'm handling the situation, then find another firm that will handle it more to your liking. I don't take clients who argue with me. It only increases the risk of harm or death if I do, both for them and for my men."

"Understood," Marlin muttered. "I'll pack a bag. Where is this safe house?"

"My men will take you there. You will bring no one from your original security team. Tell them you want them to continue patrolling your home to make it appear as though you are still there. That will keep them where I can easily find and question them if necessary, and it will also increase the chances that we catch whoever is responsible from trying again."

"You want me to have my security team house sit?" Marlin gaped at him. "On their salary?"

Liam folded his hands in front of him on the desk and stared at Marlin without a word. Either the man understood the danger he was facing or didn't.

If he didn't, Liam would cut him loose.

He either agreed to the request now, or he was going to the curb and would have to find someone else.

Marlin swallowed hard. "Fine. When will your men arrive?"

"8 AM tomorrow morning. I need time to set up everything for the safe house. I'll have some men watching the estate and the house to make sure you're not harmed in the meantime." He rose, buttoning his jacket and extending a hand to Marlin. "A pleasure to be doing business with you, Mr. Marlin."

Marlin scowled, but he shook Liam's hand anyway before turning stiffly and exiting the room, leaving Liam to himself.

Chapter 2

Liam put the matter of Mr. Marlin out of his mind the next day when Maddie showed up. She looked a little tired, and he frowned as he stopped at her desk for the usual coffee. "What were you up late for?"

She took a sip of her coffee and sighed, leaning back in her office chair. "I was just restless. I couldn't sleep."

"I see. Are you feeling all right? You aren't coming down with anything, are you?"

"No, thank you. Just a case of racing thoughts before bed." She smiled at him warmly.

The smile left a warmth in his gut, and he wanted nothing more than to come straight out and tell her he wanted more from her. Instead, he focused on the plan he'd developed and on moving slowly. "Racing thoughts about what?"

"Oh, this and that," she mumbled.

He raised a brow. "Sounds a bit vague. What's really going on, Mad?"

"Nothing." She glanced up at him, scooted closer to her desk, and began cleaning up the pens she'd left before taking off yesterday. "Really, Liam. I promise."

"All right. Do you have a minute? I wanted to ask you something."

She frowned and looked up from her desk. "About what? You sound a little nervous."

"I am," he admitted. "But I'm hoping for a yes to prove I didn't need to be."

"Okay..." Trepidation tensed the lines of her shoulders. "What's wrong?"

"Nothing. I wanted you to go to dinner with me."

"Oh." She laughed, relaxing. "That's not so bad. Are we meeting a client?"

"No. I don't need you to take notes, and it's not for business."

"Oh, okay. Well, I'm sure Trystam would enjoy dinner out."

"You mistake me, missy." He smiled gently, leaning on the desk with his hip. "I want *you* to go to dinner with me. We'll find Trystam a babysitter."

She flushed. "I...I see. You want to..."

"You work hard enough, Maddie. Let me take you out someplace fun, just like we used to do when we were all kids."

She bit her lower lip, and he forced himself to ignore the building desire to take her face in his hands and kiss her senselessly so that any doubts she had about his intentions would be erased. Instead, he stayed still and waited for an answer.

"But it's just us. Isn't that...kind of like a date?"

"Call it whatever you want," he murmured, noting the indecision and worry on her face. "I didn't want you worried or upset by a request to spend time with a woman I consider a friend."

The worry lifted, but she still didn't seem certain. "When did you want to go? I can't get a sitter on such short notice..."

"We'll figure out the best time, and I'll handle the sitter. I'll ask Mrs. Potts to watch him if we can't find anyone. She won't mind."

"We can't ask your housekeeper, Liam!" She looked appalled. "She has a life outside of working for you, and her job doesn't include watching a little boy who gets into mischief."

"Mrs. Potts likes Trystam, as you well know. I'd pay her for it too, but we'll see if we can find another babysitter."

"What will people think?" she whispered, looking away.

"What will people think?" he echoed, incredulous. "Who cares? Everyone in the office knows we're friends, Maddie. No one will care, and no one will talk, either. They know I have zero tolerance for gossip, especially in a security firm where we have to keep secrets discreetly for clients."

She licked her lips. "It's not our usual behavior."

"Maddie," he murmured.

Her gaze shot to his at the stern tone in his quiet voice.

"Are you making excuses, missy?"

The blush swept up into the delicate shells of her ears, and she lowered her gaze, hiding her pretty brown eyes. "We don't go places one on one. We're not that kind of friend to each other."

"If that's what you think, perhaps I need to try harder. I'd like us to be that kind of friend, Madison Hayes."

Her eyes widened at the use of her full first name. "W-well...if you're sure..."

"I've never been more sure in my life."

"I guess I could go. But where are we going and when? I don't know if I have anything nice enough for a personal...I mean, can one wear the same things to personal dinners as to business ones? How nice is the restaurant? If you maybe pick one—"

He pressed his index finger to her lips with a bemused smile. "Maddie, take a breath. Dress comfortably. Casual is fine. I'm not going to make a spectacle of you by taking you somewhere that makes you feel out of place or small and insignificant. Where we're going is a surprise, though. Trust me?"

She closed her eyes with a soft sigh. "Okay."

"Good girl. How about we go Friday night at six?" He pulled his finger away from her lips. "If we can't find a sitter, I'll pay Mrs. Potts. She's usually free Friday nights."

Her eyes opened, and she stared up at him with a mixture of uncertainty and warmth. "Thank you, Liam."

He smiled. "I'm the one who ought to thank you for agreeing. I thought you might not for a minute there."

She laughed quietly, cheeks pinking again. "I haven't gone out somewhere with a man one-on-one in ages. I'm not even sure I know what to do."

He gave in to his urge to touch her just a little, pressing a chaste kiss to her forehead as he picked up his coffee. "Just be yourself, missy. That's enough, I promise."

Her expression betrayed her disagreement, but she didn't argue the point with him, so he left it be. He headed into his office, leaving her to think about what she'd agreed to and smiling to himself. Step one was accomplished, at least.

Now he just had to figure out ways to hint to her that he was interested in seeing how she felt about the idea. He had a suspicion she liked him by how she reacted to his touch or the commanding note he sometimes injected into his tone, but he wanted to be certain before he risked their friendship for more.

***

She was stunned when Liam parked his Maserati in front of a little pizza place in a more rundown part of town. While they'd all grown up with relatively poor backgrounds—something that had contributed to Liam's decision to join the military—Liam no longer lived in that world. Neither did Jessica. She was the only one who did, to some extent. That Liam not only knew about a hole-in-the-wall place like this but also took her to it was astonishing.

Was this a place he took all his dates? Or was it unique to her because he thought she'd be too overwhelmed if he took her somewhere fancy? He climbed out, oblivious to her anxiety, and opened the car door for her. She let him draw her out and guide her up to the door of the small restaurant.

He opened this door, too, ushering her into the warm, inviting interior of the building. The staff stopped what they were doing to stare. They seemed to know Liam, but judging by the confusion on some of the faces and the outright delight on others, she guessed he must not bring any dates here. She wasn't *really* a date, but from the outside, it probably looked like she was, and they seemed to assume it.

"Mr. Beckett." A short Italian man with a broad smile approached and clasped Liam's hand warmly. "Good to see you. Who is this lovely young lady on your arm?"

She felt the heat of embarrassment creeping into her cheeks and then her ears, and she stared down at the floor.

Liam drew her closer, tucking her into his side. "This is Maddie. We're old friends, and she works with me."

"Ah, I see, I see." The man clapped his hands and rubbed them together. "Would you like the corner booth, Mr. Beckett? It offers more privacy."

"Thank you, Giuliano. That would be wonderful."

Liam guided her to the booth and helped her slide in. Instead of taking a seat across from her as she'd expected, he slid in next to her, keeping his warm thigh pressed against her. She bit her lip and contemplated scooting over more. Did he feel crowded? If he did, though, there was room to move, and he didn't remark on it. He'd sat this close on purpose. Her cheeks warmed. Why was he so close? What game was he playing?

He leaned in closer, whispering in her ear. "Relax, Maddie. We're just out for dinner and a little fun after."

"Why is everyone staring at me like they think I'm...like they think I'm..." *Yours*, was what hovered on the tip of her tongue, but she couldn't make herself voice it.

"I don't bring other people here." He leaned back, taking his warmth with him.

She sighed, missing the warmth even as she questioned her sanity for letting herself imagine the man, who was both her *boss* and one of her closest friends, doing more than merely whispering in her ear. This was insane.

His hand landed on her thigh.

She jumped, gasping.

He raised a brow. "Someone's jumpy. I brought you here because I really like this place, and I thought you might too. I hope you're hungry, though. They make huge pizzas."

Relaxing, she picked up the menu, letting herself indulge in a moment of weakness by leaning against him. Really, if he didn't like it, he had only himself to blame since he was sitting so close. If he did mind, he didn't say anything.

He perused the menu as if she hadn't leaned into him at all. The part of her that enjoyed pushing for a reaction wanted to see how far she could go before he scolded her, but they were in public, and she didn't want to make a spectacle of the teasing banter they shared in private.

"You've gone very quiet over there, missy," he murmured. "Are you asleep or plotting something?"

She coughed and sat up. "N-neither!"

"Mmm...plotting then. What's going through that cute head of yours?"

She ducked her head and avoided his gaze. When he said things like that, it reminded her that he was quite a bit older. Almost eight years divided them, and he wouldn't see her as a woman when he'd been taking care of her like she was his little sister all these years.

His hand returned to her thigh, rubbing in soothing circles over the thin fabric of the floral skirt she'd worn for the outing. "It's all right if you want to keep it a secret. I'm sure I'll have it out of you eventually, if not because you fessed up, then because you put the plan into action. Just know that if you and Trystam switch out my shaving cream for whipped cream again, it's your butt on the line."

She giggled, the tension easing. It was ridiculous to be so stressed about this! It was Liam. He was safe and solid, unlike so much else in her life. He'd never do anything to hurt or upset her intentionally, and however sad she might be that the mixed signals he gave off didn't mean anything, there was no reason to let that sadness stop her from enjoying this time with him.

"That's better." He smiled softly.

The waiter came to take their order, and the rest of the meal went by in easy conversation. His shoulder brushed hers as they ate and hers bumped his every so often. If it bothered him to have her so close, he didn't show any signs of it. When the meal was demolished, he paid the check, refusing to let her touch her wallet or the bill.

Once they'd made it back to the car, she bit her lip and settled into the seat. He buckled her in before she could do it and then rounded the car to climb into the driver's seat.

She smiled shyly when she found his gaze on her. "You said we would have fun after dinner...what did you mean?"

"Well..." He turned the car on, the engine purring to life quietly, and then pulled out onto the road. "It's a surprise, but I promise it'll be a good one. I hope you still like games as much as you did when you were younger."

Games? Of course she did, but what kind of games? She sat on the edge of her seat, trying not to plead with him to give her clues. He smirked when he saw her wiggling, and she stopped immediately, folding her hands in her lap as her cheeks warmed.

"It's cute that you still get so excited about surprises," he murmured, reaching over to pull her hands away from worrying at the fabric of her skirt. They'd been driving for close to ten minutes now.

"I'm not a little kid, you know," she mumbled. "I'm not supposed to be cute."

"Adults can be cute too." He pulled up in front of a large building with a neon *Arcade* sign out front.

A grin spread across her face as she processed where he'd taken her. "An arcade?"

"You used to love them when we were kids."

"You remembered?" she whispered.

"Of course I did, missy."

Tears prickled at the corners of her eyes. "I can't believe you cared enough to remember…"

"Stop that," he commanded sternly. "You know I care, Maddie. Don't put yourself down by insinuating you're not worth my attention or concern."

She flushed, and peeked up at him from underneath her lashes before he walked out. When he rounded the car to help her out this time, she didn't hesitate to take his hand. After all, she was excited to play whatever games the arcade had with Liam, and she didn't want to waste a single second. Not when he was here with her, making the night perfect and stress-free so long as she allowed herself to trust him and to enjoy it.

Chapter 3

Liam's interest in taking her out didn't stop with the trip to the arcade, though his next request included Trystam, much to her relief. As much as she'd enjoyed his attention, one-on-one time with Liam was dangerous. It tempted her to forget that he was just a good friend and one she owed a great deal to, not someone who would ever see her as girlfriend material, let alone more. Besides, there was Trystam to think of, and he would be devastated if something happened between her and Liam to cause the man to stop visiting.

"Mommy, it's a dolphin!" Trystam's squeal of delight brought her back to the present moment with her son and the man whose presence had her daydreaming.

She smiled at her son and Liam, carrying the boy on his broad shoulders as they moved through the giant aquarium. "It is, isn't it?"

"I learned all about dolphins in school this week," the proud five-year-old announced. "Did you know they're really not fish, Mr. Liam?"

Liam tipped his head up to look at the boy with a grave look. "I didn't. What else did you learn?"

"They're mammals," the boy declared. "And they breathe through a hole at the top of their heads. And my teacher says they have emotional capacities that are super close to humans."

"Impressive. What do you think, missy? Impressive?"

She smiled at him and then up at Trystam, who was holding onto Liam's head and watching her anxiously. "I think it's very impressive, Trystam. You learned a lot from class this week, didn't you?"

"I always learn lots in class, Mommy," he said, his attention going back to the dolphins with wide-eyed fascination.

She joined them at the window. "Do you think we could stay and watch them for a while? I know it's probably dull, but he's never seen a dolphin, Liam. Not in real life."

Liam pulled the amazed child from his shoulders and sat him on the bench beside the glass. He took a seat beside the child and pulled her down to sit with them. "I could watch these guys play all day. It's just a bit more fun to watch him watch them like this."

Trystam got up and ran to the glass just in front of the bench as one of the dolphins swam by, chasing after another.

She sighed in quiet contentment. "Thank you, Liam. It's not often he gets to go places this nice. I try to take him to parks and attractions, but...well, it's not really a priority, and it's hard to swing it as a single mom when I have to work. Not that I'm complaining, mind you. I like working, and I like working for you. I just..."

He reached out and took her hand in his, holding it as the two of them watched Trystam. "You just wish you had the luxury of spending this time with him while he's still young enough to be like this."

She bit her lower lip and stared down at their entwined hands. "Yeah."

"That might be possible in the future, Maddie."

"Not likely. Who wants to date, let alone marry, a woman bringing a kid along with her?"

"Well, I don't consider that a deal breaker. Trystam's a great kid, and any man should be proud if he gets the chance to be that little boy's father figure."

She felt her cheeks warm and looked away. He was just saying that because he'd known Trystam since the boy was a baby. "You're just being nice. It's easy to say it's not a deal breaker when you're talking about a kid you know. Trystam's a good kid, but most men won't care about that. They'll see him as a commitment they don't want to take on in addition to me."

His glare settled heavy on her, and she could sense his displeasure without even looking. His fingers tightened on hers when she tried to pull away. "Then you're not talking about men, sweetheart. You're talking about boys. Men don't hide from commitment."

Men like Liam didn't hide from commitment. Plenty of others did. "I still think you're just being nice. A significant other isn't in the cards for me. Even if I didn't have Trystam, I'm a little too—"

A sharp tug on the end of her ponytail grabbed her attention and drew her gaze to his. He frowned at her sternly. "You'd better not have been about to put yourself down, little girl. I don't take kindly to that, and if I have to start doing something about it, I will. Maybe we need our own version of a swear jar to put a stop to it."

She huffed. "I wasn't going to say anything that isn't true," she muttered.

He opened his mouth to reply, but Trystam returned, a big smile on his face, and put a stop to the conversation. "Mommy, can we go see the sharks too? My teacher taught me about them too."

She stood a little too quickly, pulling her hand out of Liam's sharply. Trystam's gaze wandered first to Liam and then to her, but the child didn't seem upset by the hand-holding. Usually, Liam didn't touch her in front of him. He kept his hands strictly to himself, in general, most of the time. This time had been a rare moment of public affection from her friend. Would Trystam be confused? He viewed Liam as a father, but he knew that Liam wasn't anything more than a friend, just like he knew he had a biological dad out there somewhere.

"Mommy, it's not nice to pull your hand out of someone else's. You always tell me I can't let go of yours in places like this." He pointed at Liam, who was smiling broadly. "He just wants to make sure you don't get lost, just like you always do with me."

She closed her eyes and fought back a laugh. Trystam came up with the strangest reasoning for things at times.

"Yeah, Maddie," Liam teased. "We wouldn't want to lose you, so hand in mine, missy."

She opened her eyes and sighed, extending her hand to him. When Trystam was safely holding Liam's other hand, she cast her friend an annoyed look and mouthed 'jerk'.

He smirked back and shook his head, leaning in to murmur, "The kid had a valid point, Maddie."

"He did not," she hissed back. "What's with the excuse to hold my hand, anyway? Are you just trying to get under my skin?"

His smile was too innocent. "That's for me to know and you to find out. Now, I believe a certain someone asked about the sharks."

Trystam was tugging at Liam's hand, urging him to move faster. "I saw the sign for the sharks up there!" He pointed, almost skipping in his haste to get to the next exhibit.

"They'll still be there in another five or ten minutes, kiddo," Liam chided gently. "Slow down and enjoy everything along the way. Did you see these colorful fish over here? I bet your teacher hasn't taught you about angel fish yet."

Attention successfully diverted, Trystam hurried over to the display Liam was guiding him to without protest. He stared in at the brightly colored fish with wide eyes. "They're so pretty. Did someone paint them those colors?"

Liam bent down to the boy's level, releasing Maddie's hand to point at the fish. "Nope, they're this way naturally. Isn't that cool?"

"Why are they like that naturally?" her son wondered.

"Because they swim around in the corals and need to blend in. See?" He pointed at the coral below.

"So it's like camouflage?" the boy asked.

"Just like camouflage."

Maddie watched the two of them discuss the fish with a pang of sorrow. What would it be like if Liam looked at her with so much affection? What would it be like if he ever chose to devote that same close attention to her as a woman, not just as a woman he still saw as the little girl who'd grown up while he was on tour? She wanted that more than anything, wished she had someone to lean on like that, wished Liam would be that person.

Sighing, she reminded herself for what seemed like the hundredth time that he didn't see her as a potential girlfriend or spouse. She was just the friend who gave him a chance to do something charitable here and there. He helped out of duty, not romantic affection, and as easy as it was to forget that in moments like these, she couldn't afford to forget that. Not when it would crush her heart to come back to reality if she let her dreams take her too far.

If only he had been Trystam's father, then she'd have him by her side, and she could be certain he didn't look at her as a little girl he felt responsible for.

Chapter 4

Liam received a call from the front desk informing him that Mr. Marlin had stopped in and requested to see him. He pinched the bridge of his nose with a sigh. His men gave him regular updates now that they'd often contracted out the detective work to a firm he'd worked with and moved Marlin to the safe house. He knew everything happening, particularly that Marlin was a nightmare to deal with—little surprise there. The man was petulant, spoiled, and on a power trip. He needed to be knocked down a peg, but he was a client, so with nothing more than his own pride at stake, Liam had kept his mouth shut.

The last thing he wanted was to see the pushy, obnoxious DA, but appointment or not, the man had pull and was a high-paying client. He didn't have any meetings right now and could spare thirty minutes or so. "Send him up," he told the front desk with a sigh. "Maddie will let him into my office."

He hoped the man wouldn't bully his assistant in any way. The staff on the first floor had complained about him last time he'd dropped in for the initial meeting, and he didn't want Maddie harassed.

To be certain she didn't have any trouble, he waited until he heard the elevator ding and closed out his work to go greet Marlin himself.

He reached the outer office to see Marlin standing stock still at the threshold of the office space, staring at Maddie. For her part, Maddie looked like she'd seen a ghost. She pushed away from the desk with trembling legs and forced herself to stand. "I...are you in the appointment books, sir?"

Liam was impressed at her ability to rally from what was so obviously a shock—though he didn't know why she was behaving that way—but he didn't want this going any further. He cleared his throat.

Maddie jumped and whirled about, eyes wide. If he'd thought she was pale before, she was practically white now. Her hands shook at her sides, and she looked between Marlin and him like a deer caught in the headlights. "I...I didn't hear you come out, sir."

"I can see that." Liam narrowed his eyes, examining Marlin's change in posture.

The man didn't look nearly as pushy as usual. He hadn't demanded his meeting either. In fact, he was still standing in frozen silence as if he didn't quite know what to do. When he noticed Liam's glance, he snapped out of it and returned to his usual blustery, obnoxious self. "Yes, I am in the appointment book, woman. Obviously, I am, or they wouldn't have sent me up."

Maddie flinched, her gaze falling to the floor. "Of c-course. I'm s-sorry. I didn't catch your name. Maybe there was some mistake. I j-just didn't see the appointment, that's all. I'm sure...It's probably...I didn't..."

Marlin glared at her. "Can you manage a single sentence without stuttering? Do you have any idea how annoying it is?"

She flushed, tears sparkling in her gaze as she lifted her gaze to Liam's in a wordless plea.

"Can't you hire decent help, Mr. Beckett. She certainly doesn't inspire confidence." Marlin tucked his hands into his pockets, a vicious smile on his lips. "She never has."

His eyes narrowed. This man knew her somehow. Maddie hurried to the computer, fingers shaking too violently to unlock it. When that failed, she turned to the paper record of the appointment book she kept, but she couldn't seem to locate whatever she was looking for.

Liam's fists clenched. How dare Marlin come in here and mistreat his staff, barge in uninvited and unannounced, and then criticize his secretary as if she'd been the one in the wrong? That it was Maddie, who struggled with harsh criticism and her own self-doubts, only increased his fury. "Mr. Marlin," he snapped. "Get out."

Marlin stared in shocked silence for a moment. "Excuse me?" he finally managed.

"Get. Out."

"You're kicking a paying client out over your secretary? Over *her*?" Marlin glowered at him.

Liam wasn't budging on this one. "You insulted my staff, and now you're insulting my ability to choose my staff wisely. Miss Hayes is a valued member of our staff."

Maddie quivered as she fought to keep herself under control. Liam walked over and wrapped his arm around her waist, pulling her into his side and hiding her face. His anger burned higher.

"I came for an update, and I'm paying your paycheck! You'll not kick me out over a snotty, over-sensitive woman."

"I'll kick you out because of your behavior towards my secretary and have now royally ticked me off!" Liam roared in response. "Get out before I tear up our contract and have security drag you off the premises and kick you to the curb."

Maddie shivered in his arms. He pet her hair gently and rubbed her back, trying to convey silently that he wasn't angry with her, but over the poor treatment she'd received.

Marlin shot him a nasty glare, but he spun around and marched back into the elevator. "This isn't over, Maddie. We have a lot of catching up to do, apparently. Where is the snot-nosed brat you insisted you'd keep? Or did you change your mind after all?"

When Maddie went still and tense, Liam finally put it together. He swore and released Maddie. "Marlin, if you're not gone in the next five seconds and out of my office building soon after, you're losing my protection. I don't care how much you pay me. You just made this personal, and if you want me to remain professional, you'll do what I say. Now."

The man huffed and punched the elevator button. The doors closed off their view of his annoyed expression, leaving him alone with Maddie, who was now slumped in her chair with her hands buried in her face. "I'm s-sorry." Her breath hitched. "I'm s-sorry, Liam."

He crouched in front of her and pulled her hands away from her face. "There's nothing to be sorry for, missy. He's gone. You're okay. You're okay." He reached out and wiped away her tears with his thumbs. "Deep breaths, Maddie."

She relaxed into his soothing touch with a shiver. He opened his arms for her, and she fell into his embrace without hesitation, curling into him and burying her face in his chest.

"He's Trystam's father, isn't he?" Liam asked.

The tension returned, and she tried to wiggle out of his grip. He pinched her hip in warning and tightened his grasp. "Oh, no, you don't, missy. You've avoided this with me for far too long already, and look where it's put us. I'm stuck with a client I have even more reason to hate now that I know what he's done, and I can't drop him without good reason. This doesn't count. You've been reduced to a quivering mess. Was he always this mean when you two were together?"

She shook her head, settling in his lap with a resigned sigh. "He had moments, but he never spoke to me quite like that. He...sometimes scolded me or yelled at me for embarrassing him in front of friends by talking too much or getting nervous and stammering. He could be really mean if he'd been drinking, but he...he wasn't like this sober."

Liam rubbed soothing circles into her hip with his thumb, fighting the urge to go after the other man to give him a lesson in how to treat women. "I'm glad he's not with you and Trystam, then."

"He's changed, Liam," she whispered. "He scares me. What if he insists on seeing Trystam now that he knows where we are?"

"I don't think there's any reason to worry about that, sweetheart," he murmured. "He didn't want anything to do with you and Trystam before. Why start now?"

"I don't want to see him again."

"Don't worry. I won't be letting him near you in this office." Liam kissed the top of her head. "Come on. We're going out for lunch and a coffee. I think we still have quite a while until my next meeting, and you need time to recuperate."

She let him lead her to the elevator without protest and didn't even object to the way he kept her cuddled close to his side the whole way down, which told him just how scared of Marlin she was. He gritted his teeth and swore he'd do whatever he had to in order to keep Marlin away from her.

***

Later that evening, Maddie put Trystam down to bed and poured herself a glass of wine to steady her still frayed nerves after the encounter with Alyx Marlin. She'd never imagined he would resurface or that he would show up at her place of work, of all places. In fact, she'd come to hope never to see him again at all. She had sole custody of Trystam, but seeing him again dredged up old worries about a custody battle if he ever walked back into their lives. Now he was apparently a DA a few counties over and held a lot of sway. He was also meaner, and Maddie didn't for a second think he wouldn't be more inclined to make people's lives hell if he didn't like something they'd done.

She sipped at the wine and settled onto the couch to turn on the TV. Just as she switched it on, there was a knock at the door. She frowned and checked her cell. Liam usually texted if he was coming over, and he rarely visited after Trystam was in bed, though he'd been doing a lot of things he rarely did over the last few days. He'd touched her more in the last week or two than he had in years of friendship since his return from Iraq six years ago.

There was no text, but she got up at the second insistent knock and trudged over to open the door. "It's an odd hour to visit."

"Really? It's barely after seven," a familiar, nasally voice snapped.

She gasped and tried to slam the door on him. Alyx reached out and grabbed it, leveraging it open with surprising strength. Not wanting a scene to wake Trystam or to deal with cops on her doorstep tonight, she gave in and let him in. "What do you want?" she snapped.

"I came to find out where the kid is. You might want to keep me out, Madison, but Trystam is my son too. I want to be part of his life."

"And where were you the past five years?" she snapped. "He has a father, and it isn't you."

"Is it Liam Hayes?" Alyx snorted. "Really, Madison. With your boss? I knew you'd sink low, but not that low."

She lifted her chin, tears threatening. "Get out, Alyx. I'm not sleeping with Liam. He's a good man and a good friend. He did what you should have for me and Trystam."

Alyx rolled his eyes. "Really? You think I owed you anything? I told you I wasn't ready for a kid, and I told you I had this great ADA position lined up. I was too close to have that derailed by a kid. You were pretty close to finishing up your own degree in accounting too, but I guess you gave it up for a snot-nosed brat. Now look where you are."

His gaze wandered around the small house she'd rented in derision, and she looked at it in shame for the first time. She'd never once felt so embarrassed by the small place she'd managed to rent to give Trystam a safe neighborhood to grow up in, not even when Liam or Jessica visited. They probably had twice the amount of money Alyx had, but he made her feel small in ways they never had.

"The kid could use a parent who can provide for him. I can do that now." He modulated his tone. "Be reasonable, Madison. He deserves to know his father, and a little child support wouldn't hurt anything, would it?"

Maddie flinched. "We're doing fine on our own," she whispered.

"Fine. You're doing fine," he scoffed, spreading his hands in a placating gesture. "But shouldn't Trystam get to meet his father? I'm sure he has questions."

He did. A lot of them now that he was getting old enough to understand that his situation was different from that of the children he went to school with. When the teacher talked about mommies and daddies and asked the children to share about their parents, Trystam either refused to participate or told them about Liam before bursting into tears. She'd had to leave work early to collect him a few times because of the issue.

A gleam entered Alyx's eye. "He does, doesn't he?"

She hunched her shoulders and wrapped her arms around her midsection. "Alyx, I..."

He reached out and took her chin in his slender fingers. "Stand up straight and look me in the eye. You know I hate it when people slouch and avoid looking me in the eye. Have a modicum of self-respect, Madison."

She flinched away from his touch. "D-don't touch me."

He smirked. "Stuttering again? You've forgotten everything I taught you when we were together and all the rules, too, apparently. But that's all right, *Maddie*. You'll relearn them. Go wake the kid up. I know he's here. You've glanced at the stairs every few seconds since I arrived."

Had she? She cringed, hating that she'd given away his presence to a man she didn't trust. "Please just let him sleep, Alyx," she whispered. "Come by another day at an hour when he's awake. Then you can meet him."

He nodded. "Tomorrow. Six sharp. I'll bring dinner."

She bit her lip and stared at the floor, unable to bring herself to answer or meet his eyes. Apparently an answer wasn't needed. He strode out of the house without bothering to confirm the time worked, leaving her alone in the living room.

She sank onto the sofa and knocked back the rest of her wine, tears burning her eyes and then slipping over her cheeks. She wanted to call Liam, but this wasn't the sort of thing she could tell him over the phone, so she resisted the urge and curled up to cry out the stress and anxiety of having Alyx here left inside.

Chapter 5

Liam knew something was wrong the moment Maddie walked into the office. She had dark bags under her eyes and looked like she'd been crying. He pushed away from his desk and strode out to hers. She handed him his coffee wordlessly, keeping her face carefully turned away from him.

He took the coffee and set it down on the desk. "What's wrong, Maddie?"

She tensed.

"Madison Hayes," he snapped. "We've known each other long enough to be honest with one another. Saying nothing isn't any better than lying to me in my books. If you don't want to tell me, then you tell me that. To my face."

She twisted her hands on the edges of her sweater. "Alyx visited last night."

Silence dropped over the two of them. He shoved away from the desk and raked his fingers through his hair. "I...what did he want?" He forced the words out, forcing his jaw to loosen enough to let the question escape as he paced away from the desk.

"He wanted back into Trystam's life. Insisted, in fact."

"Did he hurt you?" Liam hissed, stalking back to her.

She wouldn't meet his gaze. "Not really. He just scared me, and I was...I made him go away."

"How did you make him go away?" Liam's eyes narrowed.

"I told him he could see Trystam another day."

"There's more than that, isn't there, missy?" He crossed his arms. "Out with it."

"He wants to bring dinner over tomorrow."

Liam lost his temper at that. "Like hell he will."

Maddie's eyes widened at his cursing, something he restrained from doing around her. "He didn't wait for me to agree or refuse. He just sort of assumed I would..."

"Then he's going to have one more *unexpected* guest. I'm not leaving you two alone with him."

Maddie's gaze dropped to the gray carpet. "Why does it matter to you so much, Liam? He hasn't hurt us. I...I don't think he will as long as he gets a part in Trystam's life."

"And you think a man like that is safe for your son?" He knelt in front of her and covered her tiny hands with his. "Maddie, I love that kid like my own."

She looked away, disappointment flashing across her expression, but she didn't respond. Did she want to hear him say he loved her? Well, it was a good time for a confession anyway. He wasn't letting her give in to Alyx without making it clear she could choose him, choose a man who would cherish and care for her instead of frightening and threatening her.

"Look at me, Maddie," he ordered.

Her gaze snapped back to his.

"I love you too."

"Like a friend, I know," she mumbled. "I know you're just worried about what he might do, but really, I don't—"

He leaned up and stopped the flow of words with his mouth. He'd never been good with words, preferring actions to make his point. He'd learned to express himself verbally, too, of course, but right now, he didn't think verbal would cut it. She wouldn't listen, or she'd find reasons he didn't mean what he'd said.

She whimpered and relaxed into his touch with a soft sigh. When he tangled his fingers in her hair, she groaned and let him deepen the kiss without any protest. She'd definitely wanted this for a while. He'd suspected as much, but Maddie had been reluctant to show her emotions or her desires ever since Alyx deserted her with a baby on the way. He'd come home to a much shyer, nerdier, quieter version of her, though he'd quickly discovered how easily she babbled when nervous. He didn't dislike that version of Madison Hayes—far from it—but he missed the little girl whose emotions could be read on her face like words on a page. He hated that she felt any need to hide, at least with him.

There was no hiding now, though. She pressed against him, hands sliding up to his shoulders to anchor her against him. He had no intention of letting her go any time soon, but he didn't want to get too carried away. The first time he let that happen would be in his bed, not up against her desk where anyone could see if they walked by. He released her with a regretful sigh.

She lifted her fingers to touch her lips, eyes wide.

"Not like a friend," he murmured.

"Not like a friend."

Her agreement brought a smile to his face. "Glad I finally got that across, missy. Took long enough. Maybe now you can understand why I hate the idea of you being anywhere with Alyx alone. Besides, the man is petty, mean, and drunk on his own power. You shouldn't be left with him alone."

"But...you c-can't just show up to dinner without an invitation," she protested.

"Little girl, I most certainly can, and that is precisely what I'll do. I don't care if it's rude. This is about your safety and well-being. Can you honestly tell me you want him in your home near your son and you with no one else around?"

She lowered her gaze to the floor and lifted one shoulder half-heartedly.

"Words," he murmured.

"No. I can't."

"I didn't think so." He reached out and tipped her chin up.

"Maddie, please. Let me show you that I'm worth the chance."

She chewed on her lower lip. "I...I want to, but he's Trystam's father."

Liam scowled and crossed his arms. "And? He's nothing but the biological father, the one who donated his half and then left you with the responsibility for the result. He hasn't been here for you or for Trystam. He didn't care what had happened to you or the baby, and he taunted you with it yesterday as I kicked him out of the office. He doesn't want a second chance. He sees an opportunity to wheedle his way back into your lives for whatever selfish reason. Maybe he does want to know Trystam. Maybe Trystam is just an excuse to get you back. A man like that must hate knowing he lost something so precious."

"I...He..."

Liam raised a brow.

"Okay, he was like that when we were dating, too," she mumbled, gaze returning to the floor. "But...I can't tell him no to seeing his son, Liam. He...He does have a right."

"Says who? You have sole custody."

"But not officially. Legally, Alyx can still fight me on this. He's the sort who would fight me over it if I dug my heels in and gave him a reason. This way, maybe he'll get bored and leave when he sees I won't put out."

Liam sighed and tipped his head toward his office. "Come on. We'll continue this in my office where no one will disturb us."

She followed him inside and shut the door. "You won't take no for an answer on dinner, will you?"

"I will not," he confirmed. "But whether we go anywhere is entirely up to you. You know now that I do want you that way, and if I'm not mistaken, you *really* want to."

She wouldn't meet his gaze and rolled her lips together like she often did when she was nervous and unsure.

"Hey. Look at me, Maddie."

She did, though reluctantly.

"I'm still the same guy you've known all these years. Why are you nervous?"

"I don't know what to do." Tears filled her eyes. "I...I want to say yes, but I'm afraid if I do, he'll...he'll be angry."

"Let me handle him. Tell me what you want, not what you think you have to do to avoid his anger."

"I want you," she whispered.

"You can have me."

"But I don't feel like I can."

"Then give me a chance to change those feelings." He stepped forward and cupped her cheek in his hand. "It's simple, Maddie. Let me lead. All you have to do is take a tiny step of faith to have what you want. I promise."

She searched his gaze for a long moment, lower lip caught between her teeth. Then she nodded. "Okay."

He bent his head and kissed her once more, this time more chastely. "Thank you. I'll be at dinner."

Chapter 6

Liam showed up a half-hour before Alyx was scheduled to arrive. She let him in with a sigh, relaxing into his solid embrace after he closed the door. Trystam looked up from where he was coloring on the floor and grinned. “Mommy, is Liam staying for dinner?”

Liam smiled back at the little boy. “Yes, I am. But Trystam, I need to talk to you about something. Do you think you could listen closely for me?”

She shot him a worried look, but he shook his head slightly, a silent command not to intervene, to trust him with this. Well, trusting him had never gone wrong before. She settled back into his side and turned her attention back to her son.

The little boy’s smile had dropped, replaced with a serious look, and he nodded. “’Course I can.”

Liam released her and took her hand, pulling her over to the couch. He settled her down and then sat on the floor with Trystam. “Trystam, there are two things you need to know. One, I love you and your mommy very much. But you already know that, don’t you?”

The five-year-old shrugged. “Yeah. Mommy doesn’t like it when I tell everyone at school you’re my daddy, but you don’t mind, do you?”

Liam laughed. “No, I don’t. In fact, I’m honored that you’ve chosen to give me that position. But you know, I love your mommy as more than just a friend.”

"Like...Love, love, right?" Trystam frowned. "Like giving her a valentine?"

"Yes, like that." He glanced over at Maddie.

She felt the heat rising in her cheeks. Was he seriously trying to explain that they were dating to her son?

"Your mommy is one stubborn woman, and it's taken a lot of convincing, but she's agreed to give me a chance to be more than just a friend. Do you understand what that means?"

Trystam's frown deepened. "Like you want to be my daddy for real?"

"Eventually, but your mother hasn't agreed to that yet."

Maddie made a tiny sound of protest, but she didn't intervene when he looked over and raised a brow. He still wanted her to trust him, and Trystam didn't seem upset or worried by the prospect, though he did seem a little unsure of how to process it. Liam wasn't going to share anything the child shouldn't know. She burrowed deeper into the couch as her son also looked at her, his expression inquisitive. This wasn't how she'd envisioned this conversation happening at all.

"Maddie?" he murmured. "I'm not going to hide our relationship from your son. Nor will I hide my intentions. He deserves to know."

She bit her lower lip, but she nodded in agreement. Liam was right. They couldn't be sneaking around or pretending nothing had changed. If things worked and became serious—and deep down, she really hoped they would—then Trystam would need to know eventually. Better to give him time to adjust gradually.

"Trystam, someday, I do want to marry your mom and become your real daddy. But for now, I'm settling for being something between that and just a friend. She needs time to decide what she wants too."

Trystam nodded solemnly. "What's the second thing?"

"The second thing is that your biological father wants to meet you. He'll be here soon for dinner."

Trystam scowled. "I heard him talking to Mommy at the door last night. I don't like him."

Maddie sucked in a sharp breath. "Trystam! How many times have I told you not to eavesdrop?"

"Sorry, Mommy." The child gave her a contrite look. "But I heard the bell, and I thought maybe it was Liam."

"So what? I put you to bed." Maddie crossed her arms. "I expected you to go to sleep and stay put."

"I couldn't sleep. Tomorrow is field trip day to the zoo, and I was thinking about all the animals we'd see." Trystam pouted. "I couldn't go to sleep, and then the doorbell rang."

She sighed. "I'm not mad, Trystam. But your biological father is..."

"Mean," Trystam muttered.

"Hey! Do we name call in this house?"

"No." Her son cast her a mutinous glare. "But he deserves it."

"I'm with Trystam on this one," Liam murmured. "I think it's a fair assessment."

She huffed. "Fine...he's mean. That just means it's important you're careful around him, Trystam. You can't tell him about Liam and me. If he asks, tell him Liam's just a friend, and you can't tell him you tell anyone at school Liam's your daddy, understood?"

"Will he hurt us if I mess up, Mommy?"

She slid down to the floor and gathered her son up in her arms, tears threatening. Clutching him close, she stared at Liam over her child's head. He smiled reassuringly.

"No, baby," she murmured, kissing the top of his head. "He's not going to hurt us. Liam won't let him, and neither will I. That's why he's here. To protect us if something goes wrong."

The little boy wrapped his arms around her waist and held her tightly. "Okay."

The doorbell rang, putting an end to the conversation.

"Is that him?" Trystam murmured.

"Probably." Liam glanced at his watch. "He said six sharp, didn't he?"

Maddie nodded, moving to get up.

"Stay there." Liam stood and headed for the door. "Might as well let him know right now that there's one more person coming to dinner." He yanked the door open.

Alyx stood on the doorstep, grocery bags in hand. When he saw Liam, his expression morphed from ingratiating to furious in a split second. "What the hell are you doing here?"

Liam crossed his arms. "I came over to check on Maddie. You upset her yesterday."

Alyx glowered past Liam at her. "Did you tell him I visited, Madison?"

She held Trystam a little closer, flinching even though she knew Liam wouldn't let him do anything.

"You did." He shook his head. "You little..."

"I suggest you don't finish that sentence if you want to come in for dinner as planned."

Alyx turned his fury on Liam. "I didn't bring enough for a fourth person," he snapped.

"That's fine. I can figure something out."

"Madison, tell him to leave."

Maddie shivered at the cold tone in Alyx's voice, and Trystam trembled against her. "He's a friend, Alyx. I...I forgot about dinner when I told him he could come over."

"Then it shouldn't be a problem for him to leave if he's been visiting for a while."

"I'm not going anywhere. I said I'd figure out my own food. I did *not* say I'd be leaving." Liam stepped aside. "Do you want help with the groceries?"

"No." Alyx sneered at him. "I don't need my bodyguard helping with anything. Not the food, and certainly not my family."

Liam's expression remained cold and stony. He didn't contradict Alyx, but he also didn't acquiesce. He merely shut the door while Alyx stalked into the kitchen and then walked over to take Trystam from Maddie. The little boy wrapped his arms around Liam's neck and buried his face in Liam's broad shoulder. Maddie wished she could hide from this mess just as easily, but that wasn't an option.

"I'll go help in the kitchen."

"We all will. Trystam," he murmured to the little boy. "Remember what we said? Can you be a big boy for us and play nice with your father?"

Trystam huffed in annoyance. "I don't wanna."

"I know. None of us do, but we need you to be all grown up tonight. Please?"

"You really want me to play nice?" Trystam asked.

"I do. Tell you what. Play nice, and I'll take you to the water park with your mom this Saturday."

"Deal."

Liam let the boy down and gave him a gentle nudge toward the kitchen. Trystam wandered in and started a conversation with Alyx. To his credit, Alyx responded politely without the acidity in his tone he'd had when talking to Liam and Maddie. She and Liam joined the two in the kitchen, and a tense silence spread over the small space. Maddie closed her eyes. Well, this was going to be one long evening.

Chapter 7

Liam met Maddie at her doorstep. His hands were tucked into his pockets. She'd worn a modest one piece with a pair of shorts, but he couldn't help letting his imagination wander. When they were done with the water park today, he'd be certain to convince her to stay over at his place with Trystam. He wanted her in his bed under his roof, especially knowing that Alyx had kept stopping by when he wasn't around and that the visits had left Maddie more stressed out.

She looked more relaxed today than he'd seen her all week. Trystam bounced out the door, pausing only briefly to wrap his arms around Liam's legs in greeting before racing for the car, his towel tightly wrapped around his waist, goggles in hand. Maddie shook her head, and Liam laughed. "Hasn't he ever been to a water park?"

She shook her head. "No."

"No wonder he's so excited." He leaned in and kissed her gently, enjoying the way she relaxed into him. "Come stay at my place tonight."

"But Alyx—"

"Screw Alyx," he murmured. "You need a break, and I promised you that if you'd let me, I'd show you what it was like to be with a man who actually respected and cared for you. This is part of that."

She chewed on the inside of her cheek. "What if he's—"

"Angry?" Liam raised a brow.

She blushed a pretty pink.

"You really have to stop saying that. It's not a very good excuse."

"It isn't an excuse," she protested. "I'm worried he's going to sue for joint custody, and I don't want Trystam anywhere near him."

"Come on, Mommy!" Trystam hollered.

Liam turned to level the boy with a stern glare. "Trystam Hayes, the water park will still be there in a few more minutes. Do not yell across the driveway or interrupt adults when they're speaking unless there is a legitimate emergency."

The boy squirmed in the car, but he eventually nodded. "Sorry, Liam," he called back more softly.

"Apology accepted." He sighed and turned back to Maddie with a shake of his head. "Come on, missy. Say yes. I can handle Alyx. You've been dealing with him all week, and don't say it hasn't been stressful or exhausting. I can see it in your face at work."

"I guess I'm losing my touch if you can read me so easily," she joked weakly.

"We all reach a point where we can't hide our emotions anymore. I hate seeing you hit a point where you're so stressed and worn down that you can't even put on a convincing front with others who don't know you well. Even the receptionist who helps out when you're out for the day has asked if you should be told to take a vacation day."

She flushed. "Is it that obvious?"

"Yes, it is. Say yes, Maddie. You'll feel better with a place that's away from him and his pestering for a weekend."

She smiled shyly. "We won't be intruding, will we? I know the weekends are your only real downtime."

"I would be delighted to have you there. It's a little too quiet around my place sometimes. Since Jessica moved down to Miami for work, she hasn't visited as much, and it gets lonely."

"Okay. We'll stay. Should I pack a bag?"

"I think we've made Trystam wait long enough." Liam glanced at the little boy, who was waiting patiently, if not all that quietly.

Trystam bounced up and down in his seat and pulled his goggles on. He didn't sit still once, even when he realized Liam was looking at him with a wry smile.

"He's about to burst with excitement. Jessica won't mind if you use the things she's left lying around in the guest room, and Trystam has some things there from the last time you were over to stay with me and Jessica."

"All right." Her shoulders slumped, the tension he'd seen all week vanishing in a wave of grateful relief. Some of the usual spark of life returned to her face, and she offered him a genuine smile. "Thank you, Liam. You...You always look out for us. I really do appreciate it. More than you know."

He reached out and tugged on her braid affectionately. "And I will continue doing so for as long as you let me, missy. Ready for the water park?"

She nodded eagerly, her own mood escalating from relief to actual enthusiasm. "You know, I've never been to one either. My parents never had the money."

"Then it'll be a treat for you too." He took her hand and drew her toward the car, taking the swim bag from her shoulder and carrying it for her.

She held onto his hand tightly the whole way to the car. He pulled away to put the swim bag in the trunk and then climbed into the driver's seat.

Once they were on the road, he held her hand the whole way to the water park while Trystam colored in the back and sang along to the kids' songs Maddie played on her phone for him.

This was the perfect moment.

All of them together, all of them happy and not thinking about any of the worries from the week. He'd do anything to have these sorts of moments with Maddie for the rest of his life.

***

The park was a hit with Trystam and Maddie. The three of them flopped onto a bench to indulge in a funnel cake after a morning of slides and fun in the water. Trystam ate his third of the cake enthusiastically, watching all park visitors as they passed by, kids tugging at adults' hands as they hurried for the next ride.

He seemed content to sit and watch under the umbrella over the table, but he also seemed tired and sleepy.

Liam settled Maddie on his lap, ignoring the blush creeping up her neck as she glanced nervously at the people passing by. No one paid any attention, focused entirely on their own day.

He pressed a kiss to her shoulder and reached for the funnel cake, offering her a bite.

Her cheeks heated further, but she took the offered food with a shy smile. "Thank you. This is nice, Liam."

"Someone needs to spoil you. It's not like you do it yourself."

"Well, I...it's not like I have time."

"Precisely. Which just means I get to spoil you that much more. I'm not going to complain about that." He fed her another bite of the funnel cake.

Trystam rested his head on his arms, still watching the people even as his eyelids drooped.

"I think someone's ready for a nap."

"No, I'm fine!" Trystam protested. "We don't have to go."

"We can always come back another day, little man," Liam murmured. "But I think both you and your mother are tired."

As if to underscore the point, Trystam yawned, and Maddie let her back rest more heavily against Liam's chest.

"You're going to fall asleep right here at the table, kiddo," Maddie agreed. "Another day. We'll find time to go on the rest of the slides, okay?"

"Okay," he mumbled reluctantly. "You promise?"

"Promise," Liam told him.

Trystam yawned again. "Then I guess I could go home."

"We're going back to my place, actually." Liam lifted Maddie off his lap and stood. "Your mom needs a break, so I told her you two could come over. Is that okay?"

The little boy perked up a bit, looking a tiny bit less tired. "Really? Can I play with the Xbox again?"

"Of course you can." Liam laughed. "It doesn't see much use from me these days. Someone should play with it. But you're taking a nap first, and so are your mother and I. Everyone needs a little rest after this morning."

Trystam nodded agreeably. He took Liam's offered hand and walked alongside him to the exit of the park.

Liam bundled the child into the back seat of his car in the parking lot, buckling him in.

Maddie put the swim bag in the back and headed for her door. He opened it and helped her in, too, buckling her seatbelt before she could protest and dropping a kiss on her forehead. She smiled up at him with a sleepy, contented expression in her eyes. By the time he got back to his place, both mother and son were asleep.

Chapter 8

Maddie opened her eyes and stretched with a yawn. Liam looked up from his book and smiled at her. He remained settled comfortably against the pillows on his side of the bed, where he'd been when she'd fallen asleep this afternoon. Jessica had taken Trystam out for the afternoon to give them time alone, but she'd been so exhausted from work and dealing with Alyx that she'd had no energy for anything but a nap. A glance at the clock confirmed they only had a few hours before Trystam would be bouncing through the door, excited about wherever "Auntie Jess", as he called Maddie's best friend, had taken him.

Liam closed the book gently and set it aside. He took her chin in his hand and kissed her softly. "Welcome back to the land of the living, Sleeping Beauty."

She laughed and leaned up for a fuller kiss. "I'm sorry I fell asleep on you. What were you reading?"

"A spy novel. I needed a break from looking at reports and emails from your would-be suitor."

She scowled at the mention of Alyx. "At least he only bothers you with emails."

Liam frowned. "Is he bothering you? I know he stresses you out, but I thought things had been better the last few weeks. I've had the guys keep a tighter leash on him with the whole stalker and gang-related threats."

Shrugging, she burrowed into his side and rested her head on his shoulder. "He still comes over to see us. He's rude when Trystam's not around and seems interested in nothing but his son or ridiculing me for how I'm parenting."

Liam's frown deepened as he met her gaze. "I don't like that you let him come to your house."

"He's Trystam's father. I—"

"Have to," he grumbled. "So you've said. But you wouldn't have to if you moved on. Moved *in* with me," he murmured. "He's not going to push it with me. I have more connections than he does, thanks to how long I've been at this game."

"Move in?" She hummed sleepily. "I like the sound of it, but we're...we're still trying to figure out what we are to each other."

He slid a hand around her hip, sliding it just under her t-shirt. "*We* are not still trying to figure that out. You are. I know what I want."

"I..." She shifted under the warm, calloused touch of his fingers. "I don't know for sure what it is you want."

"No?" A wicked gleam entered his gaze, and he smirked. "Seems I haven't done a very good job of communicating then, baby girl. I want you. Plain and simple. However I can have you. I've been giving you space and haven't pushed you toward anything we haven't already discussed, but don't mistake that for reluctance on my part. There will never be a time when I don't want you, Maddie Hayes."

Her cheeks warmed, and she tried to bury her face in his chest with a shy laugh. "I never would've taken you for a sweet talker, Liam."

"I'm not." He removed his hand only to grip her by the waist and lift her to straddle his lap. "I am a man of action. If you really want to know what I want, what I'm looking for, I'm all for showing you."

She chewed on her lower lip, pressing her palms to his chest. "I don't know...Trystam—"

"Isn't here." He leaned in and nipped her earlobe. "Because my sister wanted to give us a little time alone. Probably figured we'd get to this sooner or later. She would never guess how shy you are about this stuff, little girl."

"You're not going to tell her, either!" She squirmed in spite of her sharp tone, unable to deny that what he was doing felt wonderful and, more importantly, right, like he fit her in a way Alyx never had and never would.

"No," he agreed. "I'm not."

She settled a little at that promise, sighing. "Do you really want me? Baggage and all?"

"I don't see baggage. I see beauty." He trailed his lips along the column of her throat. "And I see strength. You never see any of that, but I want to show you I do today. You promised you'd let me show you what it was like to let a real man love you."

"I've...I've kept that promise."

"I have one more thing I want to show you before I ask you for a commitment, Madison," he whispered against her collarbones. "Let me love you this way too. Let me wash away what he did and show you what it should be like. I...I need to erase him, destroy the lingering hurt over what he did to you. I need to show you your scars are a reminder of your strengths, not his cruelty."

She groaned and leaned closer, wrapping her arms around his neck. "How can I say no when you say that sort of stuff, Liam?"

He lifted his head, gaze vulnerable in a way she hadn't seen before. "Do you want to say no?"

She shook her head and lowered her mouth to his. Nothing in her wanted to say no. Everything in her wanted this man and all that he was. For this brief moment, she didn't need to worry about Alyx. Liam could be her whole world, if only for a moment. If only he could be her world forever, though. If only Alyx would disappear so that she would be free to love without repercussions. But he couldn't, and Alyx wouldn't, so she—like Liam—would take what she could get and hold onto it with a fierce protectiveness to cherish it forever.

***

When she returned home that night with Trystam, the cloud of euphoria and contentment she'd been floating on since being with Liam evaporated in a moment. Alyx sat on the doorstep, looking furious. He modulated the expression to one of subtle anger when he spotted Trystam with her, forcing a smile for the child's sake and sending the boy inside with a promise he wouldn't hold up Maddie for long.

Maddie crossed her arms and scowled. "What are you doing here?"

"Don't you ever check your phone?" he snapped. "You're as bad as you were when we were dating. Worse, actually, because now you're screwing around with some other guy." He looked her over contemptuously. "Wasn't I enough for you?"

"You *left* me, Alyx. Left me with a baby on the way so you could go to law school. And don't expect me to believe you didn't lay a few girls over the years, either. At least when I finally decided to sleep with him, I did so after being certain I was more than a one-night stand. Did the girls you slept with even care?"

His cheeks mottled red. "You've slept with him?" His voice lowered to a hissing whisper, and he took a menacing step forward. "It's bad enough that my son looks at him like a father, but now *you* slept with him?"

She balled her hands into fists and forced herself not to take a step backward. Every time they'd argued before, she'd caved. Alyx had his way every time, and she'd always made excuses. She wasn't making them for him anymore. If he couldn't take her boundaries or the fact that she had no intention of being with him again, he could leave. "You don't get to dictate who I'm with," she snapped back. "At least he's been the only one. How many have you had over the years?"

"As many as I pleased." He sneered at her. "Unlike you, I don't view being a prude as a worthy ideal."

She refused to take the bait and crossed her arms. "Go home, Alyx. I don't want you here."

"Too bad. I came to tell you I'm going to file a motion for partial custody of Trystam. He should have his father in his life."

"You are in his life."

"For now. When I go back to my usual position, I'll be two hours from here. I don't have time to be coming up for visits all the time. I'm guessing you won't bring him to me on your own, so I want weekends."

"No."

"That's precisely why I plan to file a motion. It'll be filed in a few weeks when I have the room to go public with it."

She lost it then, anger and fear driving her. "How dare you? I've been raising my son for five years without you! You can't even bother to come down on the weekends to visit him, so you want to take him away from me to make your life easier! What sort of father does that? You're a narcissistic piece of work, Alyx, and I have no intention of giving you my son any more than I intend to come back to you!"

He grabbed her wrist and dragged her closer, pulling her inside. "Lower your voice if you don't want your son to hear."

She ground her teeth, muscles trembling with the struggle not to deck him.

He pushed her up against the wall, hand going to her hip. "You won't be seeing Mr. Beckett again. Not when you have my son under your roof. I am the only man he will see you with, the only man he will ever call 'daddy' again. I know he tells the kids at school that Beckett is his father. That's going to end. You'll make it end." His grip on her wrist squeezed until she had to bite her lip to hold back a pained whimper. "If you don't obey me on this, I am going to take full custody of Trystam. You'll never see him again. You know what I do for a living, Madison. You know I could do it with a simple word to the judge."

Tears of pain and rage welled up. "You stay away from my son," she hissed.

"Oh, Madison." He reached up and wiped the tears away with a bitter smile. "You brought this on yourself, my dear. You should have known better than to keep the boy, and you should have known I wouldn't want my only living heir to grow up in this sort of tasteless place. If you'd done a better job raising him, I might not have been pushed to this. And if you weren't sleeping around with your *boss*, maybe I'd trust you to behave without this threat hanging over your head. But you are living in this little hole in the ground neighborhood, and you are frequenting Beckett's bed, so you see why I have to intervene."

"What I see is that you're a selfish pig!"

He released her wrist, and she thought he was going to move away. Instead, his hand snapped across her cheek, setting a fire blazing there. She was too stunned to cry. Instead, she dropped to her knees, her hand going to her injured cheek while she cradled the sprained, aching wrist he'd held to her chest. He sneered down at her, hands on his hips. "I think I've made myself clear, Madison. Clean yourself up and go change the sheets on your bed. I'm sure they smell like him, and I don't plan on sleeping on sheets he's used."

Terror closed around her chest like a vice, squeezing the air from her lungs. The tears flowed in earnest, and she huddled there without moving. He sighed and bent over, grabbing her by the injured wrist and forcing her to her feet. She cried out softly at the pain but tried to stay quiet so that Trystam wouldn't come to investigate. When she looked to the stairs of the small house, though, she saw him watching. She looked away, trying not to draw Alyx's attention to the boy.

"Alyx, be reasonable," she whispered. "You're under protective custody to keep the thugs after you from finding you. Think about the danger you'll be in if you stay in an unsecured location, the danger you'd be putting Trystam in. Please..."

He released with a disgusted huff. "Fine. It seems more

thinking goes on in that head of yours than it used to. I'll arrange things and return in the morning. Don't even think of running, or I'll have the cops on you for child abduction."

She trembled and backed away. "I...I'm not going anywhere."

He leaned in and pressed a kiss to her damp cheek. "Good. Stay nice and obedient, and everything will be fine, Madison. You'll see."

She waited until he'd left to move. Trystam rushed down the stairs and threw the deadbolt before running to wrap his arms around her legs. "Is he gone, Mommy?"

She sniffled and tried to pull herself together for her son's sake. "Yeah, baby. He's gone." She picked him up and held him close until the trembling in her body and his eased. "He's gone, but we...I need to call Liam, okay?"

"Will he make the bad man stay away?" Trystam whispered, tears filling his eyes when she set him down on a stool in the kitchen.

"I...I don't think so, sweetheart." She wasn't going to tell Liam anything if she didn't have to. She'd cover the bruises with makeup and pray he didn't notice because she couldn't let Alyx take her baby away from her. Even if it meant dealing with the fear and whatever harm he did to her until she could find a way to run far enough to escape his influence, she would. In the meantime, Liam's presence only provoked him. She needed to keep her distance.

Liam picked up on the first ring, concern in his greeting. "Maddie, what is it? You never call me this late."

She almost broke down then and there at the sound of his warm, deep voice, but she held it together. "I...I called to tell you I need a few days off."

"Of course," he agreed, but the concern in his tone sharpened. "Why? What's going on?"

"I need space," she whispered, eyeing her son's confused expression. "I don't...I don't want to go any further with this,

Liam. I need time to figure out how to go back to just being your employee."

The other side of the line was silent for a long time.

"Liam? I...I'm sorry."

"Don't be," he murmured tightly. "Just tell me one thing. Is this because of him? Lie to me, baby girl, and you won't like the consequences."

She almost laughed at the absurdity of the threat. He wouldn't be anything to her after she ended things, let alone someone who could offer consequences for the lie. But she also couldn't bear to lie to him. "Yes, but Liam, please don't do anything. He's your client..."

"Not as of tonight. I had a call from the investigators on the case. He's in no danger now. They've caught the men responsible."

"S-so he can go home?" Her stomach knotted with fear. If Alyx could go home, then that meant he could file that motion any day now. He'd probably file it the moment he was back in the office.

"Yes. You don't sound happy about that. What's going on, Madison?" His voice turned stern. "Do you need me to come over there and deal with this, or are you going to tell me now?"

The dam burst. Everything was just too much. She broke down into tears in front of her son with Liam on the line.

He sighed. "I'll be there in twenty minutes, Maddie. Talk to me while I drive, sweetheart?"

She tried to regain control as Trystam started crying too. "I'm f-fine."

"No, you are not." His voice brooked no argument.

She heard the quiet purr of his car's engine turning on, and then the garage door followed it. "Liam, I mean it." She tried to sound more stern, panic adding to her stress and the quiver in her voice. If Alyx found out Liam had come over here, he'd file the motion for full custody, not just partial. She didn't know if he could actually win it after so many years, but she didn't want to take the risk. "I just want space. I don't want to be with you." Her voice hitched on the last word.

Trystam continued to sob at the counter. "Mommy, I want daddy here. Liam. I want him."

Her heart broke just a little more as a second round of her own tears began. Liam wasn't just embedded in her heart; he was entwined into Trystam's too. "I know, baby, but..."

"Put me on speaker, Maddie."

She hesitated. "Liam..."

"Madison Hayes, speakerphone, right now." His voice barked at her through the phone.

Shivering at the steel in his voice, she nodded before remembering he couldn't see her and offered a soft, "Okay." She clicked the speaker button.

"Trystam?" Liam's voice came through the speaker now, softer than it had been. "What happened, kiddo?"

"He hurt Mommy," Trystam sobbed.

Maddie sucked in a sharp breath. "Trystam!"

"Thank you for being honest, little guy." He cleared his throat. "Madison, did I or did I not ask you what was wrong?"

"You d-did."

Trystam rubbed at his tears, sniffling. "Are you coming to stay with us?"

"Yeah, kiddo. I'll be there in a few minutes, but I also need to speak with your Mommy and with the...the man who hurt her. Is he still hanging around?"

"He's gone," Maddie ventured softly. "But Liam...you don't know what's at stake."

"He said he was going to take me away," Trystam howled with a fresh burst of tears. "I don't want to go with him."

"No one's taking you anywhere." Liam's voice hardened with rage. "Maddie, did he threaten to take Trystam?"

Her shoulders sagged, and tears blurred her vision.

"Madison?" Liam pressed.

"Yes," she whispered.

"Take me off speakerphone."

She obeyed with a quiet whimper. "L-liam, he told me you had to go, or he'd...he'd take Trystam permanently."

"He's not taking anything, and I'm going to kill him for this." His tone had gone from angry to deadly now that Trystam couldn't hear. "You're going to stay there. I will come to get you both when I've dealt with him. Do you understand?"

"I...you'll just make him angry."

"I'm going to make him terrified to cross me or touch either of you ever again," Liam snapped. "He's going to learn he's not the only one with connections, even if I have to call in a few favors to make him disappear for a vacation in some deep, dark hole for a while. Nobody gets away with hurting women and children on my watch, especially not *my* woman or a kid I love like a son."

"But—"

"Enough, Madison. I won't be swayed by this. He's leaving town, and there won't be any custody motion. We'll chat about hiding things like this when I get back, and then we'll talk about what you really want and what I want for our future, baby girl. What you are not going to do is leave the house or answer the door until I call to tell you it's safe. Do you understand?"

"Y-yes, sir," she whispered.

"Good girl. Tell Trystam I'll tuck him in when I come over, please." His tone softened. "Make yourself a hot cup of tea, and put on the television to distract yourself until I come home to you, okay?"

"Okay." Her voice was small and sad, but knowing he wasn't leaving her to deal with Alyx alone left a warmth in her stomach that soothed the knots, though it did nothing for the fire in her face or wrist.

"And ice whatever he did. I assume it isn't bad enough for the ER?"

"No."

"Good. I love you, Maddie. I'll call soon."

With that, he hung up. She shuffled through the motions of settling Trystam in bed and then went to the kitchen to obey his orders. With everything done, she settled in for the long wait until he returned.

Chapter 9

Liam tracked down Alyx into a local bar downtown. News of the man's freedom had traveled quickly, and his men had let him go with glee when he announced he was celebrating before he headed home. Headed home to file that motion for custody, no doubt. He stalked into the busy bar and located Alyx at the bar, already looking a little tipsy.

Grabbing the man by the shoulder, he shot the bartender—a man he'd known for a few years since he'd helped the man's son out of a scrape with drug dealers—a nod. "I think he's had enough to drink, don't you?"

The bartender gave him a nervous glance, obviously catching Liam's mood. "Liam...no violence in my bar."

"What about on the sidewalk outside?" he asked.

"You're going to have at him no matter what, aren't you?"

Alyx scoffed and downed the rest of his drink. "Think you can take me?" He took a wild swing at Liam.

Liam decked him in the jaw, sending the man sprawling. He locked eyes with the bartender. "Sorry. He attacked first. I'll take it outside."

"He deserves it, right?"

"He hurt a woman and frightened her small child. I'll say he deserves it."

The bartender's jaw hardened, and he nodded. He didn't like men who hurt women any more than Liam did. "Make sure he never comes in here or round these parts again, then. Gonna tell the boys around these parts too. They don't take too well to wife-beating cowards."

"Who are you calling a coward?" Alyx growled.

Liam grabbed him by the collar and dragged him through the crowd. "Unless you want his friends to handle you too, you'd better shut up and come outside. I want a few words with you."

Alyx let Liam drag him outside at that, but he swayed drunkenly on the sidewalk and threw himself at Liam the moment he had the chance. Liam pulled his phone from his pocket and switched on the camera, thinking of something one step better than beating the lawyer up. He dodged Alyx's blows for a while until the man noticed the camera on the phone was aiming his way. When Alyx made a move for the phone, Liam stepped out of the drunk's way and let him barrel straight into the dumpster. Then he sent the video to his work laptop as insurance and tucked the phone away.

"All right, playtime is over, Alyx." Liam hauled him up and slammed his back into the brick wall. "No one here is going to help you. If they do, everyone will shrug and say they didn't see anything when the cops show up. I have video of you assaulting and attacking me, and I am going to use it."

Alyx spluttered, face red with anger and drink. "Screw you! You're always screwing up everything around here. My girl...my chance with my son."

"Oh, no. I'm not taking any blame for anything. Well, except maybe the first...but that's beside the point, and she isn't your anything. You screwed things up for yourself the minute you ran off to law school after knocking her up. I was the one who was there for her. *I* helped change that kid's diapers, ran him to school when she was too worn down to do it, made sure she could make rent every month, and babysat when she had tough shifts. When she lost her job, *I* offered her a job so I could support her without making her feel like she was a burden because *you* didn't do your job way back then! She is her own woman, but as near as she's anybody's, she's mine because I take the time to care and be there. I am the one she called crying after you hurt and terrorized her, and I am the one her son cried for because you scared him half to death."

"I wasn't trying to scare him," Alyx muttered darkly.

"Well, too bad. You did. There'll be no more talk about custody, period, Alyx. She and that kid are under my protection. You file that motion, and the judge gets this video. How long do you think your career lasts after that? Let alone a custody battle? You're not getting your hands on that kid or on her ever again. I catch you hanging around Maddie or Trystam ever again, and I'm going to call in favors to make sure you're buried so deep under legal crap that you never practice law again, let alone make it out of the hole they'll dump you in. Do you understand?"

Alyx glowered at him. Liam glared back, unmoved. Maybe he was used to intimidating other men, but Liam wasn't other men, and his woman's safety, as well as that of a boy he'd come to consider a son, was at stake. When Alyx didn't answer, he shook the man. "Do you understand, or do I need to start making calls now?"

Alyx paled and shook his head. "I get it. I get it! I'll go."

"Good. I'll drive you to a hotel outside of town. You're not staying in my company's safe house any longer." He dragged the whining, pleading excuse of a man to his car and shoved him into the passenger's seat. "Puke on it, and I'll be sending a cleaner's bill too."

***

Liam parked in Maddie's driveway with both relief and nerves warring with one another. Now that Alyx was out of the way, he had to know what she really wanted, whether she saw a future with him. Things had been going so well the past few weeks, and he was certain she wanted him, but he was less certain if she would marry him, and he was playing for keeps, not just a few years.

He called her as he climbed out of the car, the relief winning out at the sound of her sleepy hello. "Maddie, baby, it's me. You can open the door."

He'd just made it to the stoop when she flung the door open and threw herself at him. He caught her before she could topple both of them over and held her close, fingers tangled in her hair as he pressed her to his chest. The realization that he could have lost her tonight if Alyx had kept going hit him in the gut, and he tightened his grip as a wave of anger, relief, and belated panic washed over him. She trembled against him, and he felt her tears soaking through the thin t-shirt he wore. He continued to cradle her close as they stood on her doorstep. When her trembling turned to a shiver, he scooped her up in his arms and took her inside, kicking the door shut.

With the warm light from the living room lamp spilling over her face, he could see the purple and blue bruise coming up on her right cheek, and the anger surged once more. He should've hit Alyx a few more times before he'd dragged him out of the bar. The man deserved that and so much more. Reaching out, he traced his fingers over the bruising gently. "I'm sorry I wasn't here to stop him, Maddie."

She leaned into his touch, closing her eyes. "You're here now, aren't you?"

"Yes. And he's gone. You'll never have to worry about him again. If he ever tries to challenge for custody of Trystam, he'll lose everything. One drunk rage and a few swings caught on camera sealed that fate for him. I doubt he'll risk everything to take Trystam away from you."

When she opened her eyes, tears shone there. "You really got rid of him for me?"

"I did. You make it sound like I committed a murder for you." He forced a smile. "All I did was run him out of town and take a few swings of my own after he started it."

She threw her arms around his neck and burrowed her face into his shoulder. "I don't know how I managed to get a guy so perfect," she mumbled. "I don't deserve it."

He landed a gentle smack on her butt. "Hey. No self-degradation. If I'm not about to let anyone hurt you, then I'm also not going to have *you* hurting you, even if it's just verbal. You are smart, pretty, and big-hearted, Maddie. You do deserve to be loved. You don't deserve the way Alyx treated you, and I'm going to make sure you know it." He softened his tone. "If you'll let me, that is."

She nodded, pressing closer. "I'm sorry I lied on the phone," she whispered. "I was scared. He'd threatened to…to take Trystam, and I was terrified if I let you help, he might do it."

Liam snuggled her into his chest and laid down on the sofa, grabbing the blanket from where she'd left it on the floor and settling it over both of them. He brushed her hair off her tear-stained cheeks with a sigh. "Someday, you're going to learn to trust me completely. But for now, I'll be glad you called and that you obeyed me about the speakerphone so your son could do the rest. He's a brave little kid."

"Yeah. Smart too…he knew to talk even though I was too scared to."

"Yup. He's a bright one." Liam rubbed her back gently. "Are you all right?"

"I am now that you're here." She lifted her head to look up at him. "You said you needed to ask me something?"

He nodded. "I want to know if you see yourself marrying me, Maddie. If you don't, we'll end this here. I'm not going to stay in a romantic relationship with a woman who doesn't want me. If you do, but you need time, I'm going to ask, but I'm not going to push to set a date. It's up to you. Either way, I'm going to remain the same friend you've had for years."

Her lower lip quivered. "You're really going to ask?"

"Is that bad?"

"No. I just don't want to be asked like this."

He chuckled. "Is that a roundabout way of saying yes?"

She smiled, too, despite her exhaustion and all she'd been through. "You have to ask properly, or I'm not saying anything either way."

"Fine, but I'm not waiting to get my answer, Madison Hayes. Will you marry me?"

She laid her head back on his chest. "Yes, I'll marry you. But you'd better propose when I've had time to get over what happened tonight. I want something romantic."

"This isn't romantic?"

That earned him a half-hearted smack. "No, you big idiot...Chocolates and a movie or snuggling under the stars are romantic. A proposal after you've beat a guy up on my behalf is...is..."

"Endearing? Sweet? Spectacular?" he offered teasingly.

"Okay, kind of endearing," she mumbled in agreement. "But not romantic. Ask properly, please?"

"Anything you want, baby girl. Now, let's get you to bed. It's been a difficult day." He sat up, ignoring her sleepy protests, and wrapped her in the blanket. Then he scooped her up and took her to her room. "I have to say goodnight to Trystam. You change for bed. I'll be back."

He slipped out, giving her some space to settle while he went to say goodnight to Trystam. The little boy was already asleep, but he stirred just enough to say goodnight when Liam kissed him on the forehead and pulled the blanket up to tuck it around the boy.

Promise kept, he returned to Maddie's side to find her curled up in bed, still in her t-shirt but missing the jeans, and sound asleep.

Shaking his head with a tired smile, he climbed in beside her and pulled the coverlet up to cover them both before falling asleep with her tucked into his arms.

Epilogue

Eight months later

Maddie walked down the aisle between the seats with a resplendent smile. She didn't have family to give her away, but she walked with a straight back and never wavered, her gaze fixed on him and Trystam, who stood with the rings beside him. Liam had never seen her look as radiant as she did now, with the Caribbean sun shining down on her dirty blond curls and picking out the strands of strawberry blonde, gold, and brown that wove together to showcase the full array of shades her hair held. The dress she wore was simple and elegant. The train hooked up to keep it from dragging in the sand. It hugged her hips in all the right places, and he offered an approving smile as she finally reached him and placed her hands in his.

Jessica was already dabbing at tears from her place in the first row, and his own mother was also crying. He turned his focus to Maddie and the minister with a softer smile, his own joy at having her here before him to become his wife growing as the reality finally sank in. She'd be his in name after this, not just in spirit and body. This would cement their bond in front of all of their family and friends and make Trystam his son officially as well.

The little boy stood proudly in his blue suit, holding the pillow with the rings and grinning at both of them. He'd barely contained his excitement when Liam had told him he could call Liam daddy for real at school after today. His eyes had grown wide when the plane had touched down, and they'd made the drive to the beach resort of the destination wedding. The kid had never seen anything so grand in his life, and Liam was glad he was able to both give the experience and witness his soon-to-be stepson take delight in it. The day wouldn't have been complete without Trystam.

The minister finished his short speech and launched into the vows ceremony. Maddie clutched his hands more tightly, smiling through a veil of tears as she did so. When it came time to speak her vows, however, she said them clearly, her voice never wavering. He said his in turn, and they exchanged rings.

Most of the ceremony had passed in a blur of nerves, excitement, and awe, but everything sharpened into focus when the minister told him he could kiss his bride. He dipped Maddie back and claimed her mouth with his, knowing this was only the first of many, a promise of what would come when he had her to himself. And he had a lifetime to show her what being his really meant because now she was truly and fully his.

Until death did them part, he fully intended to show Madison Hayes what it meant to be fully and completely cherished.

Doctor Billionaire Daddy (Book 4)

Blurb

Chad Gatlin is a world renowned surgeon with a fortune behind him. Most women jump at the chance to be noticed by him – except one infuriating nurse.

Chad never struggles to find a woman to warm his bed. After all, he is charming, intelligent, rich, and too sexy for his own good. When a new nurse shows up in his hospital, he cannot help but be drawn to her. But she doesn't feel the same way. After a while, he soon realizes that he wants more than just a passionate affair with Lanie.

Lanie Cooperson's ambitions will never let a playboy get in the way of her career. Once before, Lanie's chances of being head nurse were thwarted by a man she trusted and loved. Heartbroken with a career that had stalled, she vowed never to let it happen again. However, Chad seems so genuine in his attempts to woo her.

Can she take a leap of faith and give in to Chad?

Prologue

Two years earlier

Lanie Cooperson was not a woman accustomed to being laughed at or treated in a casually sexual manner that invited a sexual harassment claim. Sitting here in the office of renowned surgeon Chad Gatlin, however, she found herself face to face with both unusual circumstances. She scowled at the man she'd been admiring from the observation deck of the OR only moments earlier and crossed her arms over her chest.

His gaze dropped to her breasts despite the scrubs' modest neckline and her clear irritation with him. "You don't have to be so uptight, Lanie. On my staff, we work hard, and we play hard. The OR is where your seriousness belongs. Outside those walls, we're all well-acquainted and do not need formalities. You'll learn that soon enough."

"My eyes are up here, sir." She kept her voice level despite her rising anger. His behavior reminded her far too much of Kaiden's roving eyes before his cheating and her subsequent break up with him forced her out of her fast track to head nurse. That was how she'd come to be sitting in this chair, to begin with, and she didn't want a repeat. Even though she already loathed Chad Gatlin with every fiber of her being, she planned on sucking up as much as possible while maintaining her dignity. She intended to make head nurse somewhere. If it didn't happen on his staff in this department, it could happen in another surgeon's department as long as she didn't let him derail her career, just like her involvement with Kaiden had done. "I'm not interested in becoming 'well-acquainted' with you if that means what I presume it does."

He cocked a brow and leaned back in his chair with a sly smile. "What do you think it means, Lanie?"

"Miss Cooperson," she corrected quietly. "And I think your reputation precedes you, in numerous ways, Mr. Gatlin."

"Does it now? Do tell."

"The head nurse warned me that you were a notorious womanizer. You've slept your way through all the nurses on your staff and some of the junior doctors in the department too. Some outside of it as well, if the rumors can be believed. I don't believe in relying on rumors, so I suppose we'll stick to saying you've slept your way through most of *your* department."

"And you have a problem with that." He tented his fingers and eyed her curiously.

"Is that a question you'd like an answer to or a mere statement of fact?" she quipped back.

He grinned slowly. "A question I'd like you to answer, Miss Cooperson."

"I don't care who you sleep with on your staff." Oh, but she did. She despised him for doing it. The only people that ranked close to cheats on her list of human waste were philandering playboys like Chad. She just wouldn't say that. "I admire your work in the OR and the tight ship you run there. I watched you perform your last surgery today. It was nicely done."

His grin broadened. "I make it a point to demand nothing but perfection in my OR. You seem like you'll fit in there, at least."

But not in his department as a whole? "Is sleeping with you a requirement to work on your staff, Mr. Gatlin?"

He chuckled and shook his head. "Now, Miss Cooperson, that would open me up to a lawsuit. I might even risk losing my job.

Letting me have you is not a requirement to work for me, but most women eventually give in to my charm and allure."

"Only fools, gold diggers, and the incredibly naïve would give in to a man who will never respect them for it, Mr. Gatlin," she murmured. "I am none of those things."

A startled laugh spilled from him. "Are you mocking me, madam?"

"Is that how you perceive it?" She arched a brow. "Perhaps I am merely insulting your entire staff for being foolish or conniving enough to sleep with you and hope for something of it."

"Would you sleep with me merely for the experience, then?" He eyed her from beneath thick, dark lashes. "Is it the idea of doing it and falsely hoping for a happily-ever-after that makes you mad? Or do you simply dislike that women would be willing to sleep with me even if I didn't offer anything but that one night with me?"

She stiffened. "I think this conversation should be over. Let's leave it at 'I respect your work' and ignore how I feel about your personal life or your choice to mix pleasure and business, Mr. Gatlin."

He stood and strolled around the desk, stopping a scant inch from her and pressing his hip into the desk, hands in pockets. "I think you're just a little green, Miss Cooperson," he murmured in a low, silky voice. "You know, you might give me a chance before you judge me. On pleasure or on business."

"You'll only have a chance on the second, sir. May I be excused now to report to the head nurse?"

He leaned in and took hold of her chin, tipping her face up toward his. "I have a reputation to uphold. Are you threatening to cost me that reputation, love? You should know I don't take threats lightly and never lose once I start playing. Do you want to play knowing that?"

She pushed his hand away with a tight smile. "I think you will keep your hands off me unless I invite it because you don't want a lawsuit or, worse yet, jail time. I'll see you in the OR, Mr. Gatlin." Rising, she picked up her purse and strode out the door, leaving him to think what he would. Whatever she did or did not accomplish here, she was going to make sure she never ended up as another notch on Gatlin's belt.

Chapter 1

One year earlier

Chad took his mother's trembling, cold hands in his. He stared at the husk of a woman lying in a hospital bed in the recovery room of *his* OR after they'd discovered her tumors were inoperable and closed her back up. She was so young. Too young to find herself in this position. After all she'd fought for, the way she'd struggled to survive his father's alcoholic rages during difficult court cases, and the way she'd fought to send him through medical school after she'd left his father and taken him along, she didn't deserve to be dying of cancer at only fifty-two. She'd had him young and given the best years of her life to raising him. It wasn't fair that she didn't have a chance to see everything he'd do, see him married if he ever decided to settle down, see her grandchildren.

She opened her eyes with a dry sigh and stared back at him with tears veiling her blue eyes. "I need you to promise me something, Chad."

He swallowed past the lump in his throat and nodded, not trusting his voice to work.

"Promise me you'll never forget how frail and fleeting life is, son. I know it seems like you have your whole life ahead of you like you'll always have tomorrow to settle down instead of flitting from woman to woman like you go from surgery to surgery. You're trying to fill a void. I don't know why the void is there, Chad, but I see it." She coughed and wheezed for a moment. "I spent so long trying to fill it myself after I left your father. Now I'm dying, lonely and miserable."

"Mom, you don't—"

She held up a finger and regained her composure and her voice. "I see it and know that it will be worse when I am gone. Find someone to fill it, someone to love. Don't you dare go through life filling it with sex and liquor like your father did, and don't try to find solace in jumping from one relationship to another like I did."

He scowled. "I don't drink, Mom. You know that."

"No, but you treat every woman on your staff like toys, and I'm not sure which is worse. Doing as you do and treating them like cheap hookers or doing as I did and refusing to let yourself love any of them. Both leave you equally alone. Maybe your money and power here get you what you think you want, but ask yourself this, Chad. How many of those women want you for you?"

His mind went through each one he'd worn down and bedded over the years. Then it jumped to the one woman he still couldn't seem to wear down, the only one he really cared about having any more. *She* might want him for him if he was worthwhile, but he'd blown any shot at that when he'd behaved like a predatory jerk on her first day. To her, he was nothing but a disgusting playboy she tolerated in hopes of keeping her job. He liked their banter and enjoyed teasing her to see her flush with anger or embarrassment, but he knew that it was nothing but polite arguing for her. She didn't find any joy in it at all, and if he wanted her to want him for him, he'd need to make himself a man worth her attention and trust.

"I know that look..." His mother sighed. "Is there still one girl on your staff you've managed not to screw around with by some miracle?"

"One," he confessed quietly. "Because she hates me and all I represent."

"Why is that?" His mother raised a brow.

"I don't know. She doesn't share anything personal."

"You want her all the more because of the puzzle she represents." She sighed. "Some things never change."

"Well, it doesn't matter," he snapped. "That girl will never come to my bed. I'll never wear her down. She's colder than ice, and she hated me from day one. She only behaves politely because she respects my work and wants to keep her job. The last time she lost a job, she did so in disgrace after the surgeon she worked for made a fuss and had her sent packing."

"Yet you hired her," his mother mused. "Why?"

"Because while I don't have all the details, I don't think she actually did anything wrong." Even as he said it, he realized he'd thought so because he recognized the quiet fury blazing in the surgeon's voice when he'd told his story about her being insufferable to work with. It was the fury of a man who could not have what he wanted and had turned his anger on the one who had taken his desires away.

"Good. I think she's good for you. You need someone who challenges you. But I want your promise, Chad. Promise me that you'll settle down. You're 39 now. Find a nice girl that suits you and settle down. Don't make your father's mistakes, son. He died sad and alone."

Chad stared down at the linoleum floor tiles. "Can we not talk about this? You're dying. I don't want our last conversations centered on my love life or lack thereof."

She fixed him with a stern stare. "No. We need to talk about this. I know my time is coming up, and I want to go knowing you'll be okay. Promise me."

"I don't want to promise the impossible."

"It isn't impossible. Promise."

There was no way out of it. She wouldn't let him run from her demand or ignore it. Heaving a sigh, he nodded. "Fine. I promise you that I'll find a girl to settle with. I won't make Dad's mistakes either."

"Good." She reached out to him.

He took her hand and pressed a kiss gently to her knuckles. "Rest. You look tired."

She smiled weakly. "I'll have all the rest I need soon. I don't want to miss any moments."

His pager buzzed, and he slipped a hand into his pocket, pulling it free to read the message. Lanie had sent it, and it was brief, as usual.

OR stat. You're needed.

Groaning, he stood and pressed a kiss to his mother's forehead. "I have to go, Mom. Emergency surgery. I'll check in on you later."

"Just remember your promise, Chad." She settled in the bed with a sigh. "I know it seems hard now, but it will be worth it in the end."

He didn't know if it would be, but he'd promised her not to keep sleeping with strangers to fill the void. It wouldn't be hard. The image of a leggy woman with almond eyes and cherry lips was seared into his mind forever, and he'd tried everything to erase her. Nothing had worked, so by now, he'd given in to the concept, even if he wasn't ready to make a move.

Present day

Proving to Lanie that he was a changed man felt more impossible than surviving Mount Everest. He had promised his mother he would try to find the one he could settle with and wouldn't merely flit from woman to woman searching for fulfillment. And after watching her succumb to cancer last year, he couldn't find it in him to keep on as he had been. She'd died sad and lonely, proving to him the end result of the lifestyle he led. The days of sleeping his way through hospital staff—or any other set of women, for that matter—were gone. Chad simply couldn't stomach the thought of it, especially when all of them were poor substitutes for the one woman he truly wanted. Lanie Cooperson. The one woman who didn't want him.

He stepped into his office and glanced at her workstation. She was talking and laughing with his head nurse, Wanda McKenna, a younger nurse he'd promoted after his previous head nurse had retired. The two women had hit it off well, and he liked seeing how Lanie fit right in on his staff now. He was the only one she still had a problem with, though she hid it fairly well, sticking to subtle ribbing that she knew he didn't mind or thought he didn't notice.

Dropping his briefcase in the chair and ditching his suit jacket, he strode out the glass doors of his office space and joined the two women at the counter. "Ladies."

Wanda smiled politely and excused herself. He vaguely remembered that they'd had a brief few nights together once and wished he'd been a different man back then. Maybe Lanie would hate him less. Though he still was no closer to discovering why his sex habits needled her as much as they did. She didn't talk about her personal life, only her career. Lanie started to walk away, but he took her wrist gently and stopped her.

"Let go, Chad," she snapped. "You know I don't like being touched."

Not by men. Another confusing little thing he'd picked up on. He'd often wondered if she'd been abused, if the surgeon who'd had her fired at her last hospital had something to do with her loathing for him and his former habits. "Sorry." He let go. "Stay, please?"

She sighed and wrapped her arms around her torso. "Why? What is it you want, boss?"

You. It was on the tip of his tongue, but he knew better than to let it slip out. It would sound like he was the flirtatious jerk she'd known when she began working here. "I thought you might like to grab a coffee in the cafeteria before our shifts start."

She frowned. "Coffee?"

"It's a normal thing," he mumbled. "People do that together sometimes, you know. You make it sound scandalous."

"It is when it comes from a man who turns every sentence into something flirtatious or dirty." The frown deepened. "Why do you want to grab coffee? When I started here, I told you I wouldn't sleep with you."

"I just wanted to spend some time with you." He raised his hands in surrender. "I'm not trying to get you into bed."

"But you wouldn't mind if that were the end result," she snapped.

"Lanie, I'm a warm-blooded man. Of course, I wouldn't mind. I won't lie about that, but it isn't my goal. I really do just want to get to know you."

"Why?"

"Have coffee with me and find out?" He glanced at the clock. "We only have a half hour. Surely a half hour isn't so long that it's unbearable?"

Sighing, she dropped her arms and shrugged. "Fine. I don't get what game you're playing, but fine."

He grinned. Even though it wasn't an enthusiastic agreement, it was a truce, and he'd take it. It was progress. He'd asked her to coffee at the start of each shared early morning shift for the last four weeks after he'd worked up the courage to start, and every time, she'd politely made excuses. She never said no. She just found reasons not to go with him. "I'll try to make sure you won't regret it."

She scoffed and turned on her heel. "Let's get this over with."

He caught up with her and walked alongside her. "So...how have things been? You don't talk much about how work is going, and you never talk about things at home."

"I'm a private person."

"Or you just hate me," he shot back. "If you think you're subtle, you're not. It's clear you despise me. I just wish I knew why."

"You know why. Your habit of sleeping with anything that's female is a pretty big one."

He eyed her with a frown. "Yes, but there's something beneath that. Otherwise, why would you care?"

"Drop it." She frowned back. "I agreed to coffee, not baring my soul."

"I'm not the same man, Lanie. Haven't you noticed the changes?"

Her cheeks flushed a little beneath the bronze tan summer always gave her. "What changes? Becoming more discreet? I guess I noticed that."

He sighed. "I haven't become more discreet. I'm just not sleeping my way through staff anymore."

"Oh, you've decided to pick just one?" Her voice dripped with false sweetness. "Good for you."

"I've picked just one, all right," he muttered.

"Then what are we doing having coffee together? Or is she not the jealous type? Maybe she doesn't set the bar very high."

"Setting the bar high is certainly not the problem." He snorted. "Setting the bar too high, on the other hand, just might be. But it's clear you're not interested in having this conversation. Shall we talk about safer topics?"

"Like what?" Her lips curled into a more genuine smile. "I hope you aren't about to suggest we talk about the weather?"

He pushed open the cafeteria door and held it open for her. The place was deserted, with only a cross-looking cashier at the front counter. He led her over to look at the menu. "Not the weather. What's your favorite color?"

"Seriously?" She turned to stare at him with raised brows. "That's what you want to ask?"

He shrugged. "I thought I'd leave life-altering questions like your favorite book or movie for the second time we got coffee?"

A genuine laugh burst free, surprising him and then her. She clapped a hand over her mouth and shook her head, still struggling to keep in the laughter. He didn't mind if she laughed at his expense so long as she kept laughing like that. It was nice to hear a woman laugh genuinely instead of in that air-headed, attention-seeking way most women did when he was around.

"You can laugh," he murmured. "I know it's a bit of a lame question."

"It's not that," she finally replied. "It's the nerve you have thinking I'll agree to coffee a second time."

He put a hand over his heart. "You wound me. I'm trying very hard here, Miss Cooperson. You know my reputation. This isn't exactly easy for me."

She rolled her eyes. "What? Trying to charm your way into a woman's bed? That's second nature for you, Mr. Gatlin. Please don't treat me like anyone's fool."

That garnered a laugh from him. Second nature to charm his way into a woman's bed, yes. Into her heart? No. He'd never tried and felt more out of his depth than ever. "Pick out your coffee, woman. The clock's ticking, and I still don't know your favorite color."

She gave her order to the grumpy clerk, and he gave his before paying and guiding her to a table. He pulled out her chair, only a little disappointed when she misunderstood his attempt at chivalry, and took the seat across from him. With nothing to do then, he sat too with a little grimace.

"My favorite color is yellow," she said softly. "If you really want to know."

He leaned forward. This was the first personal information she'd shared with him—with anyone on the staff that he knew of. "Why?"

"Because it's bright and cheerful and always reminds me of sunshine." She stared down at the table. "It makes me feel a little warm inside."

"Cute."

She scowled. "Look, you asked! Don't make fun of me for liking it."

"I'm not." He sat back a bit. "I really do think it's cute. And I like that you thought about it. It's endearing."

"Then I need to work harder. I'm not meant to be endearing. Not if I want the head nurse position." She folded her arms over her chest.

He kept his gaze focused strictly on hers. Her brow wrinkled as if she'd noticed the lack of his gaze on her breasts and was confused by it. He didn't waver or react. Perhaps in time, she would notice the subtle clues he'd changed and give him a chance to show her more overtly how much he had. "You don't have to be tough to be head nurse, Lanie."

"I do in your department if I want to have it and be respected."

Her honesty hit sharply, and he looked away. "You don't really think that, do you?"

She laughed. "Of course I do! If I won't sleep with you, I have to do other things to prove I'm worthy of a promotion. Even then it might not be enough."

"Hard work is always enough to get you a well-earned promotion in my department, Lanie," he murmured, rising to throw his empty coffee cup away. When he returned, he eyed her with a frown. "Did the guy at your last workplace do things differently?"

Her cheeks lost their color, and she seemed to retreat before his very eyes, though she barely moved in the chair. She stared down at her coffee cup with pinched lips.

"Another thing to leave be, then." He sighed. "I'll figure you out someday, Miss Cooperson. Come on, then. We'll be late for work."

Chapter 2

Lanie didn't know what to make of the changes in Chad Gatlin. It was clear he had no idea how to treat a woman when his first objective was neither acquiring the next tool for a surgery nor charming her into bed, but there was something almost endearing about his mannerisms. If she didn't know he was an incorrigible flirt, she'd think he really did mean to coax her into a relationship instead of a one-night stand, but she knew Chad. However changed he seemed right now, she had no doubt he'd revert back to his usual ways, eventually.

Still, it had been a year of this sort of strange behavior from him—though the requests for company over coffee in the mornings were a recent development. He'd kept his head down, worked hard, and turned down any attempts from the others to flirt. The only nurse he seemed interested in treating with something beyond professional courtesy was her, and she didn't know how to handle or understand it.

"Lanie?" Chad tapped her on the shoulder. "We need to scrub up for an emergency. Amputation."

She winced. "Those are never fun."

"Nope." He sighed. "The guy is out and ready to go. We need to operate now."

She nodded and headed down the hall toward the OR.

He fell in step beside her. "How are you? You've seemed a little tired."

"Most nurses are tired, Gatlin. What's it to you?" she snapped.

"You don't have to be so defensive," he shot back. "I'm just asking."

"Yeah, and why is that?" She narrowed her eyes, wondering if he'd fall back on bickering or silence this time.

He went silent and crossed his arms.

"You never make sense anymore," she muttered.

"No? Sorry I don't fit in your neat little box anymore," he hissed. "Maybe it'd make more sense if you gave people a chance to change."

"People don't change. They just get better at pretending they have, Gatlin."

He glared at her. "You're the most pessimistic person I know. Who hurt you so badly that you're convinced everyone around you is incapable of being good?"

She laughed, the sound strained. "No one. I'm just observant."

"Are you, now?" His tone turned sarcastic. "That's funny, because I thought I'd shown a different side to me, but you don't seem to be *observing* that."

There was no good reply to that. She had observed it. She just didn't know what to do with it. Ever since Kaiden, she'd held firmly to the conviction that people didn't change or get better. Chad was changing, though, and even she had to admit it seemed genuine after a year of persistent differences. The women whispered about the change in the lockers, some with begrudging respect and others with irritation as they talked about how he would no longer sleep with any of them. For her part, she found herself feeling both their begrudging respect for the about-face and their frustration because she couldn't understand it. Silence was the only reply she had to his remark.

They walked together silently through the bustling halls until they reached the OR and began scrubbing up. As they did, Chad sighed. "Look, I'm sorry, Lanie. I didn't mean to be hurtful."

Her eyes widened, but she covered her surprise by turning her face away and focusing on scrubbing her forearms carefully. "It's fine."

"No. It isn't. I was rude, and I can tell the comment was hurtful."

"It wasn't." And that was the honest truth. It couldn't be hurtful because she *had* observed the things he thought she hadn't. She was just confused. "I didn't have a good answer, Chad. That's all."

He raised a brow as he pulled on a pair of gloves. "Why not?"

"Look, let's talk about this later. We have a man lying on your table waiting for an amputation. The team is ready to go, and you came looking for me instead of just paging me."

"I was in the area. I figured I'd just grab you on my way over."

"Right." She donned her own gloves. "Whatever you say, boss. Let's just get this done with, shall we?"

***

Chad watched Lanie as she scrubbed down after the surgery. It had gone without a hitch, as usual, and they'd saved more of the man's leg than he'd expected to. All in all, it was a successful surgery, but he still had a funny, discontented feeling in the pit of his stomach. Lanie was the source of it. She redid her ponytail, pulling the thick, shiny hair back and tying it off with the hair band. The side of her full lips curled up in a smirk. "See something you like, Mr. Gatlin?"

He snorted. "You know full well I do."

She turned to face him fully, the earlier irritation replaced with a sly look in her eyes. "Well, that's just too bad, isn't it? I have a look-don't-touch policy, I'm afraid."

A startled laugh escaped. "Seriously, Lanie? That might be one of the worse lines I've heard from you."

She lifted one shoulder in a dismissive shrug. "A woman can't be perfect all the time, Gatlin."

"Are you sure?" he teased softly. "You make it seem like you can."

She shifted from one foot to the other and flicked her ponytail over her shoulder, dark eyes fixing on him. "I...Is that a compliment or an insult?"

"What do you think?" He raised a brow at her and tossed his gloves and disposable hair cover in the trash.

"I think I dislike riddles. Is it a compliment or not? I want to know how I should react."

He chuckled. "That's for me to know and you to find out. No riddle. Just plain old guessing."

"You can be a real pain, Gatlin."

"Takes one to know one." He strode for the door but stopped at her side before he left. "Hey, are you free later?"

She frowned, and his heart hammered in his chest. He wanted her so badly, but more than anything, he wanted her permanently, not as a one-night fling. He liked the little spitfire, and if anyone could be the one for him, she would be. He'd never know, though, if she didn't let him try to prove himself worthy of her.

"No. Not for you." She took a step back, the teasing tone in her voice vanishing. "I don't mix work and play, Mr. Gatlin. You know that."

"Yeah..." He looked away. "Sorry. Coffee tomorrow morning, like today?"

"I don't know," she whispered, staring down at her feet. "Will it just be a coffee?"

"It can be whatever you want," he murmured, heart falling. "I know not to push my luck."

A hint of sadness washed across her face before she swept it away and looked up. "Look, it's not...I'm not trying to be rude or hurtful, Chad."

"I know." He smiled sadly. "You're just afraid. You're afraid I'll hurt you, that I'll turn out to be as bad or worse than whichever jerk hurt you the first time. It's not like I can blame you. I didn't help my case the first year you worked for me."

"No, you didn't." There was no animosity in her voice now. Only plain, simple statement of fact and an underlying hint of pain.

It was the last that cut to the quick. He never wanted to hurt her, and yet, just by being the man he had been, he'd managed to do just that. "I'm sorry, Lanie. I know you don't believe me now, but I'm going to prove it."

"You can try," she murmured. "I can't promise it'll change how I feel."

"I just want a chance. Just one chance."

"I'm all out of chances to give." She took another step back, her slight frame quivering. "I've already given too many. You proved who you were long ago."

"Back to the 'people don't change' bit again, are we?" He shook his head. "You know, my father was like you in that regard."

"Oh?" She looked away.

"Yeah. He's busy drinking his way toward an early grave." His tone hardened. "I'd really hate to watch you do the same."

She stiffened. "I'll be fine. I already told you this morning that my private life is my own. It's not up for discussion."

A nod was all he could manage. It hurt to be pushed away so forcefully. Banter, fights, and silence. Was that all that would ever be between them? He wished he could tell what she was thinking, could see if he was wasting his time or if he'd read her correctly in thinking she just needed to be shown he was worth the chance, worth trusting. Instead, he was stuck in this in-between state, unsure if she hated him or was simply terrified of wanting him too. He watched her walk away with clenched fists, forcing himself not to push too hard and not to go after her despite the burning desire to do so. She needed time if she was ever going to come to him. He had to give her that time and walk the tightrope between love and hate with her until she decided which way to fall. Only then would he know if he was hers or if he was alone.

Chapter 3

Lanie stepped into the hospital two weeks later. Chad lounged in a seat near the door, but he jumped up when he saw her with a broad smile. After a week of wheedling, he'd finally had her favorite genre to read from her. Shockingly, they had much closer reading tastes than she'd assumed, and he'd promised her he had a book somewhere at home he'd bring her. He jogged over to join her when she made a beeline for the cafeteria. His smile was shyer than she'd seen it before, and he extended a carefully wrapped package. "For you."

Her cheeks warmed, and she tried to remind herself that she didn't trust him and didn't want to get involved. She humored his daily coffee runs with her only because he was her boss, and she didn't want to lose her position over repeated hostility. Over the last few weeks, though, he'd been chipping away at her barriers, and she was floundering, unsure which way was up anymore. His efforts to please her were sweet, but not enough. They couldn't cut through her fears that he would return to his old ways like Kaiden had and leave her heartbroken. Heartbroken and out of yet another job, most likely. She'd promised herself on her last birthday when she turned 31 that she wouldn't let that happen to her again.

She stopped and turned to face him. When he held the package out again, she took the package and tucked it into her purse. "Thanks."

His smile dimmed. "Well...I thought you might open it."

"Oh..." She chewed on the inside of her cheek and tried to decide how to proceed. Did she brush him off with a bit of their usual, casual teasing? Did she push him away more abruptly? Or was silence the best response?

"Never mind," he murmured. "Never mind...I just thought you'd like it, you know? But you don't have to open it now. You probably want your coffee this early, and I'm just an obstacle to that. Come on. It's on me today."

"Chad, I..."

He waved her away, but his cheeks looked oddly flushed. "Forget about it, Lanie. We're both tired, and I shouldn't have given it to you in the middle of the lobby if I wanted you to open it. It's my fault."

She fell silent and followed him to the cafeteria. Chad never used to apologize for things, no matter how small. He did what he did and expected everyone else to get over it. He was still like that in part with others on his staff. There was no question of who was in charge, and he didn't lack confidence. With her, though, in moments that were personal and outside of the job's requirements, he seemed as awkward as she felt. A tiny smile curled the edges of her mouth, and she lowered her head to hide it if Chad was looking. It wouldn't do to let him think he might be doing something *right* for once.

He put their order in smoothly, rattling off her choice of coffee with practiced ease. He must have memorized it over the few weeks since he'd begun their little tradition. She had to admit, he paid more attention to the little details than he had before, at least as it related to personal things. Kaiden had never cared about her coffee order.

Chad guided her to a table tucked into a corner and pulled out her chair. After the first two visits to the cafeteria with him, she'd realized the disappointed, awkward look on his face always followed her subconscious refusal to take the seat he'd pulled out for her. She hadn't even considered the possibility he might behave like a gentleman, but once she'd realized he was, she'd let him help her into a chair ever since. She'd never admit it to him, but this was one little thing she *did* like about how he behaved with her. It was sweet, as odd as a word as that might be for anything Chad did.

"Only fifteen minutes today," he mused, glancing up at the clock.

She smiled into her coffee cup and waited. Every morning, it was a different question. He never pressed if she chose not to answer, but he always wanted to know something, and it was never work-related.

"Dogs or cats?"

She had to set her coffee down before she inhaled it laughing.

"What? What's so funny?" He looked confused. "Isn't it a normal question to ask?"

"Uh..." She forced herself to stop laughing. "It's just...Chad, you're not very good at asking questions that get a conversation going."

He flushed and shrugged. "Just answer the damn question, would you? Unless it's off limits?"

"No," she replied with an amused smile. "It isn't off limits. I like cats."

"Why?"

"They're quiet. They like attention on their terms, but they can also be great when you're feeling lonely or sad. It's like they have a radar and know when you need space and when you need comfort. Dogs are just all over you all the time. It's annoying. You?"

He winced. "Ah, well...I'm not sure—"

"Oh, come on! If I have to answer, so do you. Fair's fair."

"Okay, okay. I concede defeat." He raised his hands in mock surrender. "I'm afraid I'm a dog person."

She rolled her eyes and laughed. "Of course you are."

"What does that mean?" he grumbled.

"You're like a dog in a lot of ways."

He choked on his coffee and spluttered until he got his breath back. "I beg your pardon?"

"Well, you are!" She pointed a finger at him. "You wait for me to show up, and when I do, you're always there looking for attention. I swear, once you have it, you'd be thumping your tail too if you had one."

He scoffed. "Oh, please! I would not. Besides, if I'm like a dog, you're like a cat."

She narrowed her eyes. "Why do I have the feeling I won't like this comparison?"

He grinned smugly. "Perhaps because yours was insulting?"

"It was not!" she shot back hotly. "It was a statement of fact!"

"All right, then. Here's an equal statement of fact, Miss Cooperson. You're like a cat because both you and a cat only ever want attention on your terms. If it's given when you're not ready for it, you both choose to hiss or walk away. Maybe both. That and you can have quite a set of claws to you when you have a mind for it." He sat back and took a sip of his coffee. "You also, much like a cat, pretend to be indifferent about attention and affection, but secretly, you crave it. I may not know much about you, but I have learned those things from watching."

Her cheeks heated, and she dropped her gaze to the cup. "You watch me?"

"Really, Lanie? You have to ask?" He laughed. "You're losing your touch."

She took another sip of coffee to avoid the need to answer.

He leaned forward. "Come on, Lanie. You don't really think I haven't noticed you watching too."

"Not because I'm interested," she snapped. "Only because you're...you're..."

He raised a brow and waited.

"Well, you're just *you*."

"And what about that is so captivating, Lanie?"

"Nothing. You're arrogant, way too self-assured, and flirtatious. You don't seem to understand the difference between love and hate, and you clearly don't know the difference between watching out of interest and watching out of morbid curiosity."

He tsked and shook his head. "Self-deception isn't a pretty look on a woman, Miss Cooperson."

She glanced at the clock. "Oh, look. Our fifteen minutes are up."

He sighed and looked too. "So they are. But tell me just one thing, Lanie. Do you really hate me? Love and hate walk a fine line."

"I hate people like you. If you can stop being you, then maybe they'll walk a fine line," she muttered.

Deep down, though, a part of her was already beginning to wonder if that was true. Love and hate *did* walk a fine line, and Chad made it one that was easy to walk. She'd been walking it for almost a month now and was growing tired of it. Sooner or later, she was going to tip to one side or the other. The only question was, would Chad be there to catch her when she did?

"I think you're saying that to protect yourself," he murmured. "Because I think you're terrified of this, whatever it is. Don't be. I'm not going to let you fall."

"I don't believe you." She stood and tossed her paper cup into the garbage. "I'll see you later, Mr. Gatlin. I have work to do, even if you don't."

Chapter 4

Chad missed the next few weeks of coffee with Lanie. The two of them had odd hours to fill in for a few people on staff who had gone on vacation, and he found himself missing the morning chats at six AM when he sat in the cafeteria alone and realized how empty it had been without her. He used the time to think about how he might finally convince Lanie to go out with him. The coffee had been a great start, but he didn't want to press his luck. He needed something sweet and romantic to prove to her that he cared about more than sex.

Therein lay the problem, though. He'd never done romantic. He didn't take women on dates. He brought them home from work or clubs and took them however he pleased. Not one of the women he'd had over the years had meant a thing to him. Lanie was not one of those women; she meant a great deal to him. He stared morosely into his coffee and pondered the problem. Six AM was too early to be thinking about these things, but his brain was hyped up on caffeine and spinning its wheels, anyway.

What about her birthday? That was coming up at the end of the week. Maybe he could do something nice for her then. What would she like? Candies? Flowers? A card? He doubted she'd appreciate it if he threw a party for her in their breakroom after her shift ended. That would be too over-the-top for her, and it would probably earn her irritation, not her appreciation.

As he was considering the issue, the door swung open, and a

tired-looking Lanie walked in. When she saw him, a hesitant smile slipped onto her lips. She didn't bother ordering from the bright-eyed girl behind the counter. Instead, she shuffled over and joined him, flopping into the seat as he pushed it out for her with one foot.

"Are you alright?" he murmured. "You look worn down."

"I took extra shifts to cover Wanda," she murmured, pillowing her head in her arms.

Her back and shoulders looked tense with exhaustion and frustration. Without thinking, he reached out and began to work at the knots. A quiet moan slipped from her, and they both froze. He snatched his hands back, face burning.

"I'm so sorry. I don't know what I was thinking."

She sighed but didn't look at him, her shiny hair falling in a curtain to hide her face as she buried her face in her arms. "I...It feels nice, actually. C-could you work the knots out? I tried a hot shower and a hot bath. It didn't do the trick."

Hesitating, he eyed her. "I'm not going to have a sexual harassment claim sitting on my desk in a few hours, am I?"

She sniffed in dismissal. "No."

"Okay..." He wasn't going to turn down a chance to work his way into her good graces, and he certainly didn't mind the opportunity to help ease some of the tension in her body. "You should take a day off and rest. Wanda will be back soon, and we can manage."

"But I should be here. People rely on me."

He set to work on her shoulders again, digging his thumbs into any knots he came across. A soft sigh of relief and a groan were his reward. He'd never seen her so vulnerable and open with him, but he wasn't going to question it. Apparently, being tired wore down her defenses. "You have to take care of yourself before you can worry about other people."

"That's not how it works." She sounded half-asleep. "Besides, you'll be upset if I do that...Kaiden always was."

He continued kneading her shoulders, forcing himself not to pause or indicate any interest in what she'd just given away. "The surgeon from your old department sounds like a jerk."

She turned her head to look at him, pain shimmering in her gaze. "Yeah."

"What happened, anyway? You never told me." He kept his voice soft and prayed she would open up a little more.

"I don't like talking about it." Her answer was just as soft, and she turned her head away with a tired sigh. "Besides, it doesn't matter. I'm here now."

He left it be, not wanting to push too hard when she was vulnerable. He might not know how to romance a girl, but he did know enough about people to know when they were fragile, it was best not to break them. "Your birthday's this weekend."

She hummed noncommittally.

"What was that noise? You don't look forward to it?"

"It's just another day. Besides, I don't really want to celebrate turning 32, so what's to be excited about?"

He did stop working on her upper back then. "You did not just tell me you don't want to celebrate. It's your birthday, Lanie. It's worth celebrating another year alive."

She made a noise that sounded suspiciously like a sniffle. "Not really. It's just one year closer to the grave."

He took her by the shoulder and pulled her up with a scowl. "That's no way to think about it. You're going to do something fun this year."

Her jaw tensed in the mulish expression he knew well by now. "I don't have anywhere to go or anyone to go with."

"Well, you do now."

She gaped at him. Apparently she wasn't tired enough to forget that he'd never taken a woman on their floor anywhere unless it was to a hotel room or his bedroom to screw around.

"I said it," he snapped when she continued to stare in dumbstruck silence. "You do now. I'll take you somewhere."

That remark set her to fidgeting with the napkin holder. "You don't have to."

"I don't," he agreed sternly. "But nonetheless, I'm going to. I'll take you somewhere fun, and I'm going to prove to you that celebrating is way better than moping at home because you think you already have one foot in the grave."

He was shocked when tears pooled in her eyes. She blinked a few times, trying to contain herself as usual, and then stared at her lap. "Why are you doing this?"

"Because I care." He scrubbed a hand over his face. "Damn it, Lanie, I care, okay? You can't seriously be that naïve? You have to have noticed I pay attention."

"You remember my coffee order every time," she whispered, as if the simple action meant something much more to her.

"Did past men have a habit of forgetting?" he asked amusedly.

That only brought back the tears. "You don't really care," she snapped peevishly.

"If I didn't care, I wouldn't bother with taking you out for your birthday."

"I'm just the last notch you want on your belt," she persisted. "You can't have me, so you're trying a new tactic."

He crossed his arms. "Lanie Cooperson, that is unfair, and you know it! I haven't been that sort of man for over a year now. I'm tired of you refusing to see that. I think deep down, you know I'm a changed man. You're just using the past as an excuse to avoid facing the present man sitting right here asking you out."

Her cheeks tinged a dusty pink underneath her tan. "You're asking me out?"

"How many hours have you been awake?" he asked, narrowing his eyes.

"I...Maybe twenty-four now?"

He shook his head with a huff. "I don't have any surgeries for another two hours, and there's another surgeon on staff. You're going home sick, and I'm signing you out myself. You know better than to work for twenty-four hours straight. And were you coming in here for the beginning of the next shift or the end of the last?"

"Both," she admitted quietly.

He groaned. "Woman, you're going to start taking self-care more seriously from now on. You're dead on your feet; I don't need that in my OR. Come on." He helped her to her feet, and they headed out of the cafeteria.

She didn't bother to fight him on it. "But my stuff..."

"I'll bring it over when I get off tonight. You don't need it now, do you?"

"My keyring has the key to my apartment."

"Then I'll settle you in my car and come back in for it."

She opened her mouth to argue.

He pressed a finger to her lips and stopped outside the cafeteria in the deserted hallway. "Let me show you how changed I am, Lanie. No arguing on this one."

Her lips pursed against his finger, sending a shiver down his spine. He tapered the desire to have her. Now wasn't the time. Not when that wariness was mixing with her exhaustion. She didn't need more reasons to assume he was the same playboy she'd met a year ago. Finally, she nodded and relaxed.

He quickly signed her out on sick leave for the day and stopped by his office for his keys.

She looked around at the place with a morose sigh. "Surgeons really do get to have the cake and eat it, too," she muttered.

He raised a brow at her and shoved his keys in his pockets. "Someone's unusually honest when overtired. Maybe I need to get you this way more often."

Her lips turned down in a discontented frown. "You're mean."

He wrapped an arm around her waist and guided her back out the door. A few of his staff shot them confused glances, and a few of the nurses scowled at Lanie, but he ignored them. Out in the parking lot, he opened his car door for her and helped her slide into the leather seat. She curled into the armrest the moment he let go, muttering only a sleepy protest when he shifted her again to buckle her in. Then she was out like a light. He sighed and rounded the car to climb in. This woman was going to be the death of him.

Chapter 5

Chad knocked on Lanie's front door and waited nervously for an answer. She'd been so hesitant to agree to let him take her out to celebrate her 32nd birthday that he feared she would find an excuse to ditch him. When she opened the door with a slow, hesitant smile, he let out a sigh of relief. "I thought you might ditch me," he murmured, extending the bouquet of lilies and daffodils.

She took them, her cheeks flushing and adding a shy quality to her smile. "How did you know they were my favorites?"

"I, uh..." He rubbed the back of his neck. "I eavesdropped last week when the nurses were talking about the best types of flowers for dates versus gifts. You said you thought roses were cliché and preferred lilies and daffodils. I remembered when I was out looking for flowers."

She laughed and stepped aside to let him in. "I didn't think you'd actually show up. Give me a minute to change?"

"Of course." He stepped inside and tucked his hands into his pockets.

"Where are we going?"

"It's a surprise. Dress comfortably."

She raised a brow. "So we're not going somewhere super fancy?"

He tensed. Had he misstepped by choosing pizza and mini golf? She hadn't struck him as the sort to appreciate a fancy dinner and wine. "Did you want to?"

That gained a laugh. "Nope. I wouldn't know what to do with myself somewhere ritzy."

"Good." His shoulders relaxed. "Then dress comfortably. I'm not telling you where we're going, so don't beg. It won't get the location from me."

"I don't beg," she replied archly.

A flirtatious reply hovered right on the tip of his tongue, but he bit it back and looked away.

"You look like you want to say something," she prompted with a teasing lilt.

He looked up to find amusement in her gaze and a hint of a challenge. "Will you accuse me of being a flirt if I'm honest?"

She shrugged. "Once a womanizer, always a womanizer. Honestly, I'm just surprised you've gone nearly a year without a single flirtatious remark."

"Changed man, remember?" He raised a brow at her. "But if you'll allow me the single arrogance, you might not have begged anyone else. If you aren't careful, you'll discover I'm not just anyone else."

"Is that a challenge?" She crossed her arms.

The corners of his mouth pulled up with amusement. In a manner of speaking, perhaps. But he couldn't make good on it until she wanted him in her bed. He knew where the real power lay here. While he might take charge everywhere else, he knew full well he could only take control of her in a way that would satisfy both of them if she let him. "That's up to you, isn't it?"

She bit her lip and looked away. "I should go change."

"You should," he agreed mildly. "Pajamas, as adorable as they look on you, are not suitable for what I have in mind."

A glance down at her rubber duck-covered pajama pants left a smile on her lips. "Yeah, I don't think I want to go out in public like this. Normally, I'd have to kill anyone who saw me in them, but..." There was a bit of a twinkle in her gaze. "For you, I *guess* I can make an exception."

"I'm honored, mi'lady." He bowed with a grin. "Now, if you'll hurry up, dinner awaits."

"So impatient." She rolled her eyes and walked off in the direction of the bedroom, leaving him to himself.

***

Lanie didn't know what to make of this new Chad. She had to admit that this wasn't the man she'd met her first day on the job. He was relaxed, friendly, and never pushed her past her limits. She groaned and laughed at her inaccuracy as she shot for another hole and missed. "I suck at this. How are you so good?"

"My mom used to take me as a kid, and I secretly still love going to putt a few holes. I don't go much these days, though. It's not much fun when you go alone." He tucked his club under his arm and came to join her by her ball. "Here. Let me help."

She chewed on the inside of her cheek, but she nodded. After all, she could use a few pointers. He took up position behind her, the spicy scent of his cinnamon and cedar cologne tickling her senses. A tiny shiver worked its way down her spine. He tensed, his body flush against hers. Her breathing became shallower, and she sensed the heat flooding her body and pooling in her stomach before moving lower. Somehow, somewhere along the way, her hatred of him had morphed into desire as it sank in that he really had changed, despite her pessimistic view of men and people in general. She'd seen plenty of men claim they were trying to change or were different and watched as they returned to old habits. None of them could keep up a façade for a year. She couldn't deny it anymore; Chad was different.

He leaned down and placed her hands more properly on her club, his breath fanning warmth over her ear. "Like this. And then, you should take a small swing to get a feel for where the ball is. Then draw back and swing through. Don't try to stop the blow when the club hits the ball." He helped her swing the club through, sending the ball flying back toward the hole. It bounced and rolled before dropping into the hole. "There! Do you see?"

She stilled in his arms with a quiet nod. The tension crackled between them, and the way his breathing hitched told her he felt it too. She should move away, but instead, she let the moment happen and closed her eyes. How long had it been since a man had come so close to hugging her? Probably years. She hadn't let anyone close since Kaiden, and it hit her how much she'd been missing thanks to her bitterness and the snarled ball of hurt inside that she'd refused to let go of. Between that and her focus on her career, she hadn't made any time to find another to let in like she'd done with Kaiden almost four years prior.

"Should I...Do you need me to show you again?" Chad's voice was hoarse and tight.

Another chance to push him away and tell him no, but she found she didn't want to refuse the offer here in his arms. He'd asked nicely, and he didn't sound like a man who was enjoying stringing a naïve young woman along. She nodded, still afraid her voice couldn't be trusted.

He pulled away, and she whimpered at the loss of his warmth against her back before she could stop herself. His gaze flicked to her, but he hit his own ball to join hers and gestured toward the next hole. "Shall we?"

"Please."

He led the way, and she followed, heart hammering. What if she lost her chance to find love again because of Kaiden? That would be like letting him win. She wanted to move on and live life so badly, but was Chad the right one to move on with? She took a steadying breath and shook her head. He hadn't asked her out yet. They were out here because he'd felt sorry for the girl with no one to celebrate her birthday with and no reason to celebrate alone. It wasn't a date, even if he had brought her favorite flowers as a gift.

He stopped at the beginning of the next hole and set her ball down for her. "Alright. Let's try this one."

She stepped into position obediently, closing her eyes with a soft sigh when he pulled her into him and fixed the position of her hands. He helped her hit it, landing it in the hole again.

He let out a delighted whoop. "There it is! Last one is up, and you're on your own. I think you can do it."

After he shot his in two, they moved to the next hole. Using what he'd shown her, she managed to put it into the hole in two herself. A proud smile slid over her lips, and it was at that moment that she realized there was nothing left in her that hated Chad Gatlin.

They drove home with contented small talk filling the comfortable quiet of the car. She tried not to smile at the sharp contrast between this conversation and so many others they'd had. It reminded her a little of the ones they'd had in the cafeteria at work, but this seemed more intimate and less like a conversation between coworkers or friends. He pulled up in her driveway, and a twinge of disappointment flashed through her. Now the fairytale would end, and she would go back to her usual routine, lonely and wanting.

To her surprise, though, Chad clambered out of his Lamborghini and rushed around to open her door before she could finish unbuckling or open the door. He stood there with a sheepish smile and extended a hand to her. "Let me walk you to the door?"

"Where did you learn to be a gentleman? Hallmark?" The question popped out with a laugh before she could think better of it.

He winced and pulled back his hand. "Uh...Is it that bad? I'm trying, Lanie...I don't exactly know what I'm doing."

"Trying?" She frowned in confusion and reached out a hand to let him help her up. "To what? Be a gentleman?"

"No." He pulled her up and into him. "I'm trying to be romantic, woman. My efforts seem doomed to fail, but I am trying."

Her cheeks warmed, and she stared down at his broad chest and the t-shirt that didn't quite cover the muscles beneath. "You're w-what?"

"Trying to be romantic," he repeated. "I thought it was working, but if I'm just taking lines from Hallmark, maybe cheesy is all I'm actually achieving. Why is this so frickin' difficult?"

She looked up at him in shock. "Why?"

"Are you going to repeat my questions all night?" A tiny smile curled the corners of his full mouth, but there was a hint of worry in his brown eyes.

"It's so *frickin'* difficult because you've spent most of your life charming women into bed, not charming your way into their hearts." She laughed. "You didn't seriously think the two looked the same."

He let go of her with a sigh. "No, I did not. Hence the behavior that apparently seems to mimic a Hallmark movie. Cut me a little slack, Cooperson. I'm out of my depth, but I *am* trying."

She chewed on her lower lip and dropped her gaze to the sidewalk this time. "Why are you trying?" she whispered. It was the only question she really wanted an answer to right now, the only one that had been spinning in the back of her mind ever since he told her he was taking her out for her birthday. "You don't have any lack of women falling over themselves to get into your bed."

"This isn't about getting you into bed," he murmured. "And I don't want any of the others. I've had enough of meaningless flings to last a lifetime, Lanie. I want something that's real. You're real."

"So…now what?" she murmured back.

"I'd planned to wait until I had you safely on your doorstep." He took her hand and drew her up the driveway. "So that you wouldn't be cold in this chilly air when I asked you on an official date."

"Was that what this was? I thought it was a pity date."

He chuckled, the sound full and amused rather than shallow

and condescending as it often was at work. "Most certainly not! It was an excuse to get you out with me to have some fun. You did have fun, didn't you?"

They stopped on her porch underneath the light, but he didn't let go of her hand, and she didn't try to pull away.

"I did," she told him.

"Enough to go out with me for real this time?"

She nodded, holding tightly to his hand to convince herself this was real and draw strength from his solid presence for the leap of faith into the unknown she was now taking. "Don't make me regret it." She'd meant the words to come out light and teasing. Instead, they sounded like a shy, frightened plea.

"I won't." He leaned in and kissed her cheek. "I'll touch base about details in a few days when I've thought of something worthy of an official first date."

She tightened her grip on his hand as he kissed her cheek softly. "That's my goodbye kiss?" she teased, trying to take back her footing.

"Do you want more?" His voice held amusement and a faint hint of hope.

"Hmmm...only if you ask nicely."

He grinned. "May I kiss you, then?"

"You may."

He leaned in, his lips brushing hers softly. Any idea she'd had of teasing or regaining her bearings fled the moment his hands cupped her face and pulled her close. She went to him willingly, urging him to deepen the kiss. He groaned and slid his hands to her hair, tangling her locks around his fingers. Her hands drifted from his abdomen to his chest, and she rewarded him with a whimper when he gently ran his tongue over her lower lip. She wanted him more than anything, the intensity of her hatred transferring to her desire and leaving her breathless.

Instead of continuing on—she would have given him anything he asked in that moment—Chad pulled away and dropped a final chaste kiss on her lips before he let her go. "Happy Birthday, Lanie. I'll see you tomorrow, Lanie. Sleep well."

She watched him go, too embarrassed by the depth of her desire to ask for what she really wanted or to try to hold on to him. She'd taken a flying leap into the deep end, and she still wasn't sure if she was going to swim or drown.

Chapter 6

Lanie felt like she was flying when she arrived at work the next day. Chad had texted her early that morning to remind her of their usual coffee appointment and to tell her he was looking forward to seeing her. Before she could reach the cafeteria doors, the hospital's administrator waylaid her. She smiled politely, though inside, she was tamping down panic. What could he want? The chief administrator didn't stop to talk to anonymous nurses in a big hospital like this. Was she in trouble?

"Lanie," he said, hands in his pockets.

"Mr. Adams. Is something wrong?"

He glanced at the cafeteria doors. "Meeting Mr. Gatlin for coffee again this morning?"

She tensed, her own gaze going to the double doors. He'd noticed that? Had someone told him? "I didn't think it was a crime."

"It's not. But you know, if you're in a relationship with him, you have to fill out conflict of interest forms and file with HR." His gaze flicked back to her. "You aren't in a relationship with him, are you?"

She wrapped her arms around her waist. "We're just talking. Why the big deal? He has a reputation. He never gets into relationships, Mr. Adams."

"I know full well what his reputation is. That's why I'm speaking with you, Lanie. He's not the type to stick around, and I know what happened at your last hospital."

She flinched and stared down at the floor. "That wasn't my fault."

"I know that. The hospital wouldn't hire you if you'd done something wrong. But I don't think you'd be keen on repeating the error."

"None of the other nurses lost their jobs after he screwed around with them," she mumbled. "Why do you think I'd be any different?"

"Because you're too bright to let him screw around with you and toss you aside." The hospital administrator sighed. "You're in position to take over as head nurse soon, Lanie. We're moving his current head nurse to another department that needs one desperately. She wants to work NICU, and now that opportunity's arisen. The spot will need filling in a month or two, but you won't be able to fill it if Mr. Gatlin doesn't sign off on it. Are you sure you want to risk all of that with this...? With him?"

She chewed on her lower lip, unsure what to say. Chad was a changed man, but what if he wasn't changed enough? She'd also believed Kaiden was a good man, and she'd been wrong. Could she be wrong this time too? She wanted to give him a chance, though, and she didn't want to give up a chance at maybe being happy. Part of her might want to take the easy cop out that the hospital administrator offered here, but a bigger part wanted Chad. "We aren't in a relationship yet, Mr. Adams. He's asked me out, and that's all. I said yes, and if it goes further, I'll be up to your office personally to sign the paperwork if you want."

Mr. Adams heaved a sigh. "Are you certain you know what you're doing?"

"Positive." Nothing could be further from the truth.

"All right, then. If things progress, fill out the forms for HR, and make sure he does too, Lanie. I don't want an HR nightmare to deal with if it all falls apart."

She nodded briefly and walked past him to enter the cafeteria, heart hammering, and stomach in knots. Chad spotted her and rose, a broad smile on his face. He came to greet her, and his smile dropped when he saw the look on her face. He drew her toward his table and sat her down in the chair opposite his. "Lanie, what is it? You look worried and pale."

She stared down at him and then looked around automatically, checking for company. No one else was in the space besides the cashier, who was typing on her phone and popping her gum in boredom. Her gaze returned to his. "Mr. Adams just asked me about paperwork, is all."

"And that has you looking like he brought up a ghost?"

No. His mention of what had happened before had her looking like that, but she didn't know if Chad could be trusted with that yet. She didn't want to talk about it, so it was best she not mention it. "I just...I've had some bad experiences, Chad, and you have a reputation. He reminded me of that, and I...maybe we shouldn't..."

He took her hands in his. "Look, we'll do whatever you want to do, Lanie, but don't let Mr. Adams scare you out of it. We'll find a way to make it work."

"He told me I'm going to be promoted to head nurse in your department soon, if you approve." She stared down at their hands numbly. "Did you know about it?"

"No. It must be a recent development. Maybe they were going to tell me today. Why would you worry about that? You've wanted to be a head nurse for years. Isn't this good?" His brow furrowed in confusion. "We should celebrate."

"What if things go wrong between us?" she blurted out. "What if they go wrong? Is it going to cost me that promotion?"

He pulled away and went back to his own chair, frustration written all over his face. "You think that lowly of me?"

"I've seen it happen." It had happened to her.

"I wouldn't do that to you. You're an excellent nurse, and no one in my department would do a better job, Lanie. The promotion will be yours if I have any say. It doesn't matter what happens between us." He pushed the second coffee across the table to her. "Here. You'll feel better with your usual fix. Stop worrying and drink this."

She took it from him and tried to obey, but even as the notes of hazelnut and cinnamon took the edge off her worry, she still couldn't shake it entirely. She just hoped this wouldn't be another horrible mistake on her part.

***

"They told you I'm leaving, I take it?" Wanda said when Lanie arrived at the counter closest to Chad's office.

"Mr. Adams told me the news. I'm excited for you! NICU's tough, but I know you've wanted to move there for months."

Wanda grinned broadly. "Yeah, I'm really excited about it. But what about the rest of the news? Didn't you hear they want you to take my place?"

She smiled softly. "I did. If Mr. Gatlin approves."

Wanda's grin dropped. "He'd be an idiot not to...but Lanie, don't give him a reason to decide not to."

She frowned in annoyance. "Not you too! Does everyone around here know?"

"News and gossip travel fast around here. Someone in the cafeteria told us about seeing you two together. Speculation started, and then someone else heard him tell you he was taking you out for your birthday...I admit, I didn't believe them at first."

"But you do now?"

"Chad's been walking on cloud nine for a week, and he seemed happy when he stopped by the office before heading down for coffee. I know he was meeting you. He never used to drink coffee in the morning or visited the cafeteria. Now he never misses it on days when you're on shift too."

Lanie sighed. "So everyone knows. Look, it's just a date. I don't know what'll happen."

Wanda frowned. "It's not his usual M.O. But I guess you're the only one on our floor he hasn't slept with, except maybe the receptionist since she's new. Maybe he figures he needs a new approach."

She flinched and looked away. "It isn't like that."

Wanda laughed, not seeming to notice the hurt on Lanie's face. "Girlfriend, Chad Gatlin doesn't do relationships. If he's courting, it's because he wants you and can't have you any other way."

"You know, I would've agreed with you a year ago," she mumbled. "Not now. He's different."

"Yeah, and pigs fly." Wanda's laughter died, and she looked at Lanie with a frown. "You don't seriously think he's different, do you?"

"He doesn't behave like he used to. He's more serious and quiet now. Haven't you noticed?"

"His mother's death had a big impact, but not that big."

"Maybe not," she murmured.

"All I'm saying is to be careful. You're playing with fire on this one, Lanie. One wrong move, and you'll be burned."

"I'll be fine, thanks."

"And if it goes wrong? You could lose your job."

"I won't make that mistake." Lanie straightened. "Besides, I haven't agreed to be his. Just to give him a fair hearing. He's agreed it's up to me."

Wanda raised her hands in silent surrender. "If you say so."

Lanie watched her supervisor walk off with tears threatening. What if Wanda was right? What if this really couldn't work? She might lose her job if this went wrong, and nothing would happen to Chad. Once again, she would be the only party to suffer if this all went belly up.

Chad walked up to the desk. "Do you have the file for Mrs. Margrave? I needed—" His gaze settled on her. "Hey now, what's wrong? Did someone die?"

A half sob, half laugh escaped her, and she scrubbed at her

tears with the heels of her palms. "No..."

He pulled her hands away from her face. "Talk to me, Lanie. What's the matter? You don't cry much. Something set you off."

"Everyone keeps telling me it's foolish to get involved with you!" The tears pushed free again, and to her horror, she ended up in tears in the hall.

He ushered her quickly into his office and pulled down the drapes to give them a little privacy in the glass space. "Explain what's going through that head of yours."

"What if they're right?" She collapsed into a chair and buried her face in her hands. "They're all saying you aren't different, that I won't be any different. What if they're right?"

He kneeled in front of her and gently pulled her hands into his. "Look at me."

His voice was sterner than she'd ever heard it and commanded her attention. She lifted her gaze from her lap to meet his.

"I am different. So are you. Who cares what they think? They're wrong, and we're going to prove it to them." He reached up to wipe her tears away with the pad of his thumb. "Let's not worry about any of them, Lanie. It's you and me that matter. Their opinions mean nothing."

"But if they're right—"

He pressed his finger to her lips. "They aren't. No more of this sort of thinking, alright? We'll take care of the paperwork I'm sure Adams wanted filed as soon as you decide if you want me or not."

She groaned. "Wanting you isn't the problem, Chad!"

"Really?" He sounded surprised and then glad. "I thought maybe I was making more of the kiss and our interactions at the golf course than I should've. I'm glad to hear I wasn't."

"Ugh. Of course you wouldn't focus on the real problem at hand."

He leaned up and kissed her with a quiet intensity. "Darling, there is no problem at hand. Ignore them, and I'll prove to you I'm worth trusting."

She leaned into his touch with a sigh and prayed he was right. She so desperately wanted him to prove her fears groundless, but she was terrified he wouldn't too. Only time would reveal which side of her was right.

Chapter 7

The date Chad took her on turned out to be a trip to a local stable. He'd fished around about her childhood and things she'd liked doing enough in the past few days that she should have guessed, but he'd asked about so many things she hadn't been able to get a sense of what he was up to. When they pulled up in front of the stable, and she spotted the horses, she gasped in delight and turned to him with a grin. "We're going trail riding?"

"Indeed. But don't expect me to be any good at it. I've never been on a horse."

She laughed. "What? There's something the big bad surgeon can't do?"

"There is nothing he won't try," Chad shot back. "Whether he's any good is a different question. Come on. They're expecting us."

She let him open her door and walked hand-in-hand with him down the driveway until they reached the office building attached to the large barn. The feeling of his hand in hers left her warm and content. The worries she felt when at the hospital with her coworkers staring at Chad's obvious affection for her or warnings from her coworkers and supervisors melted away when it was just the two of them, as if it erased the pressure.

He opened the door and held it for her. She let go of his hand with regret and stepped inside. As if sensing her discontent with the loss of contact, he put a hand at the small of her back as they walked up to the desk and smiled down at her.

The older woman sitting behind the desk looked at them over her spectacles. "Here for the trail ride at one?"

"Yes, ma'am. I have reservations under Chad Gatlin."

She raised a brow. "You're that surgeon everyone's always interviewing and talking about."

He flushed and lifted one shoulder. "Guilty as charged."

Lanie watched with interest. His status as a hotshot surgeon wasn't often brought up in the hospital. There, it was common knowledge, and he'd personally worked with many of them. No one worried about his celebrity status, though it certainly afforded him certain perks at the hospital that others didn't get. Still, he never rubbed anyone's face in it, and no one really spoke about it. Here, though, it must be an amazing opportunity to meet someone famous, especially if one was a fan. However, this woman seemed to be nothing more than a casual observer, and she didn't fawn over him.

"Head into the barn, right through there. Our trail guide will get you started. Sign these waivers first, and then you can get going." She shoved two waivers across the desk.

She signed hers, and Chad signed his. When the receptionist had them in hand, she waved toward the big door and returned to whatever work she'd been doing when they'd come in. Chad wrapped an arm around her waist and guided her through the door. He eyed the horses saddled up and ready to go with nervous curiosity, and Lanie leaned into his side with a laugh. "Scared?"

He opened his mouth to reply when his phone interrupted them. Pulling it out of his pocket, he eyed the name on the screen. Lanie caught a glimpse of it before he rolled his eyes and declined the call, shoving his phone back into place.

"Who was that?"

"No one," he muttered. "Where is the tour guide?"

A woman with blonde highlights in her auburn hair poked her head out of one of the stalls. "Oh, didn't hear you come in. You folks must be the one o'clock's from the city."

"We are." Chad strode forward, leaving her to shake hands with their guide. "This is Lanie. I'm Chad."

The girl smiled at Chad brightly, then gave her a slightly more polite smile. "Welcome, both of you. Why don't we get you on horses? You can walk around the yard a few times to get used to yours."

Lanie raised a hand. "I've been trail riding before. If...you know, it helps?"

"Thanks for letting me know. I won't baby you. What about you, Chad?" She turned to Chad with that same bright smile.

Lanie scowled down at the ground. Chad hadn't introduced her as his girlfriend, so this girl probably assumed he was up for grabs. It left a nasty snarl of emotion in her chest, and she wanted to be anywhere else at that moment. He wasn't even rejecting the girl's advances with her right here. She began to wander off toward the horses.

Chad's arm shot out and hooked around her waist, dragging her back into his side. He didn't miss a beat while speaking with their guide. "I think Lanie might be getting impatient. Can we see our horses?"

"Of course! We'll give her a more spirited horse. You can have the tamer one, Mr. Gatlin. He's big, but he's a gentle giant."

Chad looked at their guide dubiously. "Perhaps a calmer horse for Lanie would be best. I really don't want to take her to the ER."

She kicked at the straw on the barn floor while she waited for them to get around to the riding part. One more minute of this, and she'd walk off now, leaving Chad to trail ride with the woman alone. Chad tightened his hold on her and kissed the side of her head. "You can show me how to mount properly, darling."

She huffed. "Whatever. I don't want to interrupt you while you're *talking* to her."

His attention fixed firmly on her, and he frowned. "Lanie, do you want to leave? I thought you'd enjoy this, but if you won't, we'll go do something else. I promised you an enjoyable time and intend to keep the promise."

The woman rolled her eyes and popped her gum. "Come on, folks. You paid for it, and time's slipping away."

Chad smiled at her tightly. "Give me a minute with Lanie. I think she's having second thoughts."

Lanie wanted to slap the other girl. Or maybe slap Chad. Maybe both. She couldn't believe that he'd pay attention to another woman like this or that he'd so clearly avoid calling her his. Maybe he didn't want her like he claimed he did after all. Maybe Wanda was right about him.

The worker shrugged and strode off to grab their horses. Chad turned and took her chin in a firm grasp. "Lanie, you need to tell me right now if you're going to sulk the whole ride. I have zero interest in that woman. Only in you, but if you can't see that, then we'll leave and go somewhere that won't leave you feeling out of sorts and jealous."

Tears warred with anger, and she pushed his hand away. "You didn't introduce me as your girlfriend."

He raised a brow with a shake of his head. "*That's* what you're angry about? I didn't introduce you that way because you insisted this was just a one chance sort of thing. You told me we weren't dating just because you agreed to one date."

She flushed and stared down at her feet. Okay, she had said that, but now it felt stupid. She hadn't realized how badly it would hurt not to be introduced as his girlfriend while another woman was eyeing him up. "Do you want to introduce me that way?"

He leaned in and wrapped a hand around the back of her neck, pulling her close. "I would like nothing more, baby girl, but I'm trying to respect your boundaries here."

"Oh..." Her anger deflated. "You promise you aren't interested in her?"

"I promise. Now come. You can show me how to mount whatever beast she's grabbed for me." He tugged her toward their guide, who was typing on her phone and eyeing them with an impatient scowl. "Don't let her ruin this for you."

Chapter 8

Chad took her home after every shift whenever they got off together for the next three weeks. She still hadn't let him stay over or let herself trust him fully, but she couldn't deny that she was head-over-heels with the man. He was slowly proving that he was different from than he had been before. Still, there were little things that stressed her out about him. He had odd calls at hours when she knew he wasn't on call, and he refused to answer them with her around. She had no idea if he answered them when she wasn't, but it left her on edge despite her fierce longing to go the rest of the way with him.

For his part, Chad was taking things at a maddeningly slow pace. He was the perfect gentleman most of the time, and it was driving her crazy. She wanted him to make the next move, but he'd left the ball squarely in her court. Tonight, she was done waiting. She wanted him, and she wasn't going to pretend otherwise anymore. She opened her apartment door and turned to him with a shy smile, her nerves leaving her jittery. "Chad, can...can you stay the night?"

He eyed her quietly underneath the porch light, hands tucked into his pockets. "Are you sure, darling?"

"Yes," she whispered. "I'm tired of waiting for you to make the first move."

He chuckled. "I thought you wanted slow. You still don't fully trust me."

"I trust you enough to take the next step, Chad." She reached out and took his hand. "Please...we're both off tomorrow. Maybe we can go grab breakfast together. Make it romantic and all."

"You know I'm not good at romance."

She rolled her eyes. "You're better than you think. In an awkward, endearing sort of way."

"Great...awkwardly endearing. That's exactly what every man wants to hear." He smiled, though, and let her pull him inside. "You're really sure, Lanie? I don't need you to do this just to make me stick around. I want you, sex or no sex. You know that, don't you?"

She chewed on her inner cheek. "Yeah, I know. It's not about that."

"Then what is it about?"

"Me wanting you," she admitted softly. "Please, Chad. Don't make me beg."

He drew her closer, curling strands of her hair around his fingers and tugging gently. "I do love the idea of you begging, but not right now. Not this first time." He bent his head and captured her mouth with an insistent kiss.

Nothing about the kiss left her with any delusions about who was in charge. Chad might not know how to do romance, but he did know how to be physically intimate in this way, and when it came to that, he was the one in charge, not her. She didn't really have much experience. Kaiden had been her first, and he had been a miserable experience in the end. She wanted Chad to show her something better with a desperation that surprised her, and she melted into his touch without any protest.

He sifted his fingers through her hair, yanking her head back to give his mouth better access. She moaned and gave it to him without a fight. He rewarded her with a groan of his own and then picked her up, trailing kisses down her throat to the tops of her breasts. "You're always so beautiful, Lanie," he murmured. "Where's the bedroom?"

She pointed in the right direction, and he headed there, kicking open the door when he reached it. He deposited her on the edge of the bed and stood over her, drinking in her tiny frame and how the leggings and tank top she wore clung to her body. She was glad, suddenly, that she'd worn these at home instead of her scrubs as she usually did. He made a sound of approval and then bent, taking the hem of her shirt and easing it up over her stomach and then over her breasts. Sitting up, she lifted her arms to let him pull it off.

He did so, dropping his mouth back to the swells of her breasts. "You're perfect, Lanie. You know that?"

Tingles swept up and down her body, and she surrendered to him with a gasp. He quickly slid her out of everything else she had on, taking brief moments to admire each new bit of skin revealed. Then he kissed his way up her body to her mouth. He didn't seem to be in any rush, though her own impatience was rising by the second. Finally, he kissed her earnestly and began to touch her in a way that ignited a fire deep inside instead of merely teasing her with a little warmth. Sighing, she closed her eyes and let Chad show her what it was like to be worshiped instead of merely used.

***

A few days after she'd asked Chad to stay over, he asked her to sleep at his home instead. She'd agreed readily, warmed by the idea that she'd finally be in his personal space instead of always inviting him into hers. He'd given her another evening of good food and affection with a night in his bed with numerous reminders of how much he wanted her. This morning, she woke in the warm bed and stretched with a yawn.

Chad's side of the bed was cold. Frowning, she rolled over and looked for him. He wasn't in the room, so she rose and threw on a loose t-shirt and shorts from his closet before looking for him. He'd promised that they would take a dip in the giant indoor pool he had this morning. He'd even suggested—teasingly, she thought—that they skinny dip since his staff were all off for the weekend. She'd rolled her eyes and turned him down on that one, but she was looking forward to a morning swim. He was on call, so they couldn't really go anywhere since he needed to be ready to head to work at a moment's notice, but his giant house afforded so many options she felt no need to go anywhere else.

Padding down the red-carpeted halls, she tried the kitchen first, expecting him to be up and working on breakfast. He wasn't, so she busied herself with the coffee maker. Maybe he'd taken a consultation call this morning while she was asleep. He took those sometimes. He might have received a call in for work, but there was no note, so she assumed he was around. He liked to run in the morning, so she chalked his absence up to that and set to work on breakfast.

The door opened, and Chad came into the kitchen a few minutes later. He caught her up by the waist and deposited her on the counter, pressing himself between her thighs to kiss her. "Did you sleep well, darling?"

She kissed him back with a sigh. "Yeah. Where did you go?"

"For the usual run. How are you feeling? Are you too sore for a swim?"

"No." She grinned. "You weren't *that* rough, Chad."

"I'm being considerate. Let me fuss." He kissed her cheek. "What are you cooking in here?"

"I was going to start eggs and bacon. Maybe some toast."

"That hungry? I don't usually eat that much for breakfast."

She raised a brow. "Chad, breakfast is the most important meal of the day. You know better!"

"Says the woman who usually just has coffee with me in the mornings."

She shrugged. "I eat before I come into work. I know you find it hard to believe since you always get up fifteen minutes before you have to go, but some of us do get up earlier."

He laughed. "Fair enough. I'll eat if you're planning to."

"Then you'd better let me down so I can cook."

He lifted her back down and dropped a kiss on the top of her head. "What can I do to help?"

"Uh, stand there and look pretty? The last time you helped me cook, you set off the fire alarm. I don't want to eat in a smoke-filled kitchen."

"You won't have to. I have a dozen other rooms to choose from if that's the problem. I'll handle the toast." He strode to the toaster and pulled a bag of bread from the bread holder. "I think I can manage that much."

She shrugged. "Suit yourself."

The two of them worked in companionable silence for a few minutes. She'd just taken the bacon and eggs off when his ringtone went off. He pulled the phone from his pocket with an apologetic smile and looked at the caller ID.

"Work?"

He shook his head. "Excuse me a minute, Lanie. I need to take this."

She frowned as he left the room. If it wasn't work, who was it? He never cared about taking normal calls in front of her. Even the odd ones he received were ignored when he was with her. He didn't usually excuse himself to answer. She set aside the plate of eggs and bacon to creep to the kitchen door.

I should trust him, a voice deep inside tried to reason, but she didn't listen to it. Something about Chad's behavior didn't sit right with her.

Chad was pacing in the dining room outside, his expression frustrated. "You know better than to call me like this, Rebecca. How many times have I ignored calls?"

She backed away from the door, heart squeezing and tears pressing at the corners of her eyes. Rebecca? Who in the world was that? He sounded annoyed she'd called like she had, but he hadn't hung up on her or told her not to call him again.

"You called because you want to hook up while you're in

town?" Chad sounded incredulous. "Since when has that been your M.O.? Look, don't—"

She spun on her heel and ran out of the kitchen's back door, heading into the living room on the other side. Her heart ached at what she'd heard, and she didn't trust herself to hear more without strangling Chad. The tears slid down her cheeks, and she fled upstairs to grab her stuff. She tried to ignore the rumpled sheets in his bedroom that provided evidence of last night's passions as she tossed on her sweats and jogging jacket. Snatching her purse, keys, and phone off his dresser, she hurried back downstairs and slipped out the back door. Chad was still in the dining room, pacing on the phone when she left.

Lanie drove home in a daze and settled in front of her TV. The noise filled the quiet space, but moments later, the numbness gave way to gut-wrenching tears that wouldn't stop. She felt stupid for believing Chad had changed, that she could trust his intentions. She'd done the very thing she'd promised herself all those months back; risk her job just to be another notch on Chad's belt. She trudged to her bedroom and curled up there, clutching a pillow to her chest and crying until sadness and exhaustion put her to sleep.

Chapter 9

Chad called at least twenty times in the next two days. Wanda had also called, checking in on her after her third sick day.

"Are you all right?" her supervisor and friend asked.

"No." She sniffled, the nearly constant tears that surfaced whenever Chad came to mind making a new appearance. "I can't be there right now, Wanda. Maybe tomorrow."

"Is it that bad? Chad's worried...he never worries. I think he's called a few dozen times, but he said you haven't picked up. You must've been sleeping when he called."

She burrowed deeper into her blankets and pillows, closing her eyes against the pain and the tears. "I just want to sleep, Wanda. I'm not up to talking."

Her friend's voice sharpened in concern. "There isn't anything else going on, is there?"

"Why would you think that?"

"I don't know. It's just unlike you to get sick. I mean, I know it happens, but it's just...it's unusual. And Chad seems restless, which isn't like him at all."

"Nothing else is going on."

"You sound like you've been crying." Wanda sounded suspicious.

"It's just the head cold. I'm sure it'll be better tomorrow. I'll try to be in if I'm well enough."

"Don't push yourself," Wanda replied. "Just let me know when you're ready to come back in."

"Okay, thanks."

Lanie hung up and curled up in a ball around her pillow, sobbing until she fell asleep again. She'd never felt so broken. It somehow felt worse than what Kaiden had put her through. She'd believed Chad had changed, but he'd been lying and toying with her all this time. Now she'd given him what he wanted, and he was back to business as usual. Except for the dozens of phone calls, but those could easily be explained by the fact that he hadn't finished with her and didn't know she'd caught on to his game. He still hadn't figured out that she knew he'd lied to her and wasn't going to talk to him.

She didn't know how long she drifted in and out of sleep before there was a knock at the door. Groaning, she sat up and forced herself to move. The persistent ring of the doorbell followed the knock. She threw a robe on and went to see who would be pounding down her door in the middle of the day like this.

When she opened the door, she found Chad standing there, looking worried and sleep-deprived. She froze for a moment, and then she tried to slam the door in his face. He caught it and pushed it open.

"Go away," she hissed. "I'm sick."

"I don't mind." He pushed inside and shut the door.

She backed away, pulling the robe tight. "Seriously, Chad, go away. I don't want you here."

He frowned. "You don't look sick...have you been crying?"

She wanted to curse at him for being so observant when she wanted him to go about his day without noticing anything was amiss. "No."

"You have! What happened? Are you feeling that ill? It doesn't look like you've been sleeping much." He took a step closer. "Poor baby...Is this why you took off a few days ago? If you'd told me you weren't feeling well, I would've driven you home. Come on.

Back to bed, and I'll make you some hot chicken noodle soup or some tea if you don't feel like food."

The kind façade on top of what she'd overheard was too much. "Get out!" Her voice rose. "Just get out, Chad."

He froze where he was, brow furrowing in confusion. "But...I don't...Lanie, I feel like I'm missing something here. What's wrong?"

"Everything. Just leave."

His shoulders slumped, and hurt flashed across his face. "Can't we talk this out and figure it out together? Is it something I did?"

"Yes, it is," she shouted. "And no, we can't! If you're not gone in five seconds, I'll start screaming for help. The neighbor will be over in less than a minute, and he's a cop."

Chad raised his hands, backing toward the door. "Okay, okay. I'm going...I'll see you at work, I guess. I really do want to work this out, Lanie, but I know when I'm pushing my luck by asking. I'll be here when you're ready to talk."

She crossed her arms and stared at him, tears partially held at bay by her anger. Then he was gone, and she crumpled to the floor, letting the sobs free. It all hurt so badly that she didn't know which way was up anymore. Would she ever be able to mend the brokenness inside after what he'd done to her?

***

Chad didn't know what he'd done to upset Lanie, but whatever it was, he needed to fix it fast. He hated not having their morning coffee together, not hearing her voice, and not seeing her smile. She'd returned to work today, a week after she'd kicked him out of her apartment, but she hadn't spoken a word to him beyond the ones required to do her job. She avoided him whenever he tried to talk with her, and she looked like she didn't know if she wanted to cry or hit him whenever she couldn't escape him.

He'd never felt like less of a man than he did at this moment with her ire directed at him and no idea what he'd done to put that look of anger and betrayal in her eyes. He left her alone like she'd demanded he did when he'd shown up at her apartment, but he knew he was becoming short and unusually rude with the rest of the staff as his own frustration mounted. He raked over their last moments before she'd fled, trying to decide what had happened. The only thing he could think of was the phone call, but he'd told Rebecca never to call again and had put her number on the blocked list after he'd hung up on her. When he'd gone looking for Lanie, she'd already gone, and he hadn't known what to make of it. Surely she wouldn't have run away because of a phone call that had ended with him cussing Rebecca out and demanding she forget his number like he'd wanted to forget hers?

He could tell his work quality was suffering as a result of what had happened, but it wasn't until they were in the OR that it really hit home. He stood over his patient, preparing to do bypass surgery, and his hands were unsteady, and he kept glancing around the room, looking for Lanie. There was no way he could do the work like this. He handed the tools off to his junior surgeon under the guise of having the young woman practice, but in truth, he was so distracted by Lanie's absence that he couldn't even do his work with his usual calm detachment.

The moment the surgery was finished, he walked out and cleaned up without a word to anyone. The younger surgeon looked crestfallen as he walked past her without comment on her work, but he couldn't muster up the energy to give his usual "well done," however well-deserved it was in this case. He just kept walking and went straight to his office, where he sat until the last surgery of the day was up. That was once again handed off to his junior, and he was glad it wasn't a difficult surgery. He'd done those earlier in the week while he still had a modicum of sanity. Kicking back in his chair, he tried to ignore the empty feeling inside as he watched Lanie leave for the day without a glance in his direction.

Once he was certain she'd left, he threw on his jacket and

grabbed his bag, leaving the office behind. He would go home and drink until he forgot the pain. Maybe he would find some random woman at a nightclub to take the edge off the pain. Even as the thought occurred to him, he tossed it out. He didn't even find the idea exciting like he once had. Lanie was all he wanted, the only one who left him wanting, even if she was the cause of his current pain. She was in his very soul now, and there was no way to get her back out. He told his clerk to move the elective surgeries he had for the rest of the week and to tell everyone he was taking a few days off. There was no point in being here for surgeries that his patients expected him to do if he was just handing them off to the other junior doctors. People could wait a few more days for elective surgeries that they didn't need urgently, and thankfully, he hadn't scheduled any with patients who would be seriously ill or dead if he didn't perform them now.

With that handled, he walked out of the hospital and drove home in a daze. Everything seemed darker and less appealing now without her. He found himself reaching out for her hand as he'd done every day for weeks, but she wasn't there, and his heart ached even more. He couldn't bear this agony, couldn't stand waiting fruitlessly for a call or a single clue as to what he'd done that was so bad she didn't even want to speak to him anymore. He wanted to respect Lanie's wish for space, but if he didn't have answers soon, he would go insane. Maybe a few days off would give him a more level head and allow both of them the space needed to clear the air when he returned. He could only hope it would.

Chapter 10

Chad didn't show up to work the next day, and Lanie was relieved when his receptionist told her he'd taken a few days off. She tried to hide it so that no one would know how hard his betrayal had shaken her, but Wanda knew something was off, and she'd finally had enough of keeping quiet.

Her friend pulled Lanie aside at lunch hour in Chad's office waiting room to talk. Without Chad around, the room was empty of the usual patients waiting for a consultation or test results. Lanie dropped into a chair with a tight smile and tried to look unconcerned. "What's this about? Am I in trouble?"

"No. No trouble, but we need to talk. What happened between you and Chad? Things were going great, and then they crashed and burned somehow. I have never seen that man stew so much over anything, let alone a woman." Wanda crossed her arms. "His behavior has proven me wrong. The man's head-over-heels for you, Lanie. Why are you avoiding him?"

Lanie stared down at her lap, fists clenching and tears welling as she seesawed between anger and heartbreak. "He's seeing other women on the side."

Wanda frowned. "That doesn't sound like him. Not when he's not through with a girl, and Chad Gatlin in love? I don't know, Lanie...It sounds a little ludicrous."

"I heard him on the phone. Some girl called him for a booty call. He didn't hang up. He just sounded mad she called him when he'd told her not to. He said it wasn't their M.O."

"Are you sure you understood correctly? Chad doesn't seem to understand what went wrong. He looks at you like a lost puppy that was kicked to the curb by its owner, not like a man begging forgiveness or shrugging off the infidelity."

"I..." Lanie shrank down in her seat, doubt dragging at her. "I don't know...I didn't stick around to hear the rest after that."

"So let me get this straight," Wanda said slowly. "You don't actually know if he cussed her out for calling him when he didn't want to hear from her, if he agreed to meet her, or if he just hung up and blocked her? You don't because you ran away instead of waiting for the call to end and dealing with whatever you heard?"

Her cheeks heated. "Well...you make it sound like I was in the wrong!"

"You kind of were, Lanie." As usual, Wanda pulled no punches. "He might not have done anything to cheat on you at all. He's never been like this with anyone before, and I think it's real. Even if he were cheating, you owed it to him to make sure before you ran out of respect for your promise to give him a chance. It was cowardly to run instead of facing him. You need to man up and go talk to him. He's still on leave for another day or two, so go over to his house and talk to him. Try to sort this out, and if you screwed up, apologize and fix it. You don't want to mess it up with a man who so clearly cares and wants you."

Lanie's tears won the battle with her anger. "But what if he did cheat? I can't handle that. Not again."

"That's what happened at your last job, isn't it?" Wanda pulled her to her feet and hugged her. "I'm sorry, hun. But give him a chance. Better a broken heart and knowing than a broken heart for nothing."

She nodded and hugged her back. "I'll go talk to him after my shift."

***

Chad's lights were on when she made her way up his long driveway to the mansion he called a home. A mixture of dread and relief flooded her as she spotted him moving behind his bedroom curtains. She froze on the doorstep, the urge to flee tugging at her even as she remembered her promise to Wanda. She'd promised to talk to Chad instead of continuing to run, and she needed to do it for her own sake so she could grieve and move on if she'd understood correctly.

She pressed the doorbell with a trembling finger and then snatched her hand back to wait. Wrapping her arms around her waist, she listened for his familiar footsteps. A moment later, she heard them on the stairs of the entryway. Then the door opened, and Chad stood there, hair disheveled and clothes rumpled, dark circles under his eyes betraying how little he'd been sleeping on his vacation. Was that because he was sleeping with every woman under the sun again, or was it because he was losing sleep over her? She didn't know. Biting her lip, she stared at him and tried to figure out how to start, or what to say.

"Lanie?" He looked confused and unsure if he could believe his own eyes.

"Can we talk?"

He stepped aside and waved her inside with a sad smile. "I'd like that. It's all I've wanted since you kicked me out of your apartment."

Guilt and pain washed over her, and she stepped inside, hovering to the side of the door as he closed it. She still didn't know if she wanted to stay or bolt. "I overheard you talking to Rebecca," she blurted out.

He tensed. "Is that what all this was about? If you overheard, then you know I ended the call by cussing her out for calling for the fifth time since she moved back into the city two weeks ago and then hung up. After that, I blocked her and went to find you, but you'd left. Is that call seriously what sent you running?"

"I didn't hear the rest," she whispered. "I only heard you

getting angry at her for calling when it wasn't her M.O. to call for a hookup. I thought maybe you were mad she didn't text instead so that you wouldn't have to answer the phone with me around."

"Far from it!" Chad dragged his hands through his hair with an exasperated sigh. "I can't believe this is what it's all been about. Lanie, what do I have to do to prove to you you're the only one I want? Do you want to know what I've spent the time off doing?"

She bit her lower lip and lifted her shoulder in uncertainty.

"I thought about going to a club to get laid so I could numb the pain," he snapped. "And then I realized I couldn't stand the thought of having sex with a woman who would only be a stand-in for you. So I came home and drank, slept, and wondered what I could do to fix it. But here you are, and you *still* don't trust me. You have no idea how much that hurts..." His voice softened. "Will you ever trust me?"

"I want to..." And then the whole story about Kaiden came tumbling out along with her tears.

Chad sighed and pulled her into his arms halfway through. She fought him at first and then gave in to her longing for comfort and the familiarity of his embrace, crying until she had no more left. Chad rubbed her back and made soothing noises, his anger seeming to have vanished.

"Oh, Lanie," he murmured as her tears subsided. "I'm sorry he put you through all of that, but I'm not Kaiden. I don't do that. If I were done with you, you'd know. I would never cheat. I'd just leave." He pulled away and took his phone from his pocket. "Here. Take a look at the blocked numbers list."

She took the phone after he'd unlocked it and scrolled through his contacts and the blocked numbers. The list of contacts had only a few names; hers, Wanda's, Mr. Adams, his receptionist's, and a few that looked like guy friends. The blocked list contained dozens of women's names, including Rebecca's. She looked up, the tears returning. "I'm sorry, Chad."

He reached out and wiped away her tears, pulling her in for a gentle kiss on the forehead. "I'm glad you came to me, even if I wish you would've said something sooner. Can we put this behind us, Lanie? Please? I'm miserable without you. I removed and blocked all of those numbers ages ago in an attempt to remove the worry you had over possible infidelity. Each time I got a call from an old hookup, I ignored it and then blocked the call. Rebecca slipped through the cracks. She'd called a few times that I'd missed, and she didn't leave a message any of those times, so I figured it wasn't important. She was one of the few women I spent significant time with, so I never thought she'd call for a hookup like that. I'm sorry too."

She relaxed into him and closed her eyes. "You don't have anything to apologize for. If you can forgive me, I want to put it behind us."

"Of course, darling. Forgiveness was never in question," he murmured. "I just wanted you to talk to me. Now, we'll forget all about this. From now on, we'll be transparent and open with one another to build a firm relationship. No secrets and no lies."

"No secrets and no lies," she whispered.

For the first time since Kaiden, she actually believed someone when they said those words.

Epilogue

Two years later

Lanie sat curled up in Chad's lap on the sofa in her parents' small apartment in Italy. They'd moved last year, after retiring. She and Chad had shared a few laughs over their escapades as they adjusted to living here. She was glad Chad had surprised her with this trip for their honeymoon to visit her parents.

He was laughing about some story her father was telling, but she was only half listening. Her hand rested lightly on her belly. She wasn't showing yet, but a visit to the doctor a few weeks before the wedding had confirmed it, and she'd only been waiting for the right time to share the news. With all of the family she cared about gathered in one small living room, she couldn't think of a better time to share it.

As usual, Chad noticed her distracted mood quickly. He kissed her temple and pulled her closer to rest against his chest. "Are you tired, darling? We can go back to our hotel."

She shook her head, relaxing into his embrace. "I'm not tired."

Her parents smiled at the two of them warmly. They'd taken to Chad right away, with her father claiming he was a good man because he provided for and loved her and her mother proclaiming him acceptable because he always paid close attention to her every need. Sometimes his attention could be smothering, but she loved him for caring enough to show that level of focus on her needs. It was a far cry from Kaiden and a much further cry from who he'd been when she'd first begun working on his department's nursing staff. With a baby on the way, the protectiveness he showed was bound to become more intolerable, but she reminded herself it was only a picture of how much he loved her.

"I have an announcement to make," she murmured.

Chad tensed. "It must be important. Take the mystery out of it for us, Lanie?"

Her parents waited expectantly, knowing she was never rushed into important conversations.

She took a deep breath, a smile slipping across her face. "I'm pregnant. The doctor confirmed it a few weeks ago."

The room remained still and silent for a long moment. Then Chad's face broke into a smile, and he hugged her tight with a strangled laugh. "Really?"

"Really."

"Wonderful, Lanie. I'm sure you'll be an excellent mother, and Chad will be a wonderful father as well."

She smiled back and accepted the words with a nod. The conversation turned to the baby's gender and other baby-related talk. Settling back in Chad's embrace, she reveled in the warmth of family and love, thinking how lucky she was. She never would have imagined falling for a reformed playboy, but here they were, and she was glad she had.

Actor Billionaire Daddy (Book 5)

TRIGGER WARNING

This book contains mentions of psychological abuse and threats by way of stalking behavior by an ex.

Blurb

Lowen Mcallister is a famous and rich actor. The world is his for the taking. Genevieve (Vi) Lanchester is his loyal stylist – and now she needs his help.

From the outside, Lowen's life looks like a dream that anyone would want. What they don't know is how lonely he is. He is blessed with a daughter, Emma, but after losing his wife, he feels something is missing. And he knows who he needs to make him feel whole again. He's loved Vi since he met her, but she was married then. He always thought she would fit in his family perfectly.

Vi felt nothing but pain in her marriage, seeking solace in the stability and comfort of her friendship with Lowen. So, when she found the courage to leave it behind, she thought she could start anew. If only it was that simple.

Emma's reluctance and Vi's ex prove to be barriers to their budding relationship.

What happens when her ex takes a life-threatening stance? Will Lowen step up? Will Vi trust their connection or run away?

Prologue

Two years earlier

Genevieve Lanchester clutched the signed divorce papers in her hand with a broad smile as she headed for Lowen's office in the back of the building where they'd been casting for the newest movie he was starring in. She hoped he'd be in. The need to share the news with someone burned in her chest, and Lowen was really the only friend she had—if her boss could be called a friend. With everything Arthur had put her through, she'd lost touch with her other friends. Traveling with Lowen for tours and interview trips didn't help much in that area of her life either.

Striding up to the door, she knocked and waited. Lowen pulled the door open, his dark hair tousled. He raised a brow at her. "Vi? I thought you had today off for court."

"I did." A broad grin split her face.

An answering one slowly spread across his face as his gaze dropped to the papers in her hand. "It's over?"

"I'm free," she whispered, hardly believing it. "Finally free!"

"This calls for a celebration, then!" He turned and returned to the office to grab his keys from the desk. "Come on."

"What?" She flushed and stepped out of the way as he walked into the hall. "Lowen, maybe that's a little much. I mean, I'm not sure...I haven't been...I don't think I can handle a bunch of people right now. It's been a bit of a big deal in the smaller papers. You know, *famous actor Lowen Mcallister's lead stylist wrapped up in nasty divorce*." She waved a hand with an awkward laugh. "It's dumb, but you know how the press goes wild for any hint of gossip. There's been a lot of speculation."

He stopped and pursed his lips, running his fingers through his dark hair. Then he nodded. "Then we'll celebrate privately. I've got that bourbon you really like in my home office."

She squirmed in place, biting her lip. "Maybe it's...I mean, I'm just your employee."

"So? You're more than just an employee, Vi. I'm not taking no for an answer on this one. If you don't want a celebratory bourbon, I'll find something else, but we're celebrating. That man ruined years of your life. He's not going to be the reason you fail to celebrate escaping his abusive, useless self." He held out a hand.

Well, if he was certain, maybe it was okay after all. It wouldn't be imposing if Lowen wanted to have her over, and they *did* spend a lot of time together in private when traveling. This wasn't that different. "Well...okay." She smiled shyly and took his hand.

He led her through the empty building, keeping her mind off her worries about propriety with a steady chat about the jewelry box he was carving for Emma, his fifteen-year-old daughter. She soon forgot to worry about whether she should go along with his suggestion and lost herself in listening to him regale her with tales of Emma as a child. It was really too bad that the girl had grown up without a mother, but Lowen did his best to make sure she didn't lack anything. Still, now that she was in her teen years, the truth was painfully obvious to anyone watching—Lowen was great, but he couldn't be the womanly influence Emma needed. She felt a pang of sympathy for him as she listened. He was a good man, and he tried hard. It wasn't fair that he couldn't be what Emma needed despite how hard he tried.

Lowen settled her into the passenger's seat of his Aston Martin and then hopped in on the driver's side, starting up the car with a sigh of relief. "Feels nice to walk out of work knowing I have a relaxing evening ahead."

"What were you doing in the office this late, anyway? I wasn't sure you'd still be in, but I figured I'd try. I thought...Well, I thought showing up at your home would be intruding, so I figured if you weren't there, I'd just share the news in the morning."

"I was just going over some lines for my part." He pulled out of the parking garage and onto the busy city streets. "And never think you're intruding to come to visit. I meant it when I said you were more than an employee, Vi. You're a friend, too, one of the few I have. I don't take that lightly."

She felt her cheeks warm and let silence fall between them at that. Lowen glanced at her in the dim light from the traffic outside, his expression wistful as though he wanted to say more but was holding back. He turned his attention back to the road, and they rode in silence until they reached the outskirts of the city where his giant estate sat. He parked the car and helped her out, guiding her inside.

"Won't we disturb Emma?"

"She's at a sleepover with some girls from school. We have the place to ourselves." His hand settled on her lower back, high enough to be proper but low enough to send a shiver down her spine. "Come on. The bourbon's in the office."

She couldn't help admiring the sleek cherry wood railings of the winding staircase as they walked up the stairs and then down the hallway on the thick blue and white floral carpet to his office. He pushed a heavy cherry wood door open at the end of the hall and gently pushed her inside. "Behold." He stretched an arm out dramatically with a teasing grin. "The office."

A laugh bubbled out of her, and the earlier uncertainty faded just like that. "It's magnificent."

And it was. The sleek interior had gleaming cherry wood surfaces to match the decor outside, adding a touch of old-fashioned charm to the place. His desk matched the wood but had a glass surface. She even spotted an old-fashioned quill pen and inkwell on the corner of the desk. His private sanctuary had an inviting, lived-in feel that was uniquely Lowen. She trailed to the bookcases, looking over the worn spines of the books he'd chosen to stock here, then moved on to the little table in the corner where the beginnings of the jewelry box for Emma's birthday sat.

Lowen unstopped the crystal decanter of bourbon and poured them both a glass of ice before joining her and handing hers over. "Here you are, as promised. To new beginnings."

She clinked her glass to his with a soft smile. "To new beginnings."

Soon, the two of them were laughing and exchanging remarks about their encounters with Arthur.

"Did you see his face when I told him I was through?" She hiccupped on a laugh, setting aside her third bourbon of the night. "Priceless. But I think the look on his face when I walked away with half the property and told him to keep the rest so long as he stayed out of my life was probably better."

Lowen stared at her with a smile. "I don't actually think I did. At the Christmas party last year, right?"

"Right."

"Nope. Didn't see it because I was watching you. The look on your face when you told him...I don't think I've seen a more shocked and relieved look on anyone's face." He leaned closer as they sat on the couch and reminisced. "It might have been the most beautiful thing I've seen."

She flushed and giggled. "Lowen! You can't...You're not serious."

He tipped her chin up with a finger. His dark eyes fixed on her lips. The smile on his full mouth captured her attention as well. She wondered if he'd kiss her and then suppressed another giggle. Lowen wouldn't kiss her, would he? He was much older at 42 and probably preferred experienced women, not a 27-year-old woman who had married out of high school to a boy who went from doting to abusive in less than a year. She didn't know anything outside of Arthur, and the experiences he'd offered had been sadly lacking.

When his lips landed on hers, it took a moment for her to process what was happening. Lowen was kissing her. *Her.* His stylist. The heat spread from her cheeks to her ears, neck, and chest, but she didn't stop him. Instead, she leaned into him and invited more, waiting for him to accept the invitation to take it further. A soft moan escaped her.

That small noise seemed to snap Lowen out of it. He jerked back with a groan and shoved his fingers through his hair. "I...I shouldn't have done that, Vi. Sorry. Sorry, I've made it awkward now, haven't I? Look...We should...Let's go watch a movie, yeah? I'll go pop us some popcorn. I've got that new comedy action film that came out. We can watch that."

She stared down at her lap numbly and nodded, wondering what she'd done to make him pull away. She hoped he didn't regret the kiss because she certainly didn't.

Chapter 1

One year later

Vi opened her front door and stepped outside to head to work. She tripped over a package and glanced down with a frown. Bending down, she picked up the strangely shaped package and carried it inside. It didn't have a note or address on it, and it hadn't been delivered by the post office, whatever it was. Since she had a few moments to spare, she set it on the counter and tugged the coarse brown string off the brown paper. The packaging fell open to reveal a little bird with its throat cut and a typed note in its mouth.

A screech escaped her, and she darted back, heart hammering. Who would send her something like this? Why? What was the point? She stared at the little songbird with tears blurring her vision, her hands trembling over her mouth. Her breakfast was threatening to make a reappearance, but she forced herself to get a grip so that she could look at the note she'd spotted. Perhaps that would hold answers about who had sent this sick little gift.

Plucking it out of the bird's beak with a gag, she opened it with shaking fingers. Only one sentence had been typed on its white surface, and it was plain printer paper, offering no clues about the sender's identity.

If you won't sing for me, then you won't sing for anyone.

She closed her eyes with a sob. It was probably another stupid stunt Arthur had pulled. She'd already taken out a restraining order on him after the divorce had been forced through against his wishes. He always possessed a twisted sense of humor, and this was exactly the stupid thing he'd do to scare her just to get a thrill. He'd been leaving gifts without notes, much like he'd done in the days when he'd cared about courting her favor before their wedding. She'd ignored it. She could ignore this too. It was all a dumb, screwed-up game of his, but it didn't mean anything.

She picked up the paper and the bird and threw them all into the trash. She had to get to work on time today to prep Lowen for his interview. There wasn't time to dwell on how different and scarier this particular gift seemed. She hurried out and clambered into her car, taking off for the office.

When she reached the location where they were meeting with the news channel's interviewer, Lowen was waiting in the back room for her. He'd already taken care of the things she usually did as his stylist, and she grimaced when she spotted the time on the wall. The time she'd taken to deal with Arthur's crazy little game had put her behind and left her in traffic. She'd arrived fifteen minutes late. "I'm so sorry, Lowen! I was on time, but I was held up in traffic."

He crossed his arms with a stern frown. "I'm not concerned about having to brush my own hair once in a while, Vi. Did you eat? You look a little shaky."

The realization that Arthur's stunt was still impacting her appearance and behavior left her feeling sick. She should just let go of it. He was doing it to get a reaction just like this, and she shouldn't give him the satisfaction. "I ate."

"Are you sick?" He pushed away from the dressing table and came closer, pressing the back of his hand to her forehead. "You don't feel like you have a fever."

"It's fine, Lowen. I'm fine."

He frowned, obviously not convinced. "You're a very bad liar,

Genevieve. If you've eaten and you're not sick, then why do you look shaken up and tired? Did you stay up too late, or has something happened?"

She pushed at his chest until he backed off and gave her room to breathe. Sighing, she ran her hands over the front of her pencil skirt and tried to compose herself. "I'm fine, Lowen. Really, I am. You have twenty minutes to be ready for the interview. Are you prepared?"

His frown turned to an annoyed scowl. "I hate doing these. They always want to know more than I want to share."

"The griefs of being a celebrity." She stepped closer and straightened his tie. "Don't worry about it. You'll do well, just like you always do."

He opened his mouth to reply when his mobile rang, pulling his attention away from her and the interview. With an impatient sigh, he picked up. "Mcallister."

She couldn't hear the other side of the conversation, but judging from the frustration and anger on his face, it wasn't anything good.

"Where is she now?"

There was an indistinct reply on the other side.

"I'll be there to get her in twenty minutes." He hung up with a groan of irritation and shoved the phone into his pocket. "Come on. We have to postpone the interview."

She tucked her hands under her arms with a frown. "What's happened?"

"Emma has...she and her friends were caught doing weed on school property." He scrubbed a large hand over his face. "I swear she will give me gray hairs before my time. I never knew having a teenage girl could be so frustrating."

"Well, we'd better go get her. Do you think the cops will charge her?"

"I don't know." He grabbed his suit jacket and threw it on, adjusting his cuffs and his Rolex. "But if they don't do anything,

I'll ground her for the next year for this. This is the last straw. You don't mind coming along, do you?"

"Are you sure? I mean…It's sort of a family affair."

"I'd welcome the moral support," he muttered, heading for the door. "You don't mind, do you?"

She didn't. It would keep her mind off the disturbing gift on her doorstep this morning, and it would keep Lowen from thinking to ask any further awkward questions too. She wasn't going to object to that. "Let's go."

***

Lowen tucked Vi into the passenger's seat of his Aston and then climbed in on the driver's side. His thoughts were consumed with worries about what had happened to make Vi late, putting such a pale cast on her face, and concerns about Emma. Between the two, he could barely manage to focus on driving and remained silent, clenching the steering wheel and weaving in and out of traffic.

When he had Emma handled, he would dig further to find out what was going on with Vi. She really was a terrible liar, and something had happened. Concern brought his protective instincts to the surface, and he didn't like to think too much about why he felt that way toward his stylist. Thinking about it always left him thinking about that moment in his office a year ago when he'd let alcohol prompt him to act on his desires. That single kiss had played on repeat countless times since that night, but he told himself every time not to pursue anything, even though she'd openly invited him to take the kiss further. She was dealing with a lot, and although the divorce was finalized, Arthur continued to be a problem, forcing her to file for a restraining order on him. She certainly didn't need him to add to the stress. Perhaps in a year or two—if she wanted him and hadn't found someone younger without a teenage daughter in the mix.

He pulled into the parking lot of the downtown police department with a grimace. Right now, there wasn't anything he could do about the situation with Vi. He could, perhaps, run damage control on the situation with Emma, though. Vi clambered out of the car before he could come around to help her out, a little habit of hers he had to remind himself not to comment on. She wasn't his, and he couldn't be correcting her for not letting him do things for her as if she were. It wouldn't be appropriate. If she were his, though…He'd open every door, and she'd learn to let herself enjoy the small things he could do to help her. He'd make sure she knew how special she was. Instead, he settled for beating her to the door of the building and opening that.

Inside, they went to the front desk and told the secretary on duty that they were there to pick up Emma. The woman's lips pinched in disapproval, but she disappeared to collect someone who could speak to them. An officer joined them a few moments later, nodding politely to Vi and reaching out to shake Lowen's hand.

"Are you Officer Shipton, sir?"

The officer nodded. "Yes, sir. Your daughter's in one of the cells sleeping off the high."

"What will the penalty be?"

The officer's brows rose. "I'm surprised you aren't asking what you can pay to get her out of trouble."

Lowen winced. "I'm not the average celebrity, officer, and I think she's earned her punishment. I just…I don't suppose she'll get off with community service."

"I'll talk to the judge about it." Officer Shipton crossed his arms. "She's a minor and a first-time offender. You should thank God she didn't get behind a car high, or it might be a different story. Most she'll get is a misdemeanor this time. I'll see if we can get it reduced to community service because if she's caught again, she'll end up with a felony charge."

"Can she be released to my care?" Lowen asked.

"On bail until her court date…But I think the judge could hear her case soon." The officer eyed the two of them. "If you don't bail her, she'll stay here in our cells until her hearing in a week or two."

"She'll be safe?"

"We'll keep her separate from the ones that would cause trouble. She's in her own cell for now."

His jaw tightened. This wasn't Emma's first time in trouble, though drugs were a new low, even for her. If this was her way of asking for attention, it was a poor one. She never had to ask for his attention, and to go to these depths to get what she could have without even asking left him frustrated and confused. Where had he gone wrong in raising his little girl? It was obvious Emma needed a motherly influence to guide her, someone who could balance out his usual sternness with a gentler touch to coax Emma into wiser choices. He glanced at Vi, thinking about all she'd experienced at Emma's age and realizing she stood a better chance of filling that role than anyone else in their lives right now. "Maybe she'll learn the lesson if she stays the week. Can I speak with her?"

"Sure can." The officer escorted the two of them through. "I'll bring her out."

He and Vi waited at the officer's desk for Emma. When she was led out, hope and relief dawned on her face. Then her expression turned to one of embarrassment when she spotted Vi beside him. She lowered her head with a scowl and left the officer to drag her the rest of the way to them. He pushed her down into a chair with a shake of his head. "Kid, you ought to show a little gratitude to your folks for trying their best for you."

She snorted. "You mean my dad. I don't have a mom."

The officer cleared his throat. "Well, clearly, this young lady cares enough about you to be here. Show a little respect. Otherwise, I might change my mind about advising the judge to let you off easy. Could send you to juvie for this."

Emma stiffened and fell silent.

"Could we have a minute, officer?"

The man nodded and left to talk to a colleague at another desk nearby. Lowen turned to Emma with a scowl. "Are you serious, Emma? Weed?"

"Are you going to bail me out?"

"No." He crossed his arms. "No, we are not. You're going to stay until your trial date. Maybe it'll teach you to make smarter decisions to avoid negative consequences. I love you, kiddo, but I'm not going to bail you out of your own foolishness all the time. You've got to learn to make wiser choices, and that starts now. I can't get you out of this one."

"Can't or won't?" Emma challenged.

Vi shifted uncomfortably beside him. He wrapped an arm around her waist without thinking about it, stilling her fidgeting so that he could focus on his pouting daughter. "Both. You'll be staying, Emma. That's final. Next time you do something like this, it won't be so simple to bail you out, either. I'd rather you learned from this than from real jail time for the next incident."

"It was just weed," she grumbled. "And I only had a little."

"I don't care. It's illegal and not the smart thing to do, even if it were legal. You're my daughter, and no daughter of mine is going to light up just to have fun or deal with stress. If something's driving this, we'll talk about it. If you just think this is fun, I hope that the next week in that jail cell will correct that misconception."

"You can't just leave me here!" Her voice rose. "I'm just a kid."

"Emma, your father is right," Vi murmured. "You should be thankful you have a dad looking out for you like this. Mine didn't care, and I made a lot of dumb decisions trying to deal with everything. I didn't have anyone to protect me. Please listen to your father..."

He squeezed her hip in silent gratitude for the support.

Emma scoffed. "You don't know the first thing about my life! Just because you've been working for my dad for six years and..." she stared pointedly at his arm around Vi's waist, "...may be screwing around with him, doesn't mean you have a clue what my life's like. Butt out!"

"Emma Marie Mcallister!" A low growl of warning rumbled through him. "You apologize for that right now."

Emma crossed her arms and stared back in mute rebellion. They stared at one another for a long while before it became clear neither of them would win. The officer returned, breaking the standoff. He cleared his throat and took Emma by the arm. "Time to go back to the cell. Mr. Mcallister, if there's anything you want to bring for her, feel free to stop by with it. I think we can allow her a few items for comfort's sake."

"Like my phone?" Emma snarked. "I'd like that back if we're allowing things for comfort's sake."

"That's a privilege, and we don't give it to little girls who go smoking weed," the officer drawled.

Lowen spotted Vi hiding a smile behind her hand and pretending to cough. He had to fight to hide his own amusement at the officer's response. Clearly, Emma wasn't going to wrap anyone here around her little finger like she'd done at school with the staff or at home with his own employees. It would be good for her to learn that not everyone would bow at her feet just because she carried his last name. "I'll be by with a few things and to visit, if it's allowed. Otherwise, I'll see you when we meet with the lawyer and then again in court, Emma."

Emma huffed. "I hate you!"

The officer scowled down at her. "None of that, kid. Your dad doesn't have to bring anything by. I also don't have to let you have any of it."

That shut Emma's attitude down. She became silent, sulking as the officer led her away. Lowen sighed and scrubbed his hand over the back of his neck. He and Vi left the police station in subdued silence.

"I'm sorry you had to see that," he told her when they were back in the car.

"I've seen worse," she replied mildly. "Are you all right?"

"I'll be fine." He really hoped it wasn't a lie.

Chapter 2

A week to Emma's court date passed without incident and in a blur of interviews. The word about Emma had leaked, and everyone had questions. Lowen had been tense and jittery all week, but Vi had talked him into coming over for dinner to get away from it all. Her house was out in the country. She didn't use it much when they weren't here in California, but it was a nice getaway when she needed it. Now Lowen needed it, and she was determined to be a friend in this time of need. He'd been a friend of hers many times before.

She was also determined that she wouldn't let herself be more than a friend. Ever since their kiss last year, she'd been unable to see him the same way, but she wasn't about to let Lowen know that. The embarrassment and confusion she'd felt when he'd pulled away after that kiss without taking it further wasn't something she was eager to repeat. Besides, as nice as he'd be about the letdown, she was certain he regretted the kiss, and he was her boss anyway. That made him off-limits.

There was more to it than that, though. More than held her back from even trying. Deep down, she knew she was afraid. Afraid that, like Arthur, Lowen would turn out to be a man who was not what she'd believed him to be. Even though they'd known each other for six years now and had gone through a great many challenges, she couldn't push aside the fear that people were not who they claimed to be thanks to what Arthur had done to her.

No, it was best they remained nothing but friends. She could manage friendship, and he and Emma needed her right now. She didn't need anything more from Lowen than friendship, and he didn't want anything from her besides that. She couldn't let herself forget it.

The doorbell rang, and she dried her hands off on a towel before going to the door. She was expecting Lowen, but instead, she found another brown package tied with twine. Her heart began to beat rapidly in her chest, and she bent to pick it up hastily in case Lowen pulled in and saw it. She needed to throw it away before he could see and ask questions. She wouldn't have their relaxing evening ruined by Arthur. Glancing around to see if she could catch sight of her ex, she found no one and retreated back into the house with a quiet whimper of concern.

She tossed the package into her trash can without another glance. It was just a sick game to intimidate and punish her. It wasn't anything to worry about. She shouldn't have let herself think about it when she and Lowen were meant to be enjoying a relaxing night with good food and a comedy show they could both enjoy.

The doorbell rang again, and this time, she jumped before laying a hand over her chest and taking a few deep breaths to steady her nerves. It would be Lowen this time. Arthur wouldn't risk coming back a second time now that she was already alert. She went to open the door and found a smiling Lowen on the other side. He handed her a wine bottle with a fancy label she didn't recognize.

"You didn't have to, Lowen!"

"I know." He tucked his hands into his pockets and stepped inside, closing the door and taking off his shoes before he followed her into the rest of the house. "I wanted to, though. Consider it a thank you for taking the time to cook."

"Don't thank me until you've eaten," she said. "It's not anything fancy, and I'm not the best cook."

"Simple is fine. What did you make?"

"Spaghetti casserole," she mumbled, fiddling with the ice machine to fill a bucket for the wine. "Like I said...nothing fancy."

"My mom used to make that for us on weekends." He offered her a genuine smile. "I haven't had it in years. It sounds wonderful right now."

She settled the cabernet bottle into the ice and went to pull the casserole from the oven.

"Anything I can do?"

"Do you want to set the table?" She pulled the casserole out and set it on the stovetop to cool for a moment so she could cut it.

"Sure." He began to rummage around until he had two plates and glasses.

On his way back, he stopped by the silverware drawer. He stopped digging around for forks and cleared his throat. She turned to him with a spatula in hand. "What is it?"

"I think you might have accidentally dropped a package in the trash." He bent and pulled the crudely wrapped box from the trash can.

Her heart pressed into her throat, and her stomach flipped. "Uh...No, it's empty. I didn't need the packaging."

He quirked a brow in response. "Have I told you you're a terrible liar? This isn't empty."

Her cheeks warmed. "Oh. Well...I..."

"Why did you throw it away?" He set the package on the counter. "I would've assumed you did it by accident, but now you've lied, so I'm curious."

"I didn't want it," she whispered, turning away to cut the spaghetti casserole.

"Is it another gift from Arthur?" he asked gently. "If it is, just say so. I don't need to know more."

"I don't know if it is," she told him. "If it is, he isn't labeling them. I just assume he is the one sending it because it's like all the others he used to give me when I was in high school, and he was trying to cajole me into being his."

"I see. Hasn't the restraining order been enough of a hint for him?"

"I guess not," she mumbled.

There was a quiet thud, and she turned to see that Lowen had tossed it into the trash again.

"We'll leave it at that. He has no place in our conversation this evening when we're trying to relax." Lowen opened her silverware drawer and pulled out two forks and knives, taking them to the table. "Table's set. Anything else?"

"Could you pull the salad out of the fridge?" She returned to cutting up the casserole with a relieved smile.

Unlike Arthur, Lowen understood that not everything had to be discussed, and he could take the hint when she didn't want to talk about things. She needed that from her only close friend at this moment, and she was grateful he'd given it. She really didn't want to know what was in that package, and if Lowen had insisted they open it, she wasn't sure she could've handled it. Instead, he'd set it aside and effectively given her the room to do so as well. She relaxed and took the casserole out to the table, joining him with a smile and putting Arthur out of her mind.

***

Emma was let off lightly with the requirement that she complete mandatory counseling and thirty hours of community service. Lowen made her begin both right away, knowing that it would be harder to complete the work and the counseling when he wasn't around to keep her on task. He had a tour of Europe coming up in a few weeks, and he didn't want to leave Emma unsupervised with counseling and community service left to do.

"Come on, Dad," she whined from the back of the car on the way home from the station. "I have six months to do the work. I don't need to start now."

Lowen pinched the bridge of his nose and wished he had a wife by his side to help him and support him. He'd appreciated having Vi by his side at the hearing, but he hadn't felt right asking her to drive home with him and Emma afterward, so he was on his own. He wished, not for the first time, that he had her here, that she was his partner in dealing with life in general and Emma more specifically. Right now, though, she had enough to worry about with Arthur's persistent attention and gifts. The man was leaving her stressed out and worried, and he wasn't going to add to the concerns. "You will start now, Emma. I'm going on tour in three weeks, and I won't leave you when you haven't done your community service."

"You could just take me along then instead of leaving me behind like always." She crossed her arms and slouched in the seat.

"I can't bring you along if you still have service requirements to fulfill, Emma. You know that. The judge told you it must be done before you leave the state."

She rolled her eyes. "Even if I finish it, you won't let me come. Even though this is a summer trip, just like the last one, you'll still say I have to stay home with the nanny."

"Emma, you know I'd love to have you along, but you'd be bored out of your mind."

"Genevieve will be around. She and I can do stuff while we're waiting on you."

"Genevieve is with me during interviews. There won't be anyone to watch you while I'm busy."

"I'm sixteen. I don't need a babysitter, Dad!"

"What happened last week says otherwise," he snapped. "I'm not letting you go anywhere unsupervised after what we just went through!"

"Why? Afraid I might do something to hurt your precious image in front of the public?"

He jerked the steering wheel, pulling into their driveway with a harsh laugh before parking and turning to look at her. "Do you seriously think that's what this is about, Emma Mcallister?"

She opened her mouth to reply, and he raised a hand to cut her off. "No, I don't want to hear it. This has absolutely nothing to do with my image and everything to do with wanting my daughter to be alive, well, and successful. How will your future look like with criminal charges on your record?"

Emma looked away. "It was just a little weed. We didn't go anywhere or try to drive. No one was hurt."

He climbed out of the car with a sigh and pulled open her door, taking her by the wrist and tugging her out of the car. "And thank God for that, sweetheart, but you know it's not enough. A little weed at your age is still illegal, and I don't like the trajectory. I can't stop you if you want to do it when you're legal. I can beg you to make smarter choices, but I can't stop you. Right now, you're sixteen, and I definitely can put a stop to it. Inside. Now. You're grounded for the next two weeks."

"Dad!" she whined. "I already spent a week in jail!"

"This isn't about the weed. It's to give you time to think about your nasty attitude and what needs to change before you make a really big mistake that I can't get you out of, little girl. Go on." He pointed to the house. "Don't make me take your phone and laptop too. Summer vacation's two weeks away, and you're already expelled from yet another school."

Pouting, she spun on her heel and marched to the house with a grumble. He locked the car and followed after her with a heavy sigh. This was becoming a nightmare. How was he meant to handle parenting a rebellious teenage daughter with no mother to help manage her while he wasn't able to be there? Worse still, how was he meant to deal with her as she grew into a young woman and needed him around? Maybe he should retire soon. It wasn't as if he didn't have enough money to do it. He loved the movies and set, but he hated the spotlight and was getting tired. All he wanted was to be home with his daughter, not lose all the time he had left before she'd be grown and gone, leaving him alone.

Emma slammed the door before he could reach it. He raked his fingers through his hair, wishing his house hadn't become a war zone instead of a quiet place to let down his walls. He missed the days of reading bedtime stories to her, and the time they'd spent taking solace in one another's company after her mom passed away, leaving him with an eight-year-old who didn't understand yet what had happened.

The door to the house swung open before he could turn the handle. Genevieve stood on the other side with two steaming mugs of hot chocolate. She handed him one and shut the door behind him. "Your housekeeper let me in and said I could wait for you. I figured you might need someone to vent to when you get back. I'm not too old to remember what the days of being a teen girl were like."

He took the hot chocolate with a grateful smile. "You didn't have to."

"I know." She sipped at her own hot chocolate and stared down at the rug, studiously avoiding his gaze. "But I don't feel like being home right now."

"Why not? It has to be quieter than here right now."

Emma's door slammed. As usual, she wanted to make sure they all knew how unhappy she was. He grimaced and took a long drink from his own mug. "As I said…trust Emma to make my point for me."

She finally met his gaze with a sympathetic smile. "Maybe I can talk to her."

"Give her space right now. I wouldn't go anywhere near her yet unless you want your head ripped off." He took her elbow and guided her to the living room, sinking down onto the inviting red suede cushions. "Why don't you want to be home?"

"It's too empty." She evaded his gaze but sat obediently beside him when he hooked his fingers through her belt loops and tugged gently.

"You've never complained about it before."

"I hadn't received a dead bird and ominous notes on my doorstep before, either," she said softly.

He felt awful for sending her home by herself now. Of course she wouldn't want to be there alone after what she'd been sent. He wrapped an arm around her tiny waist and pulled her close. "I should've asked if you wanted to come back here with us. I just thought you had a lot going on yourself and wouldn't want to put up with Emma. She argued and snapped at me the whole ride home."

She leaned her head on his shoulder with a tired sigh. "It's all right. I'll be fine. I just needed to be away from the place for a little while."

"Stay here tonight?" He let himself run his fingers through her loose blonde curls. "We have plenty of room."

Just like that, the tension in her body came roaring back. She sat up and scooted further away with a shake of her head, hiding behind her mug. "I can't. I'll be fine, Lowen."

He resisted the urge to comment that he very much doubted that, given how pale she seemed. Had she been gifted yet another macabre present this morning that she hadn't told him about? He wouldn't put that past her abusive ex, but she didn't seem ready to talk about it, so he let it go. She'd come to him when she was ready, and as long as he had no evidence she was in danger, he'd leave the timing in her hands.

Vi didn't need another overbearing male pushing into her life after she'd finally freed herself from the abuse of one man. Lowen might not be abusive, but he could be intense when he decided to turn his full focus onto something or someone, and he wasn't sure she was ready for that. Best to let her come to him lest he scare his little, timid bird off. In time, she would learn he wanted her and would do anything to see her happy and cared for, and then—if he had read her correctly—she would have no qualms about coming to him. He just had to be patient and let her decide.

Chapter 3

When Lowen's daughter stopped by the studio where her father was filming for his newest movie, Vi was surprised. Emma rarely came to work with her father anymore; these days, she'd seemed unwilling to be around him any more than necessary. It had been years since the teen had stopped in while her father was filming to watch or to talk to him.

"Emma," Vi said.

Emma frowned and glanced around. "My dad's not here, right? I'm doing community service in the area, and we're on lunch break."

"He's on set and won't be back for an hour or so." Vi patted the empty spot on the sofa beside her. "I'm taking a break myself. How is community service going?"

The teen eyed her. "Do you really care, or are you just going to report back to my dad? The last girlfriend he had told him everything I did that annoyed her."

Vi smiled and patted the spot again. "I'm not his girlfriend, and unless you're doing something to endanger yourself or land yourself back in a jail cell, I think we can keep whatever you want to say between us."

Emma bit her lip, surprise, and uncertainty in her eyes. "That's not what adults usually say."

She shrugged. "I'm not most adults. I'm also still *just* young enough to remember what it was like to be your age." She held her fingers up with a little space between them. "Just barely. Give it another year or so, and I might forget."

The girl snorted, but she joined Vi on the couch. "Yeah, like my dad. He used to be fun."

"You two both used to be different people, Emma." Vi took a sip of her water and poured a second glass for the younger girl. "I remember when you used to come to the studio with him on days when you weren't in school. Remember when he took you on that tour in England when you were twelve for summer vacation?"

She made a face. "Yeah. I remember sitting in interview rooms for hours and being bored out of my mind, but I guess the nights when he'd take me to see the sights kinda made up for it."

"That was a fun trip. You were a fun kid." Vi smiled sadly. "I think he misses those days too, you know."

"Wouldn't know it from how he acts," Emma muttered. "I asked him to take me with you guys on this next tour, and he told me I'm not responsible enough, and he wants me here in therapy. As if I can't do therapy online if I need to. He just doesn't want me around."

"Hon, that's not true." Vi set her water aside. "Your dad is at a loss. He knows he's not really what you need now, and he doesn't know how to be there for you right now. I think he misses having your mom around to help."

"Mom was always way better at the emotional crap than him," Emma admitted quietly. "It's like I'm talking to a brick wall when I talk to him about anything."

"Sounds like you miss her too."

"It's been ten years," the teen murmured, as if that meant she shouldn't miss her mother.

"That doesn't mean you can't miss her, Emma."

Emma's grip tightened on her cup. "It's just hard! He doesn't get it. I can't talk to him about boys or the latest mean girl at school. I can't tell him about how everyone is nice to my face but talks behind my back or the way everyone else just sucks up because he's the famous actor in the Shadow superhero films. I can't even tell him the press snaps photos or accosts me at school for interviews because if I did, he'd put a security detail on me, and I'd lose that little bit of freedom I have left."

Vi's heart squeezed for the girl. It couldn't be easy being Lowen's daughter. She'd had a small taste of how the press ate up any story and any hint of scandal surrounding Lowen when they'd dragged her messy divorce through the spotlight. She could only imagine the pressure Emma must be enduring. "He can be overprotective, I know, but it's because he cares. I get not wanting to talk to him about the kids at school or boys, though." She gave a mock shiver. "He'd probably lock you in your room for eternity if he caught wind of any interest in boys. My dad didn't care, but my mom was kind of like that, like she was trying to make up for what he wasn't." She hadn't stopped Vi from taking up with Arthur, though. "Still, as hard as he can be on you, it's better than not caring at all, Emma. I had the 'not caring at all' dad, and believe me when I say that I'd take a dad like Lowen over that any day."

Emma fiddled with the hem of her shirt. "I don't know...I wish he'd let up a little. Can...can you talk to him? I know you said you're not his girlfriend, but I'm not blind. I know he likes you. Maybe you can convince him to let me come on the tour?"

Vi choked on her water at the remark. Lowen? Liked her? Emma needed her eyesight checked. "Uh...I'm just a friend, Em. He doesn't like me. I don't think he'll change his mind just because I talked to him, either."

Emma rolled her eyes. "Seriously? You'd have to be half-blind to miss it! I've never seen him look at the one or two women he's been with since my mom like he looks at you. Seriously, it's kind of gross since it's my dad, but...I'd kill to have a guy look at me like that."

Her cheeks flamed, and the heat spread up into her ears. "I really think you're seeing things." She wasn't going to tell Lowen's kid that the man had kissed her and then run for the kitchen like he'd burned himself two seconds after.

If Lowen liked her, he had a bizarre way of showing it. Men who liked a woman generally didn't refuse an open, blatant invitation to make a chaste kiss something much more intimate and heated. Besides, she'd already screwed up one relationship, and managed to turn one man so crazed he was sending dead birds to her doorstep. What if Lowen ended up being the same? What if she ruined that too? It was better not to risk it.

Emma cast her a pleading look.

She sighed. "But I'll talk to him, Em. Now, are you going to get in trouble with your parole officer for taking off?"

Emma stood and set her empty cup on the table in front of the sofa. "No. He knows I went to see my dad on set down the road, and I promised to be back in thirty. If I hurry, I'll be back before there's any trouble. I'm not under arrest or anything. If I do my hours and see the therapist, I'm free to do as I please."

"Better get going, then. I'll talk to him, Emma, but I'm not making any promises."

"Not asking you to. I know he's a tough nut to crack." Emma offered her a rare smile. "I'm just pretty sure you'll manage to crack him. See you later, Vi."

"See you later." Vi watched her go with an amused smile and wondered if Emma was going to be disappointed. She doubted Lowen would change his mind just because Vi asked and told him Emma missed spending time with him, but she'd promised, so she would give it a try, at least.

Chapter 4

"You think I should bring Em along with us?" Lowen gaped at Vi. "Are you serious? She'll be unsupervised, and she'll get into trouble! It could cause an international scandal. That girl knows how to find trouble of unprecedented proportions."

He and Vi were sitting at a small table in a little takeout place they'd found a few weeks ago after a late night on set. They'd taken off early to get some lunch so they could pack for the trip. Vi had sprung this on him during their first real conversation in the last two weeks, and he had to admit it wasn't what he'd expected.

"Lowen, she misses you."

"Did she put you up to this?"

"She asked," Vi admitted. "But I said yes. She didn't make me do it. If you're worried, I'll keep an eye on her. When I'm not needed with you for interviews, I can take her shopping or go sightseeing to keep her out of trouble."

Lowen groaned. He didn't want to tell Vi no, especially when she seemed determined to have a yes out of him. At the same time, it was last minute. They were leaving tomorrow morning. "Is this why Emma completed her community service hours in record time? And opened up to the therapist enough for them to sign off after a few sessions?"

Vi flushed and shrugged. "She's pretty determined. I think that's proof enough of how badly she wants to go with us, Lowen.

Come on, please…It'd be nice to have a little time to spend with her. Maybe she just needs a friend right now. She won't be any trouble."

She begged so prettily. He just wished she weren't begging him to open their trip up for trouble in the form of a teenager who liked creating chaos.

"If it goes wrong, I'll take full responsibility," she promised.

He scraped his fingers through his hair. "Damn it, Vi…"

She smiled and sat back. "So she can come?"

He knew when he'd lost. There was no way he was going to tell her no when she was so excited about the idea. "You must really like that kid to argue like that for her."

Her blush returned, turning her cheeks and the shells of her ears a delicate shade of red. "Well…I just…she's got it rough in her own way, you know?"

"She has everything she could possibly want." Except his attention and a mother to be the female support she needed.

Vi's look told him she knew he wasn't being fully honest and that she knew precisely what Emma was missing. She didn't call him out on the lie, though. "Should we head home?"

He eyed her carefully, thinking then of how haggard and worried she'd seemed the last two weeks rather than about the impending trouble Emma might cause. She hadn't said anything about another package, and she'd hidden the fear they inspired better than she had the first time, but he knew they still had to be arriving, or she would have relaxed and gone back to her usual self.

Tonight, he wanted her away from the worry of when the next one would be waiting so she could relax and enjoy the trip tomorrow. "We'll stop by mine first. You can leave your car there. We'll take my car to go back to yours to pack your bags."

Her flush deepened. "That isn't needed, Lowen. I can pack my own bags and meet you at the airport."

"Not happening." This time he wasn't taking no for an answer.

"Those packages still showing up?"

She stiffened, her gaze darting to the door.

"Thought so," he growled. "You've been distracted and tired for the last two weeks. You're staying at mine so you can get a good night's sleep, Vi. No arguments."

Her chest rose with a quick, sharp intake of breath. "Lowen, I—"

He reached across the table and pressed his index finger to her lips. "What did I say?"

"No arguments," she whispered back.

"Precisely. I'm not in the habit of saying things I don't mean, am I?"

She shook her head.

"Then you know I meant that too. Come on." He stood and grabbed her jacket from the back of her chair, helping her put it back on. "Do you want to get dessert on the way home?"

"No. I'm full."

He slipped his hand through hers, placing cash down on the table for the bill. "Then we'll go home."

The ride to his place was quiet. She kept fiddling with the bottom of her jacket until he reached over, took her hand in his, and held it still. He threaded his fingers through hers with a smile. "There's no reason to be nervous. You've been to my place before."

"I've never stayed." Her voice was a tiny whisper. "You don't think Emma will mind, do you?"

"Emma will live, and she can manage, considering she enlisted you to wheedle me into letting her come along." He grinned. "I think the least she can do is be a bit understanding when I decide I want you to stay over."

"I'll be in the guest bedroom, so I guess she shouldn't be too uncomfortable," she mumbled.

"Stop worrying about what Emma will think. She already thinks we're sleeping together. How much worse could it be?"

He was rewarded for the remark with another bright blush

from the woman he'd fallen for. She really was adorable and remarkably innocent, considering all Arthur had put her through. If she only knew what he thought about the guest bedroom arrangement, he doubted she'd agree to stay. Someday, he'd have her under his own roof in his bed, not one door over in the cold guest room. Tonight, however, would not be that night.

***

Vi hated to admit that Lowen's demand that she stay over had given her the first good night's sleep she'd had all week, but she couldn't deny it when she woke up with energy and found him throwing together smoothies for the three of them. He wore nothing but a pair of sweats, and she could see a little trinity knot tattooed on his shoulder. She forced herself to look away before he caught her staring. It wasn't right to stare like this at the man who paid her bills. Emma was curled up on the couch, sleeping a little longer before they had to leave to catch their flight to England.

Lowen looked up when she sat at the gleaming granite bar and smiled. "Hey, sleepyhead. How did you sleep?"

"Well," she murmured, glancing at Emma.

"She was up too late watching chick flicks," he muttered. "But I didn't have the heart to be the bad guy by insisting she go to bed. She can sleep in the car and on the plane."

Vi raised a brow. "Oh, so she can get a bad night's sleep, but I can't?"

He turned to her, and she was reminded once again of why he looked so good in the suit he wore on set in his role as the Shadow. She bit her lip and looked away, hoping he wouldn't think she was ogling him, though she certainly was.

Lowen set a breakfast smoothie in front of her and tipped her chin up to bring her gaze to his with a knowing smirk.

She blushed, certain he knew exactly what she'd been doing and wondering why he seemed more amused than he did upset.

"She hasn't been failing to get enough sleep for two weeks straight. I think she'll live if she's more jet-lagged than usual. It'll keep her out of trouble for at least a day if she's too tired to leave the hotel rooms."

She shook her head. "Manipulative of you."

"Sometimes it's necessary to make sure no one's sanity or safety are lost."

Sipping the smoothie, she decided she couldn't really complain. She was actually relieved that Lowen had insisted she stay with him and Emma. The gifts had continued to come in the last few weeks. The threatening tone hadn't escalated, but she suspected it would only be a matter of time now before she'd stopped openly reacting to Arthur's insanity. He always took things further when he thought his theatrics were no longer gaining a response. That was the trouble with being tied up with a madman. At least now, she'd be heading to Europe, where Arthur couldn't reach her. She'd have a month or two of peace and quiet to regroup. With any luck, when they returned, Arthur would have forgotten all about her and moved on.

"What are you thinking about?" Lowen slipped onto the stool next to her.

"Just the trip," she deflected.

"Are you looking forward to it?"

"I think so." She glanced at the clock. "But you should go put a shirt on. You can't go through security like that, and we need to leave in fifteen. I'll wake up Emma and get the suitcases into the car."

He grinned. "Am I making you uncomfortable, missy?"

She bit her lip and looked away. "Of course not! I'm your stylist. I've seen you like this before. If you don't hurry up, though, we'll be late."

His laugh told her he knew she was lying just as much as she did, but he was kind enough not to call her out on it. He slid off the stool and headed for the stairs. "Oh, Vi. I'll take care of the suitcases. If you put them in the car instead, I'll have to think of some creative way to punish you for it. Can't have a woman carrying her own bags when I can do it for her."

Her cheeks warmed further. "Lowen!" she hissed.

Emma stirred on the couch. Lowen shot her a sassy smile and pointed in warning. She huffed but let it go. She couldn't be chiding him for the unusually flirtatious behavior in front of his daughter. Instead, she let him leave the room and tried to cool her flaming cheeks before she went to wake Emma so they could both finish preparing for the flight.

***

Three days passed without incident in England, full of boring interviews and press conferences or showings of the latest movie that Lowen's producers had released. Vi was finally starting to relax completely as she realized Arthur was, for now at least, unable to reach her. She spent her time bonding with Emma and helping Lowen prepare for showings, interviews, and other public appearances. Everything seemed perfect.

She hummed a little tune to herself as she pulled on her pajamas on the fourth evening. Lowen had dropped her off in her room after a nice evening with Emma. Emma had gone to her own suite—something Lowen had insisted she have for the sake of everyone's sanity—and she had settled in for an evening of reading and a glass of wine.

Just as she picked up her book and poured herself a glass, she heard a knock. Thinking it was Lowen coming to check on the next day's itinerary or Emma looking to hang out and watch TV, she opened the door. There was no one in the hallway. Frowning, she looked up and down and stepped out to search for whoever had knocked.

Her bare foot brushed a paper-wrapped box.

When she looked down, she found a little square box wrapped in brown paper and tied with twine. A low keening escaped her, and she backed away from it, slamming the door shut and pressing her back to it. Arthur was here. Somehow, he had found her and followed her to disrupt even her newfound safe haven. He had escalated it, all right, but not in the way any of them had expected.

Her stomach flipped and twisted. She forced herself to take deep breaths and reopened the door. She snatched the package up out of the hallway and brought it inside. Whatever it was, she didn't want it lying around for the cleaning staff or some other guest to find. She set it on the table and stared at it for a long while, debating whether to open it or not.

Finally, she did. When she pulled the box open, a breathless screech escaped her, and she dropped it back on the table. This time, he'd put a pair of blood-soaked songbirds into the package. They'd been white parakeets before he'd stained their feathers crimson. A blood-drenched note had been placed into one of the hapless birds' beaks. She took it out with trembling fingers, tears filling her eyes.

You're giving him what's mine!!!!
Stop now and fly back to me, and I might not have to hurt you both, little bird.

She dropped the paper into the package and raced for the bathroom, making it to the toilet just in time for her dinner to make a reappearance. She heard another softer knock at the door as she was flushing. Her stomach lurched, and she found herself clinging to the porcelain bowl and retching yet again. Had he come back to do as he'd threatened? What if he'd already hurt Lowen?

"Vi?" Lowen's deep voice filled the space outside.

Her body sagged against the toilet bowl, and she began to sob in relief. He was all right. Suddenly, she was glad she'd given him a key to her room, glad that he had come about something or just to check on her and to say goodnight. It didn't matter why he'd come in instead of waiting for her to answer, only that he was here.

His low, vehement curse brought reality crashing back. The birds. She'd left the birds sitting out in plain sight. Stumbling to her feet, she rushed to the main room. She already knew he'd seen them, but some illogical part of her brain still thought she could hide them before he did.

She found him standing in her room, staring down at the birds with his fists trembling at his sides. Stopping, she stood in the center of the little room by the end of her bed, her own body shaking.

He turned to her with a thunderous look on his face. "What is this?"

Her voice wouldn't cooperate, and instead of answering, she just collapsed onto the bed and burst into tears. He was at her side in an instant, cuddling her close and kissing the top of her head, whispering assurances in her ear. She clung to him as she let all the fear from the last ten minutes and the stress she'd been enduring for months go in a rush. When she finally stopped trembling in his arms, Lowen scooped her up and strode out of the room, down the hall, and into his suite. "I'm going to fix all of this, Vi. We'll talk about why you didn't tell me *that* was the sort of thing he was sending later."

She curled her fingers into his shirt when he tried to set her on his bed and leave. He heaved a sigh and climbed into the bed with her, curling himself around her protectively while he called the cops. The shock and exhaustion from being sick hit with a violent force, and his body heat and the thin blanket he draped over them both were all that kept her from freezing as everything went cold. It took hours before she quieted enough to sleep after the cops had asked Lowen questions and secured his promise to bring her into the station for a statement. When they left, Lowen returned to the bed and held her for the rest of the night, soothing her whenever she woke from a nightmare and singing softly until she returned to a fitful sleep.

Chapter 5

A visit to the police station yielded no results. Since they could find no fingerprints or other evidence yet to trace it back to Arthur, they promised to keep someone in the hotel for the duration of the tour stop, but they would be moving on in a few more days, bound for Italy, and then the situation would be out of the hands of the cops in England. Lowen silently fumed over the inefficacy of the police station, but deep down, he knew they would have run into the same trouble back in the States.

"Maybe we should cut the tour short and go back to California, Vi." He made the suggestion while they were cuddled up on his bed watching a show.

"I'll be fine. I can handle it," she whispered back. "I should...I should probably go back to my room now that it's been cleared."

"No. You'll be staying here in my suite with me."

"But..." She glanced around the room, which only had the one massive king-size bed.

"I'm not going to do anything you don't invite, little one," he murmured in her ear. "You'll be perfectly safe. I am not going to get any sleep unless I know you're right here with me between you and whatever else he might decide to leave at that door."

Her gaze flicked to the door, and her cheeks warmed. "Lowen, people will talk."

"About what? My intentions toward you? What we're doing? The stalker you've picked up?" He kept his lips close to the shell of her ear but resisted the urge to place small kisses along it.

She shivered, whether from his breath ghosting along her skin or at the memories of what that stalker had left, he didn't know.

"Cold?"

"N-no." Her ears turned that delicate shade of red he loved so much. "D-don't you think they'll assume we're an item? I mean...If anyone saw us, like *this*, they'd definitely assume something is going on."

"Let them assume," Lowen told her. "It doesn't do any harm if they assumed correctly."

She froze as his words sank in and then squirmed in discomfort. He knew asking her to deal with this building tension between them now, of all times, was a lot, but he was done pretending he wanted nothing more than her friendship, and he was sick of letting propriety dictate what he did. She needed a protector, but even more than that, she needed a man who would show her what love really was instead of the sick, twisted act Arthur had offered.

"Do you know..." he murmured, "...that the kiss we shared a year ago is still seared into my memory?"

The squirming ceased. Her breath was slower and less panicked, but the tension in her body didn't ease.

"Did you think I could forget?"

"I thought you hated it. That I wasn't...that my inexperience maybe made it..."

"What?" He pulled away a little. "Why would you think that?"

"I don't know...I gave you what I thought was an open invite for more, and you took off like you'd been burned. You never mentioned it again."

He groaned and pushed his fingers through his hair. "Well, I guess I made a mess of that one. Vi, I thought it would be wrong to take more with you in an inebriated, fragile state. I mean, it wasn't like I was totally sober, either. If I'd taken it further, it would've ended quickly, and I'd always be unsure if you regretted it or not. I didn't want that between us. Besides, you were just gaining your freedom from Arthur. I didn't think you needed to be tied down to another man so soon."

"Y-you mean it?"

He lifted her and turned her to straddle his hips so he could see her face. "Of course I do. I know he hurt you, love. I knew all along, and I hated it, but there wasn't anything I could do about it but be there for you as a friend. I was thrilled when you finally escaped him. You deserve the world, darling, especially after all you went through because of him. I didn't want to offer you anything less than that."

She bit her lower lip and stared down at his chest. "Arthur wasn't always cruel to me...It was good at first."

He cupped her face in his palms and lifted it to guide her gaze back to his. "Are you afraid we'll end up like you and Arthur did?"

Her bottom lip trembled. "I'm afraid he'll hurt you...I'm afraid that I'll screw everything up like I did with Arthur. He wouldn't have gone from nice to so mean if I hadn't done something wrong, right?"

"No. Don't you dare say that, baby girl. You didn't do anything to turn him into an abusive fool. He chose to be that. Even if you weren't perfect, nothing would justify what he did to you. Nothing."

The tears welled and slipped past her lashes. "W-what if I am the problem, though?"

He gathered her into his arms and kissed the top of her head. "You are not the problem, nor are you responsible for his unhinged behavior. He is both the problem and responsible for how he chooses to behave. If you decide you want to go forward with exploring the idea of us as an item, I promise it is not going to turn out like you and Arthur did."

She dropped her head to the crook of his neck and shoulder with a tiny shudder. "You don't know that."

"I do. I know what kind of woman you are and what kind of

man I am. It isn't going to end up like that." He hugged her tightly. "But sleep for now. It's been a long day."

She wiggled out of his embrace. "I can sleep on the sofa bed."

"Oh, no, you don't." He grabbed the back of her t-shirt as she tried to slide past him and off the bed. "You will stay right here on the side of the bed close to the window, little lady. I told you. If anything comes through that door, I'm going to be between you and it." He hoisted her back onto the bed and slid her onto the other side by the window, tugging the covers up over her legs. "Nothing will happen. Unless you ask for it, that is."

She blushed and slid down to lay her head on the pillow. "Night, Lowen."

He kissed her cheek and then climbed under the covers on his side. To make her feel better, he took a few of the extra pillows and slid them in between her warm body and his. Then he turned off the lights and shut the TV off before facing the door. "Night, Vi. Tomorrow, we'll ask a detective I keep on speed dial if he can look into the issue. He's helped with stalkers for me in the past."

"You think he'll find evidence to link it to Arthur?"

"He'll find evidence to link it to whatever screwed up idiot decided to play this game. If it's Arthur, he'll find out. If not, he'll find that out too."

She whimpered softly and shifted, pressing the pillows against his back. "You don't really think it's some stranger, do you?"

He turned over to face her. "No."

She shifted again, huddling closer to the pillow barrier he'd erected.

"I put the pillows up to make you more comfortable." He smirked in amusement. "If you want me to remove them and hold you, just say so, little one."

"Hold me, Lowen?"

"Any time." He tugged the pillows out of the way and pulled her into his arms with a soft sigh. Much better. This was where she belonged, even if she didn't know it yet. In time, though, she would. He just had to be patient.

***

Vi distracted herself from the worries over Arthur's next moves and Lowen's revelations by showing Emma the ropes behind set. The girl was a natural at styling and was glad for the other girl's company. Lowen had insisted she work on staff to help pay her way, and Vi found that she enjoyed working with the teen. When she had something to occupy herself, she was much more pleasant.

"So, what do you think you want to do when you graduate?"

Emma pursed her lips and finished cleaning out makeup sponges. "I think I might want to go into styling and makeup, actually. I really enjoy it, and this trip has shown me just how much I do already."

"That's great! If you don't mind my asking...how are things going with the counselor?"

Emma had continued her counseling sessions during their trip—even though they weren't mandatory—but she never spoke much about them. Vi wasn't sure if the counseling was helping or not, but she hoped Emma wouldn't shut down over the question.

"They're going pretty well," Emma murmured. "I think it's helping to have someone to talk to about all the stuff I've been dealing with."

"I'm glad."

"So...you and my dad..." Emma switched the subject with a sly smile. "You switched suites."

Vi's cheeks warmed. "It isn't like that, Emma."

"Well, what else would it be like?"

"It's...you know how I finally had the divorce with Arthur finalized a year ago?"

"Yeah."

"Well, he didn't accept the outcome, and he's..." Her chest tightened at the memory of the bloodied songbirds and the threatening notes. "He's been leaving me some threatening stuff, but no one can prove it's him yet. Your dad just offered to let me stay in his suite until it blows over."

"Oh." Emma's eyes were wide now. "Can't you just block him or something?"

"He's not texting or messaging me on social media, Emma." Vi rubbed her palms over her eyes with a sigh. "He's been leaving packages. I...I don't want to say more. But he clearly followed us, and your dad's worried. You know he can be overprotective."

Emma snorted. "That's an understatement! But I've never seen him this way with anyone except me. Not since Mom."

Vi took the cleaned sponges back to their container, avoiding Emma's curious gaze. "I don't think it means anything. Arthur's dangerous, though, so just promise me you won't put yourself at any risk if you see him. Let your father's detective and the cops handle it."

"My dad has a detective?" Emma groaned. "He probably uses the guy to keep tabs on me."

"I somehow doubt that." She laughed at the horrified look on Emma's face. "The school does a fine job of that."

"I wouldn't put it past him," Emma muttered.

"Well, for now, he's occupied with trying to figure out who's sending the notes and packages. I don't think he has any time to set the detective to watch you. That's my job." She slung an arm over Emma's shoulder. "And unless you want to watch the showing for his latest movie for a fifth time, why don't we go grab something for dinner? Just something small. I think your dad wanted to take us both to a nice meal after the showing ends."

Emma smirked. "See, he's already inviting you to dinners."

"Shush, you." Vi grinned back. "Or I'll decide not to take you for Italian gelato before dinner."

Emma pursed her lips in mock consideration. "I'll keep your secret if you keep mine. Dad would flip if he knew I was eating ice cream before dinner."

"Consider it kept." Vi mimed sealing her lips and linked her arm through Emma's, tugging the younger girl off in the direction of the front door of the theater. She knew the guards from Lowen's security detail would tag along, but she knew they wouldn't tell Lowen about the little excursion unless there was something of concern to tell him. Their secret would be safe enough, though she suspected Lowen could be wheedled into forgiving his daughter for eating gelato before dinner if Vi asked nicely enough. Lowen, she was quickly realizing, genuinely cared about her. She just hoped it wouldn't turn into a nightmare like it had with Arthur or, worse yet, become a nightmare because of Arthur.

Chapter 6

The trio checked into their hotel suites after a short trip from England to Italy. Emma's room was adjoined to theirs by a dividing door, and Lowen had canceled Vi's suite. He'd insisted she was staying with him in his. He had kept the sleeping arrangements the same, though, she noticed.

"Lowen, did you ask them to keep the single king bed on purpose?" she asked when she saw it.

"Maybe." He cast her a devilish grin. "Is that a problem?"

She flushed and dropped her gaze to the ground. "I don't know…Is there a reason I can't have my own bed?"

"Because you'll end up in mine anyway?" he teased.

The warmth in her cheeks crept to her ears. "You make it sound dirty."

"It could be," he shot back.

Her face was going to combust if he kept this up. She spun on her heel and fled to the bathroom with her toiletries. There, she focused on laying them out neatly and then fixed her makeup, giving herself a few precious moments to regroup.

"I thought we could order pizza in," Lowen called from the bedroom.

"That sounds good."

It was getting late, and she was too tired to consider a trip out for food. She heard Lowen ordering it in the background and sighed. The whole thing seemed so mundane, so ordinary. Arthur had never ordered takeout. If she didn't cook a full meal for any meals he shared with her, she paid for it later. Takeout was unacceptable in his eyes. Pizza wasn't on the list of approved meals to cook either. The contrast between Lowen and Arthur was so sharp that it brought tears to her eyes. Maybe Lowen was right. Maybe it didn't have to end badly between the two of them.

Lowen entered the bathroom and put his own toiletries on the countertop beside hers. He frowned when he saw her expression and stepped up behind her, resting his hands on her hips. "What is it? What's wrong?"

"Lowen, do you really like me?"

"I more than really like you, Genevieve," he murmured. "I think I've loved you for a very long time. Why?"

"Do you think..." She trailed off, second guessing herself.

She couldn't ask him to show her the things she'd been missing when she was with Arthur. He was her boss. She shouldn't be having this conversation with him at all, let alone considering begging him to take this further. Since she'd started sleeping in his room, the tension between them was off the charts, and she was beginning to think it would break her if she didn't do something to break it first.

A knowing look replaced his concern, and he pressed closer, sandwiching her between his body and the cold granite countertop at her waist. "Do I think what?" His voice was a low, husky murmur now. "If you want something, you'll have to ask, baby girl. You know that already. I promised, after all."

A shiver worked down her spine, but for the first time in ages, it was the good kind of shiver. She met his intense stare in the mirror and bit her lower lip.

"Well? What do you want, Vi?"

"You," she whispered. "I want you. I need you to show me what it can be like...What it's like not to be stuck with someone like *him*."

He scooped her up in his arms and carried her toward the bed.

"I thought you'd never ask, love."

He dropped her onto the bed, and she settled there on her elbows, staring up at him and unsure what to do. By now, Arthur would simply have ruched up her skirts and taken what he wanted.

Lowen wasn't Arthur. He stood between her parted thighs, staring down at her with a look of reverence and admiration. "You really are beautiful. You know that?"

She dropped her gaze away from his and squirmed.

"You are." His voice firmed. "Don't look away from me, baby girl. Eyes on me."

She obeyed with a tiny whimper as the gentle but firm command of his voice warmed her from the inside out. "I don't know what to do."

"You don't have to. Just follow my lead." His hands cupped her knees and then slid up along the bare skin beneath her skirt.

She shivered and shifted closer to his touch. He ignored her silent pleas for more and continued to explore, slipping his hands just under her blouse to pull it free from the waistband of her skirt and then sliding his fingers along her bare waist and belly.

"So beautiful, love. Sit up."

She did as asked, wondering what would come next.

He kissed her gently, the touch of his mouth to hers reminding her of the moment when he'd kissed her a year ago. This time, his hands slid higher to circle her ribcage. He was so much bigger than she was, and his hands almost managed to span around her ribcage entirely. She moaned into his kiss, begging him to give her more.

Lowen continued his maddeningly slow exploration until she thought she might scream in frustration. Finally, he stripped her of her clothes and laid her back on the bed. When he finally gave her what she wanted, she cried. For the first time, though, she cried because it was so much better than she'd imagined it could be and not because she was left hurting and wanting something her lover would never offer. Lowen was right. He really wasn't anything like Arthur.

***

There was a knock at the door early the next morning. Vi groaned and stirred. Why was cleaning services bothering them when it was barely seven? She and Lowen had forgotten to put out the do not disturb hanger for the door, but it still seemed like it was a bit too early for this. Lowen was still fast asleep, so she slipped out of bed to see what the person knocking might want. He stirred slightly but didn't wake, so she slid her feet into her slippers and walked to the door.

She opened it softly to avoid waking Lowen, but all attempts to be quiet fled when she saw the little brown package on the ground. The note was taped to the top this time.

You crossed a line last night with him, opening your legs like a common whore!!!
If he doesn't back off, he'll regret it. And so will you!!!!!

A sob escaped her, and she stepped back into the room, slamming the door shut and pressing her back to it. Her legs shook so much she couldn't stay upright, so she sank to the floor, cradling her head in her hands. Arthur always had known how to hit her where it hurt most.

Lowen woke with a start and was at her side in moments. "What is it? What's wrong, baby girl? Talk to me."

She couldn't get the words out. What would the package contain this time? Something horrible. Of that, she was certain. The words were frozen deep within her by the fear of what Arthur might have sent. He knew she'd slept with Lowen. He seemed to know everything—where she was, what she was doing, where he could send his newest "gift".

Fortunately, Lowen guessed what had shaken her up. His jaw

clenched. "He left another package."

She nodded weakly.

Lowen scooped her up and carried her to the bed. "Stay. I'll get it and call the detective I have on the case. He'll handle it. You are not to move, little girl."

She wouldn't even if she could. She just wanted to forget what had happened. Couldn't she stay in her little bubble, pretend there was no one in the world but her and Lowen? It wouldn't last forever. She knew that. She just wanted it to last a little longer than the few hours she'd had last night.

She watched Lowen as he opened the door and brought the package in, picking it up with a blanket to avoid getting any of his own DNA or fingerprints on it. The cops wouldn't find anything on it anyway if Arthur was staying true to his usual M.O. Maybe he would grow sloppy eventually. He had when they'd first begun dating, and she'd discovered it was him in time. He liked the spotlight too much to remain anonymous forever, but for now, she suspected he hadn't reached the grand gesture he had planned. There would be more, and it terrified her to think that more might mean someone getting hurt, not just a little scared or shaken up.

Emma barged in through the adjoining door of the suite next door. The sound of the door opening caused Vi to jump, her heart in her throat. When she saw it was Emma, she sighed and sagged back against the pillows. Emma's gaze flicked from her to Lowen and back. "You two are loud, and seriously...I was one room over! Did you have to do the deed with me within earshot?"

Lowen scowled at her. "Emma, knock."

She rolled her eyes and stepped back into her room, shutting the door and knocking loudly before she reentered. "Happy now?"

Despite the seriousness of the situation, her dramatic behavior brought a smile to the corners of his lips. "Do it before you come in the first time. As for your other remark...you already assumed I was sleeping with Vi. What does it matter to know we did last night in particular?"

Emma groaned and made a gagging sound. "Okay, I did *not* need to hear that, Dad! Seriously, gross...I wasn't serious when I made that remark, either. I mean, I kind of figured you were, but I didn't need it confirmed!"

Vi hugged her knees to her chest, face flaming. She hadn't meant to be loud enough that Emma could hear them in the next room. Did that mean the room on the other side had heard them too? As if the mess with Arthur wasn't enough...

She really did have the worst luck.

Lowen glanced at her and crossed his arms, his smile vanishing. "Emma, Genevieve, and I are an item. You'll have to get used to it. I'm sorry you overheard us last night. We'll try harder not to be so loud, but I like her, and I know you two normally get along. I expect you to be respectful and *not* to make her feel bad for being with me."

His daughter groaned and raked her fingers through her hair. "How the hell am I supposed to act normal around her after what I overheard last night?"

"Language!" Lowen snapped. "You'll just have to find a way."

Emma threw up her hands. "Okay, great...I'll just pretend this is all totally normal. Not weird at all! Don't worry about me. I'm not going to be scarred for life."

"Emma Mcallister, you will not be scarred for life. Knock it off with the dramatics. If you need time to come to terms with what you now know for certain, do it in your room," Lowen barked. "Vi doesn't need this right now. She's dealing with enough."

Emma's gaze fell on the package on the table, and her face went pale. "Is that...did he leave another one?"

Vi nodded miserably and dragged a pillow close to her chest.

"This is really bad, isn't it?" She looked like she might be sick.

"Yes, it is. Emma, go back to your room. I have this handled. You can come back when you're ready to apologize for adding your drama to Vi's stress."

Emma's frightened look vanished in anger. "Come on, Dad! That's not fair! I shouldn't have to apologize to her for being grossed out hearing you two having sex. I'm your daughter, and I'm only sixteen. Hello? Hearing what I did would make any kid feel a little gross."

"Lowen, she's—"

Lowen raised a hand, glaring at Emma. "You're entitled to your feelings, but you are not entitled to make someone else feel awkward, upset, or hurt because you didn't process them and respond appropriately. That is why you will apologize."

His daughter scoffed and stormed back into her room. "Then I guess I'll be in here for a long time."

Her door slammed, and Vi winced, staring down at the bedspread. "Lowen, maybe you're being too hard on her..."

"No." He joined her on the bed and pulled her into his lap. "I understand why she's weirded out, but her reaction was uncalled for. I won't let her off the hook just because it's understandable that she's feeling a little off balance."

"Lowen, maybe this won't work...If she's this upset, maybe—"

He silenced her with a kiss, though there was concern etched into his face as well when he pulled away. "It'll be fine."

She wasn't certain who he was trying to convince. Her? Himself? Both of them? She just knew that even though she let it go, for now, she had a sinking fear that this would all fall apart one way or another.

***

The rest of the day passed without incident after the detective picked up the package. He and Lowen had exchanged information about updates on the case in low voices, and then the detective had left. Lowen had a meeting with one of the funders for the movie he was shooting in a few months, so he'd reluctantly left her by herself.

She forced herself to get up. If she was going to keep herself together for the rest of the trip, she needed to do something. They were in Rome. There were things to see and do around here, and she needed to find something to keep her mind off the situation from this morning. She walked to Emma's door and knocked, hoping she could coax the girl into coming out and talking. Maybe they could sort this problem out and go sightseeing together.

"Go away," came Emma's muffled response.

"Emma..."

"I don't want to talk to you."

She didn't understand why the girl was reacting so strongly to the situation. It made sense that Emma felt a little awkward after overhearing Vi and her dad last night, but it didn't make sense that she'd be this upset.

"I wanted to see if you wanted to come with me and check out the sites?"

"No thanks. I'd rather glue my eyes together!" Emma retorted. Vi was concerned and wondered if maybe there was something more going on under the surface that Emma wasn't saying, but if there was, Vi wasn't going to get it out of her by trying to force her to talk. Sighing, she turned away from the door and got dressed.

Throwing on a pair of slacks and a blouse, she slipped her feet into her flats and grabbed her purse. She texted Lowen quickly to let him know she was heading out to walk through the touristy locations of the downtown area just so that he wouldn't worry if he returned to find her gone. She walked out of the suite, passing by two guards stationed outside. After relaying that they should keep an eye on Emma and make sure she didn't leave her room without express permission from her father, Vi headed towards the elevator.

Then she left the hotel and walked out onto the bustling streets. She made her way to a crossing and waited until the light indicated they could walk. She took her time as a group of teenagers rushed past.

Just as she was nearly to the sidewalk, a black Sedan came barreling around the corner straight at her. Onlookers screamed in warning. She turned, shock rendering her numb and useless. A strong hand wrapped around her wrist and yanked her out of the way just in time. She stared at the car as it retreated and told herself she hadn't really seen what she thought she had. Had that been Arthur's face she'd caught in the blur of motion?

The stranger who had saved her took her by the shoulders. He was saying something, but her ears were ringing, and she was shivering as it sank in that she had almost died.

"...all right, miss?" His English was heavily accented, but the words finally made it through.

"Yes," she whispered. "Yes, thank you. I'm fine."

He let her go. "Do you want I call someone for you?"

She shook her head, pulling out her phone and hitting the speed dial number for Lowen. "I'll...I have someone nearby. I'll just wait here." She motioned to the little cafe where a group of horrified diners were looking on.

"You are not good. Let me help." The man took her arm and helped her to a chair. "Do you want me to wait with you?"

"No. Please, you've done enough. Thank you for pulling me out of the way."

"No trouble, miss. Be careful." He eyed her in concern. "You are sure you not need me to wait?"

"Yes, sir. Thank you again."

Shrugging, he left, hurrying to catch a cab on the street corner. Lowen picked up on the sixth ring. Her breath hitched when he answered, and she rushed to tell him what had happened. "Lowen, I n-need you to come get me. Someone tried to run me over."

Chapter 7

After the incident with the attempt to run her down on the street, Lowen canceled everything. He had insisted they return to the States at once, where the cops would be able to handle any further threats and make an arrest once they had the evidence to tie the behavior and any crimes to Arthur or whomever was responsible. She knew, deep down, that it was Arthur, and after he'd tried to kill her on the streets of Rome, she knew that it wouldn't be long before that final grand gesture came. She prayed it wouldn't lead to Lowen or Emma being harmed and that it would only be she herself who suffered from Arthur's fury.

The note he'd left on the last package that Lowen had intercepted hung heavy in her mind, and she refused Lowen's request to take her home with him and Emma. Emma was still quiet, withdrawn, and sulky over what had happened the evening before everything went haywire, and she made no secret of her irritation and anger over their new relationship. Lowen ignored her, but the teen's behavior only added to the reasons Vi felt she had to get space.

Now that he'd dropped her off on the sidewalk and was waiting to see that she was safely inside her apartment, Vi wanted to turn back around and tell him she'd changed her mind. She gripped the handle of her luggage tightly and squared her shoulders. This was something she had to do. Maybe if Arthur thought she was distancing herself from Lowen, he'd leave Lowen and Emma alone. It was a long shot, but she wouldn't let her crazy ex hurt either of them on her account. She walked up the sidewalk to her porch and opened the door.

There, on the tiled floor of the entryway, another package sat. The note for this one was taped to the top, just like the last one.

You didn't open my gift last time. That made me angry! Open this one, or else we might have a repeat of the street in Rome.
Tick tock tick tock.

She wanted to stumble out of the house and run back to Lowen, who was still watching to see that she had gone inside and that all was well. If she did that, though, this would all be for nothing. She stepped inside, waved goodbye to him, and shut the door. The sound of his car driving off brought tears to her eyes. She didn't want to be alone in an apartment where Arthur had already found a way to enter without tipping off security. She didn't want to open his gift either. There wasn't any other choice now, though.

Setting the suitcase on the table, she picked up the package and opened it slowly. There was an ominous ticking from inside the box, and her stomach flipped, threatening to expel its contents on the floor. Had Arthur sent her a bomb this time? She pulled back the flaps and found the package contained a ball with a ticking timer and another note attached to it.

Tick tock.

Whimpering, she backed away and jerked her phone from her pocket, dialing 911. A female voice answered. "911. What's your emergency?"

"A b-bomb." Her voice trembled with unshed tears. "I came home to a package, and there's a bomb in it. You have to come quick."

"Ma'am, where are you?"

She gave the woman her address, her gaze fixed on the timer. Five minutes. Five minutes left. "It only has five minutes."

"Ma'am, I want you to leave the house right now. If you can get the neighbors out of the area next door, do it. I see you're in a duplex with a neighbor on the other side. Make sure they're not home, and then get out of the area as quickly as you can. I'll send a team."

"C-can you stay on the phone?" she begged, needing someone to ground her and keep her rising panic at bay.

"Of course. I'm right here." The woman's voice was calm and soothing. "Just go get your neighbor and get yourselves to a safe distance, hon."

She grabbed her purse off the table and ran out the door, going to the neighbor's door and banging. No one came, so she rang the doorbell a few more times and banged again. Finally, she decided they must not be home. "I don't think they're here. I've knocked and rang the doorbell a few times now."

"Then worry about getting yourself to safety. Can you do that for me?"

She took a deep breath and raced away from the duplex to the other side of the street. "Is the other side of the street safe enough?"

"It should be. The cops and a bomb squad are on their way. Just keep breathing. You're doing fine."

She tightened her grip on the phone. "How far away are they?"

"A few minutes. There's a chance they may not make it in time to diffuse the bomb, hon. Just stay where you are."

"Thank you."

"Just doing my job," the operator said.

"Still...thank you. Will you stay on the phone with me, please?"

"Sure thing, and you're welcome. Just keep breathing and stay calm."

She glanced at her watch. Two minutes left.

The two minutes came and went. "Why hasn't it gone off yet?"

"I don't know. Sometimes homemade bombs can fail. Don't go back into the house. Wait for the cops to show up."

She heard the sirens in the distance, and then the cops pulled in with a fire engine and an ambulance. A group split off to enter the house while a cop approached her. "Ma'am, are you the owner of the duplex?"

"Renter."

"I'm going to hang up now. You're in good hands, hon," the woman on the phone said.

"Thank you." She slipped the phone back into her pocket and wrapped her arms around herself.

"Any idea who might leave a bomb for you?" the officer asked.

"I..." She took a deep breath and pinched the bridge of her nose, trying to regain composure. "My ex. Arthur Mathewson. I think he's been leaving the other packages I've been receiving. I...My boss and I reported them when we started receiving them on tour overseas."

"Who is your boss?" The officer flipped open a notepad and began taking notes.

"Lowen Mcallister."

The man looked up with a raised brow. "The Lowen Mcallister?"

"Yes, sir."

"Good actor. Good man too. A friend of mine worked security for him a few years ago." The cop noted it down and glanced at the house. "When did the packages start?"

Tears filled her eyes, and she lowered her head. "He's been sending similar packages since our divorce. Not the same packaging. He's too smart for that. At first, they were nice gifts—the same sort he used to leave me back when we were first dating. Then t-the songbirds started showing up with threatening notes. I had to take a restraining order out on him last year, so he hasn't been coming around when I'm here, but I...I know it's him."

"Did the cops overseas find anything?"

"No...Lowen cut the tour short after someone tried to run me down in Rome."

"I see."

One of the men who had entered the house came back out and joined them. "Ma'am, you're fortunate. The package didn't contain a real bomb. It was a gas bomb. Your house will need to be aired out, but it didn't do any real damage. Whoever left it was trying to scare you."

"Sounds about right if it's her ex," the first cop replied. "He's been harassing her."

"You want us to bring him in for questioning, detective?"

"Yes. We'll have to wait to see if any DNA linking him to it shows up. Anything to indicate the motive?"

"The guy made overt reference to other gifts and something about a street in Rome. Does that mean anything to you, ma'am?"

She pressed a hand over her tear-filled eyes and nodded. "He's referring to trying to kill me by running me down on a street corner in Rome. It's why my boss and I cut our tour short to come back here."

"Call Mcallister, ma'am," the detective told her. "He's a good man. He'll help you out."

She wiped at her streaming eyes. "I think the escalating nature of the gifts is because Lowen and I are involved, detective. And if it is Arthur, he's going to go further. This was a warning. Next time, it could be a real bomb. He already tried to kill me once."

"We'll consider that. But I don't think he's trying to kill you just yet. If he really wanted to kill you on the street corner, he would have left a real bomb, and you wouldn't have had time to run. Keep your phone on you in case we need to bring you in for more questions. In the meantime, get in touch with Mcallister. He should keep you with him where his security can help keep you safe. We'll put officers on the house in case this lunatic leaves something else."

That wasn't much of a relief. It just meant he still thought he could force her back to him. As soon as he realized that wouldn't happen, he would take the final step. She called Lowen and prayed the cops would catch Arthur before it came to that.

***

Attempts to convince Lowen she could stay in a hotel were as futile as attempts to draw Emma out of her fuming. Lowen and Emma fought nearly every day, and Vi was beginning to think all of this would be solved if she just walked away from it all. She didn't want to leave Lowen, but Arthur and Emma both presented obstacles to being with him, and she was starting to think she was the reason his life was turning upside down. It left her stressed, out of sorts, and frightened.

Lowen asked her repeatedly what was wrong, but she refused to tell him and insisted on staying in the guest bedroom. He left it be, but she knew he wasn't happy about it. She kept her concerns to herself. Deep down, a part of her worried he might agree with her if she voiced them, and she didn't think she could stand to hear him call her the source of his current problems on top of everything else.

He'd made her take a few weeks off to recuperate from the shock the stink bomb had given her, and she spent most of her time in her room, reading and trying to avoid Emma. Today was more of the same, and she was glad she'd be returning to work in a few days. The cops had been asking more questions, but they still hadn't caught Arthur leaving any more packages. Until they had a link between him and the packages she'd been receiving, they couldn't arrest him, and she was still in danger. So was Lowen now that she was living with him. Arthur would see it as an act of defiance, and she was terrified of what the consequence might be.

In need of a snack and some water, she stood and left her

bedroom to fetch something from the kitchen. Emma was there, and she contemplated going back to her room empty-handed, but the teen spotted her before she could decide, and the opportunity was lost. Emma scowled and turned her back on Vi. "You know, you should just go home. You're making my dad worry."

Vi flinched and stared at her feet. "Emma, I'm not the enemy...You know that, don't you?"

Emma scoffed. "You're moving in, replacing my mom's stuff in his room, taking over. Yeah, you are."

Was that what this was about? "You seemed happy for us before...You were teasing me about it, and you already figured we were sleeping together. You even said he treated me like he hadn't treated anyone since your mom. Why the sudden animosity about it?"

Emma's shoulders stiffened. "I was giving you a hard time. I didn't figure you *really* liked him back. You weren't supposed to! I knew he liked you, but I figured nothing would happen as long as you weren't interested in him like that. Then..." Emma turned, her jaw clenched and arms crossed. "You turned out to like him after all. Or maybe it's just his money and protection you like. It has to be a step up to go from abusive ex to multi-millionaire actor. Maybe none of this is real at all."

Vi took a step back, throat dry. "That's not how it is. I love your father."

Vi's eyes widened at the sudden realization. This was the first time she was admitting it to herself.

"If you did, you wouldn't be here. If the threats are real, then you know being here just puts him in danger too." Emma stormed past, slamming her shoulder against Vi's as she left. "You would go if you really cared about him. Before your screwed up past costs him everything too."

"Emma..." She reached out to touch the teen's shoulder. "I offered to leave. To stay at a hotel. He wouldn't let me."

"No one's making you stay." Emma jerked free of her touch.

"He's not the boss of you, Genevieve. You know that full well. If you really wanted to go, you could, and he wouldn't be able to stop you. You want to be here because you're too selfish to give him up, even if it's for his own good."

"I...L-Lowen would bring me back, Emma. He's made it clear he won't let me leave until this mess is cleaned up."

"Don't act like you're some sort of prisoner. My father is a good man. He would let you go if you insisted." Emma flung her arm out toward the front hall. "The door's right there. He's not here to stop you. Leave if you really care."

Vi's lower lip trembled. "What did I do to deserve this, Emma?"

"You put my dad in danger and decided you could replace my mom." Emma shoved her away. "So go. Prove you love him. Walk out the door."

She didn't want to fight with Emma, and at that moment, she was beginning to think Emma was right. Maybe she really didn't belong here. Maybe it was for the best she left. She walked to the door and grabbed her purse, slipping on her shoes. Emma remained where she was, arms crossed and silent. Vi stepped outside and closed the door behind her, tears falling. Emma had made the same point about Lowen's safety that had been weighing on Vi all along. Lowen would be better off without her.

***

The first call from Lowen came the evening after she left. She had expected a little more time before he called. It wasn't as though she was always home in the evenings, though she had been going out less and less often since the bomb Arthur had sent. She sent it to voicemail.

Lowen's frantic voice filled the small hotel room. "Vi, come on. Pick up. You have to pick up. I don't know what Emma said to you, but you need to come home from wherever you're hiding. Arthur left a real bomb in my car this time. It blew up prematurely. I'm safe, but you aren't. Please, Vi...answer your phone."

Her stomach lurched, and she barely reached the bathroom before losing everything she'd managed to force down at dinner. This only confirmed her worst fear. Arthur was targeting Lowen now too, and if she didn't stay away, he'd be in danger. She needed to go home so that Arthur could see clearly that she had left Lowen. If she didn't, this was going to end with Lowen's death or serious injury. She rinsed out her mouth and rose shakily.

Grabbing her few belongings from the table, she shoved her phone into her pocket and left. She'd come back to check out in the morning, but she couldn't stay here tonight, hiding like a coward when the man she loved was in danger. She would go home and pray that it made Arthur back off on Lowen.

She drove home, heart hammering and stomach still upset. When she turned into the driveway, the headlights illuminated Lowen's hunched figure on her doorstep. She turned off the car and sat there, unsure what to do. Before the headlights clicked off, his eyes met hers for a moment, and she forced herself to get out. If Arthur was watching, then this would be the clearest indication that she could give him that she and Lowen were over. "Lowen," she murmured.

"Vi, come home. It isn't safe here. Did you get my message?" He stood and strode over to her, taking her by the shoulders. "Whatever Emma said, ignore her. I want you there, and she'll get over whatever's gotten into her."

She jerked free of his grasp, lowering her head to hide her face. "Lowen, Emma was right about everything. I'm toxic for you. Arthur tried to kill you today because you're with me. You need to go home and stay away from me."

"I can't!" He tugged his fingers through his hair. "You can't seriously expect that! You work for me, Vi. Arthur will still target me even if you walk away. He's insane, and he's not going to stop just because you put an end to what's between us. He'll want revenge. This isn't going to protect anyone."

"It will! Arthur will back off if we're not together. He might hurt me, but he'll leave you alone."

"Damn it, Vi!" Lowen's voice roughened. "I couldn't live with myself if he hurt you. I love you. Can't you see that?"

Vi's mouth opened and shut a few times, the sincerity in his voice tugging at her resolve. But she couldn't back down.

"Go home, Lowen! I don't want to see you anymore." She sucked in a sharp breath. "I quit. I don't want to work for you anymore, either."

"What?" He took a step back.

"I quit, Lowen. You'll be safe. I'll send through some recommendations of stylists I've worked with before. I won't be seeing you ever again. I mean it."

"Baby girl…" His voice was ragged with pain and exhaustion now. "This isn't the way. I can protect you, and I can damn well protect myself. Please just come home."

"Leave. I don't want to have to call the cops on you next." She ducked her head and wrapped her arms around the middle. "This is over. All of it. Just go."

Lowen tangled his fingers in her hair and pulled her head up, crushing her mouth with his. He pulled away with a low curse when she didn't respond with anything but tears. "Don't you feel anything? I thought we had a connection."

"W-we did." The tears fell faster now, and she couldn't bring herself to lie to him. "But it's over. It would kill me if you were hurt or killed because of me, Lowen. Don't put me through that."

"I won't! You just need to come home where you belong, Vi. With me."

"Go away!" She shoved past him and into the still, quiet rental house beyond. "I don't want to see you again!" She slammed the door in his face and locked it, waiting until she heard his footsteps crunching in the gravel of the walkway before she slumped to the ground and burst into gut-wrenching sobs.

Chapter 8

"Tell me you have something!" Lowen snapped over the phone.

"We've got enough to prove he's linked somehow, but we haven't figured out if he's the one who left the bomb. Until we can link him to that, the best we've got is a thin prosecution on the basis of violating the restraining order. But he can't be charged with anything if she wasn't on the premises when he stopped in." The officer sighed. "I'm sorry, Lowen. We're working on it."

"Well, work faster! She's cut me out, Detective, and she's all alone. You have to figure this out, or she'll be dead the next time he sends her a package."

"We're trying to link him to the car bomb, Lowen. We're close."

"I'll have my guy help with the case if you'll work with him."

"I'll talk to the chief about having him on as a consultant for now. Try not to worry. We have men keeping an eye on her."

"You'd better. I can't lose her."

"I understand. We're doing our best. Have a few of your men keep an eye on the situation. Give us a few more days to nail him for this. If we don't make it stick, he'll probably kill her for getting him in trouble, not just because she wouldn't come back. A guy like this would do awful things before he was done."

"I know." He closed his eyes and tried not to think about it. "I know."

"Keep an eye on your own back too. He may still come after you." Papers shuffled in the background. "Look, I have to go. I'll call if there are any updates."

"Thanks, Detective." Lowen ended the call and dropped the phone onto his office desk with a groan. He needed to call his man and then the security detail to put a man or two at Vi's home. She'd be angry if she discovered he had a guard on her apartment, but he wasn't going to let her end up dead, or worse, just because she thought pushing him away was the answer.

After a minute, he picked up the phone and called his private detective. "Mark."

"Lowen. Calling for an update?"

"I am."

"I traced down the buyer for the materials that went into the stink bomb she got and the bomb in your car. Arthur is on the list. I've also tracked down the shop he bought those songbirds from. They confirmed he's been buying the birds around the same dates that Vi received the packages with the dead ones. The last is more circumstantial, but if you add it all up..."

His heart hammered hard. "Is that enough to nail him?"

"Not for the precise bombs you two received, but it would be enough to make an arrest. They could probably find the rest of the evidence they need to prove he used the materials with a search warrant. You want me to give the local department a call?"

"Yeah. Detective Mills is running the case, and I told him I'd see if you could collaborate with them on this one. They'll take whatever you can give them. I just want her safe, Mark, okay?"

"You'll have that. You have security on her, right?"

"The cops do. I'm adding my men. How long before they can have a warrant for his arrest?"

"If the chief makes enough of a fuss, they can probably get a judge to sign off on it tonight."

"I'll make sure it happens," Lowen told him.

"I'll give them a call after you let them know to expect it. Text me once you've talked to the chief."

"Thanks, Mark. Expect that soon." He hung up and made a second call to the police department, standing up and pacing the length of the room until it connected. "Detective, Mark just touched base with an update. How fast can the chief have a warrant?"

"What did he find?"

"He finished tracking all the supplies needed for the bombs and the purchase of all the songbirds Arthur's been sending. He traced them back to Arthur."

"Quick work."

"It's been his sole focus since the moment I found out she was getting these screwed up presents. He's been working for a while."

"Have him come in and give this info to the chief directly. He'll want to hear it. If Mark can present the findings, we can have a warrant for his arrest tonight and a search warrant tomorrow."

"Thanks, Detective."

"Worry about your girl, Lowen. Once we have him in custody, I'll call, but you should go over there now to be with her, just in case. She shouldn't be alone when all this finally breaks."

"I don't know that she wants me there."

"I guarantee you she does. You've been the first person she's wanted to call in every time things went wrong, from what I hear. Just go see her."

Lowen took a deep breath and nodded even though he knew Mills couldn't see him. "Thanks, Detective. I appreciate everything you've done."

"Bye, Lowen."

The phone beeped to signal the call had ended. He slid it back into his pocket and headed for the door. Emma was sitting at the table in the kitchen, texting. She looked up and frowned when she saw him going for his coat. "Where are you going?"

"To see Vi."

"Dad, come on! She left, and it was dangerous. The cops are

handling this. Leave it."

He rounded on her, fury sparking. "Emma, I don't know what you said to drive her away, to begin with, or what your problem is, but get over it! She isn't replacing your mom, if that's what you think, and any danger she may have been bringing to our doorstep will be over soon. She's going to be in our lives whether you like it or not. Make peace with it!" Without waiting for a reply, he stalked to the door, opened it, and walked out, letting it slam behind him. He was going to find Vi and make sure she was safe, and knew it would all be over soon. This hiding and keeping him at a distance to protect him nonsense of hers ended tonight.

***

Vi had spent a miserable week alone in her apartment. After quitting her job with Lowen, she'd been left pining not only for him but for the routines she was accustomed to. Everything felt less vibrant, and a pall of fear hung over her life. When she heard the knock at the door, she immediately feared it was another package from Arthur. She hadn't seen one in the last week, but she knew better than to believe that meant they would stop without news from the police that Arthur was in jail.

Still, she forced herself to rise on trembling legs to go answer. She wasn't going to let the fear rule her life anymore. It might keep her away from Lowen—she couldn't bear the thought of letting anything happen to him because of her—but it wouldn't keep her from living her life. She was determined not to let Arthur win this, whatever happened. He would never have her back, no matter how he terrorized her.

She opened the door.

Lowen stood on the other side. Hand raised to ring the bell next. He lowered it when he saw her. "Vi."

"Lowen. I told you I didn't want to see you again."

He nodded. "It's over, Vi. Let me inside."

She bit her lip and hesitated, but finally, she stepped aside and let him come in. He strode inside and shut the door before grabbing her and pulling her into a tight hug. She let her forehead rest against his chest with a muffled sob. His hugs were something she'd missed a lot over the last week of fear and misery. "Arthur isn't under arrest."

"He will be. Come on. We're going to dinner." He pulled back and glanced around the apartment. "But before we do, the cops want you to offer a formal testimony at the trial. I got a call on the way over. They asked if I'd talk you into it."

She wrapped her arms around her middle and shook her head. "I don't want to see him again, even to see him go to jail."

Lowen nodded. "I figured as much. You don't have a choice, baby girl. That's why I wanted to be here as support when the detective calls. For now, let's fix something for you to eat. Or order in. What are you feeling?"

She sniffled and hunched her shoulders, tears pressing at the corners of her eyes. "Lowen, maybe...I don't know if I can eat right now."

He wrapped an arm around her shoulder and drew her to her kitchen table, pressing her into a chair. "We'll eat after this is done, then."

"I can't believe it's over. You aren't making it up, so I'll come back, are you?"

"No, darling, I'm not. I would never do that. I asked the detective to call and speak to you. He should call any minute now. Let's wait for the formal announcement together, okay?"

She nodded, leaning into him once he'd taken a seat beside her. Pulling her phone from her pocket, she set it on the kitchen table in front of them. They waited for a few long moments in silence, and she soaked up the comfort his presence brought while praying that she wouldn't have to give it up again.

The harsh ringtone of the cell vibrated through the small space. Vi picked up.

"Miss Lanchester?" a familiar voice asked.

"Detective."

"We have news for you, though I'm sure Lowen has already broken it. We have just arrested your ex-husband for the bomb in Lowen's car and the dead songbird packages you've received. I'm sorry we didn't inform you right away, but we were waiting to make sure the warrant would go through to arrest him tonight. We would like your testimony at the trial."

"Do you need it to nail him?" she asked, voice soft.

"We can't present all the evidence if some of it is from a witness testimony from a witness who isn't present. The accused has to be able to cross-examine. I'm sorry, Miss Lanchester."

She pressed the heel of her palm into her eyes with a sigh.

Lowen rubbed her back. "It'll be okay, baby girl..."

"I...I would rather not rehash any of it. If you're sure he'll go to prison for trying to kill Lowen, can I just stay out of it?"

"The opposition will want you on the stand. There's not really a way to stay out of it. But you'll be safe. He's going away for a very long time, and nothing he does will stop it. You'll receive the order to appear before the court once the trial date is sorted out. I have to go, Miss Lanchester. If you need anything, don't hesitate to call."

Lowen kept rubbing her back long after the phone's disconnect beep played. She stared at the black screen. A tear slipped down her cheek, then another. Then she was cradled to Lowen's chest as she cried in relief that it was over. She clung to him, thankful she wasn't alone anymore and that the awful week was finally ending.

***

Seven months later, the trial was finally over. She'd survived testifying and watched as the jury handed out a unanimous guilty verdict. Lowen had insisted they go out to eat in celebration, a moment that had reminded her of how all this had begun with a celebration of her divorce and a single brief kiss. She'd agreed with less hesitation this time.

Lowen got up from his spot in the chair across from her at the fancy restaurant he'd taken her to.

She frowned. "Lowen? What are you doing?"

He pulled a small box from his jacket pocket and knelt in front of her. "Vi, when you came into my life six years ago, you were the friend my daughter, and I desperately needed. But the more I came to know you, the more I came to see that you were more than that. You were what I needed then and what I need now. We've been through a lot to get to this moment."

Tears filled her eyes, and she covered her mouth as she realized what was happening.

"Will you marry me, Genevieve Lanchester?"

She choked on a sob. In her wildest dreams, she'd never imagined Lowen might propose to her. She'd known he wanted her for the long term, but somehow, she'd imagined he wouldn't want her for the rest of their lives. Now, here he was, proving her wrong. "What about Emma?"

"I have Emma handled," he murmured. "She'll apologize and get over it. Say yes, Vi."

"Okay. Yes, I'll marry you, Lowen Mcallister." She wiped at her streaming eyes and nodded, holding out her hand so he could slip the small engagement ring onto her finger.

He stood, pulling her with him, and kissed her thoroughly to the cheers and clapping of the other guests in the restaurant. Then he released her and gestured to a waiter nearby, who brought them a freshly opened bottle of champagne to celebrate. He held onto her hand as they sat down to have their dessert, a broad smile on his face. It was at that moment that she knew it would be okay this time. This time, she had the right one, and she wasn't going to give him up for anything or anyone.

Epilogue

Two years later

The awards ceremony night had gone off without a hitch. She, Lowen, and Emma had returned from an extended family vacation, which Lowen had been promising for nearly two months since they'd returned from their honeymoon to an annoyed Emma, who had insisted that if they were going to be a family, then they needed a family vacation since a vacation was long overdue for everyone in question. The three of them had been home for a few days and just managed to recover before heading off for the Oscars to watch Lowen receive a reward for his newest show.

The party had been a long one, and Vi couldn't wait to get out of her shoes. After all the dancing, her feet were killing her, and she and Emma had plans for a home spa night. It had taken Vi and Emma a few months to finally hash things out, and for Emma to see Vi as more of a friend than a replacement mum. Vi realized quickly that on top of everything else, Emma was scared that she wouldn't get to hang out with her dad anymore, and that his focus would shift to Vi entirely.

Though Emma's fears were understandable, they were baseless. Vi understood Emma and Lowen came as a package, and more than anything, she preferred it that way. Vi looked in the rearview mirror at her stepdaughter, sharing a grateful smile she was in her life.

Unbeknownst to Emma and Lowen, she also had big news to share, and she was slightly nervous, wondering how they'd take it. She could hardly contain herself as Lowen pulled the Lamborghini into the garage and came around to open her door.

Emma brushed past and shook her head. "Seriously, Vi, spa night isn't going anywhere. I'll still have the stuff for it when you get inside."

"Actually, it has nothing to do with spa night." Vi grinned. "I have something else I wanted to tell you both."

Lowen raised a brow and helped her inside, closing the garage door behind them. "Does this have to do with the way you've been bouncing in your seat all night and eyeing the door to the hotel ballroom?"

"Maybe." Her grin widened.

Emma scoffed. "You and your love of drama and suspense."

"Says the girl who threw a tantrum when it turned out I was interested in her father after all. After she'd already accused us of having sex." Vi could never resist giving her stepdaughter a hard time about that one.

"I keep telling you! I was giving you and Dad a hard time because it was funny. I never thought you two were *actually* doing the deed. Besides, you didn't exactly break it to me very well."

Vi wrinkled her nose and laughed. "No, I suppose not. But I will break this news better, Emma. Promise."

They all settled in the living room, Emma perched on the easy chair and Lowen sitting on the sofa. She stood in front of them, too nervous to sit despite her aching feet.

"Is your idea of breaking this news better to drive us mad with the suspense?" Emma griped.

Vi took a deep, steadying breath. "Emma, you're going to be a big sister."

Emma stared at her in silence.

Lowen opened his mouth and then closed it.

"What?" Emma was the first to manage to say something.

"I'm pregnant."

Lowen stood, a smile spreading slowly over his face. "I'm going to be a dad?"

"Umm, excuse me! You already are. I'm right here." Emma waved at him.

"A dad a second time," he amended with a roll of his eyes.

"You are." Vi couldn't stop smiling.

"How long?" he murmured.

"About a month along, they say."

He pulled her into his arms and kissed her cheek.

Emma stood too, her attention now squarely on Vi's belly. "When do we get to know the gender?"

"Not for a while yet. According to the doctor, we can't tell that until somewhere between twelve and eighteen weeks. You'll have to be patient."

Emma hugged her. "I always wanted a baby sister. But I guess if it's a baby brother, that's okay too."

Vi hugged her back and smiled over her head at Lowen, who was watching them with an expression of fondness and protectiveness. He smiled back, and she knew that whatever this next chapter entailed, she couldn't have asked for a better family at her side. Things might have been rocky at first, but in the end, she'd found the right one, and she'd found her happily ever after.

~ THE END OF THE SERIES ~

If you enjoyed the *Billionaire Daddy Series*, take a look at a sneak peek of the first book of Mountain Man Daddy Series: *Mountain Man Sheriff*.

Prologue

Lauren

I couldn't remember the last time I had been in handcuffs. I was certain that I hadn't been in the back of a sheriff's truck back then, either.

Sheriff Hollis, at least that's what he told me his name was. I have trouble trusting law enforcement these days, especially when he kept looking at me as if I was crazy. I might have screamed if that distrusting look passed across his green eyes one more time.

Fortunately, he didn't look at me again after loading me into the back of the truck. Instead, he was busy running the plates again. I thought he was only running them again to placate me. He didn't seem to believe that my ex-husband would ever tamper with documents to change the ownership of my car.

Maybe this was all karma's way of getting back at me.

I had finally packed my meager amount of things and left my controlling cop husband. When I threw a dart at a map, it landed on Willow Town. This was supposed to be my chance at a new beginning, but instead, I was being driven to the local jail.

What a way to make an impression.

Here I am, Willow Town, newly a criminal and ready to terrorize you all by stealing my own car, I thought as the sheriff drove over the bumpy back roads.

"You know, this is all a mistake. I've already told you that once. If you would actually listen to me, you might see that I'm telling the truth."

"Miss, you were trying to break into a car on the side of the road. That car back there was reported as stolen. You are either the thief or may have seen something relevant to this case. We can sort that out when we get back to the station."

"Holy shit," I said, leaning back against the seat and trying to adjust my wrists in the cuffs. "You are a real piece of work, aren't you? No wonder you're the sheriff."

"And what's that supposed to mean?" he asked, his jaw clenching as he looked at me in the rearview mirror. "If anyone in this vehicle is a piece of work, it's you. Do you honestly think I would believe that you weren't trying to break into that car? When I pulled up, you were about to throw a rock through the window."

"Because my keys were locked inside *my* car!"

I never would have been arrested if he hadn't pulled up when I tried to break into my own car. I wouldn't have had to do this if the car hadn't broken down in the first place. I had been in a hurry to get out and find out what was wrong with the engine, slamming the door before I remembered to grab the keys.

"You can't prove that. Facts are the car is reported as stolen, and you were going to break a window. While I can't question you on what I think you were about to do, I can question you concerning the stolen vehicle."

"Lucky me," I muttered, closing my eyes, and hoping it would all be over soon.

By the time the questioning was over, the sun had set in Willow Town. I was still without a car as the police tried to figure out what was happening. Apparently, my story of an ex who happened to be a corrupt cop wasn't good enough for them. I had expected as much. Cops never wanted to believe that one of their own could be corrupt—not even if they were from different counties and had never met.

Still, they had pried open the car and given me back the duffel bags that were in the back seat filled with belongings after sifting through them. My car would be held until they determined whether it was mine or not, despite showing them my insurance.

Go figure!

Rather than argue with them, I slung both bags over my shoulders and walked down Main Street. Main Street was one stretch of road that seemed to house the commercial district of Willow Town. Everything you needed was on this one short stretch of town. I tried to find my new workplace and home while looking around at the small buildings. Most of the buildings were quiet, their lights off and their curtains were drawn. It was too late at night for anyone to be awake unless they were patrons of the one and only bar in town.

When I entered *Taz* less than 10 minutes later, there was a woman with bright blue hair behind the bar. She looked up at me and smiled, speaking to one of the other bartenders quickly. She rounded the bar and joined me, wiping her hands on her towel.

"How can I help?"

"Hi. I'm Lauren...I'm looking for Kayleigh."

"Ah yes, Lauren. Pleasure to meet you." She shook my hand firmly before looking at her watch. "Thought you'd be here earlier? Did you get lost on your way here?"

"Sorry, no. Car trouble." I giggled nervously.

"Happens to the best of us," she said, smiling as she reached into the pocket of her apron and withdrew a key. "You must have had a long trip getting here. Go get some rest. The apartment is upstairs. It's small but cozy. If you need anything, come down here and let me know. I'm usually here from noon onwards."

"Thank you," I said, taking the key.

Kayleigh nodded. "I have a bar to tend to. I'll see you tomorrow night at seven for your first shift. Try not to be late."

"Thank you," I said again, turning the key over in my hand. "You don't know how much I appreciate this."

Kayleigh smiled as she walked around the bar. "You sounded like someone who was looking to start their life over. I've been there before."

Smiling, I nodded and backed away from the bar as more

patrons clustered around it. "I'll see you tomorrow night."

"Have a good night, Lauren."

I left the bar and headed to the little apartment above it. She was right; the apartment was small, but it was cozy. It was the first place I could call my own since the divorce. Curtains hung over the window, and a few pieces of furniture spread throughout the apartment. It wasn't much, but it was enough to hold me over until I could start buying my own belongings.

Instead of dwelling on what the apartment wasn't, I smiled at what it was. It was the first place I ever had that belonged to me and only me. There was no ex-husband with his name on the lease. When my head finally hit the pillow later that night, I got the overwhelming sense of finally being home.

Will Nate and Lauren ever meet eye to eye? And what happens when Lauren's past catches up to her? Will Nate be her safe haven?

Book 1 now available on Amazon!

Printed in Great Britain
by Amazon

19778665R00205